SARCAUN
THE JOURNEY

SARCAUN
THE JOURNEY

SIMONE VOLTAIRE

ISBN-13   Softcover   978-1-64961-914-3
                 eBook   978-1-64961-915-0

Library of Congress Control Number: 2021920453

Dedicated to my father, Arnauld Voltaire, for his love and support and for always believing in me.
Thank you with all my heart.

Simone Voltaire

CHAPTER ONE

Somewhere in the universe, millions of light years away from earth, Queen Xriane was sitting in the chamber of a castle located in Kreese, the main city among a group of planetary cities in the inner galaxy of Sarcaun. She was staring intensely into a round silver plated mirror that hung on a wall to her left. The queen would often gaze into this mirror to help focus her thoughts when she needed to find answers to difficult questions that were troubling her.

But on this particular day, she could not focus nor find any answers regardless of how hard she gazed into the mirror. And although it was a beautiful day outside, the atmosphere within the east wing of the castle where the queen's chambers were situated was dark and ominous. The air was thickly charged with an uncertain anticipation as the queen futilely searched for answers to the array of questions that were ceaselessly invading her mind.

As she continued to gaze into the mirror, which seemed to only reflect more gloom and darkness, a chill crept through her as she realized that the answers she desired may never come- at least not in time. Queen Xriane closed her eyes and took in a deep breath in distress.

But the queen was not alone in her distress. Moments later, there was movement at the other end of the expansive room as Nore, one of the highest-ranking gin on the planet, a counselor, moved away from where he had been leaning against the wall and crossed to the other side of the room to stand next to a window.

"Tell me, Your Majesty, what is weighing so heavily on your mind?" Nore inquired as he stood staring out of the east window, after a long stretch of silence in which each had been lost in their own thoughts.

Ironically, despite the present dismal atmosphere within the room, the sun was shining brightly outside, covering the city below with a magnificent rainbow of light that shimmered vibrantly off the tips of the crystal houses in the valley below.

When the queen did not respond, Nore slowly turned away from the window and walked towards her, stopping to stand only a few feet away from where she sat. He was a very tall, handsome and somewhat imposing man with dark skin, wild brownish red hair and piercing gray eyes. Even though he was a very soft and gentle man, one could not discern this readily as his face was sharply chiseled and his brows were deeply set in such a way that made him seem to always be scolding.

But the queen knew his heart and since he was known to be the most prominent gin on the planet, she often called on him to assist her when there were difficult decisions to be made. Not only that, but Nore was also one of the four counselors appointed to hear and decide upon the problems and issues of the people in the city of Kreese as well as in several other cities which gave him much insight into the needs and desires of the people.

Over the years, Nore had come to realize that the queen often called on him only if she was not sure of what to do or if she was uncertain of whether she was making the right decision. Otherwise, she would make the decisions herself after hearing out all sides of a particular matter. Of course, the King himself did give her his opinions and, as always, his support; yet the final decisions were always left up to the queen. Even so, Xriane appreciated the extra insight she received by discussing her ideas and concerns with Nore. After all, he was among the people more often than she and therefore had a better understanding of what their needs were and how she could best guide and support them.

Queen Xriane was a very strong and forthright woman and yet, at the same time, she was fair and was always open to ideas. Nore had come to realize that these characteristics were exactly what made her such an admirable queen. She knew her mind well and knew how to handle things responsibly. She made plans and invariably saw them through. Even at times when she knew exactly what she wanted and how she wanted things done, she never disqualified anyone, no matter who that person was. She was always willing to listen and take in ideas and make whatever changes were necessary to improve upon an idea. She was a proud woman yet at the same time humble enough to listen and hear the voice of her people when they spoke. She was very much loved and respected by all, even those who had never laid eyes on her.

Yet despite all of her wisdom and courage, Xriane very much valued the reassurance that she received from Nore. He was usually the first to know about her ideas and he was always brutally honest with her. That was what Xriane loved most about him. The king, of course, was very supportive of her in every way, but it was not the same. Over the years Xriane had grown to respect Nore's opinion and appreciated his friendship.

He was also somewhat the namesake of her youngest daughter, Norellyia, of whom Xriane was preparing herself to discuss with him. Nore was very fond of Norellyia and the queen was not quite sure of how he would react to what she was about to tell him.

"I see that something is troubling you, my Queen," Nore tried again after Xriane failed to respond to his first question. "Pray tell me what it is so that I may assist you as best as I can."

Xriane sighed and bit her lower lip. This was going to be difficult, she realized. But I might as well get it out and over with, she decided. The sooner the better; waiting was not going to change anything or make it any easier. In actuality, and if she were to be perfectly honest with herself, she had already decided on the matter. But she needed that decision reaffirmed by Nore. She slowly took in a deep breath.

"As you know, the time has come to select another Gen to send on a journey to earth," she began, "and I have given this a great deal of thought over the past few weeks." She shook her head vigorously in distress. "I do not quite know how to tell you this." She paused and took another deep breath to collect herself. "I have decided that Norellyia should be the one sent to earth." Xriane held her breath and watched Nore closely while she waited for a response from him.

At those words, Nore instantly lost his composure, something which rarely happened as he was always in control of himself. His mouth hung open as he stood there, staring at the queen in shocked disbelief for a moment before speaking.

"You are not serious, are you, Your Majesty?" he inquired, his face turning slightly pale.

"Of course, I am serious," Xriane responded, quickly coming to her feet. She had been sitting in a chair up on a platform two steps up from the main floor. She stepped down and stood facing Nore a short distance away so that her back was to the east window.

"B-but she is your daughter!" Nore stammered stupidly as he turned to face her.

"I am quite aware of that," Xriane said, sounding annoyed that he would make such a pointless statement after what she had just told him. But she wanted him to understand where she was coming from so, she added, "That is the main reason why I am sending her."

Nore vigorously shook his head. "I do not understand- why?"

"Because it is time," Xriane answered simply.

"Time? Time for what?" Nore wanted to know, not at all satisfied with that explanation and completely overwhelmed by what he had just been told. He could not believe or understand what he was hearing. This was preposterous! Impossible!! Send the princess to earth? What was the queen thinking?

"It is time for Norellyia to find out who she is-who she truly is inside and it is also time for her to understand the history of her people- that most specifically. Earth happens to hold a very vital part of our history. It is our origin, where we began. Granted, I know the earth has changed much over the course of the centuries, but it still holds a strong measure of who we are. If Elly is to become the next Queen of Sarcaun, she needs to know that history-not only know it, but experience a part of it for herself. I believe that learning about the humans, who they are and what their nature is will help Elly become a better person- and a better queen. That is what I feel and that is why she must go."

"But why send her there for? Why not just tell her about earth?"

Xriane shook her head. "That is not quite the same thing. She has heard all of the stories and has studied all of the history, which she seems to practically know by heart, but I do not think she comprehends the significance of the history earth holds."

"Forgive me, Your Majesty, but I must speak my mind. First of all, I really do not believe there is any significant history left for us to learn from on earth. That time is past. Secondly, what you are planning to do is completely out of the ordinary! Do you even realize what it is you want to do? No one of the royal house has ever been to earth since the founding of Sarcaun!"

This was not the first time that they have had a discussion along this line. Nore had always felt that it was a waste of time sending their people to earth. What was there to learn? Absolutely nothing, in his opinion- too much time had passed; there was no more history there to be of use to them. Plus, the humans had changed so little over the centuries that there was not anything about them to study or learn about on a regular basis. Send someone every two hundred or so moons to track their progress, fine, but otherwise just let it be, he had told Xriane repeatedly. He had always felt that the journeys were of no use- a complete waste of time.

When their ancestors had left earth so many moons ago, the history they had taken with them consisted of many dreadful memories of how badly they had been treated by the humans during the last several years of their life on earth. True, the behavior of humans had changed for the better since that time but Nore was convinced that it was only because they no longer had people they could control the way they had done with their ancestors. Humans had to change in order to survive and not end up destroying themselves. From what Nore could tell, they were still struggling with that change because he had watched as humans continued to abuse and destroy each other in ways that were completely incomprehensible to him.

Despite all the arguments that Nore had given Xriane against sending their people to earth, this was the one area that she was not willing to relent on. The Gens had existed on planet earth since the time of its creation before humans were even created- and witnessed the time when only two people walked the earth. Since then, they had watched the changes that have occurred in human nature from being loving and caring to outright greed and hostility. It had been the greed and heartlessness of humans that had finally forced the Gens to take action and escape after so many million years of living among the humans.

Despite all of these facts, Xriane was convinced that it was still very important to learn and study earth and its people as much as possible. There was much to be gained from it, she was certain. Trouble, Nore had told her when she explained this to him. That was all that was there to be gained.

"Well, then that will just have to change," Xriane responded fervently in response to Nore's point about how no one from the royal house had ever been sent to earth. She fixed Nore with a challenging look. The Royal Family, Xriane felt, more than anyone else would benefit from living on earth. After all, they were the ones who ruled the planet and needed most to be aware of and understand the history of their people in order to discover how to best take care of them. It was important for them to not forget who they were and where they had come from in order not to take what they now had for granted.

Nore sighed deeply, almost in defeat. "What will her father say?" he asked weakly, knowing well that arguing was not going to get him anywhere with her. He could tell from that defiant look in her eyes that she had already made up her mind. He wondered why she had even bothered telling him about her decision.

"Her father and I have already discussed this matter-"

Nore interrupted her. "And he accepted your decision?" he asked incredulously.

Xriane nodded slightly. "Yes, he agreed," she answered in a small voice, but did not elaborate further.

Nore regarded her closely. "Do you really think that Norellyia will accept this?" he asked, trying another angle.

Xriane shrugged. "She does not have a choice."

Nore laughed eerily. "You talk as though you do not even know your daughter!"

Xriane's temper flared slightly. "I know my daughter quite well, thank you."

"What? Are you going to force her to go?"

Xriane shook her head. "She will understand, you will see."

"I see," Nore replied sarcastically then continued, "Forgive me but I think you are being too dramatic about this. I am sure there must be another way to accomplish what you wish with Norellyia."

"There is no other way. You do not understand-"

Nore did not let her finish. He quickly became exasperated with her. "You are right, I do not understand." Nore heaved a deep sigh and shook his head sadly before speaking again. "Is there anything I can say to change your mind?"

Xriane shook her head. Her decision had already been made.

"Well, then, I must go." Nore felt helpless and in more ways than one. What else was there for him to do? What had been the point of all of this?

Xriane started pacing the room, something she did often when she was discontented. "Where are you going?" She did not like him leaving like this. She needed him to understand and support her but she could clearly see that that was not going to happen.

"I have things to do," Nore said, not quite answering her question. As if to say, you are wasting my time and I would rather be spending it elsewhere where I can be of some use. He was aware that something still troubled her, but could not quite put his finger on it. Why had she called him here? He wondered once more. He was missing something, but part of him really did not want to know what that was. He felt it best to leave things as they were- for now. He was certain that the truth would reveal itself in time.

Xriane turned to Nore and said, "Norellyia must not take what she has for granted. She needs to appreciate the life that she has. And I can tell you that where she is right now, she does not appreciate anything. All that must change if she is to become the next queen of Sarcaun one day."

"And sending her to earth will accomplish this?"

Xriane threw her hands up in defeat. She wanted so much for Nore to understand, without having to tell him too much. There were some things best kept to oneself, she realized. "I wish I could make you understand but I do not know what else to say."

"Why did you call me here if you have already made up your mind about this?" Nore wanted to know. He could not keep his curiosity to himself any longer.

Xriane rubbed her temple. "You know how much your support means to me in these matters, Nore."

"I am sorry, Your Majesty, but I cannot give that to you this time." There was a long moment of awkward silence between the two of them as Xriane continued to pace about the room, struggling to find the right words to say. But the words would not come. She could not bring herself to tell him the whole truth.

"Your majesty, I have a terrible feeling about this," Nore finally said, breaking the silence. Even though he was facing the window, his eyes were closed and he appeared to be in a trance. "Doors that have never been opened may unseal because of what you are planning to do and that could bring danger." Nore's voice sounded strange and far away. He slowly turned around and faced Xriane. She did not like what she saw in his eyes.

Xriane stared at him for a moment, puzzled. But then, suddenly, she began to laugh. "Danger? Here on Sarcaun, all because I am sending Norellyia to earth? Nore, please! Surely you exaggerate!"

"Have you forgotten the history of your own planet?" Nore asked sharply.

"No, I have not forgotten," Xriane answered. Her laughter immediately stopped at Nore's sharp tone. Why was he making this into more than what it was? It was infuriating. "What does any of that have to do with my decision to send Norellyia to earth?"

"Have you forgotten," Nore tried again, "about King Zirrcon-"

"Oh, please," Xriane interrupted, "those are just stories. You do not really believe them, do you?"

Nore opened his mouth to answer her but then thought better of it. He simply shook his head slightly and said, "Never mind. I must be on my way." It was obvious that her response bothered him and there was something he was holding back, Xriane could tell but she was not ready to pry it out of him. She would wait until he had calmed down and had time to absorb what she had just revealed to him.

"Yes, be on your way." Xriane, too, sounded slightly irked once more. She did not have time for this. Surely, he was just overreacting due to the shock of what she had just revealed to him. But she did not completely believe this. Nore had a special gift which was the ability to see what the future held. He was rarely ever wrong about things and sometimes his accuracy was chilling. Suddenly, the room grew cold and Xriane wrapped her arms around herself as she felt a small shiver crawl up her spine again.

Nore frowned at her. "Please, be careful," he warned. Xriane only nodded as he turned and, without another word, exited the room.

CHAPTER TWO

After Nore left, Xriane continued to pace the room. A few minutes later, she stopped in front of a large wood framed mirror and ran her fingers through her long grayish black hair.

How am I going to handle this? She wondered as she stared at her reflection. She knew that deep down inside she had made the right decision. But how was she going to convince Norellyia of this? Norellyia was the youngest of her six daughters and she was a very sensitive girl- not to mention also very impatient and stubborn. If something did not agree with her, she did not want to hear about it and she always had to have things her way.

"I am sorry, Elly dear," Xriane whispered, still staring into the mirror. "But I have to do this."

But even as she said this, Nore's words came back to her. Could this really be dangerous? She shook her head sharply and quickly dismissed the thought.

Impossible- she would know if that were so.

Xriane walked over to a hidden cabinet behind the bedroom door, opened it and pulled out an ancient book; it was tattered and torn with age. It was the book that held the majority of the planet's history that had been preserved through the generations since the planet was first discovered millions of years ago. Xriane had not opened the book in a very long time but felt the need to do so now after hearing what Nore had to say. She needed some reassurance about the decision she was making. She sat down at a long wooden table next to the window and carefully flipped through the delicate pages until she found what she sought. Taking in a deep breath she began to read.

...from the beginning of time we lived on planet earth in peace and harmony with the humans until they became aware of our powers. With the discovery of our powers, corruption began to fill their hearts and they eventually deceived us into submission by first asking us to perform menial tasks which seemed harmless to us at the time.

By the time we realized what was happening, it was too late because we had trusted the humans and had no way of directly breaking free of their control and they began abusing our powers, controlling us to fulfill their selfish and destructive desires. Soon humans began referring to us as gins and genies because of our powers but collectively we called ourselves Gens.

After a time, we became weary of the abuse of power and the suffering that it was causing us and many of those around us. Many of our kind were dead or dying due to the constant misuse and abuse of the powers we held. We realized that if we did not take action our kind would eventually no longer be able to survive. So, we banded together, desperate to find a way to freedom as we did not want any more of our children to be born into such corruption.

Because many of us were astronomers, we spent numerous days studying the stars. Being as highly intelligent and much further evolved then humans, we were very resourceful. That along with our supernatural abilities helped us to soon discover that there were other planets out beyond the stars. Some of them were within earth's galaxies, but many others were billions of miles out of the galaxy of earth, none of which were known to the humans. Upon this discovery, an expedition was immediately assembled and sent to explore these worlds out in what we eventually named the Astral Zone.

To the surprise and joy of those on the expedition, they discovered three planets near the inner circle of the Astral Zone of which one was uninhabited and very much capable of maintaining life. Several of the expedition members remained on the planet to continue research while the others came back to earth and shared the good news with those of us waiting on earth.

Over a period of time, after many studies were conducted on the new found planet and it was determined that the planet was safe and habitable, we organized ourselves and escaped from earth to the new planet out in the Astral Zone. The new home that we found for ourselves was given the name Morgea, which meant new beginning, as this was a new beginning with freedom for our people.

We lived happily on this planet for nearly nine hundred years. It was later discovered that, to the humans, gins and genies soon became a myth, passed on from one generation to the next, as there was no evidence left behind to remind the humans of us or to attest to our existence on planet earth.

But our new home, as it turned out, was not as stable as first determined and soon the planet began to rapidly move out of its original orbit. The planet eventually settled back into a normal orbit pattern but unfortunately had settled too close to the sun. The gathering heat within the planet eventually destroyed the planet by literally causing it to explode. Fortunately, many of us who had heeded the warnings of scholars who had predicted this many moons prior were able to escape before it was too late.

Sadly, though, only those of us who had been intelligent enough to listen to the Teachers who had warned about a day when our home would leave its place and be destroyed by the great star, Myzin, the sun, survived. Those of us who had listened and prepared, escaped and took shelter on a deserted part of Zirnam, another planet several million miles from where Morgea was within the inner Astral Zone that was still fairly uninhabited at that time. Some even braved themselves and went back to earth for fear that disaster would strike again should they remain out in the Astral Zone. Those who returned to earth did so carefully and blended themselves in with the humans, concealing their identities.

Through numerous researches, those of us who had remained out in the Astral Zone on the planet of Zirnam soon discovered a group of planets that formed another inner galaxy within the one in which Zirnam and another planet, Clorian, existed. We named this inner galaxy Sarcaun and it consisted of five smaller planets that orbited around a larger central planet by some sort of a magnetic force with the main source of energy being the center planet.

After studying these planets for an extended period of time, we decided that it was safe and settled first on the main planet in the center, as we wanted a home of our own and did not like living among the Zirnams for they were a strange people. Fortunately, no one on

Zirnam had ever discovered that we were outsiders and therefore no harm was done to us and we were able to live in peace during the time we lived on their planet.

We named the new planet Kreese, meaning "New Life" and after we reestablished ourselves, we sent messengers on a discrete mission to earth to find the descendants of our people who had originally fled to earth out of fear of further disaster and returned with them to our new home. Eventually we settled on all five planets that surrounded Kreese and we were able to travel and live freely among the planets. We soon set up council in each planet and identified them as planetary cities within the Sarcaun galaxy with Kreese being the main city and center of our home.

Strangely enough, as time passed and history was handed from one generation to the other, we were amazed to find that we were extremely curious about the human race, despite all the hardship that we knew many of us as well as our ancestors had suffered at their hands. Many centuries later after the discovery and settlement on our new home in Sarcaun, the Council decided that we would somehow study the humans and see perhaps if we could either learn something from or about their nature. It was decided that every fifty moons or so a Gen would be sent to earth to live among the humans and study their ways and culture. We agreed with this decision and felt that this was very important and necessary to do. After all, earth was where it all began: it was our first home, our true origin...

Xriane skipped through a few pages until she found the next section she was looking for. She read through the first paragraph carefully and felt a chill. What she was planning to do went against the guidelines that were set for choosing a Gen to send to earth. Xriane went through a few more pages but could not find the answer that she was looking for. There was nothing that could either support or explain why the decision she was making would be dangerous, as Nore had implicated.

Xriane sighed deeply, closed the book and settled herself on a windowsill that faced the eastern side of the city and stared down into the settling sunset of the city below. She went over the conversation that she had had with Nore. What she had said to him had all been true. But there was so much more to it than that-things that even King Ourak himself did not know about her despite all the years they had been together- secrets that Xriane kept deep within herself which sometimes tormented her in her sleep.

Xriane sighed sadly. Lately, every time she looked at Elly, she saw more and more of herself. Seeing such a transformation was very frightening to her. Elly's birth had been a difficult ordeal and now Xriane watched with sorrow as she turned into a difficult child more and more with each passing day, just as she had been in her youth.

Xriane remembered growing up in the small village of Korsa on the outskirt of town in the city of Aille. Her life had been simple and fulfilling for a time- until her father passed away when she was still very young. After her father's death- a father whom she had loved and who had loved her dearly- her mother, who had always been a short tempered and controlling character, soon turned cold and even more short tempered.

Having lost her father and not being able to deal with her mother's cold temper, Xriane soon became a very strong-willed child. Seeing this change in Xriane, her mother had felt that the only way to control and discipline her was to lock her up and literally starve her half to death- or insult her and smack her around, whichever her mother was in the mood for that day. Being an only child and her father dead only made matters worse for Xriane as there was no one there to defend or protect her.

Xriane smiled bitterly at the memories. Funny, she thought, how no one ever knew the horrors that took place in that small house on the outskirts of the city. People saw her pain but blamed it on her restlessness and stupidity. But nothing her mother did could stop the restlessness that was in her heart. In fact, her treatment only made things worse. Xriane became angry and defiant, not only towards her mother but towards everyone around her.

Until that one day when she ran away from home after her mother had almost beaten her to death for going to the Segrins festival against her will. Xriane could never fully remember what happened that day. All she knew was that after escaping she had passed out somewhere in the Forest of Lakes in the City of Greshan, almost twenty miles from her home in Aille. When she became conscious again, she had found herself lying on soft pillows in a cabin somewhere deep in the woods. At first, she had thought she was dreaming until she saw a man leaning over her tending to her wounds and the pain she felt when he gently touched her side was very real. Xriane had tried to get up to escape but the man had gently pushed her back down on the bed, promising that he would not hurt her. His name had been Jyarn. He had been an older man with no family. He had taken her in, loved her, and taken care of her as if she were his own. No matter what she did, he always loved her and never passed judgment on her.

As soon as she had recovered from her wounds, Xriane explained to Jyarn what had happened; about her mother and how she had run away. Without even a second thought, he packed her up along with everything he owned and left Greshan and moved to the city of Dassar, where they spent many happy years together. It had been through Jyarn that Xriane had met Ourak, then Prince of Kreese.

Jyarn had died just months after the two of them married and Xriane became the princess of Kreese; he had been so proud of her that day. Three years after that, Ourak and she became King and Queen of Sarcaun. Xriane still missed him terribly and many times over the years she had wished that he could have been there to give her advice. More often though, she ached to hear his gentle voice and contagious laugh that had enabled her to forget for a time the horrible things that she had experienced in her youth.

Xriane shifted her position as she recalled all these memories and as she now recalled the one experience that changed her life forever. Till this day, there had not been an experience more profound in her life and this was the greatest of all her secrets and the reason she so desperately felt the need to send Norellyia to earth.

It came to pass in the time that Jyarn and she lived in Dassar that Jyarn was chosen to go on an assignment to earth. Xriane did not exactly know what all of this was about during this time as she had only been a peasant girl and schooling had not been of any interest to her. But she did understand that an assignment such as this was very important and it was an honor to be chosen for it. It did not surprise her at all that Jyarn had been chosen; after all, he was the chief of the Battle man, defender of the city of Dassar and had risen to this position very quickly. He was a very intelligent and honest man and everyone loved and respected him.

Despite knowing the importance of this assignment, Xriane could not bear the thought of Jyarn going away and leaving her behind. She cried and begged him to refuse their offer, but of course he would not; he was an honorable man. After that, she would not speak to him for days and refused to eat. Jyarn was the only person that she trusted and loved. How could he leave her behind like this? The pain she felt in her heart was unbearable even though she knew she was not being reasonable. On the night before he was to leave, they still had not spoken to each other for several days. Later that night, Jyarn had come into her bedroom and woken her out of the deep slumber that she had cried herself into.

"Wake up, little one," he had said to her. "We must go, there is not much time."

"What? Where are we going?" Xriane inquired, quickly coming to life.

"I thought you said you did not wish for me to leave you behind?" Jyarn teased. "Do you not want to go on this assignment with me?"

Xriane was startled but wide awake now. "Go with you? Is that possible?"

"Completely against all regulations, but quite possible. Now come, stop asking questions."

Xriane had jumped out of bed and dressed in a flash. He warned her to take nothing with her except for the clothes she wore. They crept out of the house and made their way silently through the sleeping town. He took her to Krenam Pass, where he knew they would be taking him the next evening to send him on his journey to earth. He hid her in an empty casement behind the vestibule which they would place him in to send him to earth. He knew that all inspections had already been done that evening so that no one would be entering it except for himself when it was time for his departure. She would be safe.

"If for once you have ever obeyed me," he whispered to her sharply, "this would be the time or it will be the end of both of us. Stay here and do not make a sound. Do not move, do not even breathe more than you have to. Do you understand?"

"Yes," Xriane answered in a whisper.

"I will be back tomorrow evening when it is time for my departure, until then you must stay here." He did not give her a chance to answer or ask questions as he stepped out and pulled the casement door tightly shut behind him.

For the entire time Xriane did not move, breathe or even sleep out of fear and it seemed as though ages passed before she heard the casement door opening and saw Jyarn smiling down at her.

"Come," he held out his hand to her. "They are about to start the engine." No sooner had the words left his mouth they heard a loud whizzing sound and felt a heavy vibration beneath their feet. Jyarn led Xriane to the middle of the vestibule and held on to her tightly as a bright light began to fill the place. The sound that reverberated within the vestibule made it seem as though there was about to be an explosion at any moment. Xriane was terrified.

But in a blink of an eye, or even less time than that, if possible, Jyarn and Xriane found themselves standing in the middle of a road with the sun shining brightly at their backs and it did not take them long to realize that they were on earth.

Xriane smiled and sighed deeply. How things had changed with how the travels were made since then. But that journey was the beginning of an experience that she would never forget. One that changed her life and who she was completely forever-

The large glass door that led into Xriane's chamber was suddenly pushed open abruptly bringing Xriane back to the present time and place. A young girl with long brown hair and soft gray eyes entered the room.

"I am sorry Your Highness, I knocked several times and you did not answer. I was concerned. I did not mean to intrude."

"It is all right, Shala. What is it?"

"Dinner is ready, Your Highness," she announced politely to the Queen.

"Thank you, Shala. Do call my daughters down for me."

"Yes, Your Highness. I was just on my way to do that and stopped here first."

Xriane nodded. "Very well then, go."

Shala, who was wearing a long brown dress, left the room and walked down a white hallway until she reached a staircase at the other end of the hall. She climbed up four flights of stairs, each of which led to a different floor. On the fifth floor, she walked down the long hallway until she reached a wide glass door near the other end. She peered into the room through the clear glass door and saw a young girl sitting on the floor atop of some cushions, twirling a flower between her long, delicate fingers. Smiling, Shala slowly opened the door and peeked inside.

"Norellyia, dear, you know that your mother does not like you sitting on the floor," she said but she was still smiling as she said this. Princess Norellyia looked up at her, revealing a pair of large sea green eyes.

"Why must you always tell me what my mother does not like?" Norellyia protested, paying no heed to her words and pinning the flower up at the side of her hair. She picked up another, a yellow one, and began plucking off the petals and throwing them on the floor.

Shala gave Elly a look that said do I really need to answer that? Elly was constantly getting herself in trouble and Shala found it necessary to at least try and keep her in line.

Instead of answering her question, Shala said, "Dinner is ready. Please be downstairs in five minutes, all right?" Elly nodded but did not move from where she sat. Shala shook her head in mock exasperation and left the room. She loved the child as if she was her own, but indeed, she was sometimes too much and it seemed that she enjoyed looking for trouble. Smiling to herself, Shala continued down the hall to look for Norellyia's sisters.

CHAPTER THREE

Norellyia was a very attractive girl; tall and slender with raven black hair that fell down just past her waist. The soft curls framed her oval face and accentuated her high cheekbones and dark brows, surrounding her with an air of mystique. Her skin was a smooth, glimmering bronze and her shapely lips made her look as though she were always pouting.

Those who did not know her well would say she was a warm and gentle soul while looking into her dark green, deep-set eyes that seemed to always be filled with sorrow. But those who did know her were not deceived by her beauty and could see the fire that raged inside of her, just beneath the surface waiting to explode. Even though they could see past her beauty, they were often amazed when, for a brief moment, the storm would calm and happiness and even compassion could be seen in her deep green eyes.

Norellyia got up from the floor, stretched, laid the cushion down on a small table and walked languidly over to her bedroom window. From there, she could see the courtyard that held a garden filled with a wide variety of flowers that were always in bloom. There was a huge fountain in the middle of the garden that watered the flowers daily, keeping the air cool and fresh. All the flowers in the garden were rare and could only be found in certain areas of the planet. Elly enjoyed the fresh smell of flowers that filled her bedroom and the view from her room always helped to soothe and clear her mind. She could spend hours just sitting on her windowsill, staring out into the garden.

Sometimes she would sit for hours staring out into the garden contemplating the world that she lived in. There were times when Elly would feel that she did not fit in anywhere in her world as she often found it difficult to either understand or connect to the people in her life.

The main source of her frustration was the fact that she was the Princess of Sarcaun which meant that she would one day be queen so she felt the need to be able to connect with the people because she knew they would look to her for guidance and support. So, the fact that she felt so distant from her people was something she agonized over to the point that she sometimes found herself becoming angry and extremely agitated. For the most part, she was able to keep these feelings to herself but sometime she found herself unintentionally taking it out on others and had to fight to maintain control of her emotions.

But, surprisingly, Norellyia found that the garden was also a source of strength and peace for her. Because after the turmoil and frustrations, the sound of the fountain and the sweet smell of flowers enabled her to calm her spirit and simply enjoy the beauty of the world around her allowing her, for what may only be a short time, to forget her cares, worries and fears.

As Norellyia sat by the window looking down at the flowers, trying to sort through her thoughts, a strange sensation began to surround her. She felt odd and quite uneasy, almost as though she was about to lose consciousness.

Norellyia slowly turned away from the window and walked over to her bed, which was surrounded with gold posts filled with fresh flowers, and sat down. The strange sensation was growing stronger around her, making her feel dizzy and weak. She grabbed a pillow and hugged it tightly against her stomach. Her eyes blurred. For a split second, Elly was acutely aware that there was something extremely wrong but she was not able to focus on or detect what the problem was as she fought the nauseous feeling that was quickly overtaking her.

Suddenly, her door flew open and her oldest sister, Sora, stuck her head in the room.

"Come, Elly. You do not want to be late for dinner, do you?" Sora was a slender girl with a lithe figure and a smile that could lighten the darkest room. She looked almost like Elly with her long dark curly brown hair and hazel eyes but there were no storms behind those eyes, only love and compassion. Since she was the oldest, she always felt responsible for taking care of her sisters, doing her best to keep them out of trouble. Although where Elly was concerned, that was almost impossible.

Norellyia looked up, barely hearing her sister's words and mumbled, "I am coming. I will meet you downstairs."

After Sora left, Elly lay down on her bed and closed her eyes. Her head was pounding and she felt as though she was falling into a bottomless pit. As she closed her eyes tighter and curled up into a ball in the middle of her bed, she felt herself spinning rapidly as though she were suspended in the air by a thin thread.

Please stop! Elly silently pleaded as she hugged herself and curled even more tightly into a ball in the middle of her bed. Suddenly, her eyes began to grow heavy and her body became numb and before Elly was aware of it, she fell soundly asleep...and dreamed.

Elly found herself in a dark place. Using her hands, she felt around and soon discovered that she was in a small room that seemed to be made of glass. With every step she took the sound echoed loudly in her ears making her head ache. As she continued to walk around the room, looking for a way out, the room seemed to shrink and grow smaller with each time around until there was only room for her to stand in one place. At that point, Elly suddenly became cold and she started to find it extremely hard to breathe- it was as though the room was trying to suffocate her. Desperately becoming frantic, Elly began to push against the four walls that surrounded her hoping that she could find a way out.

Just when Elly was sure that she was going to pass out, she suddenly found herself outside somewhere, hovering above an open field with a thick, dark forest in the distance. She was gasping for air and fighting the urge to pass out. Finally, after taking in a few deep breaths, she was able to look around and was surprised to find that it was sunny and bright over the field where she hovered in the air, but in the distance where the forest was the sky was dark, menacing and cloudless.

Suddenly there came loud thundering, crashing noises from the direction of the forest and the sky lit up with flashes of light all around. Before Elly's eyes, water began to fall out of the sky to the ground as the loud booming noises continued and the lights continued to flash through the sky. But still the field where Elly was remained dry and sunny as Elly watched the disastrous event that was taking place less than twenty feet from her....

Elly awoke with a start; her heart was pounding wildly in her chest as though it were looking for a way out. What was that place? Elly wondered, remembering her dream as she wiped the sweat from her brow. Surely this was no place here on Sarcaun! For never in her life had she seen or heard of such terrible things happening here. It must have been some other place, another world I saw, she concluded. But how was that possible? She had never had such an experience in her life. Elly felt extremely weak and tired. She was sweating profusely, causing her dress to cling coldly against her body. A chill crept up her back.

But before she could acknowledge the feeling, something else pushed its way into her mind. Oh, no! Elly gasped sitting up in her bed. Suddenly her concerns about her dream vanished as she realized that she was late for dinner. She did not give herself any more time to think about what she had just experienced as she jumped out of bed and headed for the door. She admonished herself for being so careless. This, of course, would not be the first time that she had been late for dinner.

Disregarding the fact that she was still weak from her experience, Elly left her bedroom and took off down the hall. When she finally reached the large wooden doors that led to the dining room on the first floor, she paused just long enough to catch her breath then she bravely shoved the door open and stepped inside. She found her parents and sisters already at the table eating. Her father glanced up at her from where he sat.

"Elly, where have you been?" he inquired. Gratefully, Elly noticed that he did not sound upset.

"I-I fell asleep," Elly stammered. Her heart was pounding and so was her head- the pain was excruciating. "I am sorry."

Her mother regarded her closely. "Are you all right?" she asked seeing that Elly looked rather flushed, wild eyed and out of breath.

Elly nodded. "I am fine." She was still quite shaken from her experience but did not feel like sharing this with her family. It had been such a strange experience; she knew that they would never understand, especially since she herself had no idea what the meaning of it was or even why it had happened.

Her father sighed. "Well, then, have a seat." Elly stared at her father in disbelief. He had never let her off so easily in the past. There had always been a reprimand, as her father hated tardiness, along with a warning of future punishment if her behavior did not change. Quietly though, without argument, Elly went and took her seat. She began to eat as her sisters resumed their conversation.

"So, tell us, Elly, how was your day?" her mother asked a short while later, realizing that she had not spoken a word since after entering the room.

Elly shrugged. "I did not really do much today. I painted for most of the day over by the lake." Elly smiled as she thought of her paintings. Many of them could be seen hanging throughout the castle. She had been painting since she was a little girl and loved doing so with a passion. She spent as much time as she could with her art. She particularly loved painting natural scenes of the forests and lakes around the castle. Painting, for Elly was another way to relax and calm her mind or to cheer herself up whenever she felt sad or lonely.

"Do not forget to finish my painting," Kyli, the second oldest reminded her. "Del's birthday is only two days away and I want to surprise him with it." Del was Kyli's suitor. They had been seeing each other for quite some time now and it was getting serious. Elly was waiting to see them married any day now. Del seemed to be the only thing Kyli either thought or talked about lately.

"Actually, I did work on that today. I will be finished with it by tomorrow," Elly promised. "It is coming along rather well-" Elly abruptly stopped talking. The strange feeling was there again- the feeling that something was not right. The air around her was suddenly charged with electricity as if an explosion was just waiting to happen. Something was definitely wrong. Her head felt light and Elly squeezed her eyes shut for a moment to regain her composure.

Elly's mother smiled and said, "I see that you have had a busy day." She was not really paying any attention to what was being said. She was debating with herself, trying to decide when would be the right time to tell Elly about her plans. A new moon was only a few weeks away and it would then be time to send a Gen to earth. She had put off this subject long enough. Xriane reluctantly admitted that there really would never be a right time. Plus, she wanted Elly to have enough time to absorb and prepare for what was going to be happening- she did not want to spring this news on Elly at the last minute.

Knowing how vital this decision was and how the news would affect everyone in the family, the King had decided that tonight at dinner they would reveal to Elly what was planned as there was not much time before she would have to leave. Xriane had agreed, although a bit hesitantly. Her talk with Nore had greatly upset her for some strange reason and reading through the ancient book had added further to her misgivings.

Xriane pushed Nore and the ancient book out of her mind as she looked up and glanced across the table to Elly's father. The King understood and gave a slight nod.

It was time.

"Oh, I almost forgot," Elly said before Xriane had a chance to begin speaking. "Lea wanted to know if I could stop by to see her this evening. May I go?" Lea was Elly's best friend; they had grown up together and were like sisters to each other. She looked first at her mother then her father, waiting for an answer.

"You may go," her father answered, "but do not stay too late." Elly smiled at him in appreciation.

"Elly," her mother began cheerfully, finally taking over the conversation. "How would you like the opportunity to take a journey to a new place? Perhaps even to another planet?" That is putting it mildly, she added to herself wryly. But she did not know what other way to better approach this situation without making it more complicated than necessary.

Elly was astonished by her mother's question for a moment but then her eyes began to sparkle as she started thinking about the possibilities.

"Why, Mother!" she exclaimed, smiling brightly. "That is a brilliant idea! Let me see, I have always wanted to visit Clorian because I have heard so many interesting things about the place."

Xriane forced a small laugh. "No, Elly, I did not mean a planet here within this Astral Zone. I was thinking that maybe you would like to visit another planet outside of our own zone- for a change."

Elly's eyes quickly narrowed in suspicion. "What exactly do you mean by another planet?"

Xriane took in a deep breath. There was no backing out now. "I was thinking of sending you someplace different." She paused for a moment then hurriedly continued. "Some place like- Earth." She said it nonchalantly, as though it were something she had just thought of on the spur of the moment, hoping it would make the impact a little less harsh.

For a moment, there was complete silence as the queen's words hung in the air. Elly was stunned and could not believe what she was hearing. Did her mother just say she wanted to send her to earth? A cold chill swept over Elly and the pressure behind Elly's eyes increased. This was definitely wrong. Elly dropped the fork she was still holding onto her plate, shattering the silence, and sat there staring at her mother in disbelief.

"Mother, please tell me you are not serious," she finally said. For a moment, she thought perhaps she was still dreaming and had not woken out of the nightmare that had taken hold of her just before she came down to dinner. But a small voice at the back of her head informed her otherwise. This was no dream.

"Actually," her mother answered. "I am very serious about this."

Elly vigorously shook her head and rubbed her temple. "I do not understand this. Why?" She looked up at her mother; tears were already filling her eyes. Perhaps this is what she had felt earlier- that odd feeling and that even stranger dream. No wonder it had all seemed so foreign to her. Earth, of all places! The dream she had kept playing over and over in her mind and with that just the thought of going to earth horrified her.

"Elly, I think this would really be a wonderful experience and opportunity for you," her mother was saying. "It might even change your life."

Elly's face flushed. "I like my life just fine, Mother. Why do you feel that it needs to be changed? And why did anyone not bother to ask me before making such an enormous decision about my life?"

Xriane closed her eyes briefly. She had expected this reaction from Elly but was now wondering whether or not she would be able to handle it.

"Elly, sometimes in life we need to experience certain things in order to better understand who we are. I feel that the time has come for you and I also believe that there is no better way for you to pass through that experience then to send you to earth. Believe me, your father and I have given this a great deal of consideration."

"Mother, you do not have to send me off to nowhere for that to happen." Elly's voice was steadily rising and intense anger was beginning to build up deep inside of her.

"Elly, please," her mother pleaded. "Listen to me-"

"I will not listen!" Elly interrupted as she stood up and leaned towards her mother. There was fire burning in her eyes and for a moment Xriane actually felt fear as she saw herself reflected in Elly's eyes. "How could you do this to me? How could you make such a decision without even talking to me about it? This is my life we are talking about."

"If I had said anything to you earlier, you would have just said no, without even giving it a second thought."

"You are right, I would have said no," Elly told her trying to contain her anger. "And I am saying 'no' now. I will not go!"

"But you have no choice," Xriane informed her calmly.

Elly was almost in tears. She turned towards her father for help. "Father, please! Say something here."

"I am sorry, Elly," the King said softly. "But I think that your mother is right."

Elly was stunned- how could father take her mother's side on this? She was crying in earnest now. "How could you do this?" she asked her mother again accusingly, almost in defeat. She could not understand where all of this was coming from. What had she done wrong? Why was this happening to her? She felt as though she was being thrown away, abandoned.

Xriane's heart ached as she tried to reach out to her daughter, tried to make her understand.

"Elly, I am sorry if you think I am being unfair. I just wish you could understand. And even so, do not think that I am going to change my mind just because you are angry. I truly believe that this is best for you." She stopped and looked at Elly steadily.

Elly did not know what to say to this. She felt as though her whole world had just been turned upside down and she could not even begin to understand what was happening or why it was happening. She did not know what to think or how to feel. Without saying another word, she slowly got up from the table and left the dining room and headed upstairs.

I knew something was going to happen, she said to herself as she climbed the stairs. I knew something was wrong! But this is unbelievable! She shook her head sadly. Why was this happening to her? she wondered again. What had she done wrong? In her room, she lay down on her bed and quietly sobbed to herself. She was keenly aware that she was being childish and was perhaps even overreacting a bit over the whole situations but she could not help it at the moment.

It was all just such an unexpected shock and she needed time to take it all in. She never imagined that something like this would ever happen to her. In one instant her entire world had been turned upside down.

"Can I come in?" Elly looked up and found her sister, Sora, standing in the doorway. Elly turned and faced the other way, without answering; she was in no mood for company. Sora entered anyway and seated herself on the edge of Elly's bed.

"I am sorry that you are so upset, Elly. But you know that mother only wants the best for you."

"But it is not fair. How could she make such a decision without even asking me? I did not even have a chance to prepare for it."

"That is simple. She knows how stubborn you are and she also knows that talking to you would not have made a difference."

Elly grimaced. "Thank you, Sora. I can see that you are on my side on this." Elly could not help the sarcasm that crept into her voice.

Sora shrugged. "It is the truth, and you know it is."

Elly got up and walked over to her window. Indeed, she knew what Sora had said was true, but she was not ready to accept any of this. Things were just happening too fast. She needed time to think. She wiped the tears away from her eyes and suddenly realized that it was not really so much that she was going to be sent to earth that had gotten her so upset but that no one had bothered to ask her about it first- as though her feelings did not mean anything. That, she realized, was what hurt the most.

"I just know I will be miserable if I go," Elly told her sister, remembering her dream. If what she had seen in her dream was any indication of what being on earth would be like, there was no way anyone was going to make her set foot on the place!

"Oh, Elly," Sora sighed. "I am sure it will not be that bad, believe me."

"You do not know that, Sora," Elly shook her head. She wanted to tell her sister about her dream, about how she was truly feeling about this whole ordeal but something held her back. She sighed and sat back down on the bed. "It is just that I do not understand why. Why me?"

"I do not know, either," Sora answered honestly. "You would have to ask mother. It was as much a surprise to me as it was to you."

Elly shook her head. "It would not have been so bad if she at least had prepared me for this instead of just- dropping it on me out of nowhere. Honestly, Sora, I never saw any of this coming!"

"Neither did we," Sora admitted. "We were just as shocked as you were. But do not feel sorry for yourself, it will not do you any good. Look, you are not being exiled here and this really could be a wonderful experience for you, just as Mother said."

"Yes, I admit, you may be right." Yet even as she said the words, Elly knew that she did not mean them. But she was not up to dealing with her sister's optimism at the moment. "But look, Sora, I do not want to think or talk about all this right now. I am going to head over to Lea's." She got up and went to her dresser. She pulled her hair back and pinned it in place. "I will talk to you later." Grabbing a shawl off the bed, she left the room.

After Elly left, Sora went downstairs to her mother's chamber.

She knocked lightly on the door. "Mother, may I come in?"

Her mother opened the door. "Yes, come in, Sora. What is it?"

"Mother, I know that this is probably not my concern, but- is Elly going to be all right? I mean, I am really worried about her."

Xriane nodded her head in understanding. "I can see why you are concerned about her but, do not be. Your sister is very strong and I have much faith in her. You should, too."

"But she does not seem to be taking the news very well," Sora protested. As a matter of fact, Sora was not taking this news well, either. Nothing of what had happened within the last few minutes made any sense. None of it seemed right. But Sora was not one to go against her mother's words. Instead, she wanted desperately to understand. She did not believe half the things she had said to Elly. She had only wanted to calm her down.

"I know," Xriane agreed, knowing well the thoughts and confusion her daughter was facing. She got up, walked over to the window and stared outside. It was still light out and the entire east side of the city shone brightly with colors from the rays of the sun. "Elly has a lot to learn," Xriane was saying. "But I know that she can handle this." She turned and smiled at Sora. "She can handle anything if she wants to so do not worry about her."

Sora hesitated. "I do not mean to question you Mother, but is this really necessary? Sending Elly to earth I mean."

"Yes, my child," Xriane answered solemnly. "It is very necessary. Believe me, had there been another option, I would have taken it. But as I said before, Norellyia will be just fine."

"I guess that is all then." She was not convinced by her mother's words. In fact, she was even more confused by them. But without saying anything further, Sora kissed her mother gently on the cheek and left the room.

Sighing, Xriane made a mental note to tell Shala to have Elly come see her when she came home. She had seen Elly leave the castle just moments ago and had wished her father had not allowed her to go see Lea- at least not tonight of all nights. Oh well, Xriane sighed, maybe visiting Lea would do her some good and help her calm down.

Once again, Xriane settled herself on the windowsill and looked out towards the city as she surrounded herself with the memories of that time long ago when Jyarn and she had gone to earth.

Seconds after they arrived on earth, a loud noise had blasted in their ear and instinctively, Jyarn had pulled Xriane out of the street and onto the side of the road, just as a large moving vehicle passed by just barely missing them. Xriane had later learned that the big machine was a car and people used them to travel in. Xriane had been truly fascinated by these vehicles and remembered the fun she and Jyarn had the few times that they had ridden in one. It was a rather odd and archaic mode of transportation compared to what they had at home but it had been a most amusing experience.

During their time on earth, they had stayed in a small apartment in a place that was called Cambridge, Massachusetts. Jyarn had found a job working for a store clerk several blocks from where they were staying and Xriane worked with a little old lady down the street who was a dressmaker. What had fascinated Xriane the most about the people was the simple way they lived and how they seemed to find pleasure in everything they did despite the meager living conditions.

The room that they kept had been just barely a third the size of one of the rooms that could have been found in Jyarn's home in Dassar. The place had been cold and drafty during the winter and unbearably hot during the summer. Yet despite these and other misgivings that would have made any person miserable, Xriane found that instead the people were warm and open and always willing to help each other in times of need. Those who had extra always gave to those who did not have enough and needed more and many times Xriane had found herself crying as she remembered all the luxuries that she had at home of which she had taken for granted.

Through the experiences she had while on earth, the heart of stone and anger that had raged inside of her for so many years soon turned into one of love and compassion. She vowed that she would never again take what she had for granted and that, instead, she would nourish it and share it with others-others who may be less fortunate than herself.

CHAPTER FOUR

Norellyia tried to clear her mind as she stepped outside into the warm afternoon air. There were so many thoughts running through her mind that they soon began to all mingle together making her become more confused by the moment. The more she tried to clear her head, the more persistent and confused her thoughts became. As she stood leaning against a post near a flower bed in front of the castle, a small gray and blue ship pulled up next to her. She stepped inside the miniature ship and sat down.

"Kirr Sirren," she told the driver. For many years Elly had always wondered why she and her people needed the ships to travel, after all they were Gens and could be anywhere, they wanted anytime they wanted simply by thinking about being somewhere. One day she had asked her father about why they used ships to travel when clearly, they did not need them to do so. Her father had explained that each time they used their powers to travel or to do anything else, it drained a little of the powerful energy they possessed and also shortened their lives. This was primarily true for the Gens whose work required them to do a lot of traveling from one city to another.

When their ancestors realized what was happening, they decided to build ships in order to conserve their energy and not abuse the powers that they possessed. Despite this explanation, it took Elly many years afterwards before she completely understood the importance of conserving her energy and powers. Elly now understood that the energy and powers that Gens possessed was at the center of who they were and had to be protected in order for them to survive. That was one of the main reasons why the Gens had to leave earth in the first place; so that their powers would not be abused any longer.

As the ship drove away from the castle, Elly shook her head vigorously and tried distracting herself by enjoying the scenery outside. It was late afternoon and the sun was beginning to go down behind the mountains in the distance but the streets were still alive with people bustling around getting last minute affairs in order before the night set in. The orange glow from the fading sun was mesmerizing as it sparkled off the crystal houses and, for a moment, Elly was able to forget her troubles and simply immerse herself in the glow of the sun. A few minutes later, the ship took a quick turn left into a side street and soon stopped in front of a large house, bringing Elly out of her reveries and back to reality.

"Thank you," Elly said as she got out and stood in front of the house. Like all the other houses, this one was crystal and circular with two twisted posts along each side of the entryway. With the sun slowly setting, a beautiful prism sparkled off the smooth crystal exterior of the house. An old, tall, and shady sacmore fruit tree stood in the front yard in full bloom and on the west side of the house was a row of beautiful velvet pink roses with bright orange sunflowers creeping up in a vine in the background against the side wall.

Stepping up the front porch, Elly knocked lightly on the front door and waited. The door was immediately opened by a tall young woman with soft gold hair and brilliantly shiny gray eyes.

"Good evening, Madam Vasna," Elly greeted Lea's mother warmly.

"Hello, Elly! Come, Lea is in the yard." She opened the door and ushered Elly inside. "Wait here while I go call her for you."

The interior of the house was painted a soft blue with tiny flowered imprints around the top and bottom borders. The sitting room where Elly was standing was decorated in deep mauve and cream with two large mauve chairs against the farthest wall. A cream and mauve couch covered with a variety of colorful pillows shaped the contour of the opposite wall. There was also a fire burning in the room directly in front of where Elly stood, giving the house a nice, warm and cozy feeling.

Against the far wall on the other side of the sitting room stood a large glass case that took up almost the entire wall. Elly walked up to it and smiled. Inside was Lea's shell collection along with an eclectic collection of plates that Lea's mother had collected over the years. Lea loved shells just as much as Elly did. That was one of the main reasons that they were such good friends. When school was over in the afternoon, they would stop at the beach on their way home to go look for shells after which they would then head for Madam Rylem's to do some shell exchanging. Afterwards, they would take their shells home, paint and decorate them and add them to their collection.

"Hello, Elly," came a voice from behind Elly.

Elly turned around and smiled. "Hello, Lea."

Lea was the same age as Elly, beautifully tall and slim with straight brown hair and deep brown eyes. She was an only child and was spoiled by her mother beyond reason. But despite all the pampering that she had received, Lea was the most compassionate and level headed girl that Elly knew.

"Come, let us go up to my room," Lea suggested, taking Elly's hand. Lea's room was on the second floor at the end of a long hallway. The room was small but tastefully decorated in soft pink and gray. The walls were painted a light gray and were covered with paintings. The biggest one was a painting of the castle in the middle of town highlighted by the orange and yellow glow of the fading sun. She had another painting of Elly and herself at the beach collecting shells.

"So, how are you?" Lea asked as she settled on her bed.

Elly shrugged and sat down in a chair by the window. "I am all right, I guess."

"So," Lea said, settling back against her pillows. "What is wrong, Elly?"

"What makes you think something is wrong?" Elly asked evasively.

Lea rolled her eyes in mock disgust. "Please, Elly, I know you better than that."

Elly smiled at her friend gratefully and said, "I am sorry. I am really not good company right now. I decided to come see you because I really needed to get away for a little while." She paused for a moment, unsure of whether or not she should tell Lea what was happening. It did not take her long to decide.

"I might as well tell you what is happening because I am sure that you are going to hear about it any day now and I would rather that you heard this from me first." Elly paused again to compose herself then told Lea, "My mother is thinking- actually no, planning on sending me to earth. Tell me, Lea, what do you think of that?" She asked the question casually, as if it did not really matter. But inside her heart was aching. She looked at her friend closely, patiently waiting for her response.

"Are you serious?" Lea asked after a few moments of silence. She was skeptical.

Elly laughed tightly. "Funny you should ask that. That is exactly what I had asked my mother when she broke the news to me a short while ago."

Lea was not amused. "I am serious, Elly. Why?"

Elly shrugged. "I do not know. It is all very confusing to me. I am still trying to understand it all. I have not had a chance to put anything into perspective."

"This is unbelievable, Elly! Earth! You will be all right, though, yes?"

"Yes, I will be fine," Elly assured her. "I am sure that mother knows what she is doing." And as she said that, Elly knew that it was the truth. Despite all the confusion raging inside of her, Elly knew that her mother would not send her someplace where she would get hurt or someplace where she would not be safe. But knowing that did not make it any easier to accept.

Both girls fell silent for a while, each lost in their own thoughts about the news.

"On a brighter note," Lea said finally, "think about all the interesting experiences you will have. I mean, it is not everyday someone gets a chance to go to earth. Think of all the stories you will have to tell everyone when you get back!" Elly laughed for real this time. Only Lea could take such a bleak matter and make it look like the chance of a lifetime. The two girls spent some time speculating about Elly's impending journey to earth and soon Elly found herself almost warming up to the idea. Almost- but not quite completely.

Finally, Elly glanced out the window and noticed that it was beginning to get dark. "It is getting late," she said, getting up from her chair. "I best be getting home before mother and father start worrying and send the troops to search for me."

"I will see you tomorrow in class, right?" Lea asked.

Elly smiled. "Yes, of course and thank you, Lea. Thank you for cheering me up about this whole situation." Lea smiled and gave her friend a warn hug. They headed downstairs and found Madam Vasna sitting in a chair by the fireplace.

"Thank you for the invitation, Madam Vasna," Elly said politely.

"Anytime, Elly," Madam Vasna smiled. "You know we love having you over."

Elly opened the door and let herself out. Good thing I brought a shawl with me, Elly thought as a light breeze began to pick up. The ship was late. She waited in front of Lea's house huddled in her shawl for about ten minutes before the ship showed up to take her home. On her way home, Elly carefully thought through the events that had taken place during the day and tried to put everything into some logical sense but found it almost impossible to do so.

There was only one thing that Elly was very sure and clear about by the time she reached the castle. She trusted her mother and knew that she always had her best interest in mind. Reluctantly, Elly admitted to herself that maybe she was being just a little irrational about the whole thing. Once more, she went over the events of the day and this time, things started looking a little bit clearer to her...

The moment she entered the castle, Elly was immediately approached by Shala.

"Your mother wants to see you," Shala told Elly.

"Right now?"

"Yes, immediately."

Sighing, Elly walked down the corridor of the first floor and headed towards her mother's chamber. Of course, she knew what her mother wanted to see her about. She had hoped that she would have the night to sleep on things before having to face reality. She knocked on the door but there was no answer. She opened the door and peeked inside but did not see her mother anywhere.

"Come in, Elly." Elly turned her head and realized that her mother was in her bathe. Stepping inside, she took a pillow off a large chair and sat down on the floor by the window. Minutes later, her mother stepped out of the bathroom. She was wearing a purple silk robe and her thick hair was braided in two and hung over her shoulder.

"How is Lea?" her mother asked, pulling a chair up next to Elly.

"She is fine." Elly notice that her mother did not complain about her sitting on the floor.

"Elly, dear," her mother began. "I wish that you would not take this decision the wrong way-"

"No, Mother, please," Elly interjected before her mother could finish speaking. "There is something I need to say. I thought about all of this on the way home from Lea's and I am very sorry for my behavior earlier. It is just that-" she shook her head. "I was not expecting this. You took me by surprise, completely."

"So, you are not angry with me?" Xriane asked anxiously.

Elly smiled softly and shook her head. "No, Mother, I am not angry. I am just confused and- scared." The dream she had had earlier once more flashed through her head. Why was she so reluctant to share this with anyone?

"Do not be scared, my child. Everything is going to be just fine." Xriane reached over and gave Elly a reassuring hug. "I would not let anything harm you, you know that."

"I know," Elly admitted. "The whole idea just seems so strange, that is all."

"The main reason I want you to go is because you need to know the history of your people. I know," Xriane said seeing that Elly was about to protest. "You are wondering what it is you can possible learn there after so much time has passed since it was our home. But that is what you must remember; it was our home for many centuries. Earth was our first home, as a matter of fact. This is where we began and therefore it will always be a part of our lives, no matter how much time passes or what has happened. Trust me, you will understand one day. I am just relieved right now knowing that you are not upset. I was truly worried. But as for everything else, things will fall into place in time, you will see."

"I am sorry," Elly repeated. She was silent for a moment, thinking. "So, tell me mother, when do I leave?" She looked at her mother expectantly dreading the answer.

Xriane sighed. "In ten days."

"Ten days," Elly repeated. She shook her head as if she could not believe it. This was not going to be easy. Things were changing too fast.

"Look, Elly," Xriane said. "It is late. Why don't you go get some rest? We will talk some more about this tomorrow, all right?" Elly nodded and got up off the floor, putting the cushion back on the sofa.

"Good night." She leaned over and kissed her mother on the forehead. Leaving the room, she headed upstairs to her own room. Once there, she washed up, pulled on a nightgown and crawled tiredly into bed. As she lay in bed, thoroughly exhausted from the day's events, she wondered about what she would be facing in the days ahead. What is next? she thought as she felt her eyes growing heavy with fatigue. The excitement of the day had worn her out. Unable to hold out any longer, she slowly drifted off soundlessly to sleep. This time, there were no dreams.

CHAPTER FIVE

Elly woke up late the next morning. Initially when she woke up feeling the warm sunshine against her skin, she was almost able to forget the events of the previous evening. But the instant she was fully awake everything came flooding back to her. From where she lay in her warm cozy bed, it all seemed like just a bad dream- a dream that she was not going to be able to wake from. To anyone else, this would seem like just another day. But to Elly, it was the beginning of the rest of her life. Reluctantly, Elly forced herself out of bed, washed up and prepared as best as possible to face the day.

When she entered the main room downstairs, everyone was already eating and trying hard to pretend that everything was normal. No one mentioned what had happened the previous evening but Elly was sure that that was exactly what everyone was thinking about. She was anything but hungry and did not really feel like eating. But Shala forced her to eat anyway, saying how it was unhealthy to stay without eating in the morning. Once she was done eating, she grabbed her books and headed off to class along with her sisters Raina and Kyli. Her other sisters did not go to the same classes.

All day Elly's mind kept wandering from her studies and by late afternoon, she was being barraged with questions by her friends. Is it true? Was she really going to earth? They were all so excited for her. Elly was not surprised that everyone had gotten the news so quickly. News like that did not stay contained for long.

Elly understood that once a decision was made concerning who would be sent to earth, it was required that an announcement had to be made letting all people know of the decision. Apparently, her parents had made the announcement earlier that morning, which was the only thing that could explain why people in her classes already knew. Before the day was over, the whole city, if not the whole planet, would have heard the news. Elly wished that this did not have to be so public but at the same time she knew that the people had the right to know what was happening. After all, it affected them almost as much as it did her.

Finally, to Elly's relief, classes were over. She stood outside under a tree and waited for Lea and her sisters, along with some of their friends. Together, the group headed home. Since Elly and Lea lived in the same direction, they said goodbye to the other girls upon reaching the cross road and headed west towards the castle. Raina and Kyli walked on ahead while Elly and Lea followed behind them.

"Let us go down to the beach and see if we can find some shells," Elly suggested. She was not ready to go home and face the reality of what was happening in her life. She needed a distraction and the beach was always the best place to go.

"Sure," Lea agreed, knowing well what Elly was trying to do.

About three blocks from the castle was a beautiful beach. The water there was an aqua marine blue and looked serenely peaceful but actually was a deep, raging sea under the calm if a person went in too far. But it was always warm so that no matter what time of the year it was, the people living in the area could always go swimming. There was also an old shed on the beach which the girls had used as a dancing room for many years. Over the years, the girls had out grown the dancing and decided to use it for painting and other various hobbies since they both loved the old shed and did not want to see it destroyed for lack of use. During the summer, they would spend the hot days in there, talking and decorating their shells or painting.

At the beach, Elly and Lea spent almost an hour digging for shells without talking. After a while they sat down next to each other, exhausted.

"I found fourteen shells," Elly announced. "What about you?"

"Twelve," Lea answered as she leaned back against her elbows, breathing heavily. They sat there for a while staring out into the aqua marine water, each lost in their own thoughts, both were wondering about what the future held for them.

"I want to ride the horses," Elly said suddenly, jumping up, not wanting to think about anything anymore. "How about you?"

"Sure, that sounds fun," Lea said, understanding well that Elly was just trying to find ways to distract herself from thinking about what she would have to face soon: going to earth. Lea could not even imagine what Elly was feeling, but she wanted to support her in any way she could. Elly and she had grown up together and being an only child, she had always considered Elly as a sister. If this is what she needed to feel better then, this is what they would do.

The girls walked to the stables behind the castle and went inside one of them. The stable was large and airy inside and was home to over two dozen horses of various breeds. The girls had ridden the horses together many times and each had their favorite horses.

"I want to ride Maiden," Lea informed Elly, running her fingers through the mane of a jet-black horse with a white mane and white hooves.

"I will ride Blazer," Elly said, caressing behind the ears of a handsome mare. His coat, being a creamy light purple, gleamed in the sunlight. "I am quite sure that Martelly took some of the other horses to the slopes," Elly said as they mounted the horses. Martelly was the stable hand who took care of the horses. "So let us take them out to the pasture beyond the meadow, they need a good run anyway."

They led the horses out towards the meadow at a slow gallop. They were surrounded all around by gentle rolling hills covered with soft green grass peppered with colorful flowers. Elly enjoyed the feel of the wind against her skin as the horse galloped leisurely towards the pasture.

They were not far from the pasture when Blazer suddenly jerked forward wildly and in an instant the horse was galloping at full speed through the meadow at an uncontrollable speed. It all happened so fast that Elly's first reaction was panic. She sat stiffly on her saddle, gripping the reins tightly so that her hands became red, sweaty and almost numb.

Behind her, Elly could hear Lea also picking up speed trying to catch up with her. As quickly as the panic set in, it disappeared as Elly finally came to her senses and leaned forward against Blazer. Closing her eyes, she rubbed the side of his neck gently, hoping to soothe the horse. Come on, Blazer, she said, speaking to the horse quietly in her mind. Calm down, please. Within seconds, the horse quickly slowed down his pace and abruptly came to a stop. Elly sighed heavily in relief. She took a few moments to catch her breath and then slowly led Blazer into the pasture. Once there, she dismounted, leaned herself against the horse and waited for Lea, who was only a few feet behind her.

"That was close," Lea gasped, pulling up next to Elly.

"I know," Elly agreed, taking in another deep breath. Elly's heart was actually pounding from the experience, but she did not allow her friend to see her fear. Both girls had ridden Blazer and Maiden before, against her mother's wishes of course, and this had never happened. She could not understand what had caused the horse to react the way it did. She pushed the incident to the back of her mind, promising herself that she would not ruin what was left of her day. She planned on enjoying every second she had left before leaving for earth- no matter what.

Lea dismounted Maiden and soon the two horses were roaming freely through the pasture. Elly and Lea started walking through the thick bed of purple and orange flowers that were growing wildly across the field. They picked wild flowers from a gistel tree and ate kaila, a green and yellow fruit which grew on a thick old tree growing in the center of the pasture. The fruit was soft and very sweet and had always been Elly's favorite. Afterwards, Elly climbed up a mello tree where she found a cluster of red tassil fruit growing. The tassil fruit was not as sweet as the kaila, but it was very juicy. Soon, Lea joined Elly up in the tree and they sat there eating fruit until the sun began to sink behind the trees, forcing them to head back to the castle.

After the horses were brushed, put back into the stable, and fed, Lea gathered her books, said goodbye to Elly and headed home. There was no one around when Elly entered the castle except for Shala who told her that dinner would be ready shortly. Feeling a little depressed despite the excitement of the day, Elly went upstairs to wash up and prepare for dinner.

Little was said during dinner that night. Elly asked to be excused shortly after dinner was served although she had not touched her food. With her mother's permission, she quickly retired to her room. She changed and got into bed, not at all in the mood for sleeping. She sighed deeply, wondering what it would be like to live on a planet which she knew nothing of. She had read books that told tales about earth and she had also heard many stories told about the place by the elders, but nothing more.

She tried not to think too much about the dream she had had, knowing that it would only make her more anxious about going to earth. But even though she tried to ignore it, it was always there, imprinted on the back of her mind. Part of her was crying for her mother to change her mind.

She was really scared but she knew that there was no way to change her mother's mind. Once her mother made a decision about something it was almost impossible to convince her to change her mind.

It was settled.

She lay motionless on her bed and stared out the window, trying hard to count the stars on the still blue sky.

Earth.

It sounded so mysterious. Who knew what could happen there? Why think about it? She asked herself sarcastically, you are going to find out anyway- and soon.

Finally, she fell asleep in a world unknown to her, undecided.

Nine days later, Elly was lying in bed, staring blankly up at the ceiling, unwilling to face the day that lay ahead of her. I still cannot believe that this is happening to me, she said to herself as she rolled over and pulled the sheets over her head. She knew what was waiting for her. This was the day she left for earth. Her mother had talked to her about it constantly, reassuring her that everything was going to be fine.

She had learned more about the culture of humans in the past few days than in all the times she had studied about them in class. Her mother had explained that it all was essential to her survival on earth. She had to be able to blend in with the humans and the only way she would be able to do that was to learn about their current culture. She had to study about their customs, traditions, the foods they ate, the clothes they wore, lifestyles, even how they spoke- everything. Elly had been genuinely intrigued by some of the customs that humans practiced as they were very unusual while others seemed almost pointless to Elly.

She closed her eyes tightly and slowly took in several deep breaths. After a few moments, she finally forced her eyes open; she knew she was going to have to face the day eventually and doing so was not going to get any easier. Ironically, despite the gloom she felt around her, it was a beautiful day. Golden rays of sunlight shone brightly through the windows making everything in the room sparkle. She could smell the wonderful perfume of the flowers from the garden below.

It was amazing. Today was the day when the rest of her life would change forever, yet everything looked the same, was the same in fact. Forcing herself out of bed, she took a quick bath, got dressed and went downstairs where she found breakfast waiting. Reluctantly, Elly forced herself to take a few bites. This would be her last meal at home and she was determined to enjoy it.

"May I be excused?" she asked, when she finally realized that there was no way she was going to be able to keep food in her stomach. She was too anxious about what lay ahead. Her mother nodded her approval and Elly left the breakfast room. She only had a few hours left before her journey began and she did not want to spend them being closed up in the castle.

She stopped in her room to put her hair up and then she left the castle and headed out towards the beach. When she got there, she sat down on a large boulder, facing out towards the sea with the wind blowing softly against her skin. She smiled, remembering the times she had spent here with her sisters and Lea. The carefree days that they all spent here together laughing and enjoying themselves without a care or worry. Now she wondered as she sat staring at the water, if those times would ever come again.

Elly was lost in her memories and did not know how long she sat there out on the beach, sitting alone on the boulder, feeling the wonderful breeze against her skin and taking in the salt sea air. But finally, as the sun began to sink behind the clouds, she got up and reluctantly headed back for the castle, knowing that she could not stay at the beach forever and at the same time, wishing that she could. She also wished that she could see Lea again before leaving, but there was no time for that now. She had needed the time alone at the beach to calm her spirit and prepare for the journey that lay ahead. When she entered the castle, she quietly climbed up to her room, not wanting to attract anyone to her presence in the castle. Once inside, she looked around as though she were seeing it for the first time. Her warm, cozy bed, her shell collection, her paintings, all would be left with no one to enjoy or admire them. She sighed and sat down on her bed.

This is going to be even harder than I thought, she admitted to herself.

A few minutes later, there was a sharp knock at the door, bringing Elly out of her reveries.

"Come in."

The door opened and Dela, her third oldest sister, stepped in. "Elly, everyone is waiting for you," she said in a whisper. Dela was the quiet and sensible sister who only spoke when it was necessary and always said what needed to be said, even when no one else would. Unlike her other sisters, Dela took after their father. She was tall and slim with blazing blue eyes and bright red hair. Her features were sharp, almost angular, making her seem rather intimidating. People were always surprised to see how gentle she was when they met her.

Since their mother's announcement about Elly going to earth, Elly had seen a haunted and disturbed look on Dela's countenance, but she had said nothing to express what she was feeling. Even though this was peculiar everyone knew that it would be no use to try and pry anything out of her. Dela would only talk when she was ready to.

Elly stood up and looked around her room for the last time. She wondered how long it would be before she saw it again. "I guess this is it," she smiled weakly. "Come on," She took her sister's hand. "Let's do this while I still have the courage." Still holding hands, the two girls left the room and headed downstairs.

"Where are they?" Elly asked as they turned a corridor.

"In mother's room," answered Dela softly. Elly could still see that haunted look in Dela's eyes and she suddenly felt a chill.

The moment Elly set foot in her mother's room; her heart froze. It was as though until that very moment; she had not really realized or accepted the reality of what was happening in her life. Up until now it still had seemed like just a bad dream to Elly- a dream that she was bound to wake up from, she was sure. But now she realized this was real- there was no turning back. Whatever happened from this point forward she was just going to have to face it whether she wanted to or not. In that instant, a variety of mixed emotions flooded through Elly. Excitement, sadness, fear- she felt all of these things at once.

Xriane walked up to Elly and hugged her tightly. "Do not worry," she whispered. "It will be all right." Elly tried to smile as her mother brushed a lock of hair away from her face. But she could no longer conceal her emotions. Her lower lip began to quiver and tears streamed down her face. She quickly wiped them off with the back of her hand.

I will not cry, she scolded herself. I have no reason to cry. But she knew that was not true.

Her mother kissed her soundly on the forehead.

She turned towards her father who was standing by the door. She felt ashamed of having accused him of not loving her that night at the table when she first found out she was going to be sent to earth.

"Father, I am sorry-"

"Elly, shh, this is no time for apologies." He held his arms out to her.

"I love you," she whispered as she hugged him tightly.

"I love you, too," he replied.

"Elly," Sora said from behind her. Elly turned and found Sora and her other sisters standing together by the window. They too were trying to keep from crying. "We want you to have something." She handed Elly a small silver box. "It is from all of us." Elly took the box and opened it. Inside she found a necklace made of pure gold with a small crystal heart hanging from it.

"Thank you. I will wear it as a reminder of home." Elly hugged Sora fiercely then went and hugged each of her sisters in turn and then bravely turned towards her mother once more.

"Are you ready?" Xriane asked. Norellyia hesitated for a moment then nodded, not trusting herself to speak. She was as ready as she would ever be. Xriane opened a door that led into a clear glass compartment that was just long and wide enough for someone to fit inside and was fixed in the center of the room. Funny, Elly thought.

She had been in her mother's room many times and never remembered seeing such a fixture, not that it really mattered at this moment.

Xriane motioned for Elly to enter the compartment. Once inside, the door closed, locking her inside. Elly stood stiffly inside the compartment and closed her eyes, not knowing what to expect. She tried to relax but found it almost impossible to do. Eventually, though, her head became light and she started to feel as though she was floating through the atmosphere. She tried to open her eyes again but they refused to move.

For a sudden moment, she felt the same spinning sensation she had felt just prior to her nightmare. But just as quickly as the sensation started, it stopped. Her body immediately became numb, and then... there was nothing...

CHAPTER SIX

Norellyia felt strangely disoriented and her body was stiff and aching all over as though she had been lying in one position for hours. Her eyes felt heavy and she found that they refused to cooperate when she tried opening them. She lifted her head a little but it ached so much that she had to let it drop back down.

"Ouch," she whimpered as her head fell back and landed on some hard object. It took several moments before she realized that something was falling and hitting her- something cold and wet. She slowly forced her eyes open and found herself lying at an odd angle on her back with rain heavily pouring down on her. Everything around her was a dark blur. She squinted against the rain and peered up towards the sky and found that it was dark and frightening; unlike nothing she had ever set eyes on. Elly had never seen rain like this before, either, not anywhere on Sarcaun.

Where am I? She wondered. She felt cold shooting through her body as she painfully tried to stand up. Looking around, she realized that she was lying by the side of a road and there was nothing around her for miles, so it seemed. Somewhere in the distance lighting flashed across the sky and thunder crashed loudly. Elly's heart jumped.

And then she remembered her dream.

Remembering the dream motivated her and after struggling for a few more minutes she was finally able to stand. She looked around some more and saw that she was standing in a field and a short distance behind her she could just barely make out what appeared to be thick woods.

It was just as she had seen it in her dream. The field where she stood, the forest in the distance, the lightning and thunder and, of course, the rain except, it was not dry and sunny where she stood. She was soaked through to the bone. She stood for a moment in awe of the realization that she was now standing practically in the very place that she had dreamed about just shortly before she found out that her mother was planning on sending her to this strange planet.

She was on earth.

The rain continued to fall relentlessly. Norellyia had no idea what she was supposed to do from here. Her head ached and she was very cold and completely soaked even though she was wearing several layers of clothing. Rather strange clothes, too, Elly noted. She had on a pair of dark blue pants that were tight and uncomfortable, a cream colored, thick turtleneck sweater and a long, thin black coat. On her feet were a pair of white shoes that were now soaked and covered with mud. But she did not bother dwelling on the clothes she had on as the rain continued to pour down in torrents around her.

Through all the preparations and talking, her mother had never really told her what she was supposed to do once she got to earth. All her mother ever said was that she wanted her to experience life on earth and learn something from it. When she had asked her mother what she was supposed to do on earth, she had assured Elly that she would know what to do when she got there.

Well, here I am, Elly thought wryly, and I am still confused. What was she supposed to learn? Elly wondered.

Well, this certainly was a new experience, Norellyia admitted.

But she was not enjoying it at all. She was cold, aching and, of course, wet. If this was all earth had to offer her, then she was in for a long, agonizing stay on earth. Maybe I should start walking, Elly decided, desperately wanting to get out of her current predicament. But which way should I go? she wondered as she tried peering down the road in both directions through the rain. It was useless. It was dark and the rain seemed to be coming down harder by the minute. Sighing in despair, Elly finally decided to head up the road to the right.

Norellyia walked for what seemed to her like hours and as she kept walking, it continued raining harder. Doesn't anybody live around here? she wondered to herself in anguish. Maybe I am walking in the wrong direction. She was about to turn around and head back in the direction she had come from when, not far in front of her, she made out a glimmer of light shining through a window of what appeared to be a house through the rain a short distance away. Encouraged, Norellyia walked on and was soon standing in front of a house that was rather small to Elly compared to the houses she had seen back on Sarcaun.

Since it was almost completely dark and the rain was still falling in torrents, Elly couldn't really tell anything about what the house looked like except for that it was two storied and had a wide porch in the front that seemed to be made out of wood with steps that led up to the front door. There was no light shining on the front porch and if not for the light she saw through one of the downstairs windows, she would have thought that there was nobody home or that everyone was asleep.

I hope these are good people, she said to herself as she walked up the front porch and knocked lightly on the door. She was frozen stiff, wet to the bone and tired- extremely tired and as she waited for someone to answer the door, she felt herself on the verge of losing consciousness. She desperately needed to get out of the rain.

The door was immediately opened by a tall, gentle looking middle-aged woman with warm brown eyes and a scarf tied around her head, wearing a dark gray dress that fell to her ankles.

Elly opened her mouth to speak but before anything came out her eyes blurred and an excruciating pain pierced through her head and behind her eyes. Elly gripped the side of the door tightly as pain shot through her and within a few seconds Elly blacked out and crumbled to the ground at the feet of the woman who had opened the door.

Elly didn't know what was happening to her. She found herself constantly slipping in and out of consciousness. When she was awake her head swam and she felt extremely cold despite the fact that she was sweating profusely. Her body ached and her mouth felt as though it were stuffed with cotton. Elly groaned and moved her aching body hoping to find a comfortable position which she soon discovered was impossible in her current condition. The nightgown she had on was drenched with sweat and clung coldly against her skin.

She could hear distant voices around her but she was not able to stay conscious or focus long enough to find out where the voices were coming from or what they were saying. Before long, Elly was exhausted from trying to stay awake and could no longer take the excruciating pain that was coursing through her body. Giving up, she let her body relax and fell soundly asleep.

The next time Elly woke up, her head throbbed and her ears rang loudly to such a point that they hurt. Elly slowly opened her eyes and tried to focus. She moaned slightly as she moved her body and realized that she was in a bed wrapped warmly in light blue sheets. Fighting the nausea that threatened to overtake her, she forced herself to sit up in bed and slowly looked around. Next to her, to the left, was a night table with a lamp that was turned on just enough to lightly illuminate the room she was in.

She found that she was in a small, narrow room that was scarcely furnished with only a desk against the farthest wall and a chest cabinet was to the right of where she lay in the bed. There was a high window above the desk but it was dark and the curtains were closed so she could not see outside. Even so, she could hear the rain pounding harshly outside. After examining the room, it took her a moment before she realized that she was no longer wet and cold. She was nice and warm wearing a long, cotton pink nightgown with several blankets wrapped snuggly around her.

Finding herself in a strange place, Elly had the urge to go explore the place to find out exactly where she was. But as soon as she moved to swing her legs over the side of the bed her head swam and she felt pressure behind her eyes. Elly sighed as she laid back down in defeat. Apparently, she would not be going anywhere for a while.

Elly didn't remember falling asleep again but it was clear that she had because the next time she opened her eyes there was bright sunlight streaming in through the window above the desk. Elly squinted and covered her eyes against the bright light. Slowly her eyes adjusted to the light and it was only then that Elly realized that she was not alone in the room.

Turning her head to the left she found a woman sitting in a straight back chair next to the bed. The woman was watching Elly intently with warm brown eyes that were filled with compassion. Elly recognized her as the woman who had opened the door for her when she had come knocking on the door. Elly wondered how much time had passed since that time. Elly tried to sit up in bed.

"No, no," the woman said gently, laying a hand on Elly's shoulder. "You need to save your strength. Just relax, okay?"

Elly nodded and settle back down in the bed. "Why do I feel so weak?" Her mouth was dry as cotton and she found it difficult to speak.

"You were very sick with an extremely high fever when you showed up at our door two weeks ago. It's a miracle that you're even still alive."

Two weeks? Elly tried to determine how long that would have been in her world but her mind was groggy and she couldn't concentrate.

"What was wrong with me?" she asked the woman.

The woman took in a deep breath and said, "Well, a lot of things. First of all, you had a very high fever and if that wasn't bad enough, you kept slipping in and out of consciousness. We had to call the local doctor to come in and take a look at you. Even he didn't hold much hope." Elly vaguely recalled what a doctor was. She really must have been in bad shape if one had to come see her.

"Where am I?" Elly wanted to know. "And who are you?"

"I'm Adrienne Coltz. But you can call me Adria. This is my home."

"Adria," Elly said hoarsely. "Thank you for taking care of me."

"Sweetheart, we are just very grateful that you're all right." Adria smiled kindly. "Would you like some tea?" she asked Elly. "It would help soothe your throat."

"Please," Elly answered.

"I'll be right back," Adria said. She got up, left the room and came back a few minutes later carrying two steaming cups of tea. She handed one to Elly then sat back down again.

"Now, tell me, dear," Adria said as she looked intently at Norellyia, "What's your name?"

"My name is Norellyia," Elly told her. She figured that it was no use lying to the woman about this since she had been so kind to her. "But I like to be called Elly."

"All right, Elly. So, tell me, where do you live and what were you doing out there in such rotten weather? You had no identification on you so we didn't know who to call. We even filed a report with the police and put out some fliers but there was no response."

That's because I'm from a place called Sarcaun and I happen to just be here on earth for, oh, who knows how long? Elly bit her lip to keep from laughing at the thought knowing perfectly well that she could never say such a thing. Apparently, fatigue was getting to her if she was thinking like this. She realized then that she was even talking differently then she normally did. She barely recognized her own voice and the words she was speaking felt strange coming out of her mouth. This was definitely going to take some getting used to.

Elly paused for a moment and choose her next words carefully. "I have no idea," she finally answered simply.

Adria was puzzled by her answer. "What do you mean?"

Elly shook her head. "I can't remember anything. I just woke up and found myself lying on the side of a road quite a distance from here. I have no idea how I got there. I know my name, but that's it- nothing else." Elly regarded the woman closely; did she believe her? She knew that she was lying, but what else could she do, tell her the truth? That would be interesting! The woman would probably throw her out instantly- sick or not.

"You mean you don't remember anything before that?" Adria asked incredulously.

Elly shook her head.

"You poor child," Adria whispered sympathetically.

"If I have any family, I don't know who or where they are. I have no idea what I was doing or what had happened before I ended up at the side of that road."

"That is really unbelievable."

Suddenly, and for no apparent reason, Elly began to feel guilty and very self-conscious. She was lying to this kind woman who had taken her into her home and nursed her back to health and it wasn't right. What was she doing? Elly set the cup down on the night table and threw the sheets off.

"Look, you have truly been kind to me and I thank you for taking care of me. But I am better now and I really should go." Elly realized that she was babbling, but she didn't care. All she knew was that she needed to get out of the house, there was no way she could stay. Elly swung her legs over the side of the bed and her eyes swam; she had to fight hard to keep the nausea away. Apparently, she still had a way to go before she recovered her strength completely. But she was not going to let that stop her.

"And where will you go?" Adria asked, watching Elly closely as she struggled to stand up.

Elly shrugged. "I don't know- somewhere. I just don't want to impose-"

"Who said that you're imposing? I let you in and took care of you, remember?" Adria smiled at Norellyia, her eyes twinkling. "Look, I can't let you leave here when you have nowhere to go. Plus, you need to regain your strength. How old are you?" She didn't give Elly a chance to answer, but continued. "You look to be about the same age as my oldest daughter and I couldn't bear to think of her out on the street with nowhere to go, especially if she was sick. Please, stay at least until your memory comes back or until we can locate your family. At the least, please stay until you're strong enough to take care of yourself."

Elly was amazed. She never expected to receive such warmth and kindness from a stranger on earth. Maybe she had jumped to conclusions too quickly she reluctantly admitted to herself. She gave up trying to stand and looked intensely at Adria. "Do you really mean it? You want me to stay?"

"Of course, I mean it," Adria smiled warmly. "I can't let you leave knowing that you have nowhere to go and also knowing that you're just getting over a very terrible fever. I would never forgive myself if anything happened to you while you were out there all alone."

"But you don't even know me," Elly protested softly.

"You're alone. What will you do out there? Please stay. It would certainly put my mind at ease."

Elly regarded Adria closely and saw that she was being sincere. "All right, I'll stay." But she still felt guilty as she said those words.

She felt as though she was taking advantage of this gracious woman, even though she knew that wasn't really true. It wasn't her fault that she had gotten sick, she certainly never expected that such a thing would happen to her. Plus, she really did need a place to stay while she was here.

"Good because I wouldn't have it any other way." Adria reached over and gently squeezed Elly's hand.

"Thanks for letting me stay, Adria. I truly appreciate your generosity."

"No need to thank me, dear. I just did what I know is best." She stood up then and took Elly's tea cup from the night table. "Now that we have that straight, you need to get back into bed and I need to go make dinner. Do you need anything before I leave?" She pulled the sheets and blankets up and tucked Elly in.

Elly shook her head. "No, I'm fine. Thank you."

Am I dreaming? Elly wondered to herself once she was alone in the room and comfortably settled in bed. She couldn't believe that this was happening. First of all, how did she get so sick? Elly had never been sick in her life and what she had gone through had made her feel as though she was on the verge of death. Two weeks! Elly shook her head in disbelief. That was almost equivalent to something like two months in earth time back home. How could two weeks go by without her knowing it? How could any amount of time have gone by, for that matter? Despite her sickness, Elly felt like it was just yesterday that she had woken up on the side of the road that now seemed like it was miles away from here. And now here she was in a strange room, in a strange bed getting over some type of sickness. Surely her journey to earth was meant to add up to more than this!

Elly yawned and snuggled deeper into the sheets. She would need to sort things out later. All she wanted to do right now was sleep.

Over the course of the next few days, Elly kept drifting in and out of sleep. During the time that she was awake, and in what seemed like a dream, Elly got to meet the rest of Adria's family. She met Michael, Adria's husband later in the evening on the same day Adria invited her to stay. He was a tall, middle aged man with short strawberry blonde hair, soft blue eyes that lit up when he smiled and a jovial demeanor that made Elly feel at home. He too extended an invitation for her to stay with the family for as long as she needed to.

Elly met Donna, the middle child, the next day. She was a bright, spunky girl with short blonde hair, deep brown eyes, a button nose and an infectious smile. Carey, on the other hand, was the youngest and was the shy and quiet one with straight strawberry blonde hair, like her father's, deep blue eyes and a timid smile. She came in regularly to check on Elly and made sure she was comfortable but did not talk much.

Melanie, the oldest girl, was the last one to introduce herself to Elly. She had marched into the room one day carrying a large tray loaded with food- some of which Elly had not recognized.

"Hi!" Melanie had announced enthusiastically as she placed the tray down on the night table. "I'm Melanie." She had settled herself in the chair next to Elly's bed as though she owned the room. "You're Elly, right?"

"Yes, that's right." Elly had answered as she watched Melanie closely.

"So, I hear you have amnesia," was how she opened her conversation with Elly. Elly had immediately liked her. She could tell that Melanie apparently was not the type to beat around the bush. She was tall and slim with flamboyant red hair and deep green eyes with a very open manner and quick wit. Yet despite the warmth she felt towards Melanie she was keenly aware that there was something troubling about her overall demeanor. Elly soon discovered that for some reason, she became a little uncomfortable when Melanie was in the room. She wasn't quite sure why but underneath the smile and witty comments, Melanie seemed to be nervous about something, even after she was laughing.

Once, after Elly had just woken up from a nap, she caught Melanie staring down at her in a rather unusual way and even though there was a soft, friendly smile on the girl's face Elly couldn't help the chill she felt creeping up her back. But Elly tried not to be too judgmental; after all, she had just met these people and did not know any of them well enough to be jumping to any conclusions. Besides, she needed to work on regaining her strength. She was getting tired of lying in bed and wanted desperately to get out of the house and get some fresh air.

CHAPTER SEVEN

"Elly, Elly, honey."

Elly moaned softly and forced her eyes open and saw Adria leaning over her. Adria was tall like Melanie with the same flamboyant red hair. Elly found it hard to believe she was the mother of three girls; she looked young and vibrant enough to be their sister. She had taken incredibly good care of Elly and for that Elly was grateful.

"I'm going out for a little while and no one else is home right now. Will you be all right until I get back?"

Elly nodded. "I'll be fine."

"Good. I won't be long." She quickly turned and left the room.

Elly tried to go back to sleep after Adria left but found that impossible to do. After about half an hour of tossing and turning, Elly gave up trying to sleep and climbed out of bed. She put on the plush blue robe she found laid out at the foot of the bed and left the room. Outside, she found herself standing in a narrow hallway. To the left were two other doors; one on the left and one across from it on the right. She went to the door on the left and found that it was partially open.

Peeking inside, she slowly looked around the room. It was extremely small compared to her room back home, but it was beautifully decorated. The furniture was made with a smooth almond colored wood, and the sheets and curtains were a matching yellow. Several pictures and paintings were hanging on the wall; some on them were of the family.

There was also a small bookcase against one wall, but it wasn't just holding books. On the bookshelf stood a stereo, something that Elly recognized only because she remembered seeing a similar picture in one of the books her mother had made her study. There were several dozen records and tapes stacked next to it. She liked the room. Glancing up, she noticed that there was also a fan hanging from the ceiling and the room itself looked as though it had just been freshly painted a warm creamy beige. Elly figured that this must be one of the girls' rooms but couldn't figure out which one. She didn't want to invade anyone's privacy any further, so she pulled the door closed to the way it was before and continued her exploration.

Across the hall from the room she had just been admiring, she found another open door but it was dark inside. She felt around against the wall and her hand touched a switch. Flipping it upwards, a bright light came on, mildly startling Elly. To her surprise, Elly discovered that she was in what appeared to be a bathe. It was different from the ones back home but sure enough, Elly decided, as she took in the marbled sinks and pulled back the white lace curtain that revealed a small tub, this was definitely a bathe. Heading out of the bathe she stopped in front of the sink and looked at herself in the mirror above it.

"Oh, my," Elly unconsciously muttered out loud. She looked terrible. Her face was pale and haggard making her look years older than she was. Her usually bright green eyes looked lifeless and there were dark circles under them. Her hair was dingy and hung limply around her face. Elly ran her finger through her hair. She definitely needed a bathe but she would finish checking out the house first.

Leaving the bathroom, she headed down the hall to the left. The hall ended in a small entryway with an elaborate gray tiled floor that had a carpeted stairway with wooden banisters that led up to the second floor. She decided she would explore the upstairs some other time. Crossing the entryway, she found herself standing in a small room that had a low, slanted ceiling painted a soft yellow with a blue and green flowered trim. She could tell that the room was old because she could see the faded yellow paint peeling off in some places.

There was a cream sofa with burgundy throw pillows on it against the far wall and next to that was a fireplace with a mantle that held an assortment of family pictures and a small vase of flowers. At the other end of the small room was a wooden rocking chair standing in a corner with a cushion on it and in the other corner was a potted green vine. A round wooden table stood in the center of the room adorned with a centerpiece of flowers with a colorful rug underneath it.

Elly felt surrounded by warmth as she stood in the room. It had an air of homeliness to it. There was love here, she knew, and it showed.

She left the first room and continued her exploration. The next room she came upon was the living room which led directly into the dining room that was to the left. The living room was large and cozy with an arched entryway and an arched window that faced north. The cream walls brought the most out of the burgundy and cream sofa that stood against the farthest wall, opposite the entryway. There was a small coffee table at each end of the sofa bearing a potted chrysanthemum.

Above the sofa was a beautiful painting of a waterfall surrounded by exquisitely colorful flowers that Elly was not able to identify in a tasteful gold frame. There were also two matching burgundy and cream end sofas, a coffee table with a wooden base and glass top that stood on a solid burgundy rug and a lamp stood next to each end table.

The living room, on the other hand, was furnished very simply and elegantly with a mahogany dining table that seated six, a china cabinet and a gold trimmed chandelier. There was another arched window behind the dining area with burgundy and cream printed curtains that matched the curtains on the living room window. Currently they were closed, but bright sunlight was still streaming into the room from a smaller half arch window that was above the large dining room window.

Elly was on the verge of entering the next room, the kitchen, that was adjacent and to the left of the dining room when she heard noises coming from somewhere outside in the backyard. She pulled the curtain back from the dining room window and peeked outside. She could hear the noise but she was not able to see anything. She shrugged and let the curtain fall back into place.

She decided to finish exploring later and headed back to the room. Once there she searched the drawers and found that it was filled with clothes and even found several towels in the lowest drawer. In the top drawer, she found a red pair of pants and a thick pink sweater. Elly stared at the strange clothes for a few moments. She examined the pants and the blouse closely. She had seen pictures of all of these things, but actually having to wear them was something else.

Oh, well she sighed. What choice did she have? She wondered what happened to the clothes she had on when she first came here. They were not anywhere in the cabinet, that was for sure. Elly laid the clothes that she found out on the bed and headed for the bathroom.

It took her a few moments to figure out how to work the faucets in the tub, but once she did it wasn't long before she had a nice, warm bathe drawn. Elly climbed into the warm water and felt herself relaxing completely for what felt like the first time in a very long time. After she was done bathing, Elly had to force herself out of the tub. She dried herself off, pulled on the robe and went back into the bedroom where she pulled on the pants and the sweater she had found in the drawer. She was surprised to find that the clothes fitted her comfortably. Elly smiled, liking the way the soft material felt against her skin.

When she was done, she looked at herself in the full-length mirror that hung on the bedroom door and had to admit the clothes didn't look too bad on her. The colors went well with her bronze skin and dark hair. She went back into the bathroom where she found a brush and several barrettes in a small dish on the counter. She brushed her hair back and clipped it in place with one of the barrettes. She took a good look at herself in the mirror and was satisfied with what she saw. She was still a bit pale, but she certainly looked more alive than before.

She walked through the house and found a door that led out to the backyard on the other side of the house from where the living room was. Apparently, the door was not used often because Elly had to struggle to open it and when it finally gave way Elly practically fell out through the door. She was greeted by chilly air and she instantly wished she had something warmer on.

The noise that she had heard earlier was still coming from somewhere close by. She wrapped her arms around herself to fend against the chilly air and walked around to the side of the house. In the distance along the farthest end of the property, she saw a shed of some sort. A short distance from that Elly could see a young man swinging something in the air. Each time his arm went down, that terribly loud noise came again. It took Elly a moment to realize what he was doing. He was chopping wood.

Elly was sure Adria never mentioned having a son so she was curious to find out who this was. She approached the man but stopped a few feet away.

"Excuse me," she said, as the man prepared to take another swing.

The man quickly turned around, surprised at hearing someone's voice.

"Hi," he said with a dazzling white smile. "Who are you?"

I was about to ask you the same thing, Elly thought but only answered, "My name is Elly."

His eyes instantly lit up when she said her name. "Elly!! Well, hello!! It's nice to meet you. I've heard so much about you."

Elly felt awkward hearing someone she didn't even know so excited about meeting her.

He must have felt her discomfort because he said, "I'm sorry. I should introduce myself. My name is Aimer. I work for the Coltzs'." He was tall, at least six feet, and muscular with thick brown curly hair and light blue eyes that sparkled when he smiled. Despite his height he had a very boyish and trusting look about him that made Elly smile.

"Hey, what are you doing out here?" he asked. "Aren't you just getting over a fever?" To Elly's amazement, he pulled off the brown jacket he was wearing and wrapped it around Elly. "Here, this should keep you warm until you get back inside."

"Oh, no, please. I can't stay in the house any more. I need to get some fresh air." She wrapped the jacket tightly around her, grateful to have it.

Aimer chuckled and settled the ax he was holding on the ground. "Okay, but I'll only let you stay for a few minutes." He leaned back against the stump he was using as a chopping block. "I wouldn't want you getting sick again by being out here."

"I won't stay long," Elly assured him. "So, you said you work for the Coltzs'. What exactly do you do?"

"I do a little bit of everything. Mainly, though, I take care of the four horses that the Coltzs' own."

"Horses? There are horses here? Where?" Elly tried to contain her excitement. Maybe this wasn't going to be such a bad journey after all.

Aimer pointed to the right. "The Coltzs' also own that property on the other side of the fence. There's a barn and pasture over there."

Elly squinted in the direction Aimer pointed but could not see anything.

She would have to go exploring again- and soon.

"Well," Aimer said looking around. "I'm done chopping all this wood. I better get them into the shed in case it decides to start raining again."

"Can I help?" Elly asked, desperately wanting to do something with herself. She had been lying around for so long her muscles needed some exercise.

Aimer looked concern. "Are you sure? I don't want you straining yourself. You were very sick, you know."

"I'm fine," she assured Aimer. "I really would like to help."

Aimer nodded in understanding. "We just need to carry these from here to the shed over there." He pointed to a wooden structure to the left about twenty feet from where they were standing.

"Don't try to carry too much. Just take a few at a time." Motivated, Elly pulled the jacket on and got to work.

It took them a little over half an hour to carry all the wood to the shed. By the time they were finished Elly was exhausted.

"Thanks for helping me," Aimer said as they stood outside in the shed that was now almost packed full with wood. "It would have taken me much longer if I'd done it all by myself."

"It's no problem," Elly said. "Plus, working helped take my mind off of things for a while. Thank you."

Aimer smiled. "Well, you really should go back inside now. I think you've been out here long enough."

"I will in a minute, though," Elly answered. She needed some time alone to think. She could tell that Aimer wasn't happy with her response by the look on his face. "I'll be fine," she assured him. She was about to take his coat off to give back to him but he stopped her.

"Keep it for now," he told her. "I'll come by and pick it up later. Right now, I need to run to the hardware store to pick up some supplies. Are you sure you'll be all right?"

"Yes, I will. And I'm only going to stay out here for a few minutes, promise."

"All right, then, I'll see you later." He reluctantly turned away and Elly watched him until he disappeared out a gate at the opposite side of the house from where Elly had come out.

The wind was starting to pick up a little so Elly stood inside the shed for a while, thinking. It felt so strange being here. It was hard to believe that several weeks had already passed since she arrived on earth. How did she end up getting so sick? She wondered for about the hundredth time. Elly had never experienced such sickness in her life.

Thankfully, she was alive, even though a few times she had wondered whether she was going to survive. But what exactly was she supposed to do now? That question haunted her and she was not able to find an answer. Why had her mother sent her here? She was still having a hard time even believing that this was really even happening. It was almost like a dream to her. Was she really millions of miles away from home on a planet that only a few weeks ago had seemed totally unreal to her? A planet she only read about in her history class, which, she had to admit, she had found to be very fascinating to the point that she spent time outside of class studying about the history of the planet.

A lot of what she had studied concerning the history of humans had been incredible and when she had asked her teachers about some of the history, they confirmed their accuracy but explained to her that much of what her people knew about humans, humans themselves had no idea because they did not have the ability to compile history the way Sarcaunians did. If humans only knew a third of what I did, Elly thought, I wonder if they would be able to handle it. She shook her head sadly. She was doubtful that humans would ever understand.

She sighed. At least she had found a place to stay, for now anyway, and she was thankful for that. How long would it be before they asked her to leave and what would she do if they did? These were such depressing thoughts but Elly knew she had to prepare for whatever happened.

Norellyia stepped out of the shed. She stared up at the sky which was now dark and threatening to erupt into a downpour again at any moment. She tried to imagine what was happening back home.

She desperately wished she could talk to her mother again and see her sisters but she knew that this was impossible and she had no idea how long she would have to stay here before returning home. Everything she'd experienced on earth so far was so strange, so different unlike anything that Elly had ever imagined or thought possible in her life. Was all of this real or was it just some strange dream? Elly wondered. But feeling the cold wind against her skin and watching those stormy clouds in the sky made Elly realize just how real everything that was happening to her was. Elly was surprised to find that this realization both excited and frightened her.

Shaking her head, Elly headed back towards the house. On her way there, she passed a medium sized flower pot with a variety of colorful flowers planted against the side of the house. She stopped to take a closer look because she didn't remember seeing it when she first came out. Apparently, it must have rained the night before because the flower pot was filled with water. Elly stared down at the drowned flowers. They were dead- all of them.

Why did flowers on earth die? Elly wondered sadly. At home, none of the flowers in the garden ever died. Regardless of what the weather was like, they were always in bloom. Elly stood there, thinking about the beautiful flowers that grew in the garden outside her bedroom window and how wonderful they smelled. Elly wished she could be in her room now, sitting on the windowsill, feeling the cool breeze on her cheek. As she thought about these things, to Elly's surprise, the dead flowers in the garden began to bloom and grow right before her eyes. Soon all the flowers were alive with bright colors, all of them still in the puddle of water.

Elly stared at the flowers with her mouth open in disbelief. She couldn't believe what had just happened. Her mother had explained that humans were different and did not possess the same gifts, as her mother liked to call them, as they did and in order for her to survive on earth, she would have to be just like them -completely human in every way. Why then had she been able to make the flowers grow again just by thinking about the live ones back home? Was it possible that she still had her gifts even though she was on earth now? Elly was stunned by the realization.

A harsh wind blew, shaking the flowers and Elly knew that they would die again soon.

Well, Elly said to herself as she turned away from the flowers, I guess I'm going to have to be very careful around here. She smiled and entered the house again through the same side door and heard the voices the moment she closed the door behind her. They were coming from a room near the back of the house which Elly figured was the kitchen. She headed in that direction and met Adria in the living room.

"Oh, there you are, Elly," Adria said as she wiped her hands on an apron. "I thought you might have deserted us despite my offer." She smiled and held her hand out to Elly. "Come on in here. Dinner's almost ready."

Elly followed Adria into the kitchen where everyone was busy doing something to prepare for dinner. Elly's stomach grumbled as the wonderful smell of food filled her nostrils. When was the last time she had eaten a real meal? She wondered. She couldn't remember at the moment but was looking forward to the one she was going to have.

"Where's Donna?" Melanie asked as she took some silverware out of a draw.

"She went to the bakery with dad to pick up a cake," Carey answered. "Mom also needed a few groceries."

"Elly, honey?" Adria called from the other end of the kitchen. "Do you mind getting some glasses from the cupboard over there and putting them on the table?"

"Oh, no," Elly answered, eagerly heading towards the cupboard. She was glad to have something to do. "I'd love to." Soon they were all busy getting everything ready for dinner and Elly found that she was actually enjoying herself. Michael and Donna came home a few minutes later and they also helped in the kitchen. Elly was so caught up in everything that was going on around her that she didn't have time to think about or miss home.

Once the table was set, everyone settled down to eat. Elly would have been shocked by the kinds of food that were at the table if her mother had not grilled her extensively concerning the types of food humans ate. Mashed potatoes with gravy, string beans, fried chicken. The meal was delicious.

After dinner, Elly helped Melanie and the others clear the table and clean the kitchen. Washing dishes was an interesting experience for Elly. She had never even been near a kitchen back home and here she was washing dishes as though it was something she had done every day.

Adria was the one who suggested that she get some rest when they were finished in the kitchen.

"You've had a long day," Adria explained. "And you have a lot to adjust to. Plus, you are still getting over your fever so you really should go to bed."

"You're right," Elly admitted. "I am feeling a bit tired." Actually, she was feeling very tired. Her eyes were heavy with sleep. "Again, thank you so much for your generosity. I truly appreciate it."

Adria smiled and pecked her on the cheek. "It's our pleasure, honey. Now go get some sleep."

Elly said goodnight to everyone and headed to her room.

After Elly had taken another relaxing bath and was lying in bed in a pink flower nightgown she found in the drawer, she thought about the things that had happened since she arrived on earth. It amazed her how one minute she was home surrounded by her family and in the next instant was waking up on another planet where everything was so different from her own world. She had grown up surrounded by luxuries and servants all around her. Someone was always there to do her bidding-she never had to raise a finger. The simplicity of the Coltz family both amazed and fascinated her. But they were happy and very loving to each other. It was all quite simple and yet very complicated at the same time.

Elly sighed tiredly. It had been a long day. It was still hard for her to believe that she was really on earth and not safely home in her own bed on Sarcaun.

Despite the uncertainty of her present situation, though, she could feel excitement building up inside of her because deep down she knew regardless of what happened from this point forward, this truly was going to be one experience that she would never forget.

Back on Sarcaun, Queen Xriane was having trouble sleeping at night. The nightmares had started immediately after Elly had left for earth. In them, she saw the planet being torn apart, completely destroyed till there was nothing left of it. And many times, she would see Norellyia lying in her arms, barely breathing and close to death. She would wake from these nightmares, her breath short, and perspiration clinging to her skin.

The King would ask her what was wrong and she would shake her head and say, "Nothing, a bad dream that is all." She could not bring herself to tell him the truth. What she saw were not just plain dreams, she knew, they were visions, a warning to her as to what might lay ahead. What they meant exactly; she was not sure. But each time she wondered about them, Nore's words of warning would come back to her.

Danger, he had told her. Doors that had never been open would be so. Shivering, she would wrap herself in her sheets and lay back down to sleep.

She needed answers and the only way she would find them were in the dreams that came to her late at night.

After the nightmares were over.

CHAPTER EIGHT

The next morning, Elly was awakened to the wonderful aroma of food seeping into her room, pulling her out of her reveries. At first, she thought she was home in her own bed, just waking out of a distant dream. But reality quickly hit as she sat up in bed and looked around through sleepy eyes. Her heart sunk. She was on earth, in a strange house filled with people she didn't know.

But then she thought about how they took her in and nursed her back to health and welcomed her into their home so unconditionally. These thoughts brought tears to her eyes which she quickly wiped away. She was afraid if she started crying now, she would never stop. Pulling herself together, she climbed out of bed, quickly washed up and got dressed. In the kitchen, she found Adria in front of the stove.

"Good morning," Adria greeted her, giving her a kiss on the cheek. "You're up early."

"I smelled the food," Elly admitted as she took a seat at the breakfast table. "I couldn't resist."

Adria laughed. "You just hold on a minute and I'll fry you some eggs and bacon. How do you feel today?"

"Better. I'm still a little bit weak but otherwise I think I'm all right."

"I'm glad to hear that. We were really worried about you."

Just then Michael came into the room. "Good morning, ladies," he said as he planted a kiss on Adria's cheek then took a seat next to Elly. "How are you today, Elly?" He took the plate of food that Adria handed him and sat down at the breakfast table across from Elly.

"I'm fine, thank you," Elly responded. "Where is everyone else?"

"No one in this house gets up before noon on Saturdays, unless they have to," Adria answered.

"Adria and I were talking last night," Michael said as he sat down at the kitchen table to eat. "First of all, we feel that perhaps we should have a doctor come take a look at you again or take you to see one to make sure that you're all right. After all, you were very, very sick and now it seems you have amnesia. It's good that you at least remember who you are, maybe that'll help your memory return. In the meantime, we thought we'd play it safe and have a physician look at you again. We think that we should also check with the police about locating your family. So far, there hasn't been any response to our efforts. Maybe the police can check to see if anyone's filed a missing person that fits your description. Or maybe they can give us other ideas of what we can do to help you. What do you think?"

Elly froze not knowing what to say. See a doctor? Talk to police? Elly only had a slight idea of what a doctor was, she knew even less about the police. Her mother had only given her a brief explanation about them. She remembered Adria mentioning something about a doctor coming to see her and the police coming by after they found her. But what if she sees a doctor again and this time, he or she was able to see things that would make then notice that she was different? That she wasn't human at all. She wondered if that were possible. It wasn't worth taking the chance. But even though she was concerned about these things, she knew that she couldn't just straight turn down the Coltzs' suggestion. They might suspect something.

"Could we wait a few days and see what happens before seeing a doctor? I really feel fine. I'm a lot stronger and I'm sure I'm over this sickness. I don't think there's anything physically wrong with me. But if my condition doesn't change within a few days, then I'll gladly go see a doctor and go to the police." Elly held her breath.

Michael nodded; he wasn't going to push her on the matter. "That sounds fair. But in the meantime, please be careful and watch over yourself. We don't want anything to happen to you."

"I'll be careful, I promise. And thank you."

"Well, I have to go to work for a few hours today," Michael announced, getting up. "See you later, kiddo." He patted Elly on the head, kissed Adria then left the house.

"Here's your breakfast," Adria said, setting a plate of eggs and a glass of orange juice in front of Elly. "Enjoy."

A few minutes later, just as Elly was finishing her breakfast, the front door opened and Aimer stepped into the breakfast room.

"Good morning," he said.

"Good morning, Aimer," Adria answered. "Help yourself to some eggs and bacon. There's orange juice in the fridge." Elly watched as Aimer made himself at home getting breakfast. Noticing how intently Elly was watching Aimer, Adria turned to her and said, "Aimer practically lives here. We're like his second family."

She noticed that he had his jacket on. He must have come back after she went to sleep to pick it up.

"Hey, Elly, would you like to come to the stable with me and see the horses?" Aimer asked as he settled down to eat.

"I'd love to." Elly got up from the table. "I'll be right back." She left and went to her room. Elly came out wearing a blue sweater that Melanie had given her and, on her way, back to the family room she ran into Melanie coming down the stairs.

"Morning, Elly," Melanie greeted her. "Where are you off to?"

"Aimer is taking me with him to the stable," Elly explained.

"Hey, have fun. Listen, I'm going to the mall to pick up a few things later. I thought maybe you would like to come with me. It would give you a chance to get to see the town, how about it?"

"Sure, I'd love to. When are you going?" Elly was looking forward to leaving the house. Maybe that would help her figure out what her purpose here was. She was determined to find out why her mother had sent her here for. She hated thinking that her journey here was all in vain.

"I'll probably be ready to go by the time you come back from the stable."

"I'll come see you once I get back."

"You'll probably find me upstairs in my room. Have fun with the horses."

"I will." Elly left and headed back to the kitchen.

"I'm ready," she told Aimer who was just finishing his breakfast.

"Here, Elly," Adria came into the room carrying a heavy coat. "Please put this on. We don't want you getting sick again."

"All right, Elly, let's go," Aimer said. The two of them left and went out a side door which Elly hadn't seen when she searched the house yesterday. Outside it was windy and a bit chilly. Elly wrapped the coat around her tightly. She followed Aimer to the other side of the yard where there was a gate that opened onto a dirt road. There was green grass growing over several acres of land and only a few trees were scattered about.

"How long have you been working for the Coltzs'?" Elly asked Aimer as he led her through the gate.

"Three years," Aimer answered, "since I first moved out here. The guy who worked for the Coltzs' before me quit for some reason or other. They never told me why."

"That's interesting."

"I know. But I'm glad because I really love working with horses." He led her further down another narrow path that forked to the right of the main path. Elly could see the barn in the distance which they covered within a few minutes. Moments later, they were out in a clearing where there were little puddles everywhere from the rain storm the previous night.

"Is it safe to ride the horses out in this weather?" Elly asked when they reached the barn. It was still very cloudy. Elly was certain that it would probably start raining again before the day was over. Such strange weather, Elly thought.

"Yeah, it's safe," Aimer answered, opening the gate. "I always take them out farther into the pasture where the grass is thicker and there are fewer puddles." Inside the stable, Elly saw four horses; two white ones and two black ones. Elly immediately fell in love with the black one that had four white hooves and a black and white peppered mane. He was strong and healthy and there was a very majestic air in the way he stood. Elly imagined the freedom she would feel riding this horse and feeling the wind against her skin. In a way he reminded her very much of Blazer.

Aimer introduced her to the horses and she found out that the horse she liked so much was named Midnight.

"They are all beautiful horses," Elly said. "But I think I'm in love with Midnight," She ran her fingers tenderly through the horses' mane.

Aimer laughed. "I don't know why but Midnight seems to be everyone's favorite. Come on, you can help me saddle Midnight. I'll ride him today and just let the others roam for a while."

The two of them saddled the horse and afterwards Aimer led the other three horses through another gate off the side of the stable then mounted Midnight and followed the horses out into the pasture.

Elly leaned against the gate and watched as Aimer led the horses out farther into the pasture. Once there, Aimer slowly guided Midnight around the fenced in pasture several times. Soon, he was going at a full gallop. Suddenly, though, Elly could see that Midnight was becoming tense and Elly immediately knew that something was wrong. Midnight suddenly reared up wildly, and in an instant took off with Aimer down the pasture. The other three horses, startled by Midnight's reaction, scattered in different directions.

Without even thinking, Elly threw open the gate and ran into the pasture following the direction Midnight had taken off in. Don't panic! Elly told herself. This isn't the first time something like this happened! Her experience with Blazer flashed through her mind. Even so, Elly knew that if she didn't do something to get Midnight under control, he was bound to throw Aimer off.

Before Elly had a chance to come up with a solution, Midnight suddenly halted in his step, neighed loudly and reared up once more. Then, without taking another step, he stopped. Elly could see from where she stood that the horse was twitching nervously. Elly sighed deeply and wiped the sweat off her face with the back of her hand. Her heart was pounding. She quickly ran to where Aimer and the horse stood.

"Aimer!" she called out, "Aimer, are you all right?"

Aimer was as white as a sheet and breathing heavily. "Yes, I'm fine, I think." He took in a deep breath and forced himself off the horse. Elly could see that he was still in shock. Even the horse was still shaking and neighing softly.

"What happened?"

Aimer shook his head. "I don't know. This is the second time this had happened. Snowflake had the same reaction just two weeks ago." He was referring to the pure white mare, Elly had met earlier. She had seemed like such a docile creature to Elly. She couldn't imagine her behaving this way. "But this time was worse than when it happened with Snowflake," Aimer added.

Elly was absently rubbing the back of the horses' mane, trying to get him calm. Suddenly, Elly felt a chill begin to climb up her spine. Something was wrong, she knew. Something had caused the horse to panic the way he did and it didn't have anything to do with Aimer.

Nervously Elly glanced carefully around the pasture and as she turned to the left, something caught her attention. She couldn't see anything or anyone from where she was standing, but Elly was almost certain that there was someone standing at the other side of the farthest railing that encompassed the pasture which was about fifty feet away. Somehow, Midnight had sensed that person's presence even from that distance and it had frightened him. Now, why would someone's presence frighten the horse? Strange, Elly thought.

Whoever was standing near the railing was moving away. Elly could feel the presence fading and Midnight was no longer twitching. Elly turned her attention to Aimer who was slowly regaining his composure and getting over the shock of what had just happened to him.

"Tell me something Aimer, does anyone else use this pasture or live anywhere near here?"

Aimer shook his head. "No, this is a private property, only the Coltzs' use it. Why?"

Elly shook her head. "Just wondered, that's all." For no rational reason that Elly could explain, she no longer wanted to be near the pasture. The presence that she had felt around the place just moments before disturbed her and she had a haunting feeling about what had just happened.

Taking one more glance around her she turned to Aimer and said, "I think the horses have had enough for today, don't you? Plus, you need to recover from all of this." Actually, Elly did not want to be in the pasture anymore. The experience with the horse was overwhelming and she was afraid of what may happen if they stayed out there.

"You're right. Let's get the horses back into the stable."

The other three horses were together on the other side by where the gate was so it wasn't too hard getting a hold of them. Once the horses were in the stable, Elly helped Aimer brush and feed them. Afterwards, Aimer locked the gate and they headed back for the house. Elly kept her eyes opened on the way back but didn't see or feel anything out of the ordinary. If it weren't for the way the horse had reacted, Elly would have been inclined to believe that she had just been imagining things.

"Thanks for helping me with the horses," Aimer said as they neared the house.

"No problem. Are you sure you're all right?" He had been relatively quiet while they were taking care of the horses. Elly suspected he was still reeling from the experience. Who could blame him? He could have been thrown from that horse and killed. That thought alone was enough to make Elly's blood run cold.

"I'm fine, really," he assured Elly. When they entered the house, they found Adria, Donna and Carey seated in the family room, watching television.

"How did it go?" Adria asked.

Elly hesitated for a moment before answering, "It was quite an experience." She smiled knowingly at Aimer. He smiled and shook his head.

"Melanie was looking for you just a moment ago," Adria told her.

With all the excitement, Elly had forgotten Melanie's invitation to go to, what did she call it? The mall?

"I'll go let her know I'm back." Elly turned back towards Aimer and said, "Thanks for letting me see the horses." With that, she disappeared out of the family room. Once in her room, she quickly changed into a clean pair of slacks a red sweater and then headed upstairs to Melanie's room. Melanie's bedroom door was slightly open and Elly was about to knock when she heard Melanie's voice from somewhere in the room. It sounded like she was talking to someone. Elly leaned closer towards the door opening.

"Listen, if I knew where he was, I would tell you," Elly heard Melanie say in a loud whisper. There was silence for a moment then Elly heard Melanie say, "I'll see what I can find out and get back to you." Silence again. Elly figured Melanie was having this conversation on the phone with someone. "Hey, I said I would see what I can find out, didn't I? You know I want this over just as much as you do." Elly heard the click when Melanie hung up the phone.

Elly took a step back and leaned against the wall, away from the door opening. Who had Melanie been talking to? Elly wondered. And what was she talking about? Elly felt a chill and it made her think of how she felt when she had first met Melanie. She had thought then that there was something peculiar about Melanie and overhearing this conversation only affirmed Elly's initial suspicions. It was quite obvious that there was something going on and apparently Elly had somehow stepped right into the middle of it, clueless as to what was happening around her.

Mother, what have you gotten me into? Once more Elly questioned her mother's decision to send her to this planet. Elly suddenly had the sinking feeling that things were going to be getting much worse before they got better while she was here. Taking a deep breath, Elly finally knocked on Melanie's door.

"Come in!" Melanie called. Elly opened the door and found Melanie sitting at her dresser, brushing her hair.

"Hi, Elly, have a seat," she pointed to a chair over by the window. "I'll be done in a minute," Melanie told her.

Elly looked around the room and found that it was tastefully furnished with handcrafted wood with various shades of green and light brown for the sheets and curtain. The window faced to the west so Elly had a view of the pasture in the distance. Once more the incident that took place there earlier flashed through her mind.

"Elly? Elly, are you all right?"

"Oh, uh, yes, I'm fine." Elly hadn't realized that she'd drifted away with her thoughts. She forced a smile. "I'm sorry, Melanie, what were you saying?"

"I was saying that I'm ready. Come on, let's go." They left the bedroom and went downstairs to the family room where Adria, Donna and Carey were still watching television.

"Would you two like something to eat before you leave?" Adria asked, as she got up and headed for the kitchen. "It's almost lunch time anyway."

"No," Melanie answered. "We'll stop and grab something on the way to the mall."

"Well then, here, Elly," she handed Elly a small envelope. "It's for you to spend at the mall. Buy whatever you like."

Elly held herself back, hesitating. "Are you sure? You really don't have to do this."

Adria rolled her eyes in mock despair. "Elly, please, you need clothes. Now stop being shy about this." She pressed the envelope into Elly's hand. Elly accepted it with a small smile, even though she was still a bit reluctant about doing so.

"All right, already, come on!" Melanie grabbed Elly's hand and pulled her towards the front door. "Bye, Mom! We'll see you later!" She gave her mother a quick kiss on the cheek and rushed Elly out the door before Adria could say anything else.

CHAPTER NINE

Elly was taken in by her surroundings as they drove down the street. Although the atmosphere was still gray with the sun only just beginning to peek out from behind the clouds, the surrounding area was bright with colorful although small houses, each with at least one car parked in front of it. Elly understood that cars were one of humans' primary means of transportation. The airplane, Elly had heard was the other, although she had never seen a picture of it and therefore wouldn't recognize one if she saw one.

Elly was fascinated by the colorful, square like houses each with a square neat lawn and a variety of trees and flowers decorating the front of each house. They were interesting compared to the colorless, round crystal houses back home. The trees that were visible were lush and green with rain drops still clinging to the leaves and most of the houses had beautiful flowers and colorful shrubs growing in the yard. "How come your house is so far from the others?" Elly wanted to know, noticing that they had driven a few blocks before she had seen the first house.

"There's a story behind the property we live on and a rather fascinating one, too. Would you like to hear it?"

Elly nodded, yes. She could use a good story to occupy her mind because that incident in the pasture just wouldn't leave her.

"Our house used to be a huge ranch house several hundred years ago, or so we've been told. It was said that the original owner, Jake Harleson, had made his money by doing all sorts of illegal business, but no one knows for sure. The story goes that he fell in love with the beauty of the town named Belle Nobbes. She had only been in town a few short weeks before Jake met her and no one really knew who she was. But none of this mattered to Jake; he was in love." Melanie made a left turn onto another street as she continued her story. Elly was thoroughly intrigued.

"They got married shortly after meeting and everything seemed to be going fine. It's said that one night while Jake was out with some of his friends at a bar, he got drunk. When he woke up, he found himself sleeping in a dancing girl's room in the upper section of the bar, fully dressed, miraculously enough. The girl was leaning over him, placing a wet cloth on his forehead. She explained that he had passed out downstairs and that she had asked one of the guys to bring him up to her room so he could sleep off the alcohol. It was already early morning and the sun was starting to rise outside the window."

"What did he do?" Elly wanted to know.

"He left after first making the girl swear that she would never tell anyone- especially his wife about what had happened. She said that there was nothing to tell anyway. But you know how it is with small towns. Word gets around anyway and of course it eventually got to his wife who immediately confronted him about it. But unfortunately, by the time his wife heard about it, the story of what happened had changed and taken on a whole new dimension."

Elly was baffled. "What do you mean?"

"Belle believed that he had been unfaithful to her with this other girl, thus the reason why he had never told her about what really happened that night. See, when he had gotten home that morning, he had told her that he had gotten drunk and spent the night at a friend's house who both of them knew. Of course, his friend supported his story. Anyway, he apologized for having lied to her about it and swore that he had not been unfaithful to her, regardless of what anyone else had told her and begged her forgiveness."

"Did she believe him?"

"She told him that she did and said that she forgave him. But apparently, she still held it against him in her heart. She died six months after that. It's said that she cursed him upon her deathbed for his betrayal. She said that in her death, the truth would be revealed. If he had spoken the truth then he would live and prosper, if not then a curse would be on him and his house and he would lose everything and he would be ruined.

"Three months after her death he went bankrupt," Melanie continued. "He had to start selling off parts of his ranch and property. But the people who bought from him died mysteriously shortly after moving onto the land and eventually everything went to ruins. He died less than one year after Belle did, poor and lonely with only the main section of the house that you see there still standing."

"So, he had been unfaithful to her, then?" Elly deducted. Her heart felt heavy with sorrow from hearing the story. It was tragic, legend though it was.

"It would appear that way," Melanie said. "But no one knows what really happened that night. But it seems that since that time, whenever anyone tries to expand or build anything within all that empty land, something happens and the project ends up being abandoned. All of that land use to belong to him. He had bought the land wanting to build a mansion for his Belle."

"Why did your family decide that they wanted to live out there?" Elly wanted to know.

"Well, primarily because they love this town and they didn't want to have to leave also, the land we live on is one of the few places in this small town where horses can be raised and that's something my parents have always wanted to do. My father, being a contractor, bought the property right after he and mom got married and, despite the story about the place being cursed, was able to successfully renovate the property and build the house that you see there now."

"That is very impressive and they do seem very happy there," Elly admitted.

"Yes, they are," Melanie agreed. "See that there?" Melanie continued indicating something to her right. She was pointing at a structure several feet in front of them that looked like a huge house. "That's the road side cafe," she explained. "It has the best lunch dishes in town. Are you hungry?"

"Very hungry," Elly admitted. Melanie parked in front of the restaurant and then they went inside and ordered lunch. Inside, the cafe looked like a large house that had been transformed into a warm and cozy restaurant. The place was quickly filling up with people.

"I'm paying," Melanie said when she saw Elly reaching for her money. "This is my treat."

"Thanks," Elly said. She was relieved since she hadn't quite figured out how to use the money yet. She smiled at Melanie and finished off her soda. Once they were done eating, they left the cafe and headed for the mall again.

Elly studied Melanie as they continued their travel. Melanie was trying to appear relaxed and upbeat but Elly could clearly tell that she was stressed and worried about something. She could tell this by the fact that Melanie's jaw was clenched and her grip on the steering wheel was like iron. Over the past few weeks, Elly had learned a lot about Melanie and discovered that she was a rather complicated individual. She realized that the few details she knew about Melanie only scratched the surface of who this girl really was.

Melanie, Elly found out, was twenty years old and had just come back home from school a few short months ago. She had been a psychology major at a university located just outside of town. She had been there studying for two years, only coming home once in a while to visit, when, suddenly, out of the blue, she decided she didn't want to major in psychology anymore and came home to stay.

Elly, who didn't have a clue what psychology was, had wanted to know why she had changed her mind about school. Melanie had shrugged and said, "I don't know exactly why. I just know that for some reason, I'm just not motivated anymore." Elly had sensed that what she had said wasn't the whole truth but decided not to push the issue. But Elly was keenly aware that something had happened to Melanie while she was away that had led to her making such a dramatic decision about her life. Donna had explained that ever since she could remember psychology was the only thing that Melanie had been interested in. No one in the family could understand Melanie's decision, but none of them were willing to confront her about it either. They just figured she would open up when she was ready to.

Now, as she quietly studied Melanie, she was curious to find out what that reason was.

"Mel?" Elly said gently. Melanie jumped slightly in her seat. She had been very quiet the past few minutes lost in thought and had not even realized that Elly had been studying her.

"What is it, Elly?" She stopped at a red light and waited to make a left turn.

"I don't mean to pry into your life," Elly began, "but is something troubling you? You seem- distant."

Melanie shook her head slightly. "You're not prying. I am a bit distracted because I'm worried about a friend of mine."

Elly noticed that Melanie's voice changed on the word 'friend'. She spat the word out as if it was poison and her demeanor turned cold. Elly got the impression that whoever Melanie was talking about was anything but a friend but did not say anything about it.

Instead, she asked, "Would you like to talk about it? Maybe that would help."

Melanie was silent and Elly could see that she was torn up about what she should do. She needed to talk but was afraid to do so for some reason.

"Can I share something with you?" Melanie finally asked after making a left turn.

Elly nodded. "Well, sure."

"My friend's name is Brad Alwin," Melanie began. "We've known each other since grade school and he's always been my best friend. He's gotten himself into some trouble lately and frankly I don't know if there's any way he can get himself out. When this first started almost a year ago, I thought perhaps it was just something new and fun he was trying out, but now..." She trailed off and something in Melanie's voice made Elly remember her reaction to Melanie when she had first met her. She felt uncomfortable all of a sudden and her chest felt tight. Elly took in a deep breath and tried to relax as a cold chill went up her spine. She had a feeling that she wasn't going to like what Melanie was about to tell her.

"Please, go on," Elly encouraged her, ignoring the warning bells that were going off in her head. "Whatever you tell me I promise will stay with me. Plus, I'm sure that talking will make you feel better."

Melanie smiled gratefully at Elly. "As I've said, Brad and I have been friends for years and we've always been very close. We graduated from high school together and both of us got accepted to the same University. He was majoring in Physics and at first he was all about studying and being at the top of his class."

Melanie paused and took a deep breath before continuing. "About a year ago, he joined this new club that started on campus but also met at various places off campus. Not long after that Brad started to change; he was no longer the same guy I knew so well and had grown up with. In the beginning, I thought maybe he was just working and studying too hard." She paused again for a moment as she made another left turn.

"To make a long story short, I eventually found out that the change in his behavior had nothing to do with work or school but had everything to do with the club he was a part of. I won't go into the details of the sort of things this so-called club have been doing but what was upsetting was realizing that Brad was participating in almost everything they did. He's in way over his head with these people. Believe me, Elly, I've experience firsthand what being involved with this club has done to him."

Elly heard bitterness in Melanie's voice when she said those words.

"I'm starting to think that there really is no hope to ending this ordeal," Melanie concluded with a frown.

Elly was listening attentively to what Melanie was saying although she found it difficult to keep up with everything Melanie told her. She discovered that Melanie was being vague with the details of her story. What was this club Melanie mentioned and exactly what kind of trouble was this friend of hers in? Or, better yet, what kind of trouble was he causing?

"If he's so much trouble, why don't you just stay away from him?" Elly wanted to know.

"Because-" Melanie hesitated a moment then said, "because I have to do something and in order to do it, I have to deal with Brad." Her lips were set in a thin line and, if Elly was not mistaken, she looked angry.

"So, what exactly are you going to do?" Elly wanted to know seeing the grim look on Melanie's face.

"I'm working on it." She gave Elly's hand a tight squeeze. "Hey, thanks for listening to me."

Elly smiled. "Sure, no problem." But Elly could tell that Melanie was still worrying over the problem regarding her friend and she had a sinking feeling that Melanie was the one who was way over her head and just didn't know it- or just didn't want to admit it to Elly.

They both fell silent and many different thoughts started running through Elly's head all at once. There was something about what Melanie had told her that bothered her, but she wasn't quite sure what this was exactly. She knew she was missing something important. Something that could help her put together some pieces of the strange puzzle that was already beginning to form in the back of her head. She was certain that Melanie wasn't telling her the whole story.

Elly suddenly looked up and the sight that caught her eyes nearly took her breath away and made her push her worries about Melanie to the back of her mind. Up ahead of them was a huge building complex that was made entirely out of what appeared to Elly to be glass. It was several stories high and unlike anything Elly had ever seen back at home. Other tall and elaborate buildings surrounded the one that had caught Elly's attention and some of them were even taller than that one, seeming to reach all the way to the sky.

Crowds of people of all different ages and size were on the sidewalks outside and many were going in and out of the buildings. Elly had to take a deep breath to calm down and contain her excitement. She didn't want to bring any attention to herself. After all, she was supposed to be human and any strange reaction from her could cause Melanie or others to become suspicious.

"Well, here's our local shopping mall," Melanie announced as she pulled into the parking lot located in the back of the glass building that had originally caught Elly's attention. "Come on, let's see what we can find for you." Melanie found a place to park the car and soon Elly found herself being pulled through revolving glass doors by Melanie into the mall.

CHAPTER TEN

Elly stood in the main lobby and looked around the inside of the mall in awe. There were tons of people milling around all over the place. Looking up, Elly realized that the mall was separated into different floors, and each floor was packed with different shops. Elly immediately fell in love and after the initial shock wore off, Elly found herself having more fun than she'd ever had when she had gone to the markets back home. She was starting to enjoy being on earth.

Melanie guided Elly expertly around the mall, stopping at all her favorite shops and food joints. Both of them bought clothes, lots of clothes, along with many other accessories. By the time they were done shopping, both were exhausted.

"I'm hungry," Melanie said as they went downstairs from the fourth floor and exited the mall. "Let's go to Vincent's," Melanie said as they headed towards the car with their purchases in hand. "It's only a few blocks from here and it's a good restaurant. I'm working there right now while I'm out of school." Getting into the car, Melanie drove a short distance from the mall. Elly was still getting over the excitement of being at the mall.

"There's Vincent's," Melanie said pointing to a building across the street. "Let's go." After parking the car, she took Elly's hand and they ran across the street and stopped in front of the restaurant. Melanie pulled the door open but then immediately froze in place causing Elly to bump into her. Something obviously had attracted Melanie's attention. Elly was standing directly behind her and couldn't see inside.

"What's wrong?" Elly whispered.

Melanie turned slowly towards Elly and Elly could not believe the look on her face. The look on Melanie's face was nothing short of hatred, pure hatred.

"Mel, what's wrong?" Elly repeated. She couldn't believe that this was the same smiling, friendly girl she had met just a few short weeks ago. The girl who stood in front of her now was positively seething with rage.

The chill she had experienced earlier when Melanie had been telling her about Brad returned.

"She's here," Melanie said through clenched teeth, in a small tight voice.

Elly was puzzled. "Who's here?"

"Kara."

Elly was confused. "Kara? Who's Kara?"

Melanie pulled Elly around to the side of the building, away from the front entrance. "Kara," she began, "is one of the leaders of the club Brad has been hanging around with. She pretty much controls everything that goes on within the group. Over the past few weeks, Kara and I have had words, I guess you can say."

"Words?" Elly repeated cautiously, not quite understanding where Melanie was coming from.

"Well, let's just say we don't see eye to eye and we're definitely not friends. I've confronted her a few times in regards to Brad's situation which of course she denied having anything to do with it. The point is I really don't want to have to deal with her right now."

Just then, Elly heard the bell above the front entrance of the restaurant chime and turned just in time to see a tall blonde woman exit the restaurant. She was dressed all in black but was heading in the opposite direction so Elly could not see her features. A cold chill passed through her. Behind her, Elly heard Melanie let out her breath in relief.

"That was her," Melanie informed her. "I'm glad she left. I don't know what I would have done or said if I had to face her in there."

"Well, don't worry about that now. Come on," Elly took her hand and headed towards the entrance. "Let's get something to eat."

The restaurant was comfortable and airy inside with round tables covered with checkered tablecloths arranged tastefully across the floor. Elly wondered what Melanie's job was here. She had mentioned something about being an assistant manager but Elly had no clue what that meant. The concept of work was not new to Elly although it was never something she ever had to worry about herself.

With Kara gone, the restaurant was almost empty. There was only an old man sitting at a corner table by a window reading a newspaper and a young girl with short, honey blonde hair was sitting by herself at another corner table reading a book. On the other side of the restaurant, there was a tall brown-haired boy working behind a counter, having a conversation with a girl who was standing on the other side of the counter. He immediately looked up and smiled when he saw Melanie walk in.

"Hey, Mel, how are you doing?" he greeted her with a warm smile. His eyes were a deep blue and they crinkled at the corner when he smiled.

"Fine, thanks," Melanie answered smiling back at him. She leaned up against the counter. "Slow day, huh?"

"Yeah," the boy replied. "It's been like this since this morning."

"Oh, this is my- cousin, Elly," Melanie introduced, pulling Elly out from behind her, "She's staying with us for a while. Elly, this is Cory."

"Nice to meet you," Cory said as the two of them shook hands.

Elly smiled politely. She wasn't sure what it meant to be Melanie's 'cousin' but she was glad she didn't have to explain herself to him.

"What will you two have?" Cory asked.

"Two grilled steak sandwiches, salad and iced tea," Melanie answered, ordering for both of them.

"All right, have a seat. I'll bring your order when they're ready."

"Thanks," Melanie said as she led Elly away from the counter and to a table in a corner by the window. It wasn't until they sat down that Elly realized that the atmosphere in the restaurant was cold- as if all the life had somehow been sucked out of the place. Elly instinctively knew that it was due to Kara having been in the restaurant.

She had sensed something about Kara the moment she had seen her step out of the restaurant- even before Melanie had told her who she was. She hadn't been able to place the feeling but it suddenly came to her. It was the same presence she had felt while out at the stable with Aimer earlier. It had been Kara who had been standing out by the railing, watching them. The horse had also sensed her presence and panicked. Why had she been there? Elly wondered. What did she want? And why had the horse panicked? Elly definitely knew that she had stepped into something that was already in full swing that she probably had no way of stopping.

Almost like stepping into a show that has already started, without knowing your own lines, Elly thought.

Elly was afraid of what the ending of this show would be and the fact that she could end up being a part of it bothered her even more. After all, what could she do? Ignore everything and pretend that she wasn't really here?

Not a chance.

Cory finally brought their food. Elly hadn't realized just how hungry she was until then. All the excitement and shopping at the mall had given her a real appetite.

"I think we should head home," Melanie said when they had finished eating. "I promised Mom that I would have the car back by four-thirty and it's almost four now."

"All right," Elly said as they threw the trash away. Elly paid for lunch, against Melanie's wishes saying that it was her treat. After all, Melanie had spent more than enough money on her as it was.

They left the restaurant and as they rounded the corner, Melanie bumped into someone coming from the opposite direction, dropping her purse. Everything spilled out.

"I'm sorry," Melanie said as she bent down to pick up her things.

"No, I'm sorry," the person said, bending down to help her. Melanie looked up from where she was kneeling and Elly saw her mouth drop open in surprise.

"Brad?!" Melanie cried in astonishment.

"Melanie, how are you?" Brad asked. Elly stayed in the background curious as to what would happen and wanting to know who this man was that Melanie had told her about. She regarded Brad carefully, wanting to see what she could learn about him. He was tall and lean but stood kind of hunched over as if he didn't want people to see his true height. He stood with his hands stuffed in the pockets of his jeans with a crooked smile on his face. Almost absent-mindedly he reached up with his right hand and ran his fingers through his thick brown hair. He smiled and Elly noticed the dimple in his cheeks and the crinkle around his light green eyes. Without a doubt, Brad was a very handsome man.

Elly could not believe that this was the person that Melanie had told her about. Yet despite all of his good looks, there was something about him that Elly immediately did not like but she was not able to put her finger on what it was.

"I'm fine," Melanie answered, zipping up her purse. Elly could see that she was uneasy. Her hands shook as she closed her purse and she was standing stiffly in front of Brad. "How are you? I haven't seen you in a while."

"I've been all right," Brad answered. "I've been doing some work for my dad over at the garage. In fact, that's where I'm headed right now."

"I see. Oh, this is my cousin, Elly. Elly, this is Brad."

"Hi," Elly said. It was his eyes, Elly decided. Even when he smiled, they looked lifeless.

"It's nice to meet you." They shook hands and a chill instantly ran up Elly's spine when his hand touched hers. It was cold and clammy. She had to control herself to keep from forcefully pulling her hand out of his grip. "Look, Mel, I'd love to stay and talk but I've got to get over to the garage. Would you like to get together later? I really think we need to talk. What do you say?"

Melanie hesitated, but only for a moment. But then she smiled and said, "Sure. I'd love to."

Elly's heart sank. What was Melanie thinking?

Brad smiled in return. "Great. Can I pick you up at seven? My dad only needs me for about an hour or so."

Melanie nodded. "Seven o'clock would be great."

"All right then. I'll see you later. Nice meeting you, Elly." With that, Brad rounded the corner and disappeared. Elly stared after him. She then turned slowly towards Melanie who was also staring after him with a wild look in her eyes. She was shaking. Elly did not know what was happening to her.

"Mel, do you think you did the right thing?" she asked cautiously.

"Elly, I have to do this. Believe me, if there were any other way, I would take it."

Elly could hear the desperation in her voice. "But you told me yourself that he was trouble."

"Yes, but I have to find out what is going on with him and this is the only way that I can do that."

"But, Melanie-"

"Elly, please," Melanie interrupted with a slight frown, anger edged in her voice. "You are just going to have to trust me, okay?"

Elly shrugged and put her hands up in defeat. "All right, I trust you." She forced a smile.

"Look at us, already," Melanie said, trying to lighten the situation. "Who'd ever believe that we only met each other just a few weeks ago?"

Elly realized that Melanie was right. They were behaving as though they had known each other for years. It was really amazing how she had been able to fit in so well with these people to the point that she could almost say she felt at home. Things were working out better then Elly would have ever expected under the circumstances. When her mother had told her about wanting to send her to earth, she had imagined the worst as to what she would encounter when she got to earth.

Yet, despite how good things appeared, she knew that things were not as wonderful as she would like to believe. She realized this just moments ago when Brad had asked Melanie to go out with him. There was trouble up ahead, she knew, but what was worst was that she didn't know whether or not she would be able to do anything about it. Her mother had told her something about fate. But Elly hadn't believed that it meant anything.

That was until now.

Elly tried to clear these thoughts from her mind as she followed Melanie back to the car. Melanie talked to her the whole way but she barely heard what she was saying. Her thoughts were tangled in her mind like a spider's web; nothing made sense, yet everything seemed to be connected.

Finally, they reached the house and Elly sighed in relief.

CHAPTER ELEVEN

Adria was waiting for them when they entered the house. "Where have you two been?" she asked. "I was starting to worry."

"First to the mall and then we stopped at Vincent's to grab something to eat," Melanie replied.

"It was fun," Elly chimed in. "But we didn't mean to worry you."

"It's all right. I'm glad you two enjoyed yourself," Adria said. "Dinner will be ready shortly. Nothing fancy, though, just sandwiches for tonight."

"That reminds me," Melanie said off hand. "Brad asked me out on a date tonight so- I won't be home for dinner." She smiled sweetly at her mother.

"All right," Adria said. "Just be careful and please don't stay out too late."

"I won't." She hugged Adria. "Come on, Elly," Melanie grabbed Elly's hand and pulled her towards her room. "Help me pick out something to wear tonight." Elly shrugged at Adria and followed Melanie down the hall and upstairs to her room.

They dug through Melanie's closet for almost an hour before Melanie finally settled on a dark green sequin blouse and a black pair of dress pants.

"Do you really like it?" Melanie asked as she held the outfit up against herself and stared at it in the mirror.

"It's beautiful," Elly told her. "It'll look great on you."

"Then this is it." Melanie laid the outfit down on her bed. "It's almost six. I better go take a shower."

"All right, then. Yell if you need me," Elly said then turned and left the room. Going back downstairs, she found Adria in the kitchen.

"Here," Adria handed her a sandwich. "I made this for you."

"Thank you." Elly sat down at the kitchen table. "Where is everyone?" she asked.

"Dawn went to visit a friend and Carey is babysitting for the Jones'." While Adria and Elly were talking, Melanie finally came downstairs.

She looked beautiful in the dark green blouse which set off her shiny red hair and made her green eyes sparkle.

"You look beautiful," Adria said and Elly nodded in agreement. She wasn't at all happy about Melanie going out with Brad, but she had come to realize that there was nothing she could do about it. Just then, the doorbell rang.

Melanie headed towards the door, but Elly stopped her. "I'll answer it. Why don't you go grab a sweater, Mel? In case it gets chilly." Elly left the room before Melanie could respond. She wanted to get a good look at Brad before letting Melanie anywhere near him.

"Hi, Brad," Elly greeted pulling the door open. He was nicely attired in gray pressed slacks, a white dress shirt and a blue striped tie. His brown hair was combed back with only a few strands falling forwards over his forehead. Other than his eyes, which still looked cold and lifeless to Elly, he looked fine. But this did nothing to reassure her fears; she was still uncomfortable with the whole situation. What have I gotten myself into? She wondered again, miserably.

"Hi, Elly. Is Melanie here?"

"Yes, she is. She'll be with you in a minute." Elly said still studying him closely. Melanie came to the front door carrying a light green sweater.

"You look great, Mel," Brad said when he saw Melanie.

"You, too," Melanie said, forcing a smile. Elly could tell that Melanie did not really want to be going out with Brad and wondered why she was putting herself through this.

"Are you ready?" he asked.

"Yes, definitely," Melanie answered as she stepped outside, waved goodbye to Elly and pulled the door closed behind her.

Elly was on edge the minute she heard Brad's car pull away from the driveway. She couldn't understand why she was so against Melanie going out with Brad. Why did this bother her so much? She had only met Melanie a few weeks ago and Brad a few hours ago. So why were things affecting her so?

It was simple. She knew that something wasn't right and it had to do with whatever was going on between Brad and Melanie. Her instincts about things were hardly ever wrong. If she felt trouble then there was trouble. But what was it? What was she missing? Elly paced around the living room, thinking hard. Why had Melanie shared so much information with her about Brad in the first place? There was more to the whole situation than what Melanie had told her, she knew, but even before her conversation with Melanie, something had set off an alarm in her head the minute she had met Melanie.

"Elly," Adria called from the front hallway, interrupting Elly's train of thought. "I'm going out for a little while I'll be back shortly. Will you be all right?"

"Yes," answered Elly. "I'll be fine. Bye." Once Adria left, Elly lay on the couch and closed her eyes, trying to relax. It took a while but she finally felt herself drifting off into sleep.

As she slept, Elly found herself trapped in a nightmare. Once again, she was trapped somewhere in a dark room. The only light that shone into the room was from a tiny window high up near the ceiling. There was a door, but it was locked and it refused to give way as Elly pulled on it. The air in the room was thick and Elly felt as though she was being smothered. Suddenly, Elly heard voices all around her. Voices that were crying, pleading desperately. But Elly could not make out what the voices were crying about and they were coming closer, louder, closing in on her. Elly began to cry bitterly herself, begging the voices to stop. But they would not.

And then...she heard the bell.

Elly jerked up from where she lay. She was soaked with sweat and she was trembling violently. She vividly remembered her dream but she could not make anything out of it.

She heard the bell again and realized that it was someone ringing at the front door. Elly quickly got up and ran to the door. She pulled the door open and found Aimer standing on the steps.

"Hi, Elly. How- Elly! Are you all right?"

Elly blushed realizing what a mess she must appear to be.

"I'm fine," Elly assured him. "I was sleeping. I- had a nightmare." And a nightmare it was. Elly still couldn't get the images out of her mind.

"That must have been some nightmare," Aimer commented. "I just stopped by to see how everything was going. Is anyone home?"

Elly shook her head. "I'm the only one here."

"Well, then. Would you like to go for a walk with me? Maybe some fresh air would help clear your mind."

"I'd love that," Elly answered. "Do you mind waiting a minute while I change?"

"You don't need to change. You look fine, really. Just grab a sweater and come on. There's a bit of a chill out here tonight."

Elly smiled. "I'll be right back." She made a quick stop in the bathroom, washing her face with cold water to wake herself up. Then she ran a comb through her hair. After that, she grabbed a sweater out of her closet. She turned all the lights out, except for the ones in the front hall, and went to join Aimer outside.

"All right," she said to him, "I'm ready." He turned and Elly followed him down the steps onto the walkway where they headed towards the left, turning in the direction which Elly had come from when she first showed up on the Coltzs' front porch. There was a full moon out and it was the only thing that lighted their way.

"How was it down at the mall?" Aimer asked.

"Crowded," Elly answered, smiling. "But it was fun."

They were both quiet for a while as they walked on, each lost in their own thoughts. Elly thought about Melanie and wondered what Brad and she were up to. She also wondered if maybe she was just being silly, thinking that there was something wrong. Maybe she had just over reacted. After all, Melanie was a big girl; she could take care of herself.

Sadly, though, Elly found it hard to convince herself of this. Elly sighed heavily. It was all too confusing and she didn't know what to do.

"Elly? Are you Okay?"

Elly snapped out of her thoughts and looked up at Aimer. He was frowning.

"I'm fine," she answered. "I was just thinking. Trying to remember you know." It was the best- and only excuse she could come up with.

Aimer nodded. "Yeah, I see. It really bothers you, doesn't it? Not being able to remember, that is."

"Yeah," Elly whispered. "It bothers me all right." What was really bothering Elly was the fact that she had no idea what she was doing here on earth. Sure, things were going well, so it seemed, but she still didn't know what any of it meant.

Why was she here? What was she supposed to do while she was here? Then again, was she really on earth? Or was her body still locked in the chamber at home while she slept and dreamed about being on earth. Although this was possible, Elly knew that this was highly unlikely.

"Don't think about it so much," Aimer advised. "It'll only upset you more. That's probably what's giving you the nightmares."

"You're probably right," Elly answered. But she knew that it wasn't so. There was so much more to this and so many unanswered questions. "I'll try not to think too much about it."

"Do you want to head back now?" Aimer asked.

"Yes, I think we should."

"By the way, do you know where Melanie went?" Aimer asked as they retraced their steps. "Yesterday evening she had asked me to meet her tonight around seven. She wouldn't tell me what she needed to see me about, but I agreed to come by the house. I was surprised when you told me that no one was home."

Elly heard the concern in his voce. She wondered why Melanie had chosen to go out with Brad when she had already planned to meet Aimer. And how did Aimer fit into all of this? She never even considered the possibility that he may be involved with what was going on with Melanie.

But apparently, he was worried about Melanie's welfare, too.

Maybe she could learn something from him.

"She went out with Brad," Elly told him casually as though it were nothing. She wanted to see how he would react to that.

"Brad?" Aimer sounded surprised. "Melanie should know better." He added that almost to himself but Elly heard him loud and clear.

"What do you mean by that?" Elly regarded him curiously. Aimer hesitated, trying to decide exactly what he should say.

"What I know is that Brad has gotten himself into a lot of trouble in the past and I believe that he still is in trouble now. I don't know if all of the things I've heard about Brad are true but I am aware that there has been some trouble between Brad and Melanie for some time. Now, Melanie is like a sister to me; I don't want to see her get hurt again. I try to talk to her about it, but she won't listen. She knows a lot more than she lets on and that's what scares me."

"Why?"

Aimer sighed deeply. "I don't like to think about it, but I wonder sometimes if Melanie is in some kind of trouble, too. It's either she is and she doesn't know it. Or she does know and just doesn't want to tell anyone because she's afraid to. I think maybe that is why she wanted to meet me tonight. But there are times when her behavior is so at odds with the Melanie that I know that it really makes me wonder. Like tonight, for example."

Elly felt the blood drain from her face when Aimer said this to her; Aimer had just verbalized her worst fear. The thought had nagged at the back of her mind since her initial conversation with Melanie on the way to the mall but she had not wanted to have to think about or consider the possibility of Melanie being in trouble. But was there any other answer? She wondered. She remembered Melanie's reaction to Kara that afternoon and a chill crept through her.

"Melanie doesn't seem like the type of person who would get herself in trouble and I don't know Brad well enough to say anything about him. I only met him earlier today."

"That's what I keep telling myself," Aimer said. "But I still get this feeling sometimes that something is wrong."

Something *is* wrong, Elly confirmed to herself but did not share this with Aimer.

"You're just worried about her, that's all," Elly said, trying to reassure him even though she herself was not one bit reassured. Aimer was right to be concerned. "After all, you're her friend. That's what friends do, worry."

"Yeah, I guess." But he didn't sound convinced, either. They were now standing on the front porch of the house.

"Well, it's late," Aimer said. It was apparent that he did not want to discuss Melanie any more. "You should go in."

"Thanks for the walk," Elly said as she climbed up the steps. "I do feel better."

"That's good. Listen, Elly, could you do me a favor?"

Elly turned and faced him. "What?"

"Please don't tell Melanie that I was talking to you about her. She'll be furious. I promised her that I wouldn't interfere, but I just can't help it."

Elly smiled lightly. "You don't have to worry about that. I won't tell her, promise."

Aimer sighed. "Thanks. Well, then good night. I'll see you tomorrow morning."

"Good night and thanks again." Elly stood on the porch and watched as Aimer headed away from the house. Once he was out of sight, she opened the door and stepped inside. The house was still empty. No one was home. Elly checked the time and found that it was already nine o'clock.

Where is Melanie? she wondered as she paced around the living room. Shouldn't she already be home? Elly sighed. This wasn't getting her anywhere. Frustrated, she decided to go take a shower; she needed to relax.

It wasn't until after Elly had finished taking a shower and had wrapped herself in a large soft towel that Aimer's words came back to her. Again. He had said again. He didn't want Melanie to get hurt again. Meaning that Melanie had been hurt before. But when? How? And by who? Brad? So many questions but no answers. So much as for relaxing, Elly thought wryly as she dried herself off.

As she came out of the bathroom, she heard voices coming from the other side of the house. Elly quickly pulled on a nightgown and a robe and left her room. She found Michael, Dawn and Carey sitting at the kitchen table. Adria was cooking something on the stove.

"Hi, Elly," Michael greeted her. "How are you?"

"Fine, thanks." Elly forced a smile.

"I'm making some hot chocolate," Adria said from the stove. "Would you like some?"

"Yes, please," Elly answered as she pulled up a chair and sat down next to Dawn. She didn't know what hot chocolate was but it smelled delicious.

"Where's Melanie?" Carey asked.

"She went out on a date with Brad," Elly answered simply. She didn't want anyone to know how worried the whole situation was making her.

"You mean she's not home yet?" Adria asked. Elly could tell that she was concerned even though she asked the question casually.

"No, not yet," answered Elly.

"Well, that's strange," Adria muttered. She came over and handed Elly a large mug of hot chocolate.

"Don't worry, honey," Michael said to Adria. "Melanie is a big girl. She can take care of herself."

I'm not so sure about that, Elly thought to herself as she slowly sipped her hot chocolate.

"I'm tired," Elly said a few minutes later when she was finished drinking the hot chocolate. "I think I'll go to bed."

"Me, too," Carey said also getting up from her seat.

"Good night, girls," Adria and Michael said. "Sleep well."

Once she was safely in her room and in bed, Elly found that she could not fall asleep. She tossed and turned relentlessly until she was perspiring profusely.

But finally, after what seemed like hours of tossing and turning, she was able to fall asleep.

But her sleep was not peaceful. Once again, she found herself trapped in the same dark nightmare that she had been in only hours ago.

And this time, there was no one there to bring her out of it.

Elly found herself confined in a small room again. But this one was made completely out of glass. Outside, the darkness was deep and threatening. Suddenly, the air was filled with sharp shrill sounds. Elly screamed and leaned into a wall, covering her ears to block out the terrible noise. But the sounds grew louder and then there were bright red lights flashing everywhere, coming towards the room. Elly tried to find a way out, to get away from the noise and lights but there was none.

Elly began to cry bitterly as the sounds became louder and the lights grew brighter. She was trapped, she knew, with no way out....

Elly jolted out of her sleep and found that she was sitting up in her bed, perspiring so profusely that her nightgown clung coldly against her skin.

Her nightmare was clearly impressed into her mind and she found that she couldn't shake herself completely out of it.

But Elly realized that that wasn't the only thing that had sprung her out of the nightmare. There was a sound coming from somewhere within the house. It was barely audible, but to Elly's sensitive ears, it was like listening to thunder striking.

She held her breath and listened closely.

The front door was being quietly pushed open.

Silently, Elly crept out of her bed and made her way to the bedroom door. She had no idea what exactly she had in mind of doing. All she knew was that she couldn't just lay there while an intruder came into the house. Cautiously, she opened her bedroom door and stepped out into the hallway, plastering herself against the wall.

The front door closed.

There was a sound of shuffling feet as the person moved towards the back of the house.

The darkness made it almost impossible for her to see so she closed her eyes and focused. Elly got a shock a few seconds later when she was able to get a clear image in her mind of the person who was in the house.

It was Melanie slowly stumbling her way through the house towards the stairs to her bedroom. Elly was so stunned; she couldn't move at first. But within a few seconds she had regained control of herself and was quietly making her way towards the living room where she found Melanie standing in a daze, lost in her own home.

"Melanie!" Elly said in a loud whisper, "Where have you been? It's nearly two o'clock!"

Melanie turned and took a step forward. She was now standing in front of the living room window. The stream of moonlight that shone through the window fell across her face. Elly watched as Melanie stood there staring at her dumbly without recognizing who she was. It was still relatively dark despite the moonlight, but Elly could clearly see the glassy looked in Melanie's eyes.

Elly's heart hammered in her chest. Melanie seemed to be behaving as if she were drunk or stoned. Elly couldn't tell which as both were conditions experienced only by humans. Her mother had explained these things to her but she had thought that it was all just a joke when she'd heard of it. After all, why would anyone actually really put themselves in such a position and willingly do such things? But now, standing there and staring back at Melanie, Elly knew that everything her mother had told her was true. There was more to this, Elly knew but she wasn't ready to deal with any of it yet.

Elly sighed. "Mel, what happened to you?" she asked softly even though she was sure she already knew the answer to that.

Melanie's eyes shifted and then managed to focus themselves on her. "Elly?" Melanie finally said. Her voice was hoarse and thick.

"Yes. Mel, where have you been?"

Melanie considered for a moment before answering. Then finally, she simply answered, "Out." She took one step forward and Elly watched in horror as Melanie crumbled to the ground, unconscious. Elly pressed her hand against her mouth to keep from screaming.

Now what? Elly asked herself as she stared down at Melanie. She didn't want to wake anyone up, but she couldn't just leave Melanie lying there. What would her parents say if they woke up and found their daughter passed out on the living room floor fully dressed? No, she had to get Melanie to bed. The situation itself would have to be dealt with later.

She reached down and gently shook Melanie's shoulder. Melanie moaned in response and stirred. Carefully, Elly was able to get Melanie up on her feet and, with difficulty, half dragged her up to her room and onto her bed. She quickly undressed Melanie and then slipped her under the covers. Melanie was fast asleep by the time Elly was done. She left Melanie's room, closing the door behind her. Once she was safely in her own room, she crawled into bed, exhausted. Before her head even touched the pillow, her eyes clouded and she fell into a deep, dreamless sleep.

After what seemed like only minutes of sleep, Elly was awaken by a voice calling her name while a pair of hands gently shook her shoulders. She moaned, rolled onto her back and slowly inched her eyes open. And as she did so the nightmare from the previous night slowly came back to her.

Both of her nightmares.

Opening her eyes, she found Melanie sitting at the edge of her bed staring down at her with an intense frown on her face. Elly quickly sat up in her bed.

"Melanie! Are you all right? I was so worried about you! What happened to you last night? I-"

"Shh!" Melanie pressed a finger against her lips and frowned. "They'll hear you!" She glanced worriedly towards the door then back at Elly.

"What?" Elly said stunned.

"Look, Elly, I need you to promise me something."

"What?" Elly repeated again dumbly.

"You have to promise me that you won't tell my parents- or anyone, for that matter- about what happened last night." Melanie looked at her pleadingly.

Elly's mouth dropped open. "Mel, you've got to be kidding! You could have died last night."

Melanie shook her head. "Don't be ridiculous, Elly. What happened last night was- an accident. It's never happened before. It won't happen again- I promise."

Liar, Elly said silently to herself, staring at Melanie as if she were trying to see through her. It had happened before- several times- only her parents or her sisters had never caught her. Which is a wonder, Elly thought wryly, considering the state she had found Melanie in last night. But she could see that even Melanie was confused about what had happened to her. She had no idea how or why these things were occurring.

Worst things were going to be happening before this whole mess was over, Elly knew, and soon. Elly sighed deeply. Why was all of this happening now while she was here? She had only been here for a few weeks and things now seemed to be falling apart.

"Elly? Are you all right?" Melanie shook her shoulders gently. Elly's head jerked up. She hadn't realized that she'd been so lost in her own thoughts.

"Well?" Melanie prompted her anxiously. "Will you promise not to tell anyone about what happened last night?"

What could she do? After all, she was only a visitor here. It wasn't her place to go around stirring things up. She certainly didn't want to start anything with the Coltzs'. No, Elly decided, she wouldn't let herself get involved in this. It wasn't her place. Melanie's parents would just have to find out what their daughter was up to on their own.

She just hoped that when they did find out it wouldn't be too late.

"Fine, Mel," Elly said softly. "I won't tell anyone. Your secret is safe with me."

"Thank you!" Melanie reached over and gave her a tight hug. "You're a pal."

Elly did not feel like such a pal at that moment instead, she felt completely disgusted with herself.

"Yeah, sure," Without saying another word to Melanie, she climbed out of bed and headed for the bedroom door.

"By the way," Melanie said at her back, stopping her in her track. "Brad asked me to go out with him again, on Wednesday. He wants to take me to the fair and then to dinner afterwards. I thought perhaps you would like to come with us. I'm sure Brad wouldn't mind."

Elly slowly turned around and faced Melanie. She couldn't believe what she had just heard. "You're kidding me, right?"

Melanie shook her head. "No, I'm not. Elly, this is important. I have to go and I'd really like you to come. You could even ask Aimer along. I'm sure he'd like to go with you. Everything will be fine, I promise."

Elly watched Melanie closely. She couldn't tell whether Melanie was only asking her because she was feeling guilty but she could tell that Melanie was up to something, though. She couldn't believe that Melanie was actually going to see this guy again. What was wrong with this girl?

"I'll think about it," Elly said.

"No, you will not think about it. You're going and that's final. You can ask Aimer if he would like to go with you tomorrow. I'm sure he'll say yes. Really, Elly, I want you to come with us." Melanie got up from the bed and came to stand before Elly. "Please say yes."

Elly shook her head but then smiled sheepishly. Maybe she would get some answers if she went. "All right, I'll go."

CHAPTER TWELVE

"What am I going to do while you're at work?" Elly asked.

It was Wednesday morning and they were driving down the road towards Vincent's. Elly had spent the past two days exploring the rest of the town with Melanie, her sisters and Aimer. Elly was becoming familiar with the area rather quickly. The entire family had stayed home on Sunday since Adria had declared it family day. Aimer had come by later on that afternoon to exercise the horses. Elly had offered to help. The horses hadn't given them any trouble and they seemed to like having her there.

And, of course, Elly was still very concerned about Melanie. Any doubts that Elly may have had about Melanie being involved in something suspect were dispelled early Sunday morning. Elly had woken out of another nightmare Sunday morning and had found it impossible to go back to sleep. She had finally given up and gotten out of bed just at the crack of dawn. Putting on a robe, Elly had wandered out of her room and eventually found herself standing at the living room window which faced out to the back yard towards the pasture.

The sun was just starting to rise, casting an orange glow over the backyard and ensuing pasture.

Turning her head slightly to the right, Elly was able to make out the form of two people standing over near the shed talking. It didn't take long for Elly to realize that one of the people in the back yard was Melanie even though her back was to Elly. The other person, a man, was facing Elly's direction and she could see that he was somewhat agitated by whatever he was discussing with Melanie. Elly was tempted to go outside so she could hear what was being said but she knew that there was no way to do this without being seen. Frustrated, Elly had headed back to her room where she lay sleepless on her bed for a few more hours before getting up and taking a shower.

Convinced that Melanie was facing some difficult situation, Elly was actually looking forward to going to the fair with Melanie and Brad. She hoped that this would help her find out something about what was really going on.

Unfortunately, she hadn't had the chance to ask Aimer if he wanted to go to the fair with her yet. But Elly was determined to go, with or without Aimer. She wasn't about to let Melanie out of her sight. One way or another, she was going to get to the bottom of this whole mess.

"First of all," Melanie started, shaking Elly out of her thoughts, "you're going to ask Aimer to go to the fair with you." She said this as though she had just read Elly's mind. "You can find him at home. He's watching his little sister, Christina, until his mom comes home early this afternoon. His house is only three blocks down from ours, the third house on the left, it's blue. Don't worry, he won't mind if you stop by."

"Really, Mel, why can't I just go by myself?" Elly frowned.

"Because it'll be more fun if Aimer goes with you."

"But I don't think it's fair to give him such short notice."

"Trust me, Aimer is a really nice guy. He'll understand," Melanie assured her.

Elly sighed. "All right, if you insist."

"I insist," Melanie grinned as she parked the car by the curb. Elly shook her head in defeat.

"Come on," Melanie said, taking Elly's hand. They were standing in front of Vincent's. "I have a few minutes before I start my shift. I'll fix you a drink." Melanie pushed the front door open and led Elly inside.

"Well, I thought that you would never show up," a woman's voice said from behind Melanie. Melanie spun around and froze. Peeking out from behind Melanie, Elly could tell that the girl sitting up front at the counter was Kara.

Oh no, Elly muttered to herself. Here comes trouble. She regarded Kara closely trying to take in everything about her since she hadn't had a chance to study her the first time she had seen her at the cafe.

Kara was a tall and slim blonde with piercing gray eyes and a defiant appearance that clearly implied trouble to anyone who crossed her path whom she didn't like. Elly was sure Kara wouldn't think twice about hurting Melanie if she felt threatened by her for any reason. Elly took in a deep breath. This was not going to be good.

"What do you want?" Melanie asked icily.

"To talk to you," Kara said as she climbed off her seat.

"I have nothing to say to you," Melanie said and proceeded to take off her coat and gloves.

"That's good because I have plenty to say to you." Kara walked over and stood in front of Melanie, blocking her path. "If I were you," Kara began, "I would learn to stay away from things that don't belong to you." Her voice was shrill and threatening.

"First of all, thankfully, I'm not you, and secondly, I don't have anything that belongs to you." Melanie glared at Kara.

"Then why were you out with Brad last night?"

Melanie looked momentarily stunned, but quickly recovered and answered simply, "Because he asked me out and I said, yes."

That seemed to take Kara by surprise. "He asked you out?"

Melanie nodded. "Yes, he did."

Kara shook her head. "You have no idea what you've just gotten yourself into," Kara said icily. "You've messed with the wrong person again; you know that, don't you?" Kara laughed sending a chill down Elly's back. "And this time, you're not getting away with it." Still laughing, Kara pushed her way past Melanie and Elly and slammed out the door.

Elly watched her until she rounded a corner out of sight.

What had just happened here? Elly's heart was beating wildly against her chest. This can't be good, Elly thought to herself. The animosity between Kara and Melanie was almost palpable. There's definitely more to what's going on here then she's telling me, Elly concluded. And what did Kara mean when she said Melanie had messed with the wrong person again?

Elly turned towards Melanie and saw the she was shaking violently.

"Mel, what's wrong?"

Melanie shook her head. "Nothing. Kara just has a way of getting on my nerves, that's all."

Elly knew that she was lying but decided not to dwell on that.

"Look, Mel, maybe we shouldn't go to the fair with Brad tonight. We can go by ourselves some other time-"

"No," Melanie cut her off as she made her way to the other side of the counter. "We are going to the fair tonight- with Brad. Who does Kara think she is threatening me like that?" She angrily pulled an apron from a hook and tied it around her waist.

"But Mel-"

"Elly, please. She always likes to talk big. It's nothing, really. Now here," Melanie handed her a glass. "Have a strawberry shake. It's on me."

Before Elly could say anything, Cory came out from the back room. "Oh, good," Cory said. "She's gone. I'm glad you didn't have to run into her, Mel."

Melanie glanced at Elly and then said, "Yeah, me too."

"Do you need me to do anything before I take off?" Cory asked.

"No, but thanks."

"See you later, then."

"Melanie, I really think going out with Brad tonight is a bad idea," Elly said as soon as Cory was out the door.

"Look, don't worry. I'll take care of everything," Melanie assured her. "You just make sure that you remember to ask Aimer to come with us tonight, okay?"

Elly nodded sullenly.

"Good. Now, are you sure that you'll be able to find your way around without me? Do you want to take the car?"

"Yes, I'm positive and no, no car." Elly finished her shake and got up.

"Now you just have some fun," Melanie advised as Elly pulled on her coat. "Everything will be fine, all right?"

"Be careful," Elly warned her.

Melanie smiled. "I will, promise."

"I'll see you later." Elly turned and reluctantly left the restaurant.

She was afraid to leave Melanie alone, for fear of what may happen. As she headed down the street away from Vincent's, her head started spinning, making her dizzy. She stopped walking and leaned against the side of a building.

"Something is wrong, I know it," she whispered to herself. She looked around uneasily. Everything felt odd and strangely out of place and she knew that what she was feeling wasn't because she was on a strange planet.

It was something else...What was going on with Melanie? Why had she lied about what had happened to her Saturday night?

What has she gotten herself into?

When she was finally able to get a hold of herself, she began walking again. Minutes later, she found herself entering into a small jewelry shop at the end of a street corner. Inside, the small shop was filled with all sorts of jewelry closed up in glass cases. Elly found that she was captivated by the beauty that surrounded her and a lot of the things she saw reminded her of home.

"May I help you, Ma'am?" Elly looked up and saw a boy looking at her from behind one of the cases of jewelry. He was tall with blonde hair and deep brown eyes. He smiled and there was a dimple in his left cheek. Elly smiled back, knowing that her own dimple was showing.

"Yes. How much is that charm?" Elly pointed at a beautiful butterfly charm that was encrusted with colorful jewels.

"Seventy-five dollars," the boy answered. Elly frowned. How could something so small cost so much?

"It's the most expensive charm we have," the boy explained, as if reading her mind. "The jewels on it are genuine. Would you like to see it?"

"Yes, please," Elly answered eagerly. The boy opened a drawer behind him and pulled out a pair of keys. Opening the case, he carefully reached inside and pulled out the box that held the butterfly charm. He set it down in front of Elly. She ran her fingertip over it gingerly. It was exquisite.

"It's unique," the boy was telling her, "No other piece around like it."

"Thank you," Elly said, handing the box back to him. There was no way she could afford to buy such a piece of jewelry.

"I have to go," the boy said after putting the charm back in its place. He pointed towards the cash register where there were two people standing in line. "Don't want to keep the customers waiting." He flashed Elly a smile and turned to leave.

"Thanks for your time," Elly called after him.

"No problem," he answered. After the boy left, Elly still stood there in front of the case admiring the charm. After looking around the store a bit more, Elly decided to leave the store. Standing outside, Elly glanced around and noticed a small deli across the street. She hadn't been hungry when she had been at Vincent's but now her stomach wouldn't leave her alone. Crossing the street, she entered the deli and ordered a sandwich. She went and took a seat near the back of the deli to wait for her food.

"Excuse me," she heard someone say. She had been so engrossed in her thoughts that she hadn't heard anyone approach her table. Looking up she was surprised to find Brad standing in front of her.

"Well, hi there," she said uneasily.

"You're Melanie's cousin, Elly, aren't you?" he asked. Even though he was smiling, Elly couldn't help noticing once again just how cold and empty Brad's eyes were. Elly shivered slightly.

"Uh, yes, I am."

"I'm Brad, a friend of Melanie's. We met the other day, remember?"

"Uh, yeah, I remember. How are you?"

"Fine, thanks. I was just passing by the Deli when I saw you in here. I just thought I'd come in and say 'Hi'."

"That was- really nice of you."

"Did Mel remember to invite you to come with us to the fair tonight? We really wouldn't mind having you along."

"Uh, yeah, she did." So, Melanie had already told Brad about the change of plans, Elly thought. How nice.

"I understand that you might be bringing a friend along with you," Brad commented.

"Yeah," Elly said uneasily. "A friend. Is that all right?"

Brad nodded. "Yeah, that's fine."

But Elly could tell that it was not fine by the strain in his voice when he answered.

"May I sit down?" he asked. "I was thinking maybe we could get to know each other better. After all, Melanie is one of my best friends."

"Sure," Elly answered all the while wishing he would just go away. He was making her extremely uncomfortable.

The waitress came with Elly's food.

"You know something," Brad started as he made himself comfortable across from her. "Melanie has never mentioned you to me and that's funny because I've known Melanie a long time and I know her family pretty well, too." He gave her a smug smile as he leaned back and waited for her response.

"Our families had a falling out many years ago and have only recently resolved the issues that stood between us. We're working on mending our differences." What did he want from her? Brad was watching her very closely and Elly had to try hard not to squirm in her seat. His presence alone was unnerving. Elly busied herself eating, grateful to have something to distract herself with. It wasn't so much that she was hungry anymore but that she didn't want to talk to him.

"So how long will you be staying with Melanie?" His question was very incisive, catching Elly by surprise. Her mouth fell open in amazement, but just as quickly she collected herself.

"Until my parents return from their trip. They've gone away for a while. I didn't want to go with them so they allowed me to stay with my aunt instead."

Brad nodded. "I see. So will you be going to school out here?"

Elly shrugged. "Maybe."

"Where are your parents right now?"

Elly stared at him. "Down south," she answered vaguely. Brad looked away from her uncomfortably. Obviously, he didn't like being stared down even though he seemed to like doing it to others.

"Well," Brad said finally, looking at his watch. "I've got to get back to work. Thank you for the chat, Elly. Sure you'll be coming with us tonight?"

"Yes, definitely."

"Good. I'll see you then. Bye." Without waiting for Elly to respond, Brad got up and left the deli.

Elly shook her head. Talk about strange people. It was very much apparent that he did not want either Aimer or herself there at the fair tonight. She wondered why. She was even more determined now to go to that fair with Melanie- no matter what.

One thing was for sure, though, she definitely didn't like either Brad or Kara. Somehow, she was going to have to get Melanie away from both of them- before things really started getting bad, as she was sure that they would.

"I think it's time I talked with Aimer," she told herself out loud.

Leaving the Deli, Elly headed towards Aimer's house.

By following Melanie's directions, Elly had no problem finding Aimer's home. It wasn't long before she found herself standing in front of a modest one-story blue house with white trim and several large trees in the front yard a few blocks away from the Coltzs'. Elly climbed the stairs that led to the front door and rang the doorbell nervously. A few seconds later the door opened and Elly found herself standing in front of Aimer. He was dressed in an old pair of jeans and a beautiful green sweater. He smiled when he saw Elly.

"Hi, Elly," he greeted her, "what brings you here?"

"Hi," Elly said. "I'm sorry, I don't mean to interrupt anything. I can come back some other time if you like."

"No, please," Aimer said, as he pulled the door open. "You're not interrupting anything. Please, come in."

Ell tentatively stepped into the front entryway and Aimer closed the door behind her.

"You came at a good time," Aimer said as he led her into a beautifully furnished living room. "My little sister just went to take her nap." He offered Elly a chair and she sat at the edge of it nervously.

"Would you like some tea?" Aimer asked.

"Yes, please," answered Elly. Her throat was parched. Aimer disappeared out of the room and came back a few minutes later carrying two cups of tea. He handed one to Elly then took a seat across from her.

"So, tell me," he said as he settled in his seat and sipped his tea, "to what do I owe the pleasure of your company?"

"It's nothing much, really," Elly said.

"Tell me," Aimer said, leaning forward in his seat and giving her his full attention. This made Elly a bit nervous.

"This was really Melanie's idea," Elly stated. Aimer raised an eyebrow in question. Elly cleared her throat before continuing. "Brad invited Melanie to go to the fair with her and she wants me to go, too. She doesn't want me to go by myself so she suggested that I ask you if you'd like to come along with us." She stopped and watched Aimer expectantly.

"Would you like me to go?" he asked, still staring at her intently.

Elly shifted in her seat uncomfortably. "Yes, actually, I would. That is if you want to," she added.

"I'd love to go," Aimer answered.

"Really?" Elly sighed in relief. She had been so unsure about this whole arrangement. "Wonderful, thank you."

"I'm glad you asked me to go. Would you mind if I picked you up? I'm sure Brad and Melanie want to go together. We could meet them at the fair."

"That sounds good. What time?"

"Would six-thirty be good?"

"Six-thirty would be fine," she responded.

"Well then, I'll see you then."

Elly smiled heartily. But then she remembered that it was with Brad that Melanie was going to the fair with and knowing that Melanie could possibly be in some kind of trouble made the thought of going to the fair less exciting.

"What's wrong?" Aimer asked, seeing the frown that crossed her face.

Elly decided to tell him the truth. After all, he was just as worried about Melanie's well-being as she was.

"It's Melanie," she said. "I really don't think she should be hanging out with Brad. There's something very strange about him but I can't quiet figure out what it is."

"I know what you mean," Aimer nodded. "That's the same way that I feel about him."

"Isn't there anything that we can do to convince her not to see him anymore?" Elly asked desperately.

Aimer sadly shook his head. "She's got to find out who he is for herself."

She was almost tempted to tell Aimer about the incident with Melanie that had taken place the night before. Almost.

"It may be too late by then," Elly said sadly. She had no idea where that thought had come from but as soon as she heard the words come out of her mouth, she knew that they were true. She only wished that Aimer hadn't heard her say them.

"What? Do you know something?" Aimer asked anxiously.

Elly shook her head and opened her mouth. But before she could say anything, she heard someone else speak. It was a little girl.

"Aim, I'm hungry," the little girl said as she came into the living room.

She was a beautiful child, about six years old with lush corn silk hair and deep green eyes. It was hard to believe that she was Aimer's sister, they looked so different. The little girl's features looked almost alien; her eyes were unusually round surrounded by long, thick lashes. Her face was soft, almost triangular in shape with ears that were longer than normal and pointed. She looks almost like an elf, Elly thought, remembering the picture she had seen of one on the television the other day. But elves were not real, she knew they were something that humans had made up for fun. Something stirred inside of Elly when she saw the child but she didn't know what it was or why she felt this.

"Elly, this is my little sister, Christina. Chrissy, say hi to a friend of mine, Elly."

Christina stared at Elly for a long moment. Elly felt as though she was sinking into Christina's huge green eyes. The feeling was almost magical.

Finally, Christina smiled and said, "Hi, Elly, nice to meet you."

"Nice to meet you, too, Chrissy." Elly smiled back. She could tell that Chrissy accepted her as Aimer's friend and didn't hold that against her. That was good. They would be friends.

Chrissy turned back to Aimer. "I'm hungry," she repeated.

"All right, tiger, what would you like to eat?"

"Frosted flakes!" Chrissy responded instantly.

Aimer groaned. "How about some oatmeal you already had frosted flakes."

Chrissy frowned but said, "All right, I'll have some oatmeal."

"Would you like something to eat?" Aimer asked Elly.

"Uh, no," Elly answered getting up from her seat. "I really should be going. But thanks."

"Can't you stay for just a little while longer?" Chrissy asked. She looked sadly at Elly with those beautiful green eyes and Elly was a tempted to stay.

"No, Chrissy, I can't this time. Maybe next time, okay?"

Chrissy nodded and shyly turned away. Elly's heart almost broke. Why did she feel such an attachment to this child she had just met?

"I'll walk you out," Aimer offered. "I'll see you tonight at six-thirty right?" he said once Elly was outside.

"Yes, six-thirty," Elly answered. "And thanks again."

Aimer smiled. "It's my pleasure."

Elly climbed down the front steps and quickly headed down the street towards the Coltzs' house.

CHAPTER THIRTEEN

"Elly! Elly, where are you?"

Elly awoke groggily to the sound of Melanie's voice calling to her. Her head throbbed painfully and she felt a slight pressure behind her eyes. She didn't even remember having fallen asleep. How long have I been asleep? she wondered. She glanced over at the clock on her night table.

It was five-thirty.

Elly's eyes flew open as she hastily sat up in her bed.

Five-thirty! Aimer would be there to pick her up in an hour. Elly groaned. Her head swam and she had to squeeze her eyes tight and take a deep breath in order to keep from becoming nauseated.

"Elly!"

Elly got up and stuck her head out of the door. "I'm in here, Mel." Melanie appeared a moment later.

"Didn't you hear me calling you?" Melanie asked as she entered Elly's room and sat down at the desk.

Elly shook her head. "I was sleeping, I just woke up."

"So, tell me, did you ask him?" Melanie inquired eagerly.

Elly rolled her eyes. "Of course, I did."

"Well then, what did he say? Don't keep me in suspense."

"He said yes and, as a matter of fact, he's going to be here to pick me up in an hour. So, if you'll excuse me, I'll go get ready." Without waiting for Melanie's response, Elly jumped up from where she sat on her bed and started digging through her closet.

"I better go get dressed, too," she said getting up. "Brad will be here at seven. Since we're going to the fair separately, I think we should have a meeting place. Like say the hot-dog stand near the rear parking lot. Aimer should know where that is, he's been to the fair before."

"That sounds like a good idea," Elly agreed.

"And Elly," Melanie said as she stood by the door.

"What?"

"I just want you to promise me that you won't worry too much about me tonight."

A cold chill swept through Elly. "Melanie, what are you talking about. What's wrong?"

Melanie shook her head. "Nothing. I- bad timing, I guess," She shook her head again and before Elly could say anything, Melanie left the room, closing the door behind her.

Elly slowly sat down on the bed, fear coursing through her veins. What was going on here? Elly wondered. It was obvious that Melanie hadn't really wanted Aimer and her to go to the fair with Brad and herself tonight. But she was scared about something, Elly could tell. Something was going to happen tonight and Melanie was thoroughly frightened. She could feel the fear that was emanating from her.

But what exactly was going to happen tonight? What was going on?

Motivated, Elly quickly took a shower and jumped into her clothes. Grabbing a jacket, she left her room and found Adria in the kitchen preparing dinner.

"Hi, Adria," Elly kissed her soundly on the cheek.

"I hear that you and Melanie are going on a double date to the fair?" she said, handing Elly a tuna sandwich.

"Yes. I'm going with Aimer and Mel is going with Brad."

"Hope you guys have fun. I remember the fairs they used to have in South Hampton when Michael and I were young," she smiled. "Those were the good old days." She sat down across from Elly. "So, tell me honestly, how do you like it here so far?"

"I love it," Elly answered honestly. "I couldn't possibly ever thank you enough for being so good to me and letting me stay."

Adria shrugged. "What else could I do? I couldn't possibly let you go roaming the streets with nowhere to go."

"All right, enough sentiments," Melanie said entering the room.

She was wearing a black pair of slacks with an olive-green sweater.

"You both look beautiful," Adria commented, smiling.

"Thanks!" both girls answered in unison.

Just then, the doorbell rang.

"That must be Aimer," Elly said, taking her coat from the chair.

"I'll see you later, Adria." She gave Adria another kiss on the cheek.

"Be careful," Adria warned.

"And don't forget to meet Brad and me at the hot dog stand," Melanie reminded her.

"I will and I won't," Elly called over her shoulder as she made her way towards the front door. She pulled the front door open. "Hi, Aimer," she greeted him.

"Hi, Elly," answered Aimer. "You look great."

Elly blushed. "Thanks. So do you." He was wearing gray slacks with a thick navy blue knit sweater that made his blue eyes seem even bluer.

"Are you ready to go?" he asked.

"Yes, let's go." Elly stepped outside and pulled the door shut behind her. Aimer led her to his car and soon they were heading out towards South Hampton.

"So, tell me about yourself," Elly said filling in the silence that had overcome them.

"Well," Aimer shrugged. "I grew up in the city of Rance which is way on the other side of town. My parents got divorced five years ago so my mother took Christina, who was just a baby at that time and me and we moved up here to start over. I didn't think I would ever be happy here but that changed the day I met the Coltzs' and they gave me a job taking care of the horses. Apparently, the previous helper decided to move to another state and they needed someone to take his place. I was happy to do so."

"How long have you known the Coltzs'?"

"Just a little over three years." He shook his head and gave a small laugh. "I remember when I first met Melanie. She was standing on the docks at the lake-"

"There's a lake here?" Elly asked surprised.

"Sure. It's on the other side of the pasture. We'll have to take you there sometime when the weather clears up." The past two days had still been cloudy, but it hadn't rained.

"I'd like that," Elly admitted.

A frown crossed Aimer's face. "Elly, before I continue, I want you to promise me something."

Elly was puzzled. "Sure, what?"

"I want you to promise me that even when you do get your memory back- you won't forget about us out here."

"Of course, I won't forget you guys, how could I?" Elly smiled at him reassuringly. Yet she wondered what could have possibly made him think of saying such a thing. Did he know something that she didn't? Elly couldn't tell. He sighed in relief. "Now, as you were saying," she prompted him, ignoring the thoughts that were running through her mind about what he had just said.

"Oh, yeah. Melanie was standing out at the tip of the dock and I called out to her. She turned to answer, lost her balance and fell into the lake!" Elly couldn't help laughing at that.

"What did she do?"

"Absolutely nothing, can you believe it? I was sure that she was going to get angry but instead, she started laughing and she was still in the water!"

"Why am I not surprised?" Elly said shaking her head. "For the short time that I've known Melanie, I've never seen her get angry about anything. She seems to always stay calm, no matter what."

"Isn't that the truth," Aimer agreed.

"That is until she starts talking about Kara or Brad," Elly added, remembering how Melanie had reacted both times she had run into Kara at the restaurant. She bit her lip as soon as the words came out. I shouldn't have said that, she thought to herself. I'm spoiling everything.

Aimer nodded. "You noticed that too, haven't you?"

"Yes, I've noticed. Aimer, I'm really worried about her," she confided. Elly decided it was no use pretending. There was no way she was going to be able to think about anything else until this whole mess was settled and over with and who better to discuss this with then Aimer who she knew cared very much for Melanie. Who knows, Elly thought, he may be able to help me.

"I am, too," Aimer agreed.

"She said something to me tonight that was really strange."

"What did she say?"

"She asked me not to worry about her too much and then she said something about bad timing that I didn't understand."

Aimer bit his lower lip. "I hope she's not in any kind of trouble."

"What makes you think that she could be in trouble?"

"You really have no idea what's been going on here, do you? I thought Mel had spoken to you about this?"

Elly shook her head. "Melanie hasn't told me much of anything, only bits and pieces."

Aimer shook his head vigorously. "I don't know if I should be telling you any of this, then."

"Aimer!" She regarded him closely. "You care about her, don't you?"

"Of course, I do."

"Listen, I know I only met her a few weeks ago but I care about her, too. And if she is in trouble, we're going to have to do something to help her. Now please, tell me what's going on."

"You're right," Aimer agreed, "and it seems that you're the only one that I can really trust."

"Yes, Aimer, you can trust me," Elly assured him.

"I don't know what Melanie has told you but I'm sure she left out all the important parts and ended up painting a rather pretty picture for you."

"Important parts like what?" Elly wanted to know.

"Did she tell you about Brad and the group or whatever they are that he hangs around with?" Elly nodded. "Well then, did she also tell you that she was also a part of that group until about three months ago?"

Elly's mouth fell open in disbelief. "What?!" She was shocked.

"I thought so," Aimer said sadly.

"But how? Why?"

"Why? I don't know. How? Because Brad was her boyfriend at that time and he soon became the leader. Whatever he says goes. He wanted her in the group and so she was in, just like that."

Elly was confused. Brad had been Melanie's boyfriend? How was that possible? She had said that they were only good friends. "But she told me part of the reason she left school was because she couldn't stand what those people were doing and she didn't like that Brad was involved. Why would she join them? That doesn't make sense?"

"She never talked much about what happened. All I know is that Brad wanted her in, so she was in. It wasn't until Kara joined the group about four months ago that the real trouble started."

"Kara," Elly whispered. No wonder they hated each other so much.

Aimer nodded grimly. "Kara is from the old gang on the East side. It is believed that this is where the group originally started a few years back. But no one really knows for sure. No one really knows anything about this group, actually. You can't really even tell who the members are unless you're one of them or they tell you. I didn't know Brad was involved until I heard it from Melanie."

Aimer made a right turn onto another street then continued. "Anyway, when Kara joined the group here, she insisted that things be done right. Apparently, to become a member of this group, you have to be initiated. Melanie had not been initiated when she became a member so Kara insisted that if Melanie wanted to remain a member of the group she had to be initiated. Melanie came over one night crying and told me what was happening. She didn't want to be initiated but she still wanted to try and work things out with Brad, despite all the trouble the two of them had been having." Aimer did not elaborate on what he meant by that.

"From what I understand, Brad tried fighting on her behalf but Kara won over him. You have to understand, Kara has been in this type of thing since she was fifteen. This was her territory. Furthermore, she wanted Brad and the only way to do that was to get Melanie out of the picture. She knew that Melanie would never agree to be initiated; she didn't fit in. The thing was, Brad was in love with Melanie and wanted to be with her. He didn't even notice Kara when she flaunted herself at him. I think that's what set her off the most." Aimer stopped to catch his breath.

"So, what happened then?" Elly pressed. She needed to know everything. She hoped that somewhere in all of this, there would be a solution.

Aimer slowly let out his breath. "This is when it all gets sort of confusing. Melanie came to see me again about a week later and she told me that she decided to leave the group because she didn't want to go through with the initiation. That's when she decided to come home."

"Well then that's good, isn't it? Maybe she'd finally come to her senses."

"It's not so simple," Aimer explained. "From what I've heard, once you've been on the inside of this group there really is no way out. You're a member for life so to speak. I don't think anyone ever gets out in one piece- or alive for that matter."

Elly went pale when she heard this and she started shaking as if she had been drenched with icy water. And even though most of what Aimer was telling her was way over her head, Elly couldn't help the sick feeling she felt in the pit of her stomach at the moment.

This was definitely bad.

"Aimer, what are you telling me?"

"Elly, I don't think Melanie has left the group. I think she is going to let them initiate her, tonight, possibly." He said this calmly but Elly could tell that he was just as scared as she was. "Although, I don't understand why she would do that considering the trouble she could be getting herself into. If she is doing this because of Brad he is definitely not worth it. The way he's treated her-" Aimer stopped, shaking his head. Elly could see that he was angry.

Elly was having a difficult time processing everything Aimer had just explained to her. She wasn't sure she understood exactly what initiating was but she certainly didn't like the sound of it. The bottom line was that Melanie could end up hurt- or worse. "Aimer, please tell me that you don't truly believe that any of that is possible."

"I wish I could," he frowned. "But then why else would she tell you not to worry about her? And why has she been acting so strange? Something has been totally off with her ever since she came back home and I can't figure any other reason."

Elly couldn't find a better reason, either.

"We're here," Aimer said moments later. Elly turned her head and saw the bright lights from the fair in front of her. Under any other circumstance, she would have been excited about going to this fair and experiencing it. But after what Aimer had just revealed to her, excitement was the last thing on her mind. She turned back towards Aimer.

"What are we going to do?"

"Keep a close eye on Melanie," he answered. "And pray." He climbed out of the car, went around to the other side and opened Elly's door.

"Melanie said we should meet her and Brad at the hot dog stand near the rear parking lot." Elly had no idea what a hot dog stand was. She knew what a dog was. She had actually seen a few and found them to be rather interesting. But a hot dog? What on earth was that?

"I know where that is," Aimer said, taking her hand in his. "Let's go."

As Elly followed Aimer into the crowd, her mind kept going over the conversation she just had with Aimer. Elly could hardly believe what he had told her. It all seemed so unreal. The sights and sounds around her were odd and almost fluid as she and Aimer bought their tickets and then began to push their way through the crowd to get to the rear parking. Elly couldn't help the tears that ran down her face. She wiped at them quickly before Aimer could see.

How could this be happening? She wondered. It wasn't supposed to be like this! She should be having fun not worrying about facing a possible disaster.

"Let's wait here," Aimer said when they were standing close to the fencing that surrounded the rear parking lot. "This is where Melanie wants us to meet. Are you hungry?" he asked.

Elly shook her head. She was too scared and worried to think about eating.

"Oh, come on, Elly," Aimer urged. "Eat something. Worrying isn't going to do us any good. We've got to keep our heads straight, for Melanie's sake."

She nodded and forced a smile. "I guess I'll have whatever you decide to have."

"Good, wait right here, I'll be right back." He turned and headed for a stand not too far away.

While Elly was waiting for Aimer to return, she saw Melanie and Brad making their way across the parking lot towards the fair. They paid for their tickets and entered through the gate.

"Melanie!" Elly called, wildly waving her arm in the air. "We're over here!"

Melanie and Brad made their way through the crowd towards Elly.

"Hope we didn't keep you guys waiting too long," Melanie said.

Elly shook her head. "No, we just got here."

"Where's Aimer?" Melanie asked.

"Right here." Melanie turned and found Aimer standing behind her. He was holding something in both hands.

"Oh! Hi, Aimer. How are you?" Melanie greeted Aimer enthusiastically, but Elly could tell that she was nervous.

"Fine, thanks," Aimer answered. He was staring coldly at Brad.

"Uh, Aimer," Melanie said nervously, seeing the look on Aimer's face, "You know Brad, don't you?"

Aimer nodded. "We've met," he answered, but to Brad, he said nothing.

"So, guys, what's the plan?" Elly asked, trying to break the ice. She could practically taste the tension in the air. Already, things were off to a bad start.

"Well, why don't we hang out here for a while?" Melanie suggested. "Then we can leave for dinner at about nine. What do you think?"

"Good idea, Mel," Brad said, smiling. "And if we should get separated for any reason, then we should all definitely meet back here at nine. We can decide what to do from there."

Everyone agreed to the plan and as they made their way through the crowd towards the Ferris wheel, Elly couldn't help that small tremor of fear that crept up her spine.

This was going to be one long night, Elly realized.

Unfortunately, and by no accident, Elly knew, the four of them did get separated. It was eight o'clock and Aimer and Elly had just gotten off a ride called the Colossus. Melanie and Brad had been sitting in the back when they had first gotten on. Elly was certain of this because she had checked to make sure. Obviously, she had not checked well enough. How the two of them had gotten off the ride without her noticing it was a puzzle to her. Actually, no, it wasn't a puzzle, really. The ride was fun, something Elly had never experienced before. She had been enjoying the ride so much that she had momentarily forgotten about Melanie and Brad.

Momentarily.

Now Aimer and she were helplessly searching the fairground, trying to locate where Melanie and Brad could have possibly disappeared to. They had left the fair, Elly knew, she could feel it.

"Listen," Aimer said after they had been looking around for some time, to no avail. "You wait here while I go look further down, at the other end of the fair." They were standing in front of the Colossus again, hoping that Melanie and Brad might have come back. "It won't do any good for both of us to get lost in this crowd," he added, "so wait here. I'll come back and get you if I find them and if they come back here, tell them to stay put."

Elly agreed to Aimer's plan but knew that there was no chance of Melanie and Brad coming back. She sighed as she watched Aimer disappear into the crowd. Looking around nervously, Elly watched the people as they passed by her laughing and having fun. Considering the situation at hand, Elly felt depressed even though she was surrounded by happy people. She took a step back so that she could see over the heads of the people in front of her, who were crowding around a clown, when she felt herself bump into someone.

"Oh! I'm sorry!" Elly gasped as she quickly spun around to face the person that she had bumped into.

"It's all right," the guy she had bumped into said. He looked at her closely and then said, "Hey, don't I know you?"

Elly shook her head. "I don't think so."

"Yes, I do. You're Elly, right? Melanie's cousin. I'm Cory. We met at the restaurant a few days back."

"Oh, right! I remember. How are you?"

Cory shrugged. "All right, I guess. What are you doing standing here all by yourself? This is a fair, you know."

"Actually, I'm not alone," Elly answered. She quickly told Cory what had happened. "Aimer's gone over to the other side to see if he can locate them. He thought it would be best if I stayed here so that we both wouldn't get lost."

"Hmmm," Cory absently rubbed his chin. "This is really weird. I could have sworn that I saw Melanie leaving the fair with someone just about ten minutes ago."

Elly's eyes flew open in amazement. "Really? Do you know which way she left?"

"They went out through the east gate," answered Cory. Elly remembered that that was where Brad and Melanie had parked.

"I was going to go talk to her," Cory continued, "but they both seemed to be in quite a hurry to leave."

"Do you have any idea where they might be heading?" Elly asked anxiously.

Cory was pensive for a moment. "Well, I did watch them for a while because they were acting really strange. I saw them leave the parking lot and turn left, so my best guess would be that they may have been heading towards highway 38."

Elly's heart fell. Melanie and Brad were long gone, she knew, and time was running out. Elly feared that they weren't going to be able to stop whatever it was that was already in motion. Most of all, she feared for Melanie's life.

Where was Aimer?

"Elly? Are you all right?" Even in the dim light, Cory could tell that Elly had turned pale.

"No," Elly admitted. "I'm not all right."

"What's wrong? Does it have something to do with Melanie?"

"Cory, look, it's a long story and I don't really think I can explain it to you-"

"Wait a minute," Cory interrupted. "If Melanie is in some kind of trouble, I want to know. We go back a long way, you know."

Elly looked at him closely for a minute and saw that he was being sincere. He really did care about Melanie- in more ways than one. A sad smile touched her lips.

"All right," she decided. "I'll tell you what I know."

CHAPTER FOURTEEN

Aimer returned just minutes after Elly had finished explaining to Cory what was going on- or better yet, what Aimer and she believed was going on. He was completely out of breath. He had searched the entire fairground from the entrance, tracking back to the Colossus and the immediate area surrounding it with no luck. Brad and Melanie were nowhere to be found.

"I can't find them anywhere," he gasped as he leaned against a post.

"That's all right," Elly assured him. "I think Cory and I might know where they've gone."

Aimer looked surprised. "Really?" He glanced at Cory. "Hey, Cory, what's up?"

"Nothing much," Cory answered simply. "I just told Elly about the old abandoned cabin and bridge off of highway 38 and we think that this may be where they are headed."

Aimer looked at Elly quizzically.

"He knows," she answered his unspoken question. "And he wants to help. Who knows, we might just need an extra pair of hands."

Aimer readily agreed to Cory's offer to help them find Melanie.

"What makes you think that they've gone to the cabin?" Aimer asked as they made their way through the crowds towards the parking lot. They had decided that they would go separately, with Cory following behind Aimer and Elly, just in case.

"I don't know," Elly answered honestly. "It's just a feeling I've got."

The road leading to the cabin was a narrow winding road that was dark with no lights on either side. With every turn, Elly was afraid that there might be a ditch or something that they could end up falling into and she would hold her breath until the road straightened out again. To Elly, it felt as though hours passed before they reached the exit that led to the old cabin.

When they finally did reach the exit, Elly held her breath, fear running down her spine at the thought of what might lay ahead. There were no street lights in the area that they were in now. Everything was sheltered in darkness; the only light that shown was from the car headlights. Aimer cruised slowly down the road. Behind them, a short distance away, Cory's headlights could be seen.

"Do you know how to get to the cabin from here?" Elly asked, trying to peer into the darkness. Even with her keen eyesight it was useless.

Aimer shook his head. "No, it's been a while since I've been in this area. I think there are some woods located a short distance from here, I'm not sure. We're going to have to wait for Cory. He knows this area better than I do." Aimer slowed and stopped at the side of the road. Moments later, Cory pulled up behind them and got out of his car.

"We're going to have to walk from here," he said through Aimer's open window. "The cabin is hidden in the woods a short distance from here. If we get too close with the cars, they'll hear us and who know what they might do then."

"I thought you said there was a bridge here?" Elly said.

"There is. It's about two blocks east of here. Why?"

"Nothing, just thinking that's all. So, what's the plan?"

The three of them were silent. The truth was there really wasn't any plan. The only goal was getting Melanie away from Brad and whoever else she might be with safe and soundly. Of course, that would need a plan, and a good one, too. Elly groaned inwardly. This couldn't be happening!

"I have a gun," Cory said finally, breaking the silence. Aimer and Elly turned and looked at him, shocked.

"Cory, please," Elly pleaded. "I don't want anyone to get hurt."

"Yeah, but we can't just go in there unarmed. Who knows what they're up to."

"Listen," Aimer turned toward her, "I think it's best if you let Cory and I handle this. You should stay here. It's safer."

"But, Aimer, I-" Elly protested.

"Aimer's right," Cory agreed. "You should stay here. We don't want to have to worry about anything happening to you, too"

"And if we're not back here in thirty minutes, take the car and go look for help. Whatever you do please just don't go into the woods." Aimer took the keys out of the ignition and handed them to her. Elly took them reluctantly. They were useless to her; she had no idea how to drive and she wasn't going to risk getting herself killed trying. But she wasn't going to argue with them, either- that would be useless. All she could do was sit tight until the time was right for her to make her move. She was certain that no one would be coming out of those woods alive without her help.

"All right," she said to the guys. "You've got thirty minutes."

Elly chewed on her nails as she waited for Aimer and Cory to return. Until a few minutes ago, she had been able to keep track of them by the beam of their flashlight. But that had disappeared moments ago and everything was once again cloaked in darkness. Elly knew that they were now deep in the woods.

The minutes crawled by and Elly squirmed in her seat. The intense silence that surrounded her was making her feel a bit paranoid. She pressed the light button on the watch that Melanie had given her and checked the time. Only ten minutes had gone by.

How can they possibly expect me to just sit here and wait- doing nothing? Elly wondered. I need to find out what's going on before deciding what it is that I should do. I'm definitely not just going to sit here and wait!

Closing her eyes, Elly leaned back in the seat and tried to relax. Usually, it would have only taken Elly a few seconds to relax and focus her mind, but because of the tension that surrounded her, it took several minutes. Once she was relaxed, though, it was almost as if she were dead. Her breathing was practically nonexistent and her heart rate slowed dramatically.

Carefully, Elly carried herself out of her body, out of the car and into the cool night air- yes; she could actually feel the air brushing lightly against her skin- into the woods that were only about a block to the left of where the cars were parked. The woods were thick, with many trees crowded close together and even though Elly could not see them, she could feel their height and strength. These woods had survived for many years, Elly knew, and therefore held much power within the shelter of their leaves. They would guide Elly through the long night that lay ahead.

Elly made her way through the woods with absolutely no sense of direction, guided only by her instincts. She wasn't even really sure what it was she was looking for but she was certain that she would recognize it once she found it. Shortly, she came to a clearing near the other end of the woods. She continued on through the clearing and she felt almost as though she was being magnetically pulled in every direction. She was going everywhere and absolutely nowhere at the same time and even though she tried she was unable to stop the dizzying sensation that surrounded her. She was nearing her destination.

Elly wasn't sure how much time elapsed before the world came to a standstill again. Nothing was moving now, not even the air. Focusing her eyes, Elly realized that for the first time she was able to see something in front of her and she was able to hear, too. There was the sound of drunken laughter in the air. Elly then recognized that the bright light she saw not more than ten feet in front of her was the light of a fire and that there were people gathered around the fire and they were all laughing, drinking and carrying on.

Elly carefully moved in closer towards the scene and as she got closer, she recognized a face in the mist of the crowd and that recognition brought the cold chill of fear.

Leaning against a tree close to the fire, her eyes closed with a bottle in her hand was Melanie. Seated next to her was Kara.

Elly froze in her tracks too stunned to move. She couldn't believe what she was seeing. She stared hard at Melanie, hoping that by some miracle the face before her would change and it would be someone else. But that didn't happen. Instead, Elly watched in horror as Melanie slowly opened her eyes- drunken, glassy eyes-stared directly at Elly- and grinned.

Elly's eyes flew open as she snapped back into consciousness. Her breathing was heavy, almost as though she had just had the wind knocked out of her and in one sense or another that is just what had happened to her. What had she seen? What had it all meant? Elly's mind was in a turmoil. Her confusion was profound and this made her feel as though everything was slowly slipping out of her control.

Elly wasn't worried about Melanie having seen her. She was certain that Melanie's reaction was simply because of all the drinking she had been doing but the look on Melanie's face certainly had given her quite a scare.

What was Melanie doing there- with Kara of all people? Elly wondered. The impression that Elly had gotten was that Melanie and Kara hated each other. So, what were they doing drinking together late at night and in the middle of nowhere? And where were Cory and Aimer? Elly had not felt their presence anywhere in the immediate area.

Elly sighed deeply and leaned back in her seat. And here, she thought, we were worried that Melanie might be in danger.

Yet even as that thought crossed her mind Elly was certain that she was missing something. Melanie was in danger; she could feel it. What Elly couldn't figure out was what Melanie was in danger of. Elly looked at her watch again. A whole hour had already gone by.

Elly's heart pounded heavily in her chest. The boys hadn't come back. They had said to wait only for thirty minutes. Elly had to do something. It would take too long to get back in town to find help; by then it might just be too late. No, Elly decided. I've got to do this myself. We'll worry about everything else later.

Silently, Elly pushed the car door open. The air outside had cooled dramatically and the wind was starting to pick up. From what Elly understood more rain was expected soon. Not tonight, Elly hoped as she closed the door. She slipped the car keys into her pant pocket. Fortunately for her, the pockets were deep. She wouldn't have to worry too much about them slipping out. As she carefully made her way in the direction of the woods, Elly wished that she had a flashlight to take along with her. Unfortunately, the boys had taken the only available flashlight with them.

Oh, well, Elly thought, guess I'll just have to make my own light. She was disappointed that she couldn't simply count on her keen eyesight to guide her. But the darkness was too intense. She could barely make out the shape of the trees that surrounded her as she cautiously took her first step into the woods. Before she knew it, Elly was completely enveloped by the woods. At first, she tried using her hand to guide her but that soon became tiring. She felt as though she was getting nowhere and time was running out fast.

Elly stopped in her tracks and closed her eyes. She knew that what she was going to do would be risky. It might attract attention to her before she was ready since she didn't know the distance between herself and the others. But she didn't have any choice in this. Slowly, she rubbed her hands together in a circular motion until her hands felt as though they were on fire. As soon as she stopped rubbing her hands together, a small ball of bright light floated upwards out from her hands until it was just above Elly's head.

Elly opened her eyes and watched as the small ball grew bigger and bigger until it finally exploded soundlessly into a million little shards of light. The light that surrounded her was almost as bright as sunlight and Elly was able to see everything around her.

Elly smiled. If no one saw the ball of light explode, then she was safe. Because once the light exploded, it was useless to anyone else. Only Elly could see it, or see by it. Had there been someone with her, that person would once more be in darkness after the light exploded.

Once again, Elly continued through the forest. The cloud of light hovered over her head, guiding her every step.

Even though Elly had not seen anything when she had wandered through the woods a short while ago, she felt as though she knew every inch of the woods by heart. She wasn't surprised to find that she knew exactly which way to go without even thinking about it. It was often like that after she traveled out of her body. Everything always became familiar to her, almost as though the place had become a part of her.

Soon Elly reached a narrow dirt path which led straight out of the woods. Once more, Elly felt that she was nearing her destination. But this time, there was no quick getaway. She would have to stand and face whatever crossed her path. There was no turning back, either. Elly urged herself forward. Within minutes she broke through the woods and found herself in a clearing. The group was somewhere nearby; she could feel their presence.

Her guiding light was slowly dissolving. She didn't need it anyway. Less than fifty feet in front of her was the light of a fire. There were several people gathered around it. Scanning the place, Elly realized that there were less people than she had originally seen. But then, when she had first traveled here, she hadn't been looking for anything or anyone but Melanie so her estimation could have been wrong.

Now what? Elly wondered. She stopped for a moment and surveyed the area. Something in the back of her mind told her she needed to get to the bridge that Cory had mentioned but she had no idea where it was. She needed to find a way to get closer.

Elly figured that her best chance would be to simply play dumb; pretend that it was just a coincidence that she happened to be here-out in the middle of nowhere. She knew that no one would really fall for her story but at least that would give her a chance to talk to the people and try to get some information from them. She was certain that there were more people hiding around somewhere. She had to be very careful. Actually, she was tempted to just stay where she was and simply destroy all of them one by one. That is everyone expect for Melanie, Aimer and Cory, of course. But she knew that it wouldn't be right. Her mother hadn't sent her here to hurt people. She would be very disappointed if she knew what Elly had contemplated doing.

Sorry Mother, Elly thought guiltily. No, she wasn't going to hurt anyone. She was simply going to immobilize them all long enough to get Melanie away from them and also so she could find out what's happened to Aimer and Cory. She still couldn't feel their presence anywhere.

Taking in a deep breath, Elly moved out of the shadows of the woods and quickly made her way towards the camp fire.

As she got closer to the camp fire, Elly quickly scanned the place. There was no sign of Melanie or Kara anywhere. Where had they disappeared to? she wondered as a tremor of fear coursed through her. There was a skinny young man wearing a black leather jacket standing by the fire. Elly stopped right behind him and tapped him on the shoulder. The young man quickly spun around. A look of surprise crossed his face when he saw Elly standing behind him.

"Yes?" he croaked. He was drunk, stoned; he would cooperate.

"I'm sorry," Elly smiled sweetly. "But I'm supposed to meet two of my friends at a bridge somewhere around here. But it seems that I've gotten lost. Is there a bridge anywhere nearby?"

The guy looked at her dumbly. He started to perspire as Elly's eyes started to grow bigger in front of his face. He wanted to pull his eyes away from hers, but he found that he could not do that. His eyes were glued to hers and it felt as though he was being sucked into them.

"Uh," the guy mumbled, as he wiped his forehead. Time had come to a complete standstill for him. He felt as though he was on the verge of exploding. "There is a bridge here, over that way." He pointed to the left. What was he doing? he asked himself. He wasn't supposed to tell anyone anything. Who was this girl?

"Thanks," Elly smiled again. She looked closely at the guy and was saddened when she realized that this poor guy didn't really want to be here- didn't truly want to be a member of this strange group. He was here by force, not by will. "I'll remember you," Elly whispered to him, "promise." With that, Elly turned and headed in the direction that the guy had pointed to.

"Wait!" the guy called after her. But Elly paid no attention to him and before he could take a step forward to stop her, Elly vanished before his eyes. The guy stood there staring, stunned, at where Elly had been standing.

Elly found that there were still trees scattered everywhere, but they did not hinder her progress like the woods back before the clearing had. Swiftly, she made her way towards the bridge in the direction the boy had pointed. For some reason, she was certain that she would find Melanie there.

She heard the scream before she reached the bridge. Her instinct told her to run, but she knew better than that. Quietly she slipped through the shadows of the trees. She noticed that a full moon was out to the east, casting light in every direction.

So much as for a surprise attack, Elly thought sourly. But in a way, she realized, the moon was to her advantage because her eyes were adjusting to her surroundings and within moments, she was able to see everything that was around her clearly.

She was now only a few feet away from the bridge and Elly could hear rushing water. Elly paused, closed her eyes and turned her head slightly to the north, the direction where the bridge was located. She could sense that there was a river running under the bridge and a raging one, too.

Continuing through the woods, Elly finally stopped and flattened herself against a large tree just a few feet away from the bridge. She waited for a moment but did not hear anything other than the rushing water under the bridge. Peeking from around the side of the tree, she quickly assessed the situation. There were several guys and girls standing around the foot of the bridge acting like guards. Further up on the bridge was a large, bald, muscular guy wearing a sleeveless leather jacket. There was a tattoo of some sort on his arm that Elly wasn't able to identify and he was holding someone roughly by the arms.

Elly immediately realized that it was Melanie.

Elly gasped when she saw that Melanie's hands were tied behind her back and there was a piece of cloth stuffed in her mouth. It looked as though the guy was getting ready to just shove Melanie over the side of the bridge like a ragged doll.

Once she realized what the man was about to do to Melanie, she forgot all about what she had originally planned to do. There was no more time to play nice now.

Elly leaned against the tree and fiercely started rubbing her hands together. This time though, she didn't let the ball of light float into the air. Instead, she aimed and threw the small ball of light towards the group that was standing at the foot of the bridge. The minute the ball hit the ground, it exploded into a blinding orange light, making everything look as though it had caught on fire. Elly momentarily turned away from the blast and shielded her eyes. When she turned back around no one was moving and everything was still. Everything and everyone were frozen in place; everyone, that is, except for Melanie and the guy who was holding her a few feet up on the bridge. Miraculously, the blast had missed them. They were standing too far up on the bridge.

Elly gritted her teeth in frustration. I'll just have to take care of him myself, she decided. She knew if she sent another blast of light, it could send everyone who was already frozen into shock, possibly kill them. She wasn't willing to take that chance.

Leaving the shelter of the darkness and the trees, Elly quickly made her way up the bridge and towards the guy and Melanie. When Melanie saw who was coming towards them, her eyes opened wide in surprise and she managed to cough the rag out of her mouth.

"Elly!" she cried, gasping for air. "What are you doing here?"

"I'm here to get you," Elly answered simply, as she continued towards them.

"You have to leave," Melanie warned her. "It's dangerous here."

"Not without you." She was now standing in front of the guy who was loosely holding onto Melanie. He was drunk. Elly stared at him hard.

"You'll let her go, won't you?" Elly asked in almost a whisper. Without even a word, the man let Melanie go as if he had touched something hot. She fell hard on her left shoulder and groaned. Her feet had also been bound tightly with rope.

Paying no attention to the guy, Elly bent down to untie Melanie.

"Elly, watch out!" The words were barely out of Melanie's mouth when Elly felt something crack hard against the back of her head. Her eyes blurred and darkness surrounded Elly as she fell backwards. The last thing she saw was Kara's twisted, angry face peering down at her...

Elly's head throbbed angrily as she regained consciousness. Her eyes ached painfully but she forced them open anyway. Her ears were ringing and she could feel her heart beating rapidly in her chest. Taking in a deep breath, she rolled her head around a few times to relieve her aching muscles. Once her head cleared a little, she looked around and noted that she was in a dark wooden room of some sort. The only light came from a gap in the roof. She could see the moon shining brightly outside.

Elly felt that she wasn't alone. She blinked to adjust her eyes to the faint light then glanced around the room. She was able to see Aimer and Cory leaning against a wall directly across from her. Melanie was to her left, just a few inches away. Like her, their arms were tied behind their backs and their feet were bound straight out in front of them. But none of them were gagged.

I guess they figured they would let us have a few last words before killing us, Elly thought wryly.

Until coming to earth, Elly had never known what it meant to be in excruciating pain or in danger. Now, she was facing both head on and she was scared.

"We were worried about you," Elly heard Aimer say from across the room. His voice was dry and raspy. "You've been out for quite a while."

"I'm sorry guys," Elly apologized. "I know you told me to go get help, but I had to try. I was worried."

"This is no time for apologies," Cory said and gave Elly a small smile. He understood and Elly was grateful for that. "We've got to find a way to get out of here before they come back."

"What did you do to those guys back there?" Melanie asked Elly quietly.

Elly smiled despite the pain she was feeling, "Nothing."

"What are you talking about, Mel?" Aimer asked.

Melanie opened her mouth but Elly interrupted before she could speak.

"I have a better question: What are you doing out here in the first place with all these crazy people?"

Melanie sighed deeply and leaned her head back. "Look, it's a long story. I promise once we're out of here- if we even do get out of here- I'll tell all of you the whole story."

"Oh, we'll get out of here," Elly vowed, "trust me."

Just as she said that, the door leading to the room they were in slammed open and Kara stepped angrily into the doorway. The rest of her followers what was left of them- were huddled closely behind her. Brad was also there with them. Elly wondered where he had been all this time. She hadn't felt his presence anywhere throughout the whole ordeal.

Kara stepped into the room. She had a gun in her hand. Elly realized that it was Cory's gun she was holding. How ironic, Elly thought. The boys had brought it for protection and now they were probably going to end up being shot to death with it. Elly shook her head vigorously, forcing the depressing thought out of her mind.

"You!" Kara shouted aiming the gun towards Elly, "I don't know what you did to my friends out there but you're going to undo it right now!" She strode up to Elly and kicked her leg with the tip of her black boots. "Get up!"

Elly gritted her teeth against the pain. She looked coldly at Kara and said, "How can I get up with my feet bound together." With controlled anger, Kara motioned for one of the guys to untie her feet. The guy also had the decency to help Elly stand. Elly looked at him and recognized him as being the guy she had spoken to at the camp fire.

She had promised him that she would remember him and she did. She made sure that after he untied her, he stayed standing right in back of her, away from the rest of the group who were still huddled at the door.

Kara had backed up until she was back in the doorway. She still had the gun raised towards Elly.

Elly didn't believe that Kara would really use the gun. She was drunk and confused and that would be to her advantage. Her hands were still tied together in back of her. But that was going to change momentarily.

Elly rubbed her hands together. The rope fell soundlessly from around her wrists. She continued to rub her hands together.

"Come here," Kara ordered.

Elly shrugged, "All right." You asked for it, she added to herself. In one quick fluid motion, before anyone could even tell what was happening, Elly lunged towards Kara. To those around her, it looked as though she were flying through the air. At first, Kara was too stunned to react. But that only lasted for a moment. In an instant she had the gun aimed.

A shot rang out and caught Elly squarely in the left shoulder.

Elly flew backwards and in the same instant, the ball of light fell to the ground at Kara's feet and exploded, sending her flying backwards.

"Elly!" Elly heard Melanie's voice from a distance as she hit the back wall of the room and slid down to the floor.

Her head exploded. A million stars swam before her eyes and in the mist of all those stars Elly saw her mother's face smiling down at her.

At that moment, Elly instantly blacked out.

It was over.

CHAPTER FIFTEEN

Elly felt a throbbing spasm of pain shoot through her head and her eyes felt heavy and swollen as she forced them open. She shifted her left arm and immediately felt a searing pain course through it and throughout her entire body, which she found was also stiff and aching. She felt as though she had been lying in the same position for a very long time. Her head continued to ache and her mouth felt as though cotton had been stuffed inside of it; she couldn't even swallow.

When she was finally able to completely open her eyes, bright sunlight from an open window on her right greeted her, making them sting. She quickly squeezed her eyes shut again.

She suddenly sensed that there was someone in the room with her. She opened her eyes again slowly. This time, the bright sunlight did not bother her so much. She gritted against the pain and slowly looked around. She found that she was in a large room all decorated in white. There were no other colors in the room except for the bright flowers that she saw in vases all around the room.

She smelled medicine in the air, yet she had no idea where she was. The last thing she remembered was passing out against the wall at the cabin. For all she knew, she could be dead. But she ruled out that possibility because she felt herself to be very much alive. Besides, if she were dead, she wouldn't be feeling such excruciating pain in her left arm. No, she was definitely alive. So, where was she?

"I'm glad to see that you've finally woken up," she heard a woman's voice say from her left. She turned her head and found Melanie seated in a chair next to her bed. She was smiling. "We've all been worried about you. Speaking of which, I better go call the doctor-"

"No, wait," Elly stopped her from getting up. "Where am I?"

"You're at St. James hospital," Melanie answered, sitting back down.

A hospital. Yes, Elly remembered something about those. Humans took people who were sick to these places. Was she sick?

"What happened? Why am I here?"

"Don't you remember? Kara shot you when you rushed towards her at the cabin. You were bleeding quiet profusely by the time we got you here. Dr. Jainez said that you would be fine, though. But you had us worried for a while because after they operated on your arm, instead on waking up out of the anesthesia, you fell into a coma. You've been in it for almost two weeks. Nothing like that had ever happened before. No one knew what to do. Dr. Jainez said we would just have to wait it out and hope for the best." Melanie was rambling, she was so glad to see that Elly was all right. She had been terrified that she would slip away from them at any moment. She had slept at the hospital next to Elly almost every night.

Her consciousness had greatly troubled her. She felt completely responsible for what had happened to Elly- and what had almost happened to the others.

Elly smiled softly. She knew exactly what Melanie was thinking.

"It's all right, Mel. I'm fine. Don't blame yourself. You're not responsible. You didn't force me to go out there. I decided that for myself."

Melanie didn't seem surprised to see that Elly knew what she was thinking. "Yeah, but you guys went out there because you were worried about me. I put all of you in danger." Tears glistened in Melanie's eyes.

Elly reached over with her right hand and took Melanie's hand in hers. "It's all right," she repeated. "Everything's fine now." Her eyes were heavy. She was growing tired.

Melanie was looking at her oddly. "Tell me something, Elly," she said softly.

"What?"

"Who are you really?"

Elly squeezed Melanie's hand. "We'll have to talk about that later."

"Fine, but I think there's something you should know. Now that you're awake the police are going to want to talk to you."

"The police?" Elly said. Elly couldn't quite remember who or what they were.

"Yes, the police; primarily the two who have been put in charge of my particular case. They'll want to hear your side of the story. After all, you were there."

Elly was confused and tired. She was having a hard time keeping up with what Melanie was telling her. "So, what is it exactly that I should know?"

"Well," Melanie hesitated. "No one really knows what went on back there in the woods-except for you and me."

"What are you telling me, Mel?" Elly was wide awake now.

"Oh, man! The doctor and the police would kill me if they knew that I was talking to you before I notify them first." Melanie sighed deeply.

Elly could see that she was troubled and agitated by this whole ordeal.

"What I'm trying to tell you is that no one remembers what happened in the cabin. The light, the explosion, Aimer and Cory didn't mention a thing about it. Neither did Kara or her pals. Not the ones at the bridge or at the cabin and it's not because they want to hide anything- you know how vengeful Kara and her pals are."

"But when they spoke to the police," Melanie continued, "they all told the same story. Kara and her friends said that you, Cory and Aimer ambushed the place to rescue me. Two policemen had been placed to keep an eye on me for the past several weeks to see where I went and what I did, which is why the police had gotten there so fast. I guess I should mention that that's why I was hanging out with the group in the first place- I was working with the police."

"What?!" Elly interrupted. She tried sitting up but was unsuccessful because she was in too much pain and too weak. She leaned back against her pillows in defeat. "You were working with the police?" Elly asked incredulously.

Melanie bit her lower lip and nodded. "Yeah, I was. Really, Elly, it's a long story. It's sufficient to say that I almost got in too deep." She rubbed her eyes. "I'm glad it's finally over."

"All right," Elly said. "I'll let that go for now. Let's go back. What you're basically telling me is that Aimer, Cory and the others have absolutely no recollection of the actual events that took place in the woods. But the story they told the police all collaborate with each other?"

Melanie nodded. "That's it."

"But you remember," Elly said softly, almost to herself. But Melanie heard her.

"Yeah, I remember perfectly, and I know I'm not crazy! It's weird. I tried talking about it with Aimer the next day and he had looked at me as though I were crazy." Melanie laughed but there was no mirth in her laughter. "He told me that I must have really hit my head pretty hard somewhere if I had gone around all night seeing lights exploding. When we got to the hospital, the first thing he did was have Dr. Jainez check me out, just in case, he said. Can you believe that?" Melanie's face was red with anger.

"This is unbelievable."

"You mean you don't have any idea how this happened?" Elly shook her head. "I have no id-"

But then she remembered.

Just before she had passed out, she had seen her mother's face looking down at her from among the stars. She had thought that it had been her imagination playing with her but now she realized that wasn't the case.

Her mother had assured her that she would watch over her. Elly was certain it was her mother who had scrambled things up so well. Although Elly did wonder why her mother hadn't change the fact that she had gotten shot. Maybe some things just couldn't be changed, Elly reasoned. At least she was safe and was certain that no one was going to find out anything about her.

That is except for Melanie.

Elly also wondered why her mother had let Melanie remember what had happened. She would find out soon enough, Elly was sure of that.

"Elly, are you all right?" Melanie was looking at her anxiously.

"Yeah, I'm fine. Look, Mel, I'm really tired. Can we talk some more about this later?"

"Sure. But I do have to go tell the doctor and the others that you're awake. You're going to have to pretend that you've just woken up. I don't want anyone to know we've been talking."

"That should be easy enough," Elly said softly as her eyes slid shut. Within seconds, she was sound asleep again.

The doctors could not understand what had happened to Elly. They had all been amazed when they came into her room and found her awake and very alert. Everyone had been so happy, and so relieved. The doctors were calling her a miracle patient.

Miracle, right! Elly said to herself as she climbed out of the hospital bed. If she hadn't gone into that so-called "coma", which had actually been a sort of hibernation, she would have died for sure. For all the power she had, she knew that her system was unable to handle being openly exposed to human air or chemicals for too long. Her mother had explained all of this to her before she left for earth. At the time she hadn't thought that any of it was important.

Elly was starting to not be surprised to discover that she had been wrong about a lot of things. The doctors had started pumping chemicals into her since before she even got to the hospital. But, of course, Elly understood that they believed what they were doing was the only way to save her life. Luckily for Elly, her body had its own way of protecting itself. Her mother had truly prepared her well for her journey to earth.

They were finally letting her go. She had been in the hospital for six weeks- including the two weeks after coming out of the coma. The doctors had insisted on keeping her under observation just to be cautious. After all, they had never had such an experience with a patient before. Melanie and Aimer were going to be around to pick her up shortly.

Just like Melanie had warned Elly, the police had come in to talk to her the day after she woke up from the coma. The story that she told them collaborated with the one that the others had already given them. Surprisingly, they had been satisfied with the information she provided them. From what Elly understood, Kara and a few of her pals, including Brad were still hanging around in a jail cell. Apparently, there was even more to their story then met the eye.

Personally, Elly didn't really care. She simply wanted to get out of this claustrophobic place. It was starting to make her head spin. Melanie was safe and so were Aimer and Cory. That's all that mattered. As it turned out, Melanie had been working with the police to help them get information about Kara and the rest of the members involved in the club. The police wouldn't go into details, and neither would Melanie, but the members had been causing more than their share of trouble and the police had been trying to catch them for quite some time with no success. They had learned, through an unnamed source, that Melanie was close to a main member of the group and had decided to approach Melanie and asked her if she would help them and she agreed.

Melanie had admitted to Elly that the reason she agreed to help the police was so that she could get back at Brad for the way he had treated her during the time when they were going out together after he had joined the club, which at the time she had thought was only an eclectic club and not just a bunch of trouble makers. She had not been aware of just how deeply involved he had been. He was still in jail and Melanie had never expected that to happen.

Melanie had refused to explain any of the details of what had occurred between Brad and herself to Elly, but Elly had a pretty good idea of what had gone on in the relationship. Remembering the look in Brad's eyes the few times she had run into him; it was not difficult to imagine the type of abuse he must have put Melanie through. It made Elly sick just thinking about it.

But Elly now understood why she had heard bitterness in Melanie's voice so many times when she had spoken about Brad.

Elly also knew what the other reason was that made Melanie decide to work with the police; that was the only real chance she had of getting herself away from the group without being haunted for the rest of her life. She had joined the club before Brad had started treating her badly and also before she really knew who the people involved were and what they were into. Melanie had desperately wanted to get out and the police, who had been trying to break up and catch the members of the group for a while now, had used that to their advantage. They learned that Melanie had connections with the members and wanted out. So, they made a deal with her...and thus began the nightmare.

Apparently on the night that Aimer, Cory, and Elly had gone after Melanie, the two policemen who had been assigned to Melanie had lost track of her at the fair. But they got suspicious when they saw Elly and the guys leave and head out towards the freeway. The boys had already disappeared into the woods by the time the police caught up with them and they had not been aware that Elly was still in one of the cars parked by the road.

They had entered the woods and it hadn't taken them long to realize that they were lost and called for backup. By the time they had found their way to the camp, they whole ordeal was already over.

They had found Kara and the rest of her followers passed out on the ground a short distance from the cabin. Aimer and the others were free and Elly was unconscious against the back wall of the cabin, suffering from a gunshot wound in the shoulder...

Elly sighed and touched her shoulder gently. The sad thing was that throughout the whole thing, Melanie's parents hadn't had a single clue that there was anything wrong going on. They had truly felt guilty for not being more aware of what was going on with their daughter. If things hadn't ended when they did, it could have really gotten dangerous for Melanie. Members of the group, under Kara's orders, had secretly been drugging her. Melanie was doing things and acting in ways that were uncharacteristic to her and she hadn't even known this, because she barely remembered any of it in the morning. But she had known that they were doing something to her yet had been unable to stop it without making anyone suspicious.

When Melanie had shown up at the cabin that night with Brad, Kara had been there waiting for them. She had sent Brad on some errand, assuring him that she wouldn't harm Melanie because she was ready to accept her as part of the gang through her initiation. That, of course, had been a lie, but Brad had believed it.

Once Brad was out of sight, Kara had knocked Melanie out and then had one of her guys inject her with a huge dose of drugs. Her plan had been to kill Melanie on sight, but she decided to have some fun first. She would kill her afterwards. If Elly hadn't shown up when she did, Melanie would have been thrown in the river that flowed under the bridge and left to drown. Of course, the police did not know that it had been Elly that saved Melanie's life. As it was, no one other than Elly and Melanie really knew what happened that night- a matter that still bothered and confused Elly. But she wasn't ready to deal with that yet. She had more than enough to deal with for now.

What the police and Melanie wouldn't tell her about what had been going on, she filled in for herself. All of it seemed rather unreal.

She had experienced so many things in such a short period of time that it was all too much to take in all at once. She had been concerned about what would happen when she went to earth, but there was nothing that could have ever prepared her for any of this.

Sighing, Elly stuffed the last of her nightgowns into the bag of clothes that Adria had brought for her and sank back down on the bed. Her left shoulder still ached from where she had gotten shot, but otherwise, she was perfectly fine. Another miracle, the doctors were baffled.

Elly couldn't help laughing to herself. It was strange. She had fought so hard against coming to this place but now she found that a part of her was actually starting to like it here- despite the experience that she had just gone through.

Aside from all the tragedy that encompassed their lives, humans were rather fascinating and their world was filled with many wonders. Humans had a magic unlike anything she had ever seen in her life. Yet Elly found that they took that for granted. Elly even wondered if they even really knew their own potential. From what she had seen, that was highly unlikely.

She couldn't wait to go back home and tell her sisters about her experiences. They'd never believe that she had actually gotten shot! Elly smiled bitterly, nothing like a good story to take home. But she wished that all of it could have been different. There was too much pain sewn into one story. No one should have to endure so much pain. Elly's thoughts were interrupted as the door squeaked open and Melanie stepped inside.

"Ready?" she asked Elly, eyeing the night bag packed on the table.

"Yeah, I'm ready." Elly grabbed the night bag off the side table and the two girls left the hospital.

CHAPTER SIXTEEN

For the next week, everyone at the Coltzs' pampered Elly. They wouldn't let her do anything and Adria even insisted on bringing her breakfast in bed. Aimer stopped by a few times to see how she was doing and brought her flowers. Elly had taken quite a liking to him. It was strange, yet wonderful to see the way they had taken her in and accepted her without any questions. The issue of her "amnesia" was never mentioned by any of them since the time Michael had wanted to take her to see a doctor. I guess they figured I would bring it up when I was ready to deal with it, Elly concluded. Seeing the kindness the family had bestowed on her brought tears to Elly's eyes.

Elly stretched out on her bed and smiled. She had spent the morning down at the stable with Aimer and the horses and later on that afternoon, she had gone shopping for groceries with Adria. It was now late evening and Elly was thoroughly exhausted.

Elly felt her eyes growing heavy with sleep and she willingly gave in to her exhaustion.

But it felt strange once her eyes were closed. Elly did not feel as though she was sleeping. She felt as though her body was drifting up into space, being carried away on a tide of some sort. It was almost as though- Elly jerked out of her sleep and sat up in bed, her heart racing. She knew immediately what would happen if she were to lie down and go back to sleep.

Her time on earth was up. She was going home.

Not yet, please! Elly pleaded. I'm not ready to go! But she knew that there wasn't anything she could do to stop it. Yet it didn't feel right to just disappear without leaving a trace. After all the Coltzs' had done for her, she just could not bear to do that to them.

Elly heard a soft knock on her door.

"Come in," she called, as she swung her legs over the side of the bed. The door opened and Melanie came into the room. She was wearing a beautiful white nightgown.

"Hey, Mel," Elly greeted, "how are you?"

"Oh, I'm fine. How are you?" She went over and sat down next to Elly on the edge of the bed.

"I'm all right, I guess," Elly answered tentatively. "What's on your mind, Mel?" she asked. Actually, she knew exactly what was on Melanie's mind. She had been avoiding the subject since she returned to the house, but knew that there was no way she could avoid it now.

Melanie didn't beat around the bush- she got straight to the point.

"Remember the conversation we had at the hospital?" she began, "there was a certain question I had asked you and at the time you told me that we would talk later. Well, later is now and I'm ready to listen and I want to know everything."

Elly sighed. She didn't want to do this but she figured it was the least she could do since in the morning there would be no trace of her.

"All right, Mel," Elly said, coming to a decision. "I will tell you who I am. But first, you have got to swear to me that you will not ever tell anyone what I'm going to reveal to you."

Melanie laughed. "Elly, you don't have to worry about that! Who am I going to tell? No one would believe me, anyway."

Elly realized that what Melanie said was true. There was no one to tell and no one would believe a word she said. Her secret would be safe.

Taking a deep breath, Elly began her story.

"Billions of years ago, when this planet was first created, my people lived on this planet- it was our home." she began.

"Your people used to live here?" Melanie asked incredulously. "But who are your people exactly. Who are you? What are you?"

"I am what your people would call a genie. Actually, I'm just a higher form of a human being. But we refer to ourselves as Gens collectively, humans called us gins and genies and we still call ourselves that since that is what we were first known as."

Melanie stared at Elly in unbelief and shock. "You're a genie? Are you serious?"

"Yes," Elly answered. "I am a genie. But a genie is more than what humans imagine us to be."

Melanie was silent for a moment as she absorbed what she had just been told. "Are there still genies living here on earth?" she wanted to know.

"Yes, but not many. We prefer to be on our own."

"Why did your people leave earth?"

"It was mainly because men started treating us badly and took us and our powers for granted so that after a while, we were forced to flee the planet. We went and found another planet many billions of miles here, out in the Astral Zone, and made it our home. We were glad to be away from humans."

"What's the Astral Zone?" Melanie wanted to know. She was thoroughly intrigued by what Elly was revealing to her.

"It is called the Astral Zone because of the fact that it is past many galaxies. The Astral is the main galaxy zone but there are many other zones within it. My home is located in the Nigran Tau zone. There are only two other planets there beside ours: Clorian and Zirnam. And, of course, Myzin, our sun-"

"Wait a minute! You mean to tell me that the sun that we have is not the only sun?" Melanie was astonished.

Elly couldn't help laughing. "Of course not! Your sun is only one of many suns. If your sun was the only sun that existed then we would not be able to live as it is not bright enough to even reach to the outer limit of where the Astral Zone begins. There are many other galaxies besides our own and our sun Myzin is not bright enough to reach to them, either. Therefore, there are many suns as there are many galaxies out beyond the stars that shine brightly in the dark night sky. Far beyond what any human mind is capable of imagining."

"Wow! That is incredible," Melanie shook her head in amazement.

"Anyway," Elly continued, amusement showing in her eyes from seeing the look on Melanie's face from what she had just revealed to her. "Several centuries later, our first planet, which had been named Morgea, exploded. It was said that it had traveled to close to Myzin which thus caused the explosion. Those who had been aware of the planet's path around the sun and had noticed the change in its position had warned that something like this could happen. Unfortunately, not many people headed the warning. Those who did though, were able to flee the planet in time. They took refuge on the planet Zirnam, which was still relatively uninhibited during that time.

"Many centuries later, we discovered a cluster of planets out in the Nigran Zone, which is actually several million miles from where Morgea had originally been, out in the Zar, the third zone of the Astral. There were six planets all together and five of them formed what could be roughly described as a star with the largest planet, the sixth one in the center. After it was discovered, we called this galaxy of planets Sarcaun. It became our new home and eventually we inhabited all six planets so they became more like six separate planetary cities to us as we were able to freely move among each one of them. To this day, we no longer refer to them as planets but as cities that exist within Sarcaun instead."

In the air, with her index finger, Elly drew the five points that roughly appeared to be the shape of a star with a sixth point in the center. Melanie looked at her in awe.

"The center city, Kreese, is where the main resources for all the other five planetary cities are located," Elly explained. "The other five cities: Aeshern, Morgea, named in memory of our first home, Dassar, Greshan and Corsa all lead, in one way or the other, to the center planet."

"Exactly who are you?" Melanie inquired. She was completely taken in by what Elly was revealing to her. "And where are you from?"

"I am Princess Norellyia, from the city of Kreese," Elly pointed to the center of the star, "the youngest daughter of Queen Xriane and King Ourak."

Melanie's eyes almost protruded out of her head when she heard that. "You're a Princess?" she asked incredulously. "This is too unbelievable."

"You do believe me, though, don't you?" Elly asked solemnly.

Melanie looked at her directly and answered, "Yes, I do believe you, I guess. I mean, after the things I saw you do, how can I not believe you?" She was pensive for a moment and suddenly a look of confusion crossed her face. "Wait a minute; you said your people were on this planet in the beginning, when this planet was first created. How is that possible?"

Elly hesitated for a moment. She wasn't sure if she should reveal what she knew to Melanie.

"Come on, Elly. Don't you trust me?"

"Of course, I do." Elly took in a deep breath. Where should she begin?

"We were there in the beginning, when the earth was first created and we lived here for millions of years before humans were created-"

"How did your people come into being," Melanie interrupted, "Who created you?"

Elly shook her head. "You know what, Mel, I don't know if I can answer your question in a way that you would understand but I'll try." Elly paused for a moment to gather her thoughts. "There's a power out there, Melanie, One through whom all things are created and for whom all things exist. He is the One that created the heavens, the earth, all of the stars, moons, suns and planets- including the one I call home. He is also the one who created us- you and me both."

"You mean God," Melanie said.

Elly nodded, "Yes, most humans know him as God. But we know him simply as the Power, the source of all things."

"So, your people already existed before he created humans?"

"Yes, we did, although no one is certain exactly how many years passed before man was created."

"I have read the Bible and know what is written about the creation but is there anything you can tell me about how we were created?"

"Well, what I'm going to tell you is what our ancestors wrote in the ancient books that have been written over the course of billions of years. It is written in the ancient book of Hezron that the first man created, Adam I believe his name was, was created straight from the earth and being so was very strong and dark skinned. I believe your people would say he was black. Eve, the woman, on the other hand, was created later from a portion of Adam's rib and therefore was white as the bone from which she was created."

"That's pretty much parallel to how the creation is written in Bible except the Bible doesn't mention anything about what color they were. Are you sure about this?"

Elly nodded. "I am very sure. I have read the ancient Hezron book many times and am very familiar with the ancient history of earth. It is also written that from these two all other races came into being. So, in essence all humans are connected to each other and therefore people really should respect and love one another. That being the case, there is something about humans that I find very strange."

Melanie had been listening intently to what Elly was telling her and was overwhelmed by what she was hearing. "What do you find strange?" she managed to ask while she was still trying to process everything Elly had told her.

"I find it strange how humans can harbor hatred against each other and continually go around trying to find ways to destroy each other. I've noticed that even those among the same race and ethnic background try to destroy each other at times. Why is that?"

Melanie shook her head sadly. "I don't know, Elly. And to tell you the truth, I've never really thought much about it. But now that you mention it, it is strange and sad. But Elly, I can't help but wonder- why is it that humans don't know any of this, especially the part about Adam and Eve being black and white?"

"Well, that is a complicated question. All I can tell you though is that everything written in what you call the Bible is true, but very much incomplete. This is because Emmanuel, who I believe you know as Jesus, did come into this world to teach and enlighten people but unfortunately was not given the opportunity to teach or reveal to people all that he desired. But after his crucifixion and before he returned to his Father, he revealed a wealth of information to his disciples.

"But because of the fear and dissention that occurred among the disciples after Jesus ascended," Elly continued, "much of the information he passed on to them was lost. Also, after Jesus' Ascension, the disciples dispersed in all directions, leaving not only each other but much of their lives and belongings behind. So, the Bible was written with the information the disciples were able to save as well as with what they were able to remember but much has been left out or forgotten because of the chaos and confusion that occurred and was still occurring during that time."

Melanie was mystified. "Elly, are you sure about all this? Quite frankly, everything you have told me is very unbelievable and is too much for me to take in."

Elly smiled sadly, "So you don't believe me."

"I don't know, Elly. You've given me a lot to think about. But since we're on the subject of the Bible, there are quite a few things that I've always wondered about. For instance, why did God have to test Abraham by telling him he had to sacrifice his son? Does a rainbow really represent a covenant God made with us? I've also always wondered about Jesus' dying on the cross. I could never understand why they say he died-"

Elly raised her hand to stop her from continuing. "Melanie, one question will always lead to another and it would take me several lifetimes to answer all the questions I see going through your mind. I have answered all the questions that I am able to answer for you right now. But one day, when the time is right, all of your questions will be answered."

"Really?"

"Yes, I promise. Now, my time here is nearing its end and I must prepare to leave."

"What do you mean?" Melanie asked, confused.

"Melanie, you will not see me again after tonight," Elly explained as she leaned forward and took Melanie's hand in hers. She closed her eyes for a moment. "I will be leaving, returning to my home. But I have a feeling that I will be returning here someday. Believe me when I tell you that we will see each other again."

"When will you be returning?" Melanie inquired.

"One day," Elly shook her head, "but I'm not sure exactly when. It will be many, many moons from now." A thought began to form in the back of her mind, but Elly shook her head and dismissed it. She would think about that later. When it was time. "But do you think your parents would allow me to stay with then again, if I were to come back and needed to?"

"I'm sure they would," Melanie assured her. "They really care about you, you know."

"I wouldn't know what to say to them about-"

"Don't worry about it," Melanie interrupted, reading her mind. "I'll take care of everything, all right?"

She looked at Melanie fondly. "I will miss you greatly. You have truly been a friend."

"And you have truly been my friend. I will never forget what you did for me. But do you really have to go?" Melanie asked squeezing Elly's hand tightly. There were tears in her eyes.

"Yes. I don't have a choice in this matter. The decision has been made. Will you be all right?" She could see that Melanie was still very confused by what she had just revealed to her. Maybe she had revealed too much. But it was too late, now. It was done.

"I'll be fine," Melanie assured her. "Tell me something," Melanie continued, as she wiped at her eyes with the back of her hand. "What does your home look like?"

Elly closed her eyes and rubbed her hand together until a bright light shone around them. Then, opening her hands like the covers of a book, she said to Melanie, "Look inside."

Obediently, Melanie peered down into her hands. The light around Elly's hands sparkled and a picture began to form. Once settled, Melanie could see the bright orange and purple light of the setting sun that caused brilliant colors to reflect off of the pure crystal houses. She saw a glimpse of the deep green woods and valleys along with the clear waters of the beaches. Tall mountains capped the plains filled with beautifully colorful flowers and she saw the castle surrounded by rich green woods, valleys and an abundance of colorful flowers.

"It's beautiful!" Melanie sighed as the picture began to cloud over.

Elly smiled softly. "Yes, it is beautiful," she agreed. Until that moment, Elly hadn't realized just how much she missed her home. She turned away from Melanie and peered out of the window. It was dark out and the moon was beginning to rise. "It is time," she said in a low voice, facing Melanie again.

"Should I go?" Melanie asked. Her voice was shaking.

"Yes, but first, I need you to swear to me again that my secret is safe with you."

"Oh, it is!" Melanie cried, fiercely hugging Melanie. "I swear."

"Go now," Elly said, gently pulling herself away from Melanie.

"I'll miss you," Melanie said and kissed Elly on the cheek. Without another word, she got up and left Elly's room.

Elly waited several minutes with her eyes closed before she moved from where she sat. Finally, she got up, went to the bathroom and took a long soothing bathe. Afterwards, she put on her favorite nightgown, a pale blue one that Adria had bought for her while she was in the hospital, and slipped into bed. Closing her eyes, she quickly fell into a deep, dreamless sleep, leaving everything behind her.

CHAPTER SEVENTEEN

Elly opened her eyes slowly and instantly felt the sting from the bright sunlight that streamed in from a large window on her left, blinding her for a moment.

Once her eyes had adjusted to the light, Elly looked around and realized that she was lying in a huge bed and covered with what felt like silk sheets. Her body ached as she slowly sat up and looked around. The sheets were royal blue. On the other side of the room was a gold trimmed dresser with a matching mirror hanging above it. There were also colorful pillows all over the place and the room was filled with beautiful flowers in antique vases. And there against the wall, by the bedroom door, was a shell collection inside an elaborate glass case.

This was her room and this was her bed she was lying in. Elly smiled and hugged a pillow against her chest.

She was home.

She got up from her bed and walked over to the window. She pulled back the pale-yellow curtains and peered outside. There below her stretched the flower garden; the fountain was on, making the flowers glisten in the sunlight.

It was a marvelous sight. Elly was overjoyed to be home. No matter how comfortable she had started to feel on earth, this was her home and this was where she belonged. I should go find mother, Elly told herself. But she stood there by the window, enjoying the beautiful sight before her. After a few minutes, she reluctantly left the room and headed downstairs for her mother's chamber.

Elly's hands shook as she knocked on her mother's door. She was so excited; there were tears in her eyes.

"Come in," she heard her mother call to her from inside the room. It was wonderful hearing her voice again. Slowly, Elly eased the door open and peeked inside. Her mother was sitting by the window.

"Elly!" her mother cried when she saw her. "Thank goodness you are back safely!" Elly entered the room and silently hugged her mother. She was crying in earnest now.

"Come now, Elly," her mother said, taking her face between her hands, "do not cry. It is all right. You are home safe and sound."

But Elly could not stop crying. She stood there for a few more minutes in her mother's arms as the tears ran freely down her face.

"I never realized how much everyone and everything here meant to me," Elly sniffed, finally getting a hold of herself. "Until now."

"There, you see?" her mother said as she took Elly's hand and led her to a sofa. "And you thought going to earth would be a waste of time." She smiled at Elly sheepishly and Elly could not help laughing.

"You were right, Mother," Elly confessed as she leaned her head back against the sofa. "Going to earth truly was a wonderful experience." She was about to start telling her mother everything she had experienced since the moment she set foot on earth, but then she realized that it would be useless to do so.

"You were there with me, were you not, Mother?"

Her mother brushed the hair away from her face. "Yes, of course, my child. I was with you. Did I not I promise you that I would be?"

Elly nodded solemnly. "I guess I just had not understood what you were telling me then. But I do now."

"That is good. Now come, let us go share the good news with your father and sisters!"

Later that evening, as Elly was preparing to go to bed, she heard a knock on her door. She was exhausted. She had spent the day ceaselessly answering her sisters' questions about what she had seen and done on earth. They had been relentless but Elly had enjoyed the attention. Now, though, all she really wanted to do was go to bed and get some rest. It had been a long day and she was planning to go see Lea first thing in the morning.

Earlier, when Elly had finally had a chance to breathe, she had asked her mother about Melanie. She was confused as to why Melanie had still remembered everything that had happened during the confrontation with Kara and her followers when the others who were there did not remember a thing.

"Melanie is a very special girl," her mother had told her but she had not bothered to elaborate any further. This, of course, had only caused Elly to become more confused and curious. She was determined to find out exactly what her mother had meant by those words. She would just have to be patient- which would not be easy for Elly.

Another knock sounded on the door, this time more sharply, bringing Elly back to the present.

"Come in," she said as she took a brush to her hair. The door opened and her mother entered the room.

"I am sorry to bother you, Elly," her mother apologized as she took a seat at the edge of Elly's bed. "I know that you are tired. But what I have to tell you is really important. I just could not wait until morning to tell you."

Elly turned and faced her mother. "What is it?"

"There is a reason why your father and I wanted you to come back home now besides the fact that you had been gone for so long," her mother began.

"So long?" Elly said incredulously. "What do you mean? I have only been gone for what? Two months almost? In earth time that is. I don't know what that equates to here."

"That is almost three years," her mother told her. "But that is not the point." Xriane continued without giving Elly time to take in what she had just told her. "The point is that we have a problem at hand and because of that we felt that you should be here, with your family, not in another galaxy. Besides, I believe we may need your help in this matter." As a matter of fact, Xriane knew for sure that they would need Elly's help. But she did not want to frighten Elly with too much information all at one time. She would take things slow but she did want Elly to be prepared.

Elly was perplexed by her mother's word. Nothing she was hearing made any sense to her. She had been gone for almost three years which to her had only seemed like a few months and now there was a problem?

"Problem? What problem? What are you talking about, mother?" Elly inquired.

Her mother sighed and shifted positions. This was not going to be easy. "I do not know if you remember Lanaya. She used to play with you quite a bit when you were little. She loved you almost as if you were her own daughter. Your sisters used to be jealous of you because of that." Xriane smiled at the memory then continued. "But now, you might know her better as Princess Lanaya Trasell of Aeshern." It was a tradition that went back many centuries which required that when a person was named as a Princess or Prince, their name was changed once they were crowned. More often than not, they were named after their mother or father if they were no longer living. Lanaya's mother's name had been Trasell.

Elly knew of Aeshern's Princess. In fact, Elly remembered as far back as she could, how she used to always say that one day, she wanted to be like Princess Lanaya. Of course, that was before she found out that she herself was a Princess. But even so, Lanaya had always been a fascination for her and she never really understood why.

"I know who Princess Lanaya is. But I do not remember her as a child."

"You were too young then to remember," her mother told her. "Anyway, while you were away, she contacted us and explained that there was some sort of trouble in Aeshern." Her mother stopped and took in a deep breath. "She explained that for a short period of time, Prince Navar had disappeared and no one had been able to find him. He showed up again a few days later lost and disoriented. He told the people who found him and took him home that he had no idea what had happened to him. But ever since that time, strange things have been happening in Aeshern, unexplainable things and Prince Navar has not been himself since; his behavior has been unpredictable and erratic. We have been investigating this situation thoroughly but have not found any answers."

"When you say strange things, what exactly do you mean?"

"Well, for instance, riots are happening almost everywhere throughout the city and several attempts have been made against the lives of a few of our higher officials in Aeshern and that is just to name a few things. There is such chaos and discord happening in the city right now you could not even begin to imagine. Things have settled down a little over the past few weeks but we are still highly concerned about the situation and have not been able to find any answers or suitable solutions."

Elly's mouth fell open in utter amazement from what her mother was telling her. She could not believe what she was hearing. "Are you serious?" Elly inquired, even though she could tell just by the look on her mother's face that she was indeed very serious. But Elly did not know what else to say or ask at the moment. She was still recovering from the initial shock of what she had just been told. Riots in Aeshern? Unbelievable.

"Unfortunately, yes," Xriane answered. "I am very serious. As it is, the entire city has turned upside down; people there hardly know what to do with themselves. Prince Navar was found after his disappearance disheveled and disoriented in the middle of the Adalain valley barely able to speak. He was immediately taken to the castle and physicians were sent for. They examined him and concluded that no physical harm was done to him; he was only mentally distraught by whatever he had experienced during his disappearance- which, by the way, he has refused to talk about."

Xriane let out a sigh then went on with her story. "At first, despite the fact that he refused to talk about his experience, the prince was very cooperative about having an investigation put under way and also about having extra personnel security posted. But recently, he has become stubborn and impassive about the whole situation. He has ordered the extra security to be dismissed and has even halted the investigation to discover who or what is behind this whole ordeal. The entire city has been turned upside down because of this situation and now, Prince Navar simply wants everything to go back to being the way it was before—as though nothing had happened. The point that I am trying to make is that we do not believe that things are really back under control. Either Prince Navar is hiding something or he is truly an idiot."

"First of all," Elly began, "I do not understand why anyone would want to harm Prince Navar." Elly did not know Prince Navar very well personally but from the few conversations she had had with him over the years, she was able to tell that he was a very kind and compassionate man. Everyone spoke highly of him and all of Aeshern loved him.

Why, then, would anyone want to cause him harm, or anyone else on the planet, for that matter?

"Neither do we," Xriane admitted. "That is why we want to find out what is going on. Nothing like this has happened here on Sarcaun in many, many centuries." Xriane was pensive for a moment; she was remembering the warning Nore had given her when she had first decided on sending Elly to earth. She felt a chill.

"Where do I fit into all of this?" Elly asked, remembering that her mother had said there might be a way for her to help.

"Well," Xriane started slowly. "We evaluated the situation while you were still on earth and discovered a possible strategy that may help us find some answers. Of course, you can decline if you do not feel that this is something you would be comfortable doing. But please keep in mind that this may be the only way to get some answers about what is going on over there." Xriane paused momentarily, trying to find the right words. Finally, she continued. "We felt that the only way we could really find out what was happening is if you went to Aeshern and paid the prince a visit."

Elly stared at her mother in disbelief. "Mother, you cannot be serious about this!"

Xriane rubbed her forehead in frustration. "Elly, I am very serious about this."

"You mean to tell me, the entire city is in turmoil, someone apparently tried to harm the prince and you want me to go there and see the prince? What am I supposed to do?"

"Elly, we need some answers, otherwise this can get out of hand very fast and the prince is not cooperating with us. We just need you to try and find out what is going on there."

"Mother, you know this is impossible."

"Elly, please," her mother pleaded. "Do not be difficult about this. We really need your help in this matter."

"Fine, then." Elly stood up and started pacing. "Answer this for me: why me? Why should I be the one to have to go?" First going to earth, now this! When was this going to end? Elly fumed inwardly.

Xriane hesitated a moment not sure of how to respond, should she tell Elly the truth or make something up?

"As you know, Elly," Xriane began, deciding to be honest with Elly. She deserved nothing less than the truth considering the responsibility she would be taking on- if she agreed to do this. "One day soon you are going to become queen of Sarcaun. The time has come that we must start thinking about the proper marriage alliance for you." Xriane chose her words carefully as she continued. "Recently, in fact, just before your return, and before chaos broke out in Aeshern, Prince Navar expressed his interest in you to your father and me." Xriane took a deep breath. "He wishes to be a suitor for your hand in marriage."

Elly's mouth fell open in disbelief. "A suitor? Are you serious?" She seemed to be asking that question a lot lately. How had her life gotten so complicated in such a short time?

Xriane nodded in response, not trusting her voice to speak at the moment.

"Well- what did you tell him?" What was going on here? Elly wondered. I go away and the whole planet turns upside down. Elly almost started laughing at the sound of that but bit her tongue. All of this was too overwhelming.

"Of course, we told him that it would be up to you," Xriane assured Elly seeing the panic in her daughter's eyes. "We gave him our approval, yes. But we made it quite clear that the final decision would have to be up to you."

Elly let her breath out in relief. "Thank you. You had me worried for a moment." Elly shook her head in disbelief of all that she had just heard. She had left her home in peace and now it seems that there was only chaos. How could so much change take place in what appears to Elly to have been such a short time? A small chill ran down Elly's spine. Strangely enough, she was sure that this was only the beginning. She felt that things were going to end up getting worse before they got better. Oh, please, Elly silently prayed to herself. Not again!

"Elly, we love you," her mother was saying. "We would never force such a thing on you. But we do need you to help us out here. Surely, you can see why we feel that you have a chance of getting some answers concerning this situation if Navar does have answers that he may just be hiding from us."

"Yes, I can see why," Elly admitted grudgingly. Navar would not suspect that she was there for any reason other than to meet him in order to determine if she wanted him as a suitor. Elly stood up and walked to her window. The stars were shining brightly in the dark night sky and there was a cool breeze. She closed her eyes and felt the cool air against her cheeks. There was so much to consider. But she knew what she had to do.

"So, Elly, will you do this?" Xriane asked hopefully after giving Elly a few minutes of silence so she could think things through. "Will you go to Aeshern and see if you can find out what is really going on over there?"

"Do I have a choice?" Elly asked settling back in her seat. She sighed and did not wait for her mother to answer. "Yes, mother. I will do it. So, please tell me, what do you have planned?" Elly asked. How ironic! She had asked Aimer and Cory the same question when they had gone out to rescue Melanie. This was not going to be easy, Elly knew. How had her simple life gotten so complicated in such a short time? She wondered again. She prayed that all of this would end soon so she could settle back to the peaceful life she had before all the chaos began which actually started when her mother had decided she was going to send her to earth.

Xriane smiled in relief. "I will contact Lanaya tomorrow and get back to you," Xriane told her "All right?"

Elly nodded. "Fine."

"Good, then, get some rest. We will talk some more in the morning." She kissed Elly on the forehead. "And Elly, I assure you, you will be safe there."

Elly smiled. "Yes, I know that mother."

After Xriane left, Elly sat on her windowsill and stared out into the darkening sky. It amazed her to see how quickly things had changed in her life. She had experienced things that were beyond her imagination. Had someone told her that her life was going to take on such a turn, she would have never believed it! Looking back, it seemed as if her life up to this point had only been a dream. Elly sighed and shook her head in confusion as she closed her curtains, turned out the lights and haggardly crawled into bed. There was a long day ahead and she needed to rest so that she would be able to face it.

CHAPTER EIGHTEEN

The next few days were very hectic for Elly. Everyone was talking about her trip to earth and everyone wanted to hear about it. It was not until almost three days later that Elly had finally been able to find time to go see Lea, who had been anxious to talk to her since her return. Elly spent almost the whole day over at Lea's not really because she wanted to, but simply for the sake of being able to get some rest, away from the crowds of people who had been following her everywhere she went, plying her with questions. It still amazed her to realize that she had actually been gone for almost three years instead of just a few months. It was no wonder everyone was so excited. But she needed a break and sought refuge at Lea's house for a day.

Elly had spoken to her mother earlier the following morning after their initial conversation. Xriane had explained to her that she was going to get in touch with Lanaya as soon as she could and get everything in order. As soon as that was done, Elly would then be leaving for Aeshern. Of course, Elly herself was in no rush to leave, after all, she had just gotten home after being away for quite some time. True, Aeshern was part of her home, but it just was not the same.

On the morning of the fourth day after her return, Elly woke up early with a splitting headache. It was just barely dawn outside so she tried going back to sleep but found that to be useless. The headache persisted and grew worse within minutes. Groaning, Elly climbed out of bed, took a quick bathe and headed downstairs. Entering the breakfast room, Elly was surprised to find that it was already occupied by her mother and another woman. Elly could not make out who the woman was since she sat with her back facing the door. All Elly could see was the woman's long, shiny, light brown hair.

Elly wondered what was going on; no one in the castle ever got up this early. Elly immediately knew that something was wrong for she could feel tension in the air.

Xriane looked up from where she sat across from the woman and saw her daughter standing in the doorway. "Good morning, Elly," her mother greeted her, forcing a smile. "Why are you up so early?"

"I could not sleep," Elly answered, still standing by the door. She could not help wondering what she had just stepped into. Her mother had obviously been having a serious conversation with the woman. Elly could see the grave expression on her face even though she was trying to hide it.

"Maybe it is good that you are awake already. Come here, Elly," Xriane beckoned to her. "I want you to meet someone."

Elly cautiously stepped into the room. The woman, who until then had been sitting motionless in her seat, stood up and slowly turned to face Elly. Never in her life had Elly seen anyone so strikingly beautiful. There was an air of mystery about this woman who now stood before Elly. She was tall and slender with a softly triangular face, high cheek bones that accentuated her beauty even more if that was possible, full lips that seemed ready to erupt in laughter at any moment and bright blue eyes which Elly instantly knew could see right through her to her very soul. Elly also saw timeless age and wisdom reflected in those eyes. The woman wore a long, dazzling dress of gold that hugged every inch of her slim figure.

"Elly, this is Princess Lanaya Trasell of Aeshern," Xriane introduced.

Elly extended her hand. "Nice to meet you," she said, unable to stop staring at the woman.

"Oh, Elly, please," Lanaya laughed, revealing a set of perfectly white teeth, "do not be so formal!" She leaned over and hugged Elly fiercely. "My, look at you!" Lanaya stepped back, pulled her dark brown hair that fell almost to her feet to one side and admired Elly. "You are not the little girl I remember who used to love when I bounced her on my knees. You have turned into a beautiful woman, Elly."

Elly laughed, embarrassed. "Thank you, Princess Lanaya." That was quite a compliment coming from a woman who was the pinnacle of beauty herself.

"Please call me Lanaya, Elly. I really would like us to be friends."

Elly smiled but did not say anything. She was preparing herself for what would come next.

"Elly, dear," Xriane said, as if on cue to what Elly was thinking. "Lanaya was just asking me when you would be ready to come to Aeshern. She really is looking forward to having you as a guest."

"Yes, indeed," Lanaya interjected as she took Elly's hand and led her over to sit on a sofa at the other end of the room. "This trip most certainly will not be all business, you know." Lanaya laughed, sounding like a little girl. "After all, I am sure we can keep an eye on what is going on with Prince Navar and have some fun at the same time, can we not?"

"Yes, I guess that would be possible," Elly said not quite sure if she agreed with that. This matter was way too serious for games. What was Lanaya trying to hide from her?

"Listen, Elly. I am not going to belittle this situation in anyway." She said this as though she had read Elly's mind. "We must learn as much as we can as to what is going on with Prince Navar and within the city. But we have to be careful and act as though nothing is amiss. We do not want him suspecting our motives for seeing him, do you understand?"

"Yes," Elly answered. "I do. But there is something about this whole thing that bothers me. Why is Prince Navar even interested in me? I have only met the man twice, I think."

"Elly, this may surprise you but every eligible man from Counselors to Princes will soon be interested in you. After all, you are to be the next Queen of Sarcaun."

"That is why when the time comes, you must choose carefully," Xriane interjected. "But let us not worry about that right now," Xriane quickly added seeing the panic that was rising within Elly. "The time for that has not come and when it does your father and I will be here to help you."

"Yes," Lanaya agreed. "Right now, we need to concentrate on the problem at hand. Do you think that you would be ready to leave for Aeshern today, Elly?"

"Uh-yes. Yes," Elly replied, coming back to herself. The conversation was taking the wind out of her. Things were happening too fast. But Elly was ready to do her part, even if she did not quite understand where things were leading to. She would find out soon enough, she was certain of that. "Let me go upstairs and pack. I will not be long."

Within hours, Elly was ready to leave for Aeshern. Once more, the family gathered in her mother's chamber to see her off. But this time, there were no need for tears. In fact, her sisters were begging Xriane to let them go with Elly. But, of course, their mother said no. They would have to wait for another time. This trip was for Elly alone.

Once all the goodbyes were said, Lanaya led Elly out of the castle and into the awaiting ship.

"Re alste?" the driver asked. He was speaking Lumerian, the language spoken by the majority of people on Aeshern, but Elly understood every word perfectly. It was a gift. She could understand just about every language spoken on the planet with the exception of a few that were not very common and were only spoken by a handful of people on Sarcaun.

"Travers, Casne id Noer, Aeshena," answered Lanaya as they entered the ship. They were heading for Noer castle, Lanaya's home. Once they were settled in their seats, the driver spun the ship around and headed north away from the castle.

"So, did your mother fill you in on all the details?" Lanaya asked as the ship picked up speed.

"Yes," Elly answered, "pretty much." Soon the ship was traveling so fast that everything outside was a blur. Elly never knew that a ship could travel so fast. Her stomach was not taking it very well.

"Are you all right?" Lanaya asked, seeing that the color had drained from Elly's face.

"I will be fine," Elly assured her, taking in a deep breath. "It is the speed of this thing that is all."

"Do not worry; we will be in Aeshern in no time. Just try to relax." Elly leaned back in her seat and closed her eyes. Next to her, Elly heard Lanaya begin to sing what Elly recognized was an ancient song which she did not know the words to. Without realizing it, Elly's body instantly began to relax. Within seconds, she was sound asleep.

"Casne id Noer!"

The voice boomed in Elly's ears, causing her to jolt out of her sleep. She looked around her and found that everything was in darkness.

"Where are we?" she asked Lanaya, rubbing her forehead. The headache was back again and her throat was parched. It had miraculously disappeared some time ago, but now it was persisting even worst then before. Elly wondered what it was that was causing her to have such intense headaches. She had never had them before.

"We are in the city of Travers at Noer castle," Lanaya answered as she led Elly out of the ship. There were lights streaming outside through huge trees that were lined up close together. Lanaya pushed a large gate open and led Elly inside.

Noer castle loomed in front of Elly, beautiful in the light of the full moon that shone behind it. It was surrounded on all sided by enormous trees and flower gardens, and a water fall. And even though it was night Elly was still able to see the beauty of the castle.

"This is absolutely breathtaking!" Elly exclaimed.

"Wait until you really get a look at it in the morning," Lanaya said with a smile as she led Elly to the front door and ushered her inside. There were no lights on in the castle except for one in the front hall.

"You must be exhausted," Lanaya remarked. "I will take you to your room now. The grand tour can wait for tomorrow."

Indeed, Elly was tired. She could feel her eyes weighing down and her body was aching.

"Come." Lanaya walked down the hall and then up a flight of stairs to the second floor. Flicking on a light, Lanaya led her down another hall until she reached a set of double doors to the right. She pushed the bedroom doors open and turned on the lights. "This will be your room while you are here," she told Elly, holding the doors open.

Elly stepped inside and looked around. The room was exceptionally large, and everything in the room, including the walls, was a yellowish gold. There was a hanging mirror on the far wall and the bed, with its curved gold post and bright yellow sheets, was turned facing the east window. There were vases of flowers on the dresser and night table, and beautiful paintings all over the walls. On the right was another room which Elly quickly discovered was a washroom.

"There is a regular bath across the hall," Lanaya explained. "In case you want to bathe."

Elly shook her head. "Not tonight. This really is a lovely room," Elly said, smiling at Lanaya. "I like it. Thank you."

"Good. Now go to sleep."

"All right. Good night." She kissed Lanaya quickly on the cheek. Smiling, Lanaya left the room, closing the door behind her. After drinking a glass of water to cool her throat from the water pitcher on the night table, Elly quickly washed up, changed into a long white silk nightgown, turned the lights out and crawled into bed. Sleep came before her head even touched the pillow.

CHAPTER NINETEEN

Elly woke up the next morning to bright golden sunlight streaming in through her window, and a persistent knock on the bedroom door.

"Come in," Elly croaked, rolling over onto her stomach. Lanaya entered the room wearing a navy-blue dressing gown.

"Wake up, Elly!" she said cheerfully as she settled herself on the edge of Elly's bed. "We have got a full day ahead of us."

"I would rather just stay here and sleep," Elly grumbled. The trip to Aeshern had completely worn her out.

"Sorry," Lanaya said, pulling the sheets back. "But that is not one of your choices. Here, I will make your life a bit easier. I am going to fix your bed and find you something to wear while you go take a nice bath. How does that sound?"

"Sounds good," Elly agreed, pulling on her robe.

"Do not fall asleep in the tub, please," Lanaya warned with a smile as Elly made her way to the door.

"Very funny," Elly made a face at Lanaya and left the room. Half an hour later, she came back feeling completely refreshed.

The bath had been a terrific idea. Her headache had receded considerably and was only a slight pulse at the back of her head. Lanaya was nowhere in sight when Elly entered the bedroom but the bed had been neatly made and Elly found a magnificent peach dress made out of satin laid out on the bed for her along with a pair of peach satin sandals. It was a wraparound dress that pinned at the shoulders with two silver brooches. It was the traditional style of dress worn by women on Aeshern, but only royalty and the rich could afford to wear silk and satin. Once dressed, Elly admired herself in the mirror and was satisfied with the effect the dress made of her figure. Leaving the room, she went downstairs in search of Lanaya.

As she stood in the front hallway, she heard voices coming from the west wing of the castle. She walked in the direction that she heard the voices coming from until she came to a large open room near the front of the castle which turned out to be the breakfast room. Lanaya was seated at the head of a long glass table surrounded by beautifully carved wooden chairs on all sides.

"Well, good morning, Elly," Lanaya greeted her. "I was afraid that you might have gone back to bed. Come," she motioned Elly towards a chair. "Join me for breakfast. Afterwards, you and I will leave and head for the prince's castle. By the way," she continued as Elly settled herself at the table, "that dress looks absolutely marvelous on you."

"Thank you," Elly smiled brightly.

Just then, a lovely young woman carrying a silver tray piled high with a variety of foods entered the breakfast room. Her skin was pale, and she had silver white hair and dark blue eyes. Her features made her look very delicate and frail.

"Elly, this is Zarlash," Lanaya introduced, "She helps me run the castle."

The woman bowed slightly and said, "It is a pleasure to meet you, Princess Norellyia." Her voice was almost a whisper.

"I am pleased to meet you, too," Elly replied. "But please, call me Elly."

Zarlash smiled. "As you wish."

"While you are here," Lanaya said, taking a marchiem, a fluffy white roll with hot syrup poured over it, from the tray in Zarlash's hand, "I am sure Zarlash would love to show you around the villages. As you know I am sure, we have some very beautiful gardens here in Aeshern. What do you think, Zarlash? Would you have time to show our friend around sometime?"

"I would be delighted to," Zarlash answered, enthusiastically.

"Well, then," Elly said, as she took a roll from the tray. "That is settled. Have a seat, Zarlash, and join us for breakfast."

After breakfast, Lanaya convinced Elly to leave the castle for a while and take a ride with her through the city.

"Are you ready?" Lanaya asked Elly, as she tied a blue silk scarf around her neck. She checked herself in the hall mirror and was satisfied with what she saw.

"Yes, I am," answered Elly.

"All right then, we must leave now. Zarlash," Lanaya called in the direction of the kitchen. "We will be back in time for lunch."

"It will be ready upon your return," Zarlash assured Lanaya.

Lanaya pulled the front door open and allowed Elly to go out in front of her. The castle and its surroundings were even more magnificent in the warm sunshine, Elly noted. Casne id Noer. The castle of Gold. The place sure did live up to its name. The entire castle was made of gold along with just about everything around it, including the walkway. The fountains were running and the beautiful gardens were packed full of colorful flowers. Most of them were rare and could only be found in certain areas on Aeshern. Mesmerized by the sight before her, Elly reluctantly followed Lanaya to the awaiting ship and got inside.

"Where are we going?" Elly asked as the ship took off and headed east, away from the villages and Travers city, out towards the mountains and valleys of Aeshern.

"We are going to surprise Prince Navar with a visit," Lanaya answered.

The prince's castle was located deep in the Valley of Adalain, famously known for its lush woods and flowery pastures. A few small villages dotted the area that made up the Adalain Valley.

There was a popular tale that said that the Valley was named after the beautiful Princess Adalain who lived in one of the villages long ago. She had been murdered by her husband, Prince Maler, because a seer had told him that she had been unfaithful to him. He had scattered the ashes of her body out in the valley afterwards. As it turned out, what the seer had told him had been a lie. He had told the prince this only to spite him because the prince had killed his son, accidentally as it was, in a brawl. When the prince had found out about this, he had wept bitterly and out of remorse had declared the valley sacred, to be named after his late wife Adalain.

Since then, it was said only beautiful things grew in the valley now known as Adalain. And, indeed, there was no other valley to be found on Sarcaun as beautiful and picturesque as Adalain. The prince's final wish before he died was to be buried deep in the woods of Adalain where he had strewn the remains of his wife's body. But no one knew exactly where in Adalain they had buried him, or even if he had even been buried there.

Elly was always amused by this story and often wondered if there was any truth to it.

"We are here," Lanaya announced a few minutes later, as the ship began to make its decent. Elly came out of her reveries and, looking out the window and in the distance, she could see the gleaming silver peeks of the Adalain castle. It was surrounded by huge trees and gorgeously colorful vines all covered with flowers. Minutes later, the ship landed at the front gate. Elly got out and stood in front of the silver gate that was almost ten feet high.

"Coonar laim," Lanaya said the driver. The driver nodded and took off.

"Come, Elly." Lanaya pushed the gate open inward, took Elly's hand and led her down a narrow brick pathway that ended right in front of the huge oak double entry door. Lanaya rung the bell and waited. Standing next to her, Elly was glancing about the place in awe. Within minutes, the door was opened by a tall man with a narrow face and long brown hair pulled back in a tail. A smile broke across his face when he saw Lanaya.

"Princess Lanaya," He exclaimed taking her hand. "What a delightful surprise!" He soundly kissed the back of her hand.

"Good day, Tal. How are you?" Lanaya greeted him.

"Very well, thank you. And who, may I ask, is this lovely young lady?"

"This," Lanaya said, pushing Elly forward, "is Princess Norellyia."

Tal's eyes opened wide in surprise. "The Princess Norellyia?" he inquired. "The youngest daughter of the King and Queen?"

Lanaya nodded. "Yes, indeed."

"I am honored to finally make your acquaintance, Princess Norellyia," Tal exclaimed, kissing her hand repeatedly. "I have heard so much about you!"

"Well, uh, I am pleased to meet you, too," Elly replied nervously, as she gently pried her hand out of his grip.

"Please, come in," Tal quickly ushered then into the front hall.

"Is Prince Navar in?" Lanaya inquired.

"No, I am sorry. You just missed him. He is out making some last minute arrangements for tonight's gathering."

"Gathering? What Gathering?" Lanaya asked, confused.

"You mean you did not get the prince's invitation?" Tal asked sounding even more baffled than Lanaya was.

"Invitation? No. When was it sent?"

"Eight days ago, I do believe," Tal answered.

"Eight days? Well, I have been rather- busy these last few days. I may have over looked the invitation."

"But you are going to come, are you not?" Tal inquired, sounding worried. "Prince Navar would be truly disappointed if you did not make an appearance. And of course," he turned towards Elly, "the invitation is extended to you. Prince Navar would be devastated if you did not come. He has wanted to meet you for so long. So, will you come?" He glanced anxiously at Elly then at Lanaya. Elly looked at Lanaya not knowing what to say.

"Well, of course we will be here," Lanaya assured Tal. "We would not dream of missing such an event."

Tal relaxed when he heard that response.

"I thought I heard a familiar voice," someone said from behind Elly and Lanaya. Elly turned and saw an elderly man with bluish white hair and gray eyes making his way towards them.

"Caspan," Lanaya smiled. "How nice to see you again."

"The pleasure is all mine," Caspan said as he kissed Lanaya on the cheek.

"Caspan, I would like you to meet Norellyia. Princess Norellyia."

"My, my!" Caspan cried taking Elly's hand in his. "Look at you. You were just a baby the last time I saw you. Now you are all grown up and quite lovely, I might add." Elly blushed. "I am Caspan, Navar's father," Caspan introduced himself. "I am delighted to have you in my home."

"Thank you," Elly said politely.

"Now, I heard Tal here telling you about the gathering. You both are coming right?"

"Yes, of course," Lanaya answered.

"Why are we standing around here?" Caspan inquired. "Come, let us go into the drawing room. Tal, bring us some drinks and cake."

"Yes, sir," Tal answered and disappeared.

"Tell, me," Lanaya said as Caspan led them down the hallway and into a large drawing room decorated in gray and peach. "Why is Navar having this gathering?"

"It is a pre-festival gathering," Caspan explained as they sat down. "In preparation for the Maizan Festival."

The Maizan festival was celebrated just after two full moons circled the city of Morgea, named after their first home planet, in celebration of the finding of Sarcaun. There were lots of festivities during this time and everyone gathered together off the island of Crepe in Morgea to celebrate. The festival was only sixteen days away. Quite frankly, Elly had almost forgotten about it due to the sudden commotion that had recently entered her life starting with the trip to earth. But as a child, she remembered how she had always looked forward to the Maizan Festival. For some strange reason, Elly realized that she was not quite looking forward to this one. She could not help wondering why.

"Quite frankly," Caspan was saying, "I do not think this is a good time for the prince to be throwing any kind of a gathering, especially with what has been going on around here. But he says that everything is under control. But I am not inclined to agree with him completely. You know how Navar is."

"Yes," Lanaya said, "I do. Once he gets something into his head, it is quite impossible to make him change his mind. He has always been one to do what he wants when he wants to do it."

Caspan nodded. "I just hope that everything really is under control. If not, then there is a lot of trouble up ahead." The look on his face was grim.

Tal entered the room with a large tray filled with food and drinks. He quickly went around and served everyone then left the room again. Everyone was quiet for a few minutes, each lost in their own thoughts.

"But I must also admit," Caspan continued once Tal was gone, "that lately, Navar has not quite been himself."

"What do you mean by that?" Lanaya asked, leaning forward curiously.

Even Elly was paying full attention.

Caspan scratched his chin thoughtfully. "I am not sure exactly," he confessed. "But there is just something about him that is not quite right. I can feel it at certain times whenever I am near him. I started feeling like this since just after the time he disappeared and was found again a few days after. It is quite strange, really."

"Does he do things differently now, is that what bothers you?" Lanaya asked, now completely taken in by what Caspan was saying. Even so, she sipped her drink as she spoke hoping Caspan would not see how anxious she was about what he was telling them.

Caspan hesitated before answering. "Not really. I mean, he does, but the problem is way beyond that. It is more like his aura has changed. When I look at him, it is like looking at someone else who looks like Navar, but it is not really him." He sighed deeply. "I know what I am saying does not quite make sense. But I just cannot express my feelings about Navar clearly enough."

"It is all right, Caspan." Lanaya assured him. "I think I understand what you are trying to say. But you have to understand that what you are experiencing right now may just be because of the tension that has been going on. It has made everyone a little bit jumpy and cantankerous in a way. Once things settle down for good, I am sure you will feel differently."

But Elly observed that there was no conviction in Lanaya's words. Something was definitely bothering her. Obviously, Caspan had not noticed this because he smiled at Lanaya thankfully, relief showing in his eyes.

"Look, Caspan, we would love to stay and talk some more," Lanaya said getting up, "but we really must get going. After all, we have to get ready for the gathering tonight."

"Why, of course! I look forward to seeing the both of you tonight." He led them to the front hall. "And it has most certainly been a pleasure meeting you, Elly." He kissed her hand lightly.

"What time will the gathering officially be starting?" Lanaya inquired.

"Early this evening," answered Caspan. "But feel free to come at any time. I am sure Navar will be delighted to see you- both of you."

Lanaya kissed him lightly on the cheek. "We will come as soon as we can. And look, please do not worry too much about Navar. I am sure he is going to be just fine."

"Those words sound very reassuring coming from you," Caspan told Lanaya.

Lanaya smiled. "We will be seeing you later, I promise. Take care of yourself." With that, Elly and Lanaya left the castle and got into the awaiting ship parked at the front entrance and headed back to Travers City.

It was late afternoon when Elly and Lanaya finally returned to Noer castle. Lanaya had insisted on buying new clothes to wear to the gathering. After apologizing profusely to Zarlash for missing lunch, and after informing her that they would also be missing dinner, Lanaya quickly ushered Elly to her chamber on the fourth floor so that they could prepare for the gathering.

"What do you think, Elly?" Lanaya asked holding up a light pink dress with flowery pattern against her.

"It is beautiful," Elly answered. "You will look great."

Lanaya looked at the dress critically for a few moments, then decided against it and threw it into a chair across the room. Elly sighed in distress. At this rate, she thought, we are never going to make it to the gathering in time!

"How about this?" Lanaya held up a midnight blue high collared dress.

"Definitely not!" Elly answered, making a face. Lanaya threw the dress onto the corner chair. Within five minutes, she discarded twelve other dresses. They were all over the floor of the chamber.

"Now, this is the dress I want to wear!" Lanaya exclaimed, pulling out a dress from underneath the pile of dresses that was still considerably high on the bed. It was a soft cream velvet dress with a high lacy neck and a full skirt. There was also lace around the cuffs and bottom edge of the skirt.

"Yes," Elly agreed, "it is absolutely marvelous. You must wear it." At this point, Elly would have been happy with any dress Lanaya pulled out. They had been at this for almost an hour and Elly was getting tired.

"Good, I am glad that is settled. Now, it is your turn and I have the perfect dress for you." Lanaya reached over the side of the bed and pulled out a package that Elly had not seen before. She handed it to Elly. Carefully, Elly opened the package and discovered a gorgeous purple dress inside that was made out of lace with lace around the hemline, waist and neck which was cut low both in front and back. The long skirt of the dress swirled down to her feet and tied in a simple bow in the back.

"When did you get this?" Elly asked as she held the dress up against her and admired it in the mirror that hung on the chamber door.

"While you were looking at the trinkets in the market across the street," Lanaya answered smiling, "Do you like it?"

"Like it? Oh, I love it! Thank you so much!" She gave Lanaya a tight hug and kissed her on the cheek.

"Well, then, in that case, we have a gathering to attend."

CHAPTER TWENTY

The sun was just going down behind the horizon when Elly and Lanaya reached Adalain castle. They could see the festivities that had already started out in the gardens from up in the air. Once they landed, Lanaya quickly grabbed Elly's hand and dragged her through the crowd of people that were out front by the entrance hall.

"After I introduce you to him," Lanaya whispered to Elly pulling her into an empty corner of the hall. "I need you to keep him occupied for as long as possible because I am going to search this place to see what I can find."

"How do I do that?" Elly asked, bewildered.

"Be creative," Lanaya hissed quickly as she saw Tal coming towards them.

"Good evening, ladies," he greeted with a smile. "I was starting to think that you were not going to make it."

"Oh, we would never miss this," Lanaya assured him as he took their shawls. He informed them that Prince Navar could be found in the East Bay room. He had been delighted to hear that they were coming, Tal explained, and was anxiously waiting to meet the Princess.

"Well, then," Lanaya said, "let us not keep him waiting much longer!" Once again, she took Elly's hand and began to guide her through the castle. She finally stopped in a large room near the other end of the castle that was made almost completely out of glass and furnished in gray and black. The room was packed with people.

"It looks like the prince has invited the whole planet to this gathering!" Elly commented as Lanaya searched the room for the prince.

"Yes," Lanaya agreed, "it sure does look that way. Oh! I think I have spotted him. Come." Lanaya pulled her through the crowd behind her.

"Prince Navar!" Lanaya called as she waved in his direction. Elly crammed her neck to see who Lanaya was calling to.

Hearing his name being called, the prince, who was standing by a window and enjoying the view outside, turned around to see who it was. Elly gasped when she saw him and Lanaya could not help the smile that crossed her face at Elly's reaction.

The prince was tall, muscular with a very aristocratic face. His cheekbones were high and his jaws strong and slightly angular. His dark brown hair was thick and lush and fell just past the nape of his neck. He was an incredible sight to behold. Yet despite his overly handsome features, Elly was disheartened to find that his eyes, which were a dark piercing gray, seemed rather cold and empty. Elly shook her head. You should not jump to conclusions, she warned herself. You need to be objective about this.

Prince Navar smiled when he saw Lanaya coming towards him, revealing a set of perfect white teeth.

"Princess Lanaya," he said, as he made his way towards her, "how good to see you." He kissed her hand then leaned over and kissed her on the right cheek. "I am so glad to see that you could make it." He spotted Elly then, standing just behind Lanaya, as though she were trying to conceal herself from him.

"And you must be Princess Norellyia," he said, stepping around Lanaya.

"Uh, yes," Elly answered clearing her throat. "I am Princess Norellyia. But please call me Elly."

The prince took her hand in his. "You have no idea how long I have waited for this moment," he told her as he kissed her hand. Elly thought she was going to faint at his feet. She could see that he was a very charming man.

"Well, uh, I am pleased to meet you, too." Elly smiled nervously.

"Come, will you join me for a drink?" Prince Navar inquired. Elly glanced at Lanaya who quickly nodded her approval.

"I would love to," Elly said and was surprised to find that she really meant it. She nodded slightly.

"Right this way." Navar took Elly's arm in his and led her through the crowd, towards the table at the other end of the room. Elly realized that he had not even bothered to excuse himself to Lanaya.

"So, tell me about yourself," the Navar said as he poured Elly a drink.

"There is not much to tell," Elly shrugged.

"Is this your first time coming to Aeshern?"

Elly nodded. "Yes, it is."

"How do you like it so far?"

"I have only been here one day almost, but I love it already. It is a very beautiful city."

"I am glad to hear that. By the way, what made you decide to come out here in the first place? Had I been aware that you were coming I would have made myself more serviceable to you." He asked the question calmly, as though it was just an afterthought but Elly sensed what he was trying to do. He was searching for information. Apparently, her arrival here was causing the prince to be suspicious of her for some reason. Elly did not have time to wonder why.

Without the slightest hesitation, Elly responded, "It was a spur of the moment idea. I had not really planned it. Lanaya had been requesting that I come visit her for quite some time now and really this was the perfect opportunity. I am sure you have heard about my travel to earth."

"Ah, yes," Navar's face lit up. "I did indeed. Quite extraordinary."

"Yes, it was. Well, anyway, the attention I was getting from it was just too much to take. So," Elly shrugged, "I contacted Lanaya, and thankfully she was very much willing to let me come stay with her for a short while so that I could get away."

Navar smiled. "Yes, I can understand your wanting to get away." He was satisfied with her answer, Elly could tell. She saw the muscles in his neck relax and he took in a deep breath.

I wonder what he is hiding, was the thought that ran through Elly's mind. There was no doubt in her mind now that something was going on and she was sure Prince Navar knew all about it.

"Would you like to take a walk with me through the gardens out back?" Navar asked, pulling Elly away from her thoughts.

Elly glanced out the side window. The sun had almost completely set but there was still some light out. Be creative, she heard Lanaya's voice echo in her ears. It was then that she realized that Lanaya had disappeared and left them alone. Navar did not even seem to have noticed. Or if he did, he did not bother mentioning it.

"Sure," Elly answered, smiling sweetly at Navar. "I would like that."

Navar led her outside through a sliding glass door. There were still some people outside, but not many. Most had gone back into the castle in search of food and drinks.

"Please forgive me, Navar," Elly said, "I am not trying to be meddlesome, but I am concerned about you. I heard from my mother just after I had decided to come out here that you had disappeared for several day during which time no one knew where you were. Is this true?" Elly knew that her words were not entirely true. But she wanted the prince to stay away from any suspicions about her presence on Aeshern.

Navar nodded gravely. "Yes, unfortunately it is."

"And from what I understand, you are not willing to do anything to either protect yourself or find out what happened or who is responsible. Why is that?"

"I do protect myself," he answered. "And I would give anything to find out who is responsible."

"So, then, what is the meaning of all of this?" Elly inquired, gesturing towards all the people who were crowded in the yard and inside the castle. "The person or persons who are responsible for your disappearance could be here at this very moment just waiting for the perfect opportunity to do harm to you."

Prince Navar sighed. "You did not come here tonight simply to chastise me, did you?"

Elly blushed. "No, but I figured I might as well do so while I am here. We are all very concerned about you, you must understand that."

Navar laughed pleasantly. "I appreciate your concern, really, I do. But there is nothing to worry about, everything is under control, trust me."

"What exactly do you mean when you say that?"

"Look, this is supposed to be a happy event. I really do not want to talk about these other matters right now, do you understand that?" There was a note of anger in his voice.

Elly turned her head and glanced towards the side entrance.

Where was Lanaya?

"Yes, I understand perfectly," she answered. What an idiot! She thought to herself. He was apparently more good looks than brains. Suite yourself, Navar! If you want to get yourself killed, then by all means, go right ahead. Who am I to stop you?

"Listen, Elly, I am concerned about this whole situation, also," Navar explained, as though he had read her mind. "It is just that I am not willing to let my life come to an end because of one unexplainable incident. Personally, I think I may have just wandered off somewhere and gotten lost for a few days and become disoriented which would explain why I cannot remember anything. I am probably the one responsible for what happened to me."

"Then how do you explain all of the strange riots and general chaos that have been occurring here since that time?"

"These are all coincidences, I am sure. Trust me, Elly there is nothing for you to fear."

Elly was not convinced of this, but did not say anything to Navar. The one thing Elly was certain of, though, was that she could not trust this man. On the outside, Prince Navar seemed to be normal and very rational. Not only that, he seemed to be a perfect gentleman.

But there was something about him that did not quite sit well with Elly. First of all, the prince seemed to be too perfect- rather unreal in a way. Elly glanced at him out of the corner of her eye. He looked like what humans would call a Greek god with his bronzed skin, tall stature and piercing eyes. Of course, he expected everyone to believe everything he said and never question him. He enjoyed being in control, Elly could tell.

Elly smiled. He was so transparent.

"What is on your mind?" Navar asked seeing the smile on her face.

Elly shook her head. "Nothing in particular. It is a beautiful night out."

"Yes," Navar agreed, "it is."

"There you are, you two," Elly heard a voice call from behind them. Turning around, she spotted Lanaya making her way towards them. "I was wondering where you had disappeared to," Lanaya said when she was standing in front of them.

"Do you need something?" Navar asked, smiling at her pleasantly. Elly flinched. It was apparent to her that Lanaya's interruption had annoyed him as there was an edge to his voice even though he was smiling. Elly could tell that Lanaya had notice the change in Navar by the brief look of shock that appeared on her face. But that was gone in a flash and Navar did not seem to have noticed.

"Actually, yes," Lanaya admitted facing Navar, acting as though nothing was wrong. "I would like to ask you about something, if you do not mind."

"Not at all," Navar said. "Go right ahead." He relaxed a bit.

"I was talking to someone inside," Lanaya commenced, "and he mentioned something to me about the Fenora Reig and it made me realize that you did not have your traditional game this season, why is that? I know how taken you are by that game along with everyone else on Aeshern."

Navar regarded Lanaya with a blank look on his face. It was as if she had been talking to him in a language completely foreign to him. Elly regarded Lanaya quizzically, but she ignored her look. Elly then realized that Lanaya must have found something out or else she would not be out here acting this way. As far as Elly knew, there was no such thing as the Fenora Reig.

"The Fenora Reig?" Navar said stupidly having been caught completely off guard.

"Yes," Lanaya said as if she did not understand the baffled look that Navar was giving her. "You know, what is it that you men like to call it- the Fore."

"Oh, that!" Navar cried, laughing uneasily and trying desperately to regain his composure. "Well, you see, since I decided to have this gathering, I figured the Fore could be held off till next season. I have been planning this for quite some time, you know." Navar smiled at Lanaya, but it was strained. For some reason that Elly could not understand, Prince Navar had suddenly become very tense in their presence. She could even see small beads of perspiration on his forehead just below the hairline.

"Oh, I see," Lanaya answered, nodding her head as if everything was clear to her now. "And of course, that all makes perfect sense. No use having both a game and a gathering at the same time. It would really be too much."

Navar relaxed once more, apparently thinking he was in the clear.

"Yes, I think it does, too. In fact, I have some people working out the details for this year's Fore as we speak."

"Do you really?" Lanaya inquired. "Well, that is good. I am glad you had not forgotten about it. It is one of my favorite past times."

"Well then let me do the honor of inviting both you and Elly beforehand."

"Thank you, Navar. That is very generous of you. And of course, we accept, we would not miss it for anything!"

All this time, Elly was lost to what was taking place in front of her. She had no idea what Lanaya was up to.

"Elly, dear," Lanaya said, turning towards her. "It is getting late; we really must go. Are you ready?"

"Uh, yes, I believe I am."

"Do you really need to go so soon?" Navar inquired.

"Unfortunately, yes," Lanaya answered. "I promised Zarlash I would come home early and bring some sweets for her. She is probably still waiting up for us."

"All right, then. Elly, how would you like to come by the castle tomorrow for lunch?"

"Yes, that would be lovely," replied Elly.

"She will have to check on that, though," Lanaya interjected quickly. "We do have quite a few things planned for tomorrow."

Elly turned towards Lanaya. Where was all of this coming from? Hadn't Lanaya said that they needed to spend as much time with the prince as possible? "Lanaya, we-"

"Hush now, Elly. I will see what I can work out for you, all right?" Lanaya looked at her sternly. Something was wrong, Elly was certain of this because nothing Lanaya was saying made any sense.

Elly nodded but said nothing.

"Good. Then I guess this is good night." She leaned forward and kissed Navar gently on the cheek. "I had a lovely time," she said, "thank you for inviting us."

"The pleasure was all mine," Navar answered kissing her hand.

"Good night, Elly." He turned to Elly and kissed her on the cheek. "I am glad we finally got the chance to meet. Hopefully we will get to know each other a bit more during your stay here on Aeshern."

Elly blushed. "I had a lovely time, Navar. Thank you."

"Come, Elly, we best get going." Lanaya took her hand.

"Good night," Elly said to Navar over her shoulder as Lanaya led her away.

Navar waved and smiled.

"What was that all about?" Elly hissed once they were in the castle and making their way towards the front door.

"Be still," Lanaya ordered. "I will tell you everything once we are out of here. And believe me, you will not like one word of what I have to say!" she assured Elly as they reached the front door. Tal was nowhere in sight. Grabbing their shawls out from the hall closet, they exited the castle and waited out in the front garden for the ship that was to pick them up and take them back to Travers City.

CHAPTER TWENTY-ONE

"All right, Lanaya," Elly said while she lounged in a chair in Lanaya's room, sipping a cup of tea. "What was all that about back at Navar's place?"

They had just gotten back to the castle a short while ago and, to Elly's disappointment, Lanaya had insisted that they change and have some tea before she started telling Elly what she discovered at the Adalain castle. Elly had immediately thrown off her dressed, slipped into a comfortable nightgown and robe then headed straight for Lanaya's room. Lanaya had just finished making the tea and was still wearing her gown when Elly had come into the room.

"Elly, dear, I really do not quite know how to tell you this," Lanaya remarked as she unzipped her dress.

"Just keep it simple," Elly told her, kicking off her slippers.

"Well, first of all, as I am sure you already know, there is no such thing as the Fenora Reig." Lanaya threw her dress on the bed and pulled on a plush pink robe.

Elly had pretty much figured that out but she had not been sure. But even so, hearing Lanaya say it was rather strange and she wanted to be sure she understood what Lanaya was telling her. "Do you mind clarifying that for me?"

"The Fenora Reig does not exist- at least not to anyone I know," she added to herself as she picked up her own cup of tea. "I made that up just to get a reaction from Navar. Believe me, I only had a suspicion before and really hoped I was wrong. For weeks I have been trying to figure out why he, as well as the people, has been behaving so strangely. I have not figured it all out yet, but from what I witnessed tonight I now have no doubt that the person we spoke with tonight was not Navar. Elly, something strange is definitely going on in that castle and I hope we can find out what it is before it is too late." Lanaya stopped to catch her breath.

"Wait a minute," Elly held up her hand. "I am lost here. Please slow down and give me the details. How did you come to such a conclusion?" Nothing Elly was hearing made any sense. She was becoming more confused about this whole situation by the minute. Besides the answer Navar had given about the Fenora Reig, Elly had not noticed anything significant that would have led her to the conclusion Lanaya was coming up with.

"Let me start from the beginning." All this time Lanaya had been pacing up and down the room. Elly felt a slow throb beginning at the nape of her neck and wished that Lanaya would stop pacing so much. It was making her dizzy. Lanaya finally stopped in front of the tall window that faced the east garden and stared out for a few minutes without saying a word. Elly thought it best to keep quiet but had to fight to keep all the questions that were running through her head to herself. She realized that she would probably learn more than she desired before the night was over.

At last, Lanaya settled down again in a seat across from Elly.

"After I left you with Navar," she began, "I started mingling around and talking to the other guest in hopes that I could get some information out of someone there who either knew or heard of some information that no one else had been made aware of. It did not take me long to realized how useless that was. Everyone was talking about and repeating the same things, nothing new that I had not already considered or looked into. I finally sneaked out of the guest rooms and began searching the other parts of the castle. I was not sure of how much time I had, since I did not know how long you would be able to keep Navar busy. But I figured it would be worth taking the chance." Lanaya paused briefly, gathering her thoughts, and then continued.

"I honestly did not know what exactly I was looking for so by the time I got to the third floor, I was just about to give up and head back downstairs when I heard voices coming from a room farther down the hall away from the stairs. Quietly, I tiptoed back down the hall towards the room. I heard the voices again and realized that they were coming from an open door halfway down the hallway. I stood away from the door opening and listened closely; I had not quite decided how I was going to handle this situation yet. The people inside were talking again but I could not hear what they were saying. I found this to be very strange as my ears are very sharp and I have the ability to hear things from a great distance."

Lanaya paused again and this time, Elly watched as the color slowly drained from Lanaya's face. Elly was sitting on the edge of her seat, every muscle in her body tense as Lanaya resumed her narrative.

"It did not take me long," Lanaya continued, "to realize that the problem was not that I could not hear what they were saying because I could hear them perfectly. The problem was that I could not understand what they were saying. The language that they were speaking was not Lumerian or any other language that I would be familiar with. And believe me, I am very well versed in every language that is spoken on Sarcaun."

Elly was baffled. "What do you mean? What exactly are you trying to tell me?"

Lanaya rolled her eyes in exasperation. "Elly, listen to me, the people in that room were not Sarcaunians!"

Now it was Elly's turn to be exasperated. "Come on Lanaya, you do not know that for sure."

"Oh, yes I do," Lanaya assured her. "Let me finish telling you what happened and then you can tell me what I do not know."

Elly was almost afraid to hear the rest of Lanaya's story but said nothing as she resumed her narration once more.

"As I stood outside the door, realizing all of these things, I was indecisive about what I should do. Should I go or should I stay and listen a little longer in hope that maybe I could somehow learn something anyway, despite the fact that I could not understand a thing that was being said in there? But I quickly decided that standing around was definitely not an option. That was too dangerous. So, I figured the best thing for me to do was to pretend I was lost."

Elly shook her head in confusion. "What? Pretend you were lost? What exactly did you do?"

Lanaya took in a deep breath and closed her eyes. "I quietly eased back a few paces from the door and then approached it as if it were the most natural thing, pulled the door open and went in."

Elly flew to her feet. "What! Are you insane?"

"Elly, there was no other way for me to find out what was going on in there," Lanaya tried to explain.

"So, you just walked in there as though it were nothing?"

"Exactly," Lanaya conceded. "I pretended I was lost and apologized profusely. I explained that I was just a tired guest looking for a place to take a rest and that this room was the only one that I had found open."

"What did they say?" Elly settled back in her seat realizing that reprimanding Lanaya about this now was not going to do any good- it was already done.

"Oddly enough, they did not say anything to me. There were six of them in there sitting around a long wooden table that was cluttered with paper, all of them men, and they just stared at me as if I were the strangest creature."

"Then what?" Elly prompted.

"When I realized that they were not saying anything, I just apologized one last time, smiled and left the room, leaving the door open, just the way I found it. I was on the verge of just bolting down the hall, when it occurred to me that that would not look natural, it would make them suspicious. I decided to continue on down the hall. As I did so, I tried the other doors but they were all locked, which was no surprise to me. Surely enough, when I finished checking the last door and headed back the other way to go downstairs, there was one of the men standing in the doorway watching me. When I got to where he was, I smiled politely and was about to step around him but he stepped out in front of me instead and blocked my way."

Elly gasped. "What did you do?"

"I started to apologize again, but he held up his hand and stopped me. In halting Lumerian he apologized for scaring me and explained that they were special guards sent to protect and watch over Navar. I, of course, pretended that I was delighted to hear that he was a guard and was relieved to know that Navar was not taking the situation lightly. He then said 'No one is to know of our presence here, can I trust you to keep this confidence?' I assured him that he could and that I would even make sure that no one else would come around to disturb them from their duty of protecting Navar." Lanaya paused and took in a deep breath. "He smiled and said thank you and immediately went back into the room and closed the door."

Elly let out a sigh and realized that she had been holding her breath practically the whole time Lanaya had been talking. "Do you think he believed you?"

Lanaya nodded. "Yes, I do. But there was something so very strange about him."

"What do you mean?"

"For all intent and purpose, he looked normal. He was dressed in the traditional guard uniform, as were all of the others. But his eyes are what got to me. They were cold and empty. Even when he had smiled at me it had been cold, it was scary," Lanaya was searching for the right words to express what she had experienced. "The aura that I felt around the man I spoke to was completely foreign and his eyes- it was almost like looking into the eyes of a snake, do you know what I mean?"

A cold chill went up Elly's spine. "Yes," she answered softly. "I believe I do." She remembered the look she had seen in Kara's eyes when Melanie and she had seen her at the restaurant. Cold and distant with absolutely no emotions.

"So, what does it all mean?" Elly inquired, forcing herself out of the past so that she could concentrate on the current dilemma at hand.

"I do not know. But what I do know is that whatever is going on in that castle right now is wrong, all wrong. The men I saw in that room tonight were not Sarcaunians, of that I am certain. The man who spoke to me could barely even speak Lumerian. And if they were there to protect Navar, what were they doing hiding in a room on the third floor? On top of that, Navar's behavior was completely out of place when I spoke to him. As far as I am concerned, only an impostor would not know that the Fenora Reig does not exist otherwise why would he cover it up like that?"

Elly did not have an answer to any of Lanaya's questions.

Lanaya continued, "The main question would be: when did the impostor take over?" Lanaya was pensive as she got up and started pacing again. "Caspan said that Navar started acting strange right after he came back from having disappeared for a few days. It must have happened during that time."

"But why?" Elly asked. "Why would someone want to step in and take Navar's place? Why had he disappeared in the first place? And if the person we spoke to tonight is an impostor where is Prince Navar, I mean the real Prince Navar? What is going on here, Lanaya?" Elly was getting angry. There were so many questions, and not enough answers.

"I do not know, Elly, but I am going to find out," Lanaya promised. "But to answer your first question, I do not believe that someone has actually taken Navar's place physically. I think the better chance is that Navar is being controlled somehow. Outwardly, he looks like Navar and still is Navar but mentally and otherwise it is not Navar."

Elly had to laugh. That sounded so ridiculous! "Come on, Lanaya," Elly said, "This is becoming absurd."

"I am being very serious here," Lanaya informed her. "Think about it, Elly. No one would ever suspect anything. Here he disappears for a few days and nobody knew where he was. He is eventually found somewhere out in the Adalain valley completely disoriented. When he returns, he acts a little strange which would be expected under the circumstance. I think it is safe to conclude that during the time that he was missing something happened to him; someone or something just stepped in, literally speaking, and took over or maybe someone hypnotized him to gain control, who knows. No one would be the wiser of it."

Elly silently regarded Lanaya. There was a stern look on her face.

She was not joking about any of this.

"But that does not make sense," Elly said for about the hundredth time. "Why?"

Lanaya closed her eyes and rubbed her forehead for a few moments. Suddenly her eyes flew open. "I do not know why I did not think of this before." She got up from her seat and went into her closet. "Actually, part of me was hoping that this whole thing was just a terrible misunderstanding which would eventually clear up. Nothing that was going on here seemed real until tonight." She came out of the closet dressed in a long black cloak wrapped around her. Turning towards Elly, she said, "There is only one person who can give me the answers I need."

"Where are you going?" Elly asked, getting up from her seat.

"I have to go see someone. You stay here. Do not bother waiting up for me. This might take a while." Lanaya grabbed her purse from the bed and headed downstairs with Norellyia in tow.

"Can I come with you?" Norellyia asked.

"No!" Lanaya answered sternly. "Make sure you lock the door behind me. Do not open it for anyone." She hugged Elly and kissed her on the cheek. "Do not worry. I will be back as soon as I can." With that, Elly stood and watched as Lanaya disappeared out into the darkness. Once she out of sight, Elly quickly pushed the doors closed and turned the lock.

"Elly! Elly, wake up!"

Elly groaned as she opened her eyes. Someone was shaking her vigorously, forcing her out of her slumber. She did not remember having fallen asleep. She had been sitting on the window seat in her room watching for Lanaya and must have drifted off.

"What is it?" She moaned as she rolled her neck to relieve the ache from having slept leaning against the window. She got up, stretched and sat down at the edge of the bed. Lanaya sat down next to her, a worried expression etched on her face. Glancing out the window, Elly noticed that it was barely light out.

"I am sorry to wake you like this," Lanaya apologized. "But it is urgent."

"What is it?" Elly was still trying to wake up and clear her head.

"You must leave here at once," Lanaya informed her.

"What!" Elly was fully awake now. "Why?"

"It is not safe here for you. You must return home at once. I already contacted your mother. She will be expecting you." Lanaya was already beginning to pack Elly's belongings into her bags.

"Lanaya, what are you doing? What is going on?"

"Elly, please!" Lanaya said sharply. "This is no time for questions! You will be heading out as soon as you are packed. There is already a ship waiting for you out front to take you home."

Elly sighed, realizing that it would be useless to either argue with or question Lanaya. Confused and with a heavy heart, Elly began to help

Lanaya pack her bags. Once they were done, they carried everything downstairs and out into an awaiting ship.

"Elly," Lanaya said, once everything was packed and Elly was ready to go. "I am sorry that things have to be like this. But this is for your safety, which is most important. I hope you do not hold this against me, because it is not my doing. I cannot give you the answers you want right now. But you will have them when the time is right. But I want you to leave knowing that I am your friend and always will be. I just hope you will still be mine."

"Of course, I will," Elly replied with tears in her eyes. "I understand." Of course, that was not true, but Lanaya did not need to know that. She hugged Lanaya fiercely then stepped away and entered the ship. From the window, she waved goodbye to Lanaya.

The sun was just beginning to rise over the castle in the east as the ship took off and headed towards Kreese.

CHAPTER TWENTY-TWO

Once Elly reached home, she headed straight for her mother's chamber before even going up to her room to unpack. Despite what she had told Lanaya she was quite disturbed by the whole situation and she was determined to get some answers. She knocked loudly on her mother's door and waited, rather impatiently, for her mother to let her in.

"Norellyia! how good to-"

"Mother, what is going on?" Norellyia quickly inquired, cutting her mother off. Xriane was surprised by her daughter's outburst.

"What are you talking about dear child? Come, sit down." Elly sat down in a couch across from her mother.

"Why did Lanaya have to hustle me back here- practically in the middle of the night- without even an explanation?"

"Norellyia dear, it is obvious that you are exhausted from your long journey. Perhaps you should get some rest. You are overreacting, really!" Xriane tried to smile but did not quite make it. There was fear in her eyes.

"Do not humor me, Mother!" Elly fumed. "You are treating me like a child and I do not like it."

Xriane sighed. "Elly dear, this early on, there is no solid information that I can give you and it would be of no use for me to worry you prematurely. But believe me, as soon as we have some real answers, you will be one of the first to know. Please, Elly," Xriane said, holding up her hand to keep Elly from responding. "Trust me. Now please go lay down for a while. You really do need to rest."

Disregarding her mother's request, Elly inquired, "Does everyone else around here know what is going on except me?"

"No, Elly, other than yourself, only your father and I know. Your sisters only know what they have heard from the rumors. They do not even know the real reason we sent you to Aeshern. They think that you just wanted to get away and, quite frankly, I would like to keep it that way."

Elly regarded her mother closely for a few moments then finally she said, reluctantly, "Fine. I will go take a nap." She wanted to say something more but then changed her mind. Silently, without a backwards glance, she left Xriane's room and headed upstairs.

Xriane sighed in relief once Elly was out of the room. The poor child, she thought. Already so lost and confused- and worried. She had a right to be, too, Xriane admitted to herself. If she knew the whole truth, she would be more than just worried. She would be horrified. Xriane had taken the warnings she had received lightly and because of that had put Elly's life at risk by sending her to Aeshern. She had believed that Elly's presence would help to calm the rage that was taking place in Adalain as well as possibly provide some answers but, unfortunately, she had been wrong. She had been foolish to underestimate what she had seen.

Nore had been right, she admitted to herself sadly. Sending Norellyia to Earth had been dangerous. It had opened the door to things that Xriane would have otherwise believed to be impossible. How could I have been so stupid not to listen to him? Xriane scolded herself. He warned me!

But something else bothered Xriane. Why had the seer been able to reveal everything to Lanaya? She had believed her dreams to be whole but obviously, they had not really been so. Why? It was because of the dreams that she had risked sending Norellyia to Aeshern. Something in her dreams had told her to do so, and she had.

She could have gotten killed! Xriane paled at the thought. If Lanaya had not gone to the seer and Elly had remained on Aeshern for a few more days, who knows what might have happened. Xriane did not want to think about this. Apparently, she could not simply rely on her dreams, they could trick her easily. The force at work was more powerful than she was. She had to be careful. She would also have to search for answers elsewhere.

Xriane got up and left her chamber.

There was work that needed to be done and she had to do it fast. She hoped that it was not too late.

For the next few days, Elly tried to distract herself by spending time at the beach with Lea, her sisters, and a few other friends. Even though it was fun and relaxing, it did not quite keep Elly's mind from the many questions she had that were unanswered. She had absolutely no doubt that there was a serious situation at hand. She wished that she could get some answers but her mother was not talking and she had no way of contacting Lanaya without her mother finding out about it. She would just have to wait and that bothered her immensely.

The only thing that could keep Elly's mind distracted was the coming of the Maizan festival; everyone was busy with the preparations for it. The festival was the biggest event for all Sarcaunians and everyone worked together to get things ready. The festival lasted for several days, and within the course of the next five days, Norellyia and her family would have to take a few trips to the island of Crepe in Morgea to make sure that everything would be set in time. There was much work to be done.

Yet, despite the excitement that was occurring around her, Elly could not shake the gloom that hung over her head. It was amazing to Elly how quickly her life had changed. Now, it seemed that not only was her life changed, so was her home. Prior to going to earth, her life had been simple and tranquil and there was always peace on Sarcaun. Now every time Elly turned around, she was hearing about riots breaking out unexpectedly all over Aeshern. They had started just days after Elly had left and appeared to be spreading to other cities. Elly wished she could change things back to the way they were before but she knew that that would be impossible. She hoped that everything would work out soon so that things could get back to normal.

Now as Elly sat on the high stool facing the window in her room, she forced the gloom out of her mind by thinking about the first time she had gone to the Maizan festival. She had been very young then, only a few years old, but she remembered it all so clearly almost as if it were yesterday. She remembered the games, the rides, and the tons of food that had been set out on mile long tables. Across the island there could be heard the sound of laughter, singing, and dancing. It was a time when everyone simply put all their troubles and worries away and enjoyed themselves.

Perhaps the main reason Elly remembered the first festival she had gone to so well was because it was also there that she had discovered a few of the powers that she possessed. Or, better yet, gifts, as her mother liked to call them. She had discovered that she could make something happen (or not happen) by simply using her thoughts. That, of course had saved her from almost killing herself when she had fallen fifteen feet off from the Sargo. Her mother had been furious after that and had given her a long, but well-deserved scolding.

That was when she had also discovered that she could read people's minds, which had been very unnerving at first, and had taken a while to adjust to. She did not really have any control over it, it just happened. She would be talking to someone and the next thing she knew, she could tell what they were thinking. But this did not happen with everyone and sometimes Elly wondered why that was.

Elly smiled at these memories. She had always known that everyone on the planet had at least one special gift or ability. But it always surprised her when she saw just how many gifts she possessed. It was strange really. Sometimes, Elly felt almost as if she were an outsider, even though no one else seemed to mind that she was so different and her mother had warned her that there would be more.

Elly sighed and wondered what else was waiting for her out there. Lately, whenever she looked in the mirror, she was frightened by what she saw, but she could not understand why that was, either. It was a sign, Elly knew, but she had no means of deciphering it and she certainly did not have the nerves to tell anyone about it. She would just have to be patient and wait. She just hoped that she was doing the right thing by keeping quiet.

Elly shook her head and tried to clear the clouds that were crowding her mind. This was not the time to start questioning herself. "Elly!" Sora's voice interrupted Elly's thoughts. She turned and found her sister standing in the doorway of her room.

"What is it?" Elly asked sounding a little annoyed at the intrusion.

"The Counsel is here," Sora answered, her voice filled with excitement.

"Already?" Elly said as she jumped off the stool, her annoyance forgotten. "Oh, I will be down in just a minute." Elly quickly brushed her hair, pulled on her gold sandals and hurried out of the room.

The Counsel, who happened to be the family that headed all the major preparations for the festival, were close friends of her mother's and they sometimes came to stay at the castle in the days before the festival to help with the final preparations. It had been quite a while since they had come to stay. Elly had still been very young the last time they stayed at the castle before the festival. They were very much like family to Elly and her sisters and Elly always enjoyed when they came to visit.

"Elly, you are just in time," her mother told her as she entered the Guest Hall on the second floor.

"I was just talking about you. Garna, you remember Elly my youngest daughter?"

Garna, who had been sitting on a couch behind Xriane, stood up. She was a woman of average height, just a few inches shorter than Elly, with a round open face, thick golden-brown hair and ocean blue eyes. She was wearing a silver gown that loosely hung down to her feet.

"Of course, I remember," Garna said pleasantly as she came towards Elly. "You were still just a little girl the last time we were here." She gave Elly a warm hug. "Now look at you." She held Elly at arm's length and smiled. "You have grown to be a very beautiful young woman. Your mother must be very proud of you!"

Elly turned towards her mother and smiled. She had not realized until that moment just how much her mother really meant to her. She suddenly felt guilty for the way she had reacted towards her mother on her return from Aeshern. I will apologize later, Elly promised herself. Garna's two daughters, Liana and Nyline, were also in the room sitting on the sofa. Nyline was a slender girl with long silver brown hair and dark brown eyes. She had a dimple on her forehead, making her face seem as though it were shaped like a heart. Liana, on the other hand, was the exact mirage of her mother except she was a little taller and slimmer.

Elly remembered that the three of them use to love playing together, running through the castle and making a lot of noise. Parlin, their father, was in the room across the hall talking to Elly's father, King Ourak.

Elly's sister came into the room and they all sat and talked for a while before they got to work on finishing the preparations for the festival.

It was five days later and the sisters were crowded in Sora's room, since it was the largest, helping each other get dressed for the festival. Everyone had stayed up late the night before making last minute preparations but there was so much excitement in the air that no one had time to feel tired. There were only a few more hours before it would be time for all of them to head off to Crepe Island.

Elly entered the room wearing a beautiful, long soft yellow gown. The dress looked spectacular against Elly's smooth, bronzed skin, which was exposed at the shoulders, and ravishing black hair, which she had piled high on her head with only a few strands loose to frame her face. The dress hugged her figure perfectly and fell past her ankles. She had put on a pair of red heeled shoes to match the red lace that was embroidered around the neck, sleeve, and hem of the dress that encircled her feet. A pair of red string earrings added the finishing touch.

"You look gorgeous," Raina said, and everyone agreed with her.

"Thank you," Elly smiled at her sisters appreciatively.

A few minutes later, their mother came into the room. She was dressed in a light purple dress embroidered with white satin. Her hair, which was usually braided and pinned back, was hanging in loose curls over her shoulders.

"Are you girls ready?" she inquired.

"Yes, we are," Sora answered for all of them.

"Good, because Garna and the others are waiting for us. We should not keep them waiting much longer."

The girls filed out of the room and followed their mother downstairs then outside to where a large ship was waiting for them. Garna, her two daughters and their father were already inside. As soon as everyone was inside and seated, Xriane gave the driver the signal to take off. Within seconds they were on their way to the island of Crepe in Morgea.

CHAPTER TWENTY-THREE

Crepe Island had been transformed over the course of the past few weeks in preparation for the festival that was now in full swing. Lights were strung all across the island and many colorful tents were erected to house the many shops, among other things. There was entertainment for every one of every age, games with prizes, and most of all there was lots of food. Elly enjoyed meeting the many interesting people who came from every planetary city of Sarcaun to participate in the festival and the food that was spread out on long tables throughout the island were spectacular. Elly could not remember ever eating so much food all in one day except for when she was at the festival.

Stepping out from the ship that had just landed on the island, Elly stood for a moment and took in the lights and excitement and smiled. She was ready to have some fun and just forget all her worries and fears for a while.

Later on, during the day, Elly went in search of her parents. She had not seen them since they had first reached the island. The sisters had hung around together at first, along with Lea and some other close friends. Soon afterwards, they had separated and gone their own way, blending in with their friends both old and new. Elly and Lea had met a pretty girl named Arielle upon arriving at the festival. She was the daughter of the second Host, Croste Dore, who was in charge of overseeing the entire festival. She had introduced Elly to three of her closest friends, and for several hours the girls had toured the island together. Now, Elly was exhausted and all she really wanted to do was find some place to sit down and get some rest.

After searching around for a while, Elly spotted her parents sitting at a table under a large sacmore tree at the east side of the island. There were two other people sitting at the table with them. Looking closely, Elly realized that the man and woman sitting at the table were inner galaxy people from the planet Clorian. Elly was not surprised at this. Many years ago, the Clorians had been in trouble, having been attacked by the other Inner Galaxy planet Zirnam. Zirnam had wanted to overtake Clorian, but Clorian had fought back, defending itself as best as it could.

In the end, Clorian was left with barely enough food and water for the people there to survive on and Zirnam had lost interest. The King and Queen of Sarcaun at that time had freely given their help to the people, aiding them to get back on their feet. Since then, the Clorians had been close allies with Sarcaun and it was a tradition to invite a few Clorians, those from the Royal house of Cloria, to come to the Maizan Festival as a sign of peace and friendship to the Clorian people. Right now, her parents were probably talking about politics of some sort with these two Clorians concerning the welfare of both their homes.

Elly decided that maybe this was not a good time to bother her parents. She was about to turn and head in the other direction when her mother saw her and waved for her to come join them. Groaning inwardly, Elly went and joined her parents. So much as for getting some rest.

"This is my youngest daughter, Norellyia. Elly, I would like you to meet some people," Xriane said when Elly was standing next to her.

"This is Norla," Xriane introduced the woman seated across from her. "She is the Queen of Clorian."

Norla extended a thin pale hand from under a long red cloak. The Clorians were well known for their pale white skin and cat like eyes that were deeply shadowed.

"A pleasure to meet you," Norla said in a deeply accented voice while offering Elly a smile. Elly smiled back in response as she shook Norla's hand. Norla's face was thin with bright blue eyes that had black lining around the pupils, giving her eyes an eerie effect. Her ears were sharply pointed and her long red hair hung loosely around her face.

"This is Prince Troy," Xriane said, continuing the introductions. Elly could not help but stare at the young man who was now standing next to Norla. He looked nothing like his mother. He did not even look like a Clorian. If not for his cat like eyes and pointed ears, Elly would not have believed that he was from Clorian.

Troy was tall and muscular with bright green eyes and lush blue hair that fell just below his shoulders. He had a cleft in his chin, and soft full lips that made him look as if he always had a smile on his face. He wore a dark blue uniform that emphasized his pale skin and blue hair.

"A pleasure to meet you, Elly," he said in a deep throaty voice as he reached for her hand.

Elly almost lost her tongue at the sight of him, but quickly regained herself. "A pleasure meeting you, too," she answered as Troy kissed the back of her hand. When he looked at her, his eyes were twinkling as if he was silently laughing at her and Elly felt herself blushing.

"Elly," Xriane said with amusement in her voice. "This is Prince Troy's first visit to Sarcaun. Why don't you take him around to see the island? I am sure there is still plenty of it that you have not seen yourself."

"Well, I would love to, if you like," Elly answered hesitantly. She glanced nervously at Prince Troy. She was not surprised to discover that she was no longer tired.

"I would truly be honored," Troy answered, a smile playing on his lips. He came around to join Elly on the other side of the table. "Come," he said gently, seeing how Elly was frozen to the spot where she stood. "I saw some interesting things on my way over here. Those strange looking balloons floating inside that cage near the First Walk, what are they for?"

"Oh!" Elly cried, coming alive. "It is a game. See, if you can break enough balloons with the little pins they give you, you win a prize!"

"Well, then," Troy grinned, "let us go see what we can win!"

A short while later, Elly found that she was having the time of her life with Troy. He was fun to be with and quite easy to talk to, as it turned out. Elly had been uncertain as to how she should act around him or what she should say. But Troy quickly put her at ease after winning his first prize at the Hazanage, as it was called. He selected a beautiful silk doll dressed in purple for his prize and handed it to Elly with such ceremony that it was comical. It was as though he was handing her a precious stone instead of a simple doll. He was so proud of himself for winning it that Elly could not help but laugh.

It was easy from that point on. They played games and ate everything in sight. Troy was so thrilled with the island that it made

Elly ashamed to know that she had taken all of it for granted for so many years. She was seeing everything from a whole new perspective that made the island seem alive and exciting in a way she would have otherwise never believed was possible.

"All right!" Elly said laughing as she leaned up against a pole. "I need a break!"

Troy looked disappointed. "Elly, please," he groaned. "We have not even started yet."

Elly rolled her eyes skyward. "Lands, Troy! Where do you get your energy from?"

"The sun," Troy answered, his eyes teasing her.

"Well, the sun is going down," Elly pointed out to him, going along with his jest. "Should you not stop and take a rest?"

Troy shook his head in mock disbelief. "I, for one, do not need rest. But since it is quite apparent that you do, why don't you wait for me here while I go get us something to drink?"

"That is a good idea," Elly conceded.

Troy disappeared within the crowd and Elly settled herself on a nearby stool to wait. In a bag at her feet, she held nine prizes of various assortments, all of them won for her by Troy. She smiled. She had never had so much fun all in one day. It was a day she would never forget- and for more reasons than one, too.

Suddenly, out of nowhere, Elly felt a strange presence around her and she quickly turned her head to the left and then right but saw no one at first.

He was standing next to her, to her right, before she even realized it.

"Good day, Elly," Navar said, smiling slightly.

"Navar!" Elly's heart jumped at seeing him. Where had he come from?

"I see you have been having some fun," Navar said, glancing at the bag at her feet, not noticing the shocked look on Elly's face. Or maybe he did notice and just did not care. It was impossible to tell- his face was very impassive.

"Uh, yes," Elly answered nervously. Elly regarded him closely and noted there was something strange and out of place about him that

Elly could not quite figure out. If he were a human being, Elly would have said he was drunk, disoriented.

Suddenly, Elly felt cold. All the things Lanaya had said to her about Navar that last night she was on Aeshern came flooding back into her head like a tidal wave.

He was not himself, possibly hypnotized. That is what Lanaya had said.

Was there some truth to those words? Elly wondered.

Get a grip! Elly chided herself. This is no time for disillusions. As if reading her mind, Navar said, "I have been wondering, why did you leave Aeshern so abruptly? Lanaya never did clearly explain that to me. We never did get the opportunity to have lunch together." He said this casually, but there was hardness in his voice that would have made Elly jump had she not been so thoroughly frozen by the fear that had begun to creep into her veins.

"Well, you see," Elly said her mind spinning quickly. She did not dare tell him the truth. Yet she wondered if he did not already know.

Another chill shot through her at that thought.

"My mother was not feeling well," she quickly explained trying to swallow her fear, trying to convince herself that she was being over reactive and irrational. "And she wanted me to come home and be with her. I protested of course," she said, forcing a smile. "I wanted to stay, really. But she insisted I come home immediately." Elly shrugged and frowned as though to say, it was out of my hands, out of my control.

"I see," Navar nodded as though to say that he was satisfied with her answer. But his eyes said otherwise.

"Would you mind taking a walk with me, Elly," he asked suddenly, as though he had just come up with the idea. But Elly was sure that he had planned all of this ahead of time.

"Uh, well, I would love to but I cannot. I am waiting for someone."

"Who?" Navar's eyes shot with fire.

"A friend," Elly answered simply. "I am sorry."

"Do not be," Navar told her, "Because you do not have a choice in this matter. You and I have something to discuss and if you know what is good for you and for everyone on this island, you will be a good girl and just come with me." With that, he grabbed Elly's right arm and yanked her off the stool crushing her against him.

"What are you doing?" Elly's voice was high with fear. What was going on here? And where was Troy? It was starting to get dark and the island was so noisy that no one paid any attention to them.

"Not a sound out of you!" Navar warned her as he started pulling her through the thinning crowd. "Or believe me when I say that you will live just long enough to regret it!"

"Where are you taking me?" Elly whimpered as tears began to stream down her cheeks. What was happening to her? This had to be a nightmare! If only she would wake up! But deep down inside, Elly knew this was not a dream, the nightmare was real and there was no waking from it.

"You will find out when we get there," Navar answered simply.

Navar dragged her out of the crowd and farther out until they were in a clearing some distance away, leaving the noise and people behind them. To the east, the sun was slowly sinking behind the mountains, bathing the island with a bright orange glow.

"Now," Navar said as he threw her to the ground, "I am going to talk and you will listen. I am going to give you a choice, be grateful of that choice and if I were you, I would choose wisely." Navar paused to catch his breath. Elly was too stunned to say anything.

"You are lucky that I am even giving you a choice. I am giving you a choice only because I have been in love with you since the day you were born. I have watched you from a great distance and I knew then that you would be the one to rule with me, at my side when the time was right. But, like I said, the decision is yours. Even I do not have a choice. The time is finally come and I cannot ignore it!"

Elly was confused by all that Navar was saying. Nothing made sense. His voice boomed like thunder and he paced about impatiently as he spoke, as though he were a caged animal that was being tormented.

He must be mad! Elly thought, but said nothing as she slowly scooted herself on the ground until she was sitting up.

"I wished that it did not have to be this way, but the time is here. I did not choose the time. It presented itself, so, I grabbed it. I have waited too long to let such an opportunity pass! But before you decide, Elly, be aware that there are a thousand ships from Zirnam waiting in the sky to attack the island on my signal. Now, this is your choice: either you come with me and rule with me or I will be forced to destroy the planet and everything that is on it while you watch me do it. Then, when I am done, I will have the pleasure of slowly killing you myself and watching you die!"

He laughed then, the sound of it echoing eerily in the silence that surrounded them. "But if you join me and stand at my side, I will not destroy the planet, but only damage it enough so that in time it will end up destroying itself anyway. The choice is yours!" he concluded with a flourish of his hand.

Elly was stunned and her blood ran cold. She could not believe what she was hearing. This was a nightmare beyond belief.

"What has happened to you, Navar?" Elly asked angrily as she slowly stood to her feet. "Why are you so bitter? Why are you turning against your own people?" Her voice rose with each question. She circled him until her back was towards the direction they had originally come.

"These are not my people!" Navar yelled viciously and Elly could practically see the blood boiling in his face and the veins rising from his neck. "These people betrayed me and put me into prison and there is no way in Land's name I am going back!"

Elly was confused by his words. "I do not understand! What are you saying?"

"You do not need to understand!" He started pacing about furiously again, looking once more like a caged animal. "I have not forgotten what they did to me and now it is time for them to pay! I want these people to suffer just as much- no, more- more than what I suffered for all this time!"

Elly gasped in disbelief. "But, why?" Elly asked, her voice barely a whisper as tears began to fill her eyes once again.

Navar did not answer her question. Instead, he turned to her with his eyes gleaming with anger and said, "I am giving you a chance to live through this because I still love you. Why that is I do not know. But it is there. Be assured that if you turn against me instead of joining me- again I will hunt you down and destroy you in such a way that you will never believe possible. But before I do that, I will let you live long enough to see your parents and the rest of your family die in pain and misery! Now choose! What will it be, Norellyia?" He stood and stared down at her, waiting for her answer, evil oozing out of every pore of his body.

Without even thinking, Elly turned and fled, running as fast as her feet could carry her until she was lost once more in the crowd. She glanced behind her once but saw no one following her. She kept running; perspiration streamed down her face and mixed in with her tears.

"Elly! Elly, stop!" She felt someone grab her arm and pull her aside. Elly spun around and found herself facing her sister, Sora.

"Elly, what is wrong?" Sora asked, seeing Elly's pale face.

"Where are Mother and the others?" Elly inquired not even answering Sara's question. There was no time.

"Why? What-"

"Where are they?!" Elly screamed, cutting her off.

"They are at Tames Square," Sora answered, stunned by her sister's outburst.

"Follow me, Sora." Elly grabbed Sara's hand and took off running again. She was so shaken with anger that she could not control herself. She would have never believed that anything like this could ever possibly happen- not even in her worst nightmare. Yet, here she was running for her life and hoping with all her heart that something could be done to save the lives of the others here on the island that Navar had threatened to destroy so harshly.

No, he had not threatened that he would do so. He had promised it. Elly was gripped with a fear that was beyond her comprehension and this made her feel something that she had never felt before in her life.

Hatred.

The word shocked her as it echoed in her mind. Elly never thought she would possibly ever be capable of hating another being. But there it was, pushing its way into her heart. She no longer recognized herself for the hatred she felt for Navar at that moment blocked out everything else in her mind and in her heart. Elly had never known what it meant to hate someone. It was a word only spoken by Sarcaunians but rarely ever felt, for they were loving, not hateful beings.

But all of that had changed for Norellyia in just a matter of minutes. Hatred burned inside of her like a furnace and Elly was afraid that nothing would ever be able to remove its stain from her heart.

That thought scared her even more than the hatred itself that had begun to fester inside of her.

Elly quickly pushed her worries from her mind. She had something more important to think about now.

They were less than thirty feet from Tames Square when Elly heard the first shot ring out. Spinning around sharply, Elly caught sight of the Hazanage, the first place she had gone to with Troy, and the booths that surrounded it as they exploded into a million pieces, setting everything on fire.

People starting screaming, panicking from the unexpected attack that had taken place. Elly glanced up and stopped dead in her tracks at what she saw, so did Sora.

Above them hovered perhaps a hundred Zirnam fighter ships, like bees over a hive. Elly had been too paralyzed with fear to look up when Navar had mentioned the ships to her and seeing them now made her blood run cold.

The entire sky was a blanket of the Zirnam's white and black ships all poised and ready to attack on command. They just hovered there in the sky, waiting.

Waiting for Navar to give them his signal.

Elly knew that the first blast had just been a warning to make the people aware of their presence. Now they were just bidding the time till the real battle started. Such a battle as it was: hundreds of armed ships against several thousand defenseless people.

Snapping quickly out of her shock, Elly grabbed Sora's hand and once again headed towards Tames Square at a full run. Their passage was harder now with everyone panicking and running around screaming, trying to find safety.

And Elly suddenly remembered that there was safety on the island. Safety in the large underground basements and tunnels still left from the Crozium war, the only war that Sarcaun had ever fought, by her ancestors many centuries ago on the island. They had been left in tack as storage and historical sights of a sort. And at that moment, Elly was extremely grateful for their existence.

Maybe, there was hope after all!

Elly pushed her way forcefully through the crowd with Sora following behind her. They were finally able reach Tames Square. It was a large art center in the middle of the island where shows were held and paintings displayed. Elly had not gotten the chance to explore Tames Square.

Thanks to Navar, I am not going to get that chance, Elly thought to herself bitterly.

"Elly, there is Mother!" Sora cried. Elly turned to her left and saw her mother and the rest of her family, minus her father, huddled in a corner of the Trius Stage. Her mother was frantically waving to the two girls.

"We have been so worried about you two!" Xriane exclaimed as she hugged her daughters in relief.

"Mother, Navar-" Elly began, but Xriane did not let her finish.

"I know my child, I know. Listen, this is not the time or place to discuss this matter. We need to get the people and ourselves to safety. Then we can talk."

Elly looked at her mother, stunned. Had she known all along? Elly wondered. That was unthinkable!

"Elly, please," Xriane pleaded seeing the look on Elly's face. "We need to organize ourselves, but carefully. Elly, I do not like asking you to do this, but due to the grave situation we are in, I need you to help secure the island. First, I need you to make sure that the gates on the North side of the island are guarded and shut. The people should only enter the basements through the West and South entrances, for safety purposes. Your father and Norla have gone to the Cresna with Bowe to organize the men." Bowe was the Master Battle man. "Norla said her people will help, of course. But as of now there is no way of reaching them without interference from the Zirnams. You will have to do this alone because I need your sisters to help with other security matters. Do you think you can do this?"

Elly nodded affirmatively. "Where is Troy?" she inquired.

Xriane frowned. "Was he not with you?"

"Yes, but we got separated. I will have to look for him on my way to the North end."

"Elly, please be careful!" Xriane warned. "When you are done, meet us in the Brigade Basement, do you remember where that is?"

Elly nodded in response.

"We will talk then," Xriane promised. "Now go before it is too late. Time runs short. And be careful!" Xriane warned her again.

Compulsively, she reached over and hugged Elly. Without another word, Elly turned and disappeared into the crowd.

CHAPTER TWENTY-FOUR

Why are they not attacking? Elly wondered in frustration when she was out in the open. Looking up, she could see the ships still hovering in the air like a swarm of bees. The noise that emanated from the ships was deafening, causing the ground to vibrate. A fluorescent green light glowed around the ships, making it possible to see them even though it was dark.

The people were quickly beginning to regain their senses and move in the right direction towards the basements. Those who were not going to the right place were quickly gathered together by Elly and made to follow her as she headed towards the North end. She would leave them at the West end before continuing on. After leaving the people who were with her in the safe hands of the West end guards, Elly turned and headed for her destination once again.

It was then that she spotted Troy. He looked dazed, lost and was walking about in a circle amongst the crowds. Elly heaved a sigh of relief at the sight of him.

"Troy!" Elly called out to him. He spun around quickly and smiled when he saw her. She ran over to him and was shocked to discover that he had an ugly blue and black bruise on the left side of his face.

"Troy! What happened to you?" Elly exclaimed.

"I was attacked," Troy explained as he gingerly touched the bruise on the side of his head. "After I left you and turned the corner, I was grabbed from behind by two men. Before I could defend myself, they knocked me out. When I came to, I found myself in a back alley several feet from where I had been attacked. I retraced my steps and came to find you, but you were gone." He regarded her quizzically. "Where were you?" There was no accusation in his voice, only curiosity.

Elly's heart fell. "I will explain everything to you later," Elly promised. "Right now, I have something to take care of. Will you come with me?"

"Of course," Troy answered taking her hand. "I just need to know one thing: is my mother safe?"

"Yes," Elly assured him, "she is."

Together, the two of them made their way to the North end. Once there Elly explained to the guards that the gates and basement entrances were not to be used by order of the Queen. Without asking any questions, they secured the gates and basement locks and began directing the people around the place to the other security areas.

"How come the people cannot enter the basements through these doors?" Troy inquired.

"Because these are the easiest entrances to the basements," Elly explained. "There are traps down there so if anyone enters through them, they will die before getting anywhere. No one but my mother, father and I know about this, for emergency purposes such as this, of course."

Troy nodded in understanding. "Now what do we do?"

"We need to get back to the basements at the South end of the island. That is where your mother and my family are."

"Then we better get going." He looked up and stared at the ships that were lingering over the island. "I have a feeling that the Zirnams are not going to be waiting around much longer before they decide to attack."

And he was right.

They had not gone more than a few feet when the first shot since the original blast minutes ago, came down shattering the booth right in front of them to pieces. Troy grabbed Elly's hand and pulled her down behind the canopy of another stand. All around them, people began screaming and shouting in alarm as the Zirnams continued firing at everything in sight, people included.

How could this be happening? Elly found herself wondering. This was insane! But it was happening all the same and at this point there was not really anything that she could do.

Except keep herself and Troy alive.

"There is no way we are going to make it back to the South end!" Troy informed her over the chaotic noise that surrounded them. "We will have to find some place to hide until this is over."

But Elly knew that this was not going to be over anytime soon.

"We have to go!" Elly insisted. "They will worry if we do not reach them soon!"

"But Elly, there is no way!" Troy protested. "They will kill us!"

"Not if I can help it," Elly muttered. "Follow me," Elly said to him as she began to crawl along the side of the canopy. Reluctantly, Troy followed.

But they did not get far. The south end of the canopy, where they had been hiding just moments ago, caught on fire from a shot and was coming towards them at full speed.

"Run!" Troy screamed, when he saw the blaze in back of him. Grabbing Elly's hand, he pulled her away from the canopy. They were just barely out of reach when the fire rushed by them, taking the whole tent down. Elly could actually feel the warmth of the fire as Troy pulled her back.

"We will never make it!" Troy gasped.

"Yes, we will!" Elly said indignantly. "Come!" Elly took Troy's hand and then began to retrace their steps back the way they had come.

"Where are you going?" Troy asked, confused but Elly did not answer as she continued on.

Finally, she stopped. "There," she pointed downward. They were standing in front of a large trap door in the dirt. "This leads to the basements."

"But is this not part of the North end basements?" Troy asked incredulously as he realized what she was contemplating to do.

"Yes, it is," Elly answered as she pulled on the rusted handle of the door. It finally gave away with a loud shriek and swung open. Troy peered down over Elly's shoulder, but saw only darkness.

"We will need light," Elly said.

"I will find something. Stay here." He disappeared but was back within a few seconds caring a large flame torch. Fortunately, he had also been able to find a small roll of lighting flint and fluid for it in case the torch started to die out.

"The flame throwers booth is right in back of us," he told Elly. "I think it is the only thing that is still somewhat standing out there. I will go down first," he said when he saw that Elly was ready to start descending ahead of him. "Hold this." He handed Elly the torch and she held it close to the opening.

There was a rusted metal ladder that led down into the basement. Troy lowered himself onto the ladder then took the torch from Elly as he continued his decent. Once he reached the bottom, he signaled for Elly to climb down. She lowered herself down and carefully pulled the trap door closed above her before continuing. She held her breath until she was standing safely next to Troy.

"Watch you step," she warned Troy, as they looked about the place. They were in a barren tunnel constructed of stone and metal that was rusted with age.

"Which way should we go from here?" Troy inquired, still holding the torch and trying to get a scope of the place, which was difficult because the light was not bright enough to cover the entire tunnel.

"There," Elly pointed to the right. "Stay close to the side," she advised him, "the traps are somewhere close to the middle of the floors. We should be safe as long as we stay close to the outer walls."

They walked along silently for what seemed like hours, feeling their way with their hands as well as with the guidance of the torch light, not knowing if the next step they took would plunge them down into one of the traps. Elly was only aware of the trap doors in the middle of the basements but could not be a hundred percent sure that there were no other traps in the tunnels.

"How will we know when we are in the clear?" Troy asked as they stopped to light the torch that was beginning to fade out.

"We should be coming to a cellar door soon," Elly explained. "It is safe once we get through it."

Suddenly, she felt something slither against her right leg. Looking down, she saw a snake wrapping itself around her ankle. Troy instantly reached for the snake and Elly screamed loudly as her heart pounded in her chest and jumped back, away from the wall, towards the center of the tunnel. And instantly the floor beneath her gave way and she found herself falling through one of the trap doors. The snake slid from her ankle.

Troy grabbed her arms to stop her from falling and Elly screamed wildly.

"It is all right," Troy soothed her, "I have got you. Now stay still!" He carefully set the torch down next to him and slowly began to hoist Elly up from the hole until she was standing once more against the wall.

Elly's breath came in short gasp as she leaned against the side of the tunnel and fought to regain control of herself.

"Are you all right?" Troy inquired. Elly nodded. She was still breathing hard. "I told you this was dangerous," he reminded her.

"I know," Elly admitted, beginning to calm down. "But what other choice did we have?"

Troy did not answer her question. Instead, he asked, "What is down there?" He held the torch over the hole but could see nothing but darkness below.

"The stories say that below the basements lies the pit of eternity. Once you fall through, you never stop falling. There is no end to the pit. It goes on forever." Elly shook her head in disbelief as she realized how close she came to finding out whether or not those stories were true.

"Let's get out of here, now!" Troy said, seeing the ghastly look on Elly's face. Taking her hand in his, he picked up the torch and started walking again, being careful to stay close to the wall.

They finally reached the cellar door at the other end of the tunnel. The door to the cellar was so old and rusted that it took several minutes of both of them pulling at it with all their strength before it finally gave way.

They were greeted by several guards with guns on the other side.

"At ease," Elly said to them, without a trace of fear in her voice. Recognizing who it was, the guards put away their arms.

"We were just being careful, Your Highness," one of the guards said. "I apologize."

"No need to apologize, Crisdar," Elly informed the tall muscular guard. "You were just doing your job. That is good. Where is my mother?"

"Follow me," Crisdar said, "I will take you to her." Crisdar made his way through the crowd of people that were packed in the basement and Elly followed with Troy close behind her. Crisdar led them through several mazes of tunnels and a few other basements that were also packed with people until he came to a solid metal door.

He knocked on the door three times. The door was pulled open and King Ourak stood in the entrance. Crisdar moved aside, revealing Elly and Troy who were standing behind him.

"Elly!" the King exclaimed hugging her tightly. "Thank goodness you are safe. Troy." He shook Troy's hand warmly. "Come," King Ourak ushered the two of them inside. "The others are in the back room waiting. Let us not keep them much longer. We have a great many things to discuss tonight."

CHAPTER TWENTY-FIVE

Elly and the rest of her family, along with Troy, Norla and Bowe, the master Battle man, were sitting in what was known as the underground Hall of Drase which had been used as a headquarter during the Crozium War many centuries ago. The war had been fought with a planet called Haran, which was located millions of miles from where Sarcaun was. No one on Sarcaun had even been aware of the planet's existence. But apparently, they had been very well aware of Sarcaun. Haran attempted to take over Sarcaun, specifically targeting Morgea, and had failed, but not before they had nearly leveled almost every city to the ground.

The underground tunnels and the Hall that had been built underneath them are what had enabled the people to survive and had given the warriors a chance to reorganize themselves so forcefully that the Harans were taken by utter surprise when the attack against them took place. Until that final attack, Haran had believed that they were successful in over taking the planet. But because the plan had been so well organized and the Harans were unprepared, it gave them no choice but to retreat for fear of their own planet being destroyed.

Elly knew about the tunnels but had only heard stories about the Hall of Drase and never believed it actually existed let alone believe that one day she would find herself inside the Hall, which was almost fifty feet underground beneath the tunnels, trying to find a way to fight for the life of her family and all the people on the planet.

In the main room of the Hall, Elly was sitting next to Troy, still as a statue, stunned by the things that she had just heard over the past hour since she and Troy had arrived. She was stunned because she had just come to realize that she had been the cause of the destruction that was now taking place on the planet above them. No one had said so, but that was how Elly saw the whole picture.

Her mother had just finished explaining that when Elly had left the atmosphere of the Nigran Zone to go to earth, her power and energy had allowed the gate of Infersity, where the spirits of the dead, the evil spirits of the dead, to be more precise, are known to be held, to open. Yet only one spirit managed to escape before the gates closed again.

It was that same spirit that was now somehow controlling Navar and causing such extreme devastation on the island. But Xriane would not say who it was or why it was out to destroy the planet.

"You will have your answers soon," she assured them.

So, she was to blame, is what Elly felt. Indirectly, perhaps, but still to blame.

Xriane was currently explaining to them about the visions that she had had since the day after Elly had left for earth. In her visions she had seen the planet being destroyed over and over again, in various ways. She had later realized that they had not only been visions, but also warnings as to what was to occur. She had not believed them to be possible.

Until recently.

"And now, it may be too late," Xriane concluded sadly. "Do not blame yourself for this, Elly," Xriane said to her daughter seeing the expression on her face. "You are not responsible for this. If anyone is, I am. After all, I was the one who insisted that you had to go, even though you did not want to and despite the sharp warning that I had received from Nore. He was right and I was stubborn not to listen to him."

Xriane frowned, remembering the conversation that had transpired between her and Nore when this whole affair had started. Since that time, Nore had never mentioned another word to her in regards to the matter. Until the chaos had started erupting in Aeshern, that is. When the trouble had started, Nore had directly confronted Xriane, reminded her of his earlier warning, and advised her to immediately bring Elly back home before it was too late. Xriane had not even bothered to take the time to ask him what would be too late. Instead, she did exactly as he advised and brought Elly home.

"But why did you send me to Aeshern if you knew what was happening?" Elly inquired.

"Because I truly believed that your presence would stop the chaos from continuing. The dreams had told me so. I later realized that it had all been a trick, worked out by Navar himself so that he could get to you. Had it not been for Lanaya, who knows what would have happened had you stayed in the city for much longer?" Xriane shook her head in despair and shivered at the thought. She had put her daughter's life in danger and would never forgive herself for that.

Elly was still puzzled. "What did the dreams show you that made you believe sending me there would solve the problem?"

Xriane sighed. "I cannot explain it to you. But you will understand soon." She was holding something back from them, Elly knew. For some reason, she also refused to tell them who was really behind this whole disaster or if the man who claims to be Navar was not really him.

"So, what do we do now?" Sora asked, fear mirrored in her eyes.

"There is only one thing that can perhaps give us a solution to this dilemma. We must contact the Keepers to see what they have to say."

The Keepers were said to be the Spirits of Old that protected the planet and only the queen knew how to communicate with them. Elly had never witnessed the rite that was used to call the Spirits nor had she ever been in their presence. Despite the present situation, Elly could not help feeling curious about the Keepers. She had studied about them in school and understood that they were very powerful and could take on many shapes and forms. But she was not aware of any time when there had been a need to call them directly to ask for their assistance. All of that was about to change right before her eyes.

Xriane got up and disappeared through a door that was directly behind her which, until that moment, Elly had not been aware existed. She appeared again a few minutes later carrying a thick, ancient gold book with a red silk book mark inside of it that Elly had never seen before. Xriane sat down, placed the book on the table in front of her and began to randomly flip through the book until she found what she was looking for.

"Kyli, will you turn the lights down for me, please?" Xriane asked. Kyli did so and after the lights were dimmed, Xriane instructed everyone to stand up and hold hands with each other around the table.

"It is important," Xriane instructed, "that no matter what happens we must maintain a tight circle. Do not let go of each other's hand under any circumstance." Once she had advised the group of this, Xriane closed her eyes briefly and then softly began reciting ancient words from the book that Elly could not understand.

Suddenly, and for no apparent reason, Xriane stopped reading from the book, closed her eyes and started humming softly. In an instant the atmosphere in the room changed and to Elly's amazement, as she glanced up, it was as though she could see through the walls of the tunnels clear to the sky and she was frightened by what she saw for the clouds were dark and menacing, charged with lightning and electricity.

A strong wind blew into the room and sent anything that was not anchored down flying in the air, except for the ancient book which remained on the table, unmoving as though nothing had changed. The force of the wind almost knocked Elly off her feet and she had to fight to maintain her grip on Troy's hand. Elly felt panic rising inside so she closed her eyes and tried to focus on staying calm. Panic was the last thing she needed right now.

In the mist of the harsh wind and charged electricity, Elly heard a loud, commanding voice ask, "Who calls the Spirits from their place of protection?"

"It is I, Xriane, Queen of Sarcaun," Elly heard her mother respond in a voice equally as strong. She tried to open her eyes so she could see who her mother was speaking with but her eyes refused to open no matter how hard she tried.

"Why have you called us here?"

"As I am certain you are aware, the planet is under attack and in need of your help and protection now more than ever. Please tell us how to stop the destruction."

"Who has brought such peril to this place?"

"I have," answered Xriane without even hesitating. "I had been fore warned but I did not listen. Please, do not let my people suffer because of my ignorance."

"You know well, Xriane, that there are consequences that must be considered."

"I am prepared to face my responsibilities," Xriane answered and Elly could hear the slight fear that crept in her voice.

"Very well, then. We will send someone to you who will be able to put an end to this catastrophe." With those words Elly instantly felt the presence of the Spirits disappear and all was calm again. It was almost as though they had never been there.

Elly slowly opened her eyes and was relieved to see that everyone was still standing. The circle had not broken.

"Did you hear them?" she whispered to Troy, squeezing his hand tightly in hers.

"Hear what?" Troy asked.

Elly opened her mouth to answer but slowly looked around the room again and seeing the look on everyone's face told her clearly, she was the only one who had witnessed the exchanges between her mother and the Spirits.

That was strange, thought Elly. She turned towards her mother hoping to get some answers but her heart skipped a beat as her eyes reached her mother who was standing directly across from her. She was standing stiffly, staring at Elly with a dazed look on her face.

"Mother?" Elly whispered, fear creeping down her spine. Elly stood there shaken as she watched her mother's body slowly begin to transform before her eyes. Her body and posture changed, her hairs changed and soon, without even blinking her eyes, Elly was staring into a pair of sharp sea green eyes, not her mother's eyes but someone else's solemn green eyes.

Elly's heart leapt as she stared at the person who now stood where her mother had been just moments ago. There in her place stood a tall slim woman with sharp green eyes, raven black curly hair, and an aura of strength that was unmistakable. If Elly did not know better, she would have sworn that she was looking at herself in a mirror.

The woman who stood at the table where Xriane had just been looked exactly like Elly. Were it not for her eyes, Elly would not have believed she was looking at someone other than herself. Her eyes told a different story, a story that was old and timeless at the same time.

Elly was transfixed to where she stood, shocked.

"Safriem es cornea," the woman said in a low voice, looking intently at Elly. Elly did not understand her for she did not know the ancient language. "I am Lurcia, the first queen of Sarcaun, greetings." She gave a small nod.

"What brings you to us?" King Ourak asked, taking control of the situation. Elly was surprised to see that he was not a bit fazed by what had just transpired before them. It was as if he had expected this all along although Elly knew that was not possible.

Lurcia's solemn eyes blazed as she spoke her next words. "The evil spirit of King Zirrcon Tuscany has escaped the imprisonment which I had set him in so many centuries ago within Infersity." Lurcia stopped and took a deep breath. "He has returned to finish the destruction he had started when he ruled the planet. But that will not be so," Lurcia added fiercely. "Because I am here and I will find a way to put an end to him once and for all, in one way or another, I promise you."

Elly heard Lurcia's words as if from a great distance because everything around her was beginning to spin around her head. She could no longer see straight. She felt dizzy as the blood drained from her head, down to her feet. Quickly she broke away from the circle, rubbed her forehead and sat down in her chair. Everyone followed her lead and sat down, too.

Elly started mumbling and shaking her head. "I do not understand it. I just do not understand." Actually, she did understand. Everything was now quite clear to her. She simply did not want to believe it. This is not happening, she kept telling herself. This cannot be real! She knew now why her mother had believed that her presence in Aeshern could bring things back to order.

Lurcia looked at Elly steadily and said, "My child you must understand. You are the one who is in the most danger here."

"But why?" Elly asked genuinely confused.

Lurcia smiled sadly. "Do you not see? Look at me."

Elly did so reluctantly and in doing so, something came to her. But she was not quite sure what it was. The pieces refused to fall into place.

"You resemble me in just about every way," Lurcia explained, seeing the confusion in Elly's eyes. "You remind him of me. That is why he is so determined to destroy you," Lurcia raised her hand to stop Elly's protest. "Even if you had taken his side, he would have destroyed you still, eventually. That is all that matters to him. This war he is fighting, it is not everyone else he wants to destroy, it is you and you only he wants destroyed. Woe, to everyone else who gets in his path."

Lurcia paused to catch her breath, anger burned in her eyes. "The problem is he cannot destroy me directly. But he is doing the next best thing that will satisfy him. Destroying the planet which he knows I love so dearly and after he has done that, he will come after you and destroy you, too. That, to him will be a symbol of my own destruction."

"What about Navar? Can you free him from Zirrcon's control?" Elly asked Lurcia.

Lurcia shook her head sadly. "I cannot save him. It is too late and too dangerous. I will not take such a chance. Whatever happens from this point forward, Navar will be lost to us."

Elly was surprised to find that she was saddened by this. After all, it seemed Navar was a victim just as she was.

"Why did Zirrcon choose him?" she wanted to know.

"I believe it is because Navar is of his blood, a grandson of many centuries past. Taking control of him was easier than trying to take control of anyone else. And another thing you need to understand is that since Zirrcon is controlling Navar, he sees himself as Navar not as Zirrcon. So technically it is Navar that we are dealing with here." Elly nodded in understanding.

"How did Zirrcon escape from Infersity is what I would like to know," King Ourak said and everyone nodded in agreement with him.

Lurcia sighed and shook her head in dismay. "He was still alive when I put him in Infersity many centuries ago. I was able to discover that he died after a time, having been tortured by the other spirits about him. But his power still remained with his spirit when he died because of where he was and who he was, being that he died while already in Infersity. You may not be aware of this, but the gates of Infersity can be opened if someone of the Royal house travels outside the astral belt, as you did when you traveled to earth, Elly. Traditionally this would not be a problem unless there are spirits in Infersity that still have some amount of power, as was the case with Zirrcon. So, when you passed out of the atmosphere when you were sent to earth, your powers and energy caused the gates to open and his spirit was able to use his powers to escape, as if he were still alive and not just a spirit."

"And the worst part," Lurcia continued, "is that once the gates opened as long as you were on earth there was no way to close them. That is why it was crucial for you to return to Sarcaun once the trouble started: so that the gates would close and prevent any further disaster from occurring. We are very fortunate that only one spirit escaped while the gates were open. Of course, none of this was revealed to me until it was too late. I had no way of knowing such a thing would or could ever actually happen when I had first placed him in Infersity many centuries ago."

Elly shook her head in utter amazement at what she had just heard.

"So how did you manage to put him there while he was still alive?" Elly wanted to know. She was still trying to process all the information Lurcia had revealed to them.

"That," Lurcia said softly, "I cannot reveal to you. It should suffice to say that I was given the power to do so, so I did it. Believe me when I say it was much of a sacrifice to do so. But I had no choice. He would have surely destroyed the planet had I not done so."

Everyone was silent as they took in everything that Lurcia had just told them. Elly's heart was pounding in her ears and a thin film of perspiration clung to her skin.

"For the safety of the planet, and for the sake of your life, you must leave this planet as soon as possible," Lurcia continued, looking directly at Elly.

"No!" Elly cried indignantly. "I will not turn my back while my home is in jeopardy!"

"Staying here will only put you in more danger along with everyone else. If you leave here for just a little while, there may be a way to stop him."

"How?" Elly asked.

Lurcia shook her head. "Do not worry yourself with that. You must leave here at once!"

But Elly was certain that there was nothing to be done to stop Navar.

Nothing. Regardless of where she went, it would never end.

"My mother and I can find a way to sneak her out from here and take her back to Clorian with us," Troy volunteered. "She should be safe there."

Lurcia nodded in approval. "That is an excellent idea. Thank you, Troy." She turned towards Elly. "Please, let us not fight about this. There is not enough time."

Elly nodded in defeat. "Where is mother?" she asked in a small voice, trying hard not to start crying.

Lurcia paused, not knowing exactly how she should answer this question. Finally, she said, "She is in the spirit world where I was before being sent here. In order for me to be here, someone has to keep my place so that the Gates of Infersity will remain sealed as I am one of the gate keepers."

"My mother is where?!!" Elly cried incredulously jumping up from her seat. This situation was getting even worse by the moment.

"Do not worry," Lurcia said soothingly as she reached across the table to hold Elly's hand, hoping to calm her down. "She is safe."

CHAPTER TWENTY-SIX

Above on the island, smoke had filled the air and darkened the sky from the destruction caused by the Zirnams. Nothing was left standing and almost the entire island had been burned to the ground and what had not been was in shambles. Dead and wounded bodies were scattered everywhere and panic was running through the island. Those who had survived the attack were currently in the process of putting together makeshift camps to attend to the wounded.

The cries from the children and wounded pierced through Elly's heart as she stood on the remnants of a tent that had once held charms and trinkets taking in the destruction that surrounded her. Her eyes burned with tears as she watched a small child limping in tears from out from one of the camps; his clothes were tattered and he had a bandage around his broken left arm. Moved by the little boy, Elly took a step in his direction but felt someone grab her hand, stopping her in mid stride.

"Elly, we have to leave," she heard Troy say from behind her.

Taking in a deep breath, Elly reluctantly turned away.

It was nightfall and Troy, Norla and she were making their way through the rubble of the island towards Cresna where the Battle men were located. The Zirnam ships had retreated from the island, but they would be back, Elly knew. To attack somewhere else or finish what they had started here on the island. Either way, Elly was certain that more disaster lay ahead.

During the attack, the Battle men had managed to shoot down a few of the Zirnam ships. Currently, Bowe and a group of technicians were in the process of seeing if they could get one to work so that

Troy could get Elly safely off the planet without being noticed by the Zirnams. As a rule, the Zirnams would never attack one of their own, no matter where the vessel was headed, and the fact that the ship they were using was damaged would be to their advantage as the Zirnams would most likely just assume it was returning to the home planet for repairs.

It was their only hope of getting off the island alive.

Tears streamed down Elly's cheeks as she continued to gaze at the destruction that had taken place on the island. She desperately wanted to stay to help those who were wounded and to see that the dead received a proper burial. It was the least she could do but she knew that it was out of the question. It would be too dangerous. Right now, Navar was probably just sitting back somewhere, just waiting for the perfect opportunity to strike again.

After what seemed to Elly like hours, they finally reached the Cresna. Bowe was waiting for them out in the front hall.

"We repaired her as best as we could," he explained as he led them inside. "I am sure she is stable enough to take you to Clorian, but be careful just in case."

Inside, they found a Zirnam fighter ship. Elly was surprised to discover that up close the fighter ship was not as big as she had expected it to be. Considering the damage that had been done on the island, Elly had expected much more than the gray and black sleek ship that was only about twenty feet long. One side of it was still badly damaged from where it had been shot down but otherwise it was still in tack. Several technicians were milling around it, checking out all of its functions to make sure it was prepared for their trip. Bowe took Troy aside to explain to him how the ship worked while Norla and Elly waited by the entrance.

"Do not worry so much, Elly," Norla said giving her shoulder a squeeze. "Everything will work out fine. I promise."

"Thank you, Norla," Elly said, forcing a smile. But she was not really encouraged by those words. Nothing will ever be the same again, Elly concluded silently. Nothing.

"All right, we are ready to go," Troy said, joining them by the door. Quickly, the three of them climbed on board, with Troy sitting at the control. Minutes later, they were out of the Cresna and flying through the air at full speed.

"These ships are not much different from our own," Troy said to Elly who sat in back of him. "These are just a little bigger, that is just about it." Elly nodded in response, too scared to speak. She just hoped that they could make it to Clorian without any interference.

As time passed, Elly tried to relax herself, seeing how the trip was going quite successfully. But she could not.

Elly found her thoughts drifting to what was taking place back at home. Everything that was happening seemed very strange and surreal to her. She thought back to all the stories she had heard in her ancient history classes about the tyrant king Zirrcon, the first King of Sarcaun. It was said that he had tortured the people; giving them nothing and taking everything, treating them like slaves. The people had suffered for many years, powerlessly dying at the hands of King Zirrcon. Even Queen Lurcia had been kept as a prisoner in the castle, unable to do anything to help her people.

Then, one day, Queen Lurcia had suddenly disappeared and no one knew what had happened to her. Soon after that, the King had also disappeared without a trace and with his disappearance the people were finally free from his tyrant hold. Once the people were freed from Zirrcon, a new king and queen were appointed and everything eventually became normal again and the planet was restored. But no one was ever able to discover what had happen to King Zirrcon or Queen Lurcia. Elly's father had questioned Queen Lurcia about her disappearance, but she had refused to answer any of his questions. All she would say was that she did what she had to do to protect her people and the planet.

Oh well, Elly sighed. I guess I will never know the whole story. Maybe no one would ever know.

"We are in Clorian," Troy told Elly excitedly a few minutes later. Anxiously, Elly peered out the side window. The sun was just beginning to set in Clorian and in the dim sunlight Elly could see a magnificent castle in the distance situated on a plush green hillside that was peppered with blue and yellow flowers and cushioned in the soft pink and purple glow of the setting sun. A clear blue stream circled the whole of the castle down below the hill on which it stood.

"Amazing," Elly whispered in awe. "It is beautiful!"

Troy lowered the ship in what Elly later found out was a guard station a half a mile away from the castle. Getting into one of their own ships, they flew back to the castle and entered through the left wing.

"You must be exhausted," Norla said to Elly once they were inside. "You need to get some rest." She turned to Troy and said, "Take her up to the fifth floor and get her settled in. I will have someone bring you some food later on," she informed Elly.

"Thank you," Elly said, giving Norla a quick hug. "Thank you for everything." Norla smiled then waved her away. Quietly she followed Troy as he led her up several narrow flights of stairs.

"Here you are," Troy announced, opening a door near the end of a long, dark hallway on the fifth floor. "My room is right over there." He pointed to another room a few doors down the hall. He then reached inside the dark room where Elly was going to be staying in and waved his hand against the side wall. Instantly there was light inside the bedroom. Elly tentatively stepped inside.

The room she found herself in was large yet very scarcely furnished. There was a large bed fitted with royal purple sheets against the far wall with a wooden night table next to it and above the bed on the wall hung a painting of a young girl. Elly could not restrain herself from staring at the painting. The girl looked familiar to her somehow, but she could not quite figure out how or why. Those deep green eyes.

"My sister," Elly heard Troy say from behind her. She turned slowly and regarded him. Yes, she could see the resemblance. But there was something else.

"You have a sister?" Elly inquired, trying to push the strange feeling that was nagging at the back of her head away.

"Had a sister," Troy answered sadly.

Elly looked puzzled. "What do you mean 'had'?"

"She is dead," Troy answered softly. "She died some time ago."

Idiot! Elly scolded herself. She should have known. "I am sorry," Elly said.

"Do not be," Troy gave her a small, sad smile. "You had no way of knowing."

"How did she die?" she inquired without even thinking. Something told her she needed to know.

Troy shook his head. "It is a long story." He forced another smile. "I will tell it to you sometime, but not now. You need to get some rest."

Elly looked away from him and stared into the room. "This was her room, yes?" she asked not looking at Troy. She already knew the answer.

"Yes- it was-"

"Maybe you should give me another room," Elly interrupted as she turned and faced Troy once again. There was a tight knot in the pit of her stomach and she immediately knew that she would not sleep well in this room.

"No, that is not necessary." He smiled at her again, this time genuinely. "She would have liked you; I know. Please stay. Plus, I want to be able to keep an eye on you and none of the other rooms are suitable for guest at the moment."

Elly hesitated, but only for a moment, and then said reluctantly, "All right, I will stay here,"

"Good. Now please, get some rest. There is a washroom through that door over there," he pointed at a door located opposite the bed. "And feel free to use whatever you need that is in the room. Have a good night, Elly." With that, he took her hand in his, kissed the back of it lightly before he turned away and headed back down the hallway.

Stepping into the room, Elly gently closed the door behind her. The only other furniture in the room besides the bed and night table was a wooden desk with a straight back chair against the right wall. There was also a closet at the other end of the room and a window to the left of the bed with heavy silk gray curtains pulled closed, shutting out any natural light that could have possibly entered the room.

Quickly, Elly crossed the room and pulled the heavy gray curtains that hung over the tall window next to the bed open. She needed some natural light in the room to keep from feeling as though she were trapped with no way out. Crossing the room, she went and looked in the closet and was surprised to find that it was filled with clothes. She reached inside and touched one of the dresses and felt a small shockwave of electricity go through her body as her fingers cradled the soft material.

She instantly pulled her hand away as it dawned on her that the clothes in the closet were that of the girl in the picture. The clothes had belonged to Troy's sister. How could she possibly wear them? She rubbed her forehead in distress knowing that she did not have a choice in the matter. She had not had time to go home to pack anything to bring with her and the only article of clothing she had was the yellow gown she was wearing which was now filthy and torn in several places. She needed something clean to wear.

They are just clothes, Elly reasoned to herself. They cannot harm me.

Coming to this conclusion, Elly swiftly stripped off her gown. She rummaged through the closet until she came upon a silk blue night gown that also had a matching robe. Slowly, she slipped the robe on. Elly stood there a moment as if she was waiting for something to happen. But nothing did. She almost laughed at her foolishness. She then laid the nightgown on the bed to wear later after she had washed up. Just as she was pulling the closet door closed, Elly noticed the bedroom door slowly being pushed open out of the corner of her eye. In the doorway, a young girl with wild blue hair and matching eyes stood holding a tray piled high with food.

"Oh! Hello," Elly greeted the girl, smiling cheerfully. "Norla must have sent you. Thank you for bringing me food. I really am starving!" She waited for the girl to say something. But, instead of responding, the girl simply walked into the room, set the tray down on the desk, and then walked back out of the room without even a backwards glance at Elly.

How strange, Elly thought as she closed the door which the girl had left standing open. It was as if she had not even heard me.

Shrugging, Elly sat down at the desk to enjoy her meal which consisted of meat, which tasted delicious even though she could not identify exactly what it was, a salad made of a variety of colorful fruits, and sweet cakes. After eating, Elly was barely able to keep her eyes open so she quickly washed up and climbed into bed. She was immediately overtaken by exhaustion from the long, emotional day she had just experienced. Yet, being in a strange place made her weary so she was not able to fall asleep easily. After what seemed like a long time of tossing and turning, she was finally able to sleep.

And she dreamed...

In her dream Elly saw a young man and woman walking through a field covered with beautiful flowers that filled the air with a sweet fragrance. There were lush green mountains in the background to the left and bare ragged hills that looked menacing and very dangerous in the distance to the right. It was a wonderfully warm day and the sun was shining brightly through the crystal clear blue sky.

The young woman was tall and very beautiful with long, corn silk yellow hair, deep green eyes that twinkled when she smiled and as she walked through the field she laughed, revealing a set of perfectly white teeth. The young man, who walked with a slight limp, was older with olive skin, soft curly brown hair and piercing gray eyes. He was wearing a dark gray riding outfit and in his left hand he carried a cane. The couple walked lazily through the field for a while until the woman decided to sit down somewhere out in the middle of the field and motioned for the man to join her. So, they sat there for a while, talking and laughing, enjoying the day.

But suddenly, the man said something to the woman that caused her to become angry and her face creased with shock and disbelief at what the man had just told her.

Instantly, the weather changed. The flowers withered and died and soon the once beautiful field was bare, with only sand covering the terrain. The sky, which had been beautiful and clear just moments ago, became overcast with dark, angry clouds, hiding the sun, turning everything a dull gray. The air became thick and humid, charged with electricity as though a storm was moving in. Yet the air was still and windless.

The woman became even angrier as she sat there and began yelling sharply at the man who had now stood up to hover above her. He yelled something at her and the woman leaped to her feet, fire flashing in her eyes. She said a few more words to him then turned abruptly away, heading out of the field. The man followed behind her, slowed by the limp in his left leg, still yelling at her in frustration. But the woman paid him no heed. She marched on until she came to a stable which she entered and came out a few seconds later with a black horse in tow. It did not have a saddle on; only the reins were in place. She quickly climbed the horse and started galloping away.

The man also went into the stable and came back out with a horse. This one was chestnut brown and was saddled and ready to go. He climbed on and took off at a full gallop after the girl.

They did not notice the man who was standing on a hillside not far from them, watching.

The man yelled something to the girl who was now only several feet ahead of him. She quickly glanced back at him and there was a look of horror on her face. Determined to increase the distance between them, she dug her feet into the horse's side, urging him to go faster. Her palms were starting to become hot and sweaty, causing her grip on the reins to slip repeatedly. Tears began to fill her eyes, blurring her vision.

Soon she was out of the field and found herself galloping through rocky terrain with jagged peaks on every side. Looking out of the corner of her eye, she realized that there was someone else following them but she did not stop to worry about that because the man was quickly gaining on her.

The horse's hoof slipped on a rock, causing her speed to falter.

The woman knew that she should not be pushing the horse so hard on such rocky terrain, but she had no choice. There was no other way out.

The horse slipped again, but still she urged him on as tears earnestly spilled down her cheeks now.

But suddenly, the horse jerked to a stop, almost causing her to fly off his back. The horse stopped only for a second, though. Only long enough for her to hear the man's words ringing clearly in her ears. Only long enough for her to turn and see the devilish countenance of his face as he said those words. Long enough for the fear to settle into her bones.

Then, without warning, the horse began to buck wildly, uncontrollably, spinning around in every direction, shaking violently without stopping. The girl's heart was racing as she pulled tightly on the reins, trying to control the horse. But it was no use because she was not strong enough and the horse was too wild. Suddenly, the horse gave a violent twist and the girl immediately lost her grip on the reins causing her to fly backwards off the horse through the air. Everything seemed to be happening in slow motion and the girl felt as though she hung in the air for hours. But then in the next instant she found herself rushing towards the ground at full speed and from that point it was not long before she heard the loud crack as she landed sharply on her back on top of one of the jagged rocks.

She laid there on the cold, rocky peak without moving, shock and fear mirrored in her eyes as she felt the ravishing pain that was coursing through her body. She did not even try to move, not only because she could not, but because she knew it was too late.

Out of nowhere, a raging wind began to blow, disrupting the stillness in the air.

Slowly turning her head to the right, she was able to see the man who had been chasing her galloping away without even a backward glance and as her eyes began to close, she saw the other man that had been following them galloping his way towards her at full speed.

As he came closer, she recognized his face and a sad smile touched her lips.

When he finally reached her, he jumped off his horse, his blue hair blowing wildly in the harsh wind and his eyes dark with anger. When he was close to her, she reached up and took his hand, gritting her teeth against the pain that racked her body. Gently, he lifted her off the jagged rocks and cradled her in his arms. Blood trickled out of her mouth.

The man started crying bitterly, burying his face in her hair as he rocked her slowly back and forth.

She suddenly let go of his hand, too weak to hold on. She laid there in his arms feeling the strength seep out of her. She no longer felt any pain, only sadness filled her heart.

The man raised his head and started screaming, screaming at the top of his lungs. His screams echoed through the air and had anyone been there to hear them, they would have felt chilled to the bone.

He screamed as he knelt there on the hill, watching the girl slowly die in his arms.

Elly woke up with a start and found that she was sitting in an upright position on the bed and her heart was pounding wildly. Her body was covered with perspiration, causing the nightgown to cling coldly against her skin. She took in a couple of deep breath and tried to calm her racing heart. She then swung her legs over the side of the bed and turned on the lamp that was perched on the night table. She was shaking violently, but she forced herself to look at the painting of the girl that hung above the bed.

The girl from her dream.

Christina! her mind cried out suddenly. The girl reminded her of Aimer's little sister. That is why it had looked so familiar to her earlier.

The girl with long corn silk yellow hair, deep green eyes and rosy pink cheeks and lips.

Troy's sister.

But why did she remind her of Christina? Elly could not figure that out, after all the girl in the painting and in her dream were years older than Christina. It did not make any sense. And that dream- Elly began to cry uncontrollably, her body shaking as though she had just been drenched with freezing water. Elly knew that what she had experienced had not only been a dream. Although there had been no sound, no voices, she had sensed everything as though she had been there to witness the scene herself. She knew that what she had seen had actually taken place a long time ago. Being in the girl's room had somehow enabled her to tune in to her past, a rather frightening one at that.

Elly sat at the edge of the bed for a long while, trying to regain control of her emotions. She was confused and scared by what she had just experienced. In all of her years nothing like this had ever happened to her. Tired of trying to rationalize the situation, she finally got up, walked over to the window and pulled the curtains back. It was dark outside and not a single star shone in the sky. She wondered what was going on at home as she stood there peering out into the darkness.

After what she had just experienced, Elly did not want to stay in the room any longer and, at the same time, she was afraid to go out from it. Although she was exhausted, she was afraid to close her eyes and sleep again. Afraid of what might be waiting to appear behind her closed lids. She went into the washroom and splashed some cold water on her face but after a while, she could no longer keep her eyes open. Giving in to her exhaustion, Elly crawled back into bed and closed her eyes, falling soundly asleep before her head even touched the pillow.

This time, there were no dreams, only darkness.

CHAPTER TWENTY-SEVEN

When Elly woke up the next morning, bright sunlight was pouring in through the window as she had forgotten to pull the curtains closed after going back to bed after her nightmare. Her body was tired and she felt strangely disoriented as she rolled over, stretched and forced her eyes open. For a moment, she thought she was at home safe in her own bed.

But as she looked around the room groggily and realized where she was the events of the last several hours came rushing back, making her feel weak and nauseated. She had hoped that what had happened had only been a bad dream. Sighing in despair, she curled up in the bed, not wanting to face the day. Eventually, she forced herself out of bed, washed up and was pulling on a dark blue dress she had found while rummaging in the closet that buttoned at the neck and fell to her feet when she heard a knock at the door.

"Coming," she called as she finished pulling on the dress. Opening the door, she found Troy standing in the hallway.

"I am going downstairs to breakfast. Would you like to join me?"

"Yes, I would. Can you give me just a moment?"

"Of course."

Going back into the bedroom, she pulled on a pair of blue sandals she found in the closet and quickly pulled her hair back and tied it with a ribbon she had found in the washroom. Leaving the room, she followed Troy down the hall to the left and down several flights of stairs to the first floor.

Opening a set of double doors halfway down the hall, he stepped aside for Elly to enter before him and she found herself standing in an elaborate breakfast room that took her breath away. There were tall, paneled windows on both side of the room from one end of the room to the other for a total of twelve windows all together that allowed exquisite sunlight to fill the room and sparkle off on the two crystal chandeliers that hung from the ceiling ten feet apart from each other. The curtains in the room were a deep blue with rose prints that were barely visible adding to the beauty of the material. In the center of the room was a long elegantly hand carved wood table that could seat at least twenty people at once. Three places were set at the other end of the table and Elly saw that Norla was already seated and waiting for them.

"Good morning, Elly. I hope you are feeling well today," Norla greeted her as Troy pulled out a seat for her.

"Yes, I am fine," Elly answered, not really being completely honest. She was still rattled by the dream she had last night but was not about to share that with anyone.

Troy took a seat across from her and she enjoyed a wonderful breakfast of wild berries and sugared bread with cream that melted in her mouth instantly. She had never tasted any of the food that was brought to her and she reveled in experiencing such new taste. The food was almost enough to distract her from thinking about the disaster that had taken place on Sarcaun that brought her here in the first place.

After having breakfast with Norla, Troy volunteered to show her around the castle. After guiding her through the various parts of the castle and explaining to her how to get around, Troy took her outside to see the vast expanse of land that surrounded the castle. Outside the castle was just as magnificent as the inside. Elly had been too tired the night before to marvel at the elegance. It was built completely out of a brown-red brick with trellises and balconies elaborately sculpted throughout the structure. Beautiful vines were growing against the walls and bright pink and purple flowers were in bloom on the vines. Elly took pleasure in admiring the castle as Troy walked with her around its parameters.

"I have been meaning to ask you," Elly said as they strolled through a grassy field behind the castle that was beginning to bloom with flowers, "about the girl who brought me my dinner last night." For some reason, the girl had stuck in her mind and would not go away. The girl's strange behavior had somewhat disturbed Elly.

"Who was that?" Troy asked as he picked a beautiful purple flower from the grass and handed it to Elly.

"I do not know who she was," Elly answered, twirling the flower between her fingers. "That is why I wanted to ask you about her. When she came into my room last night, I spoke to her but she did not respond to me." Elly looked thoughtful for a moment then said, "It was as though she could not hear me."

"That must have been Jerran who came to your room last night." Troy explained. "Jerran is deaf and mute."

"You mean she cannot talk or hear?" Elly asked, astonished.

Troy nodded. "She had problems when she was born- very complicated ones. Within a few years of her birth, she lost both her voice and her hearing. But you can communicate with her, through your mind but that takes time to master. Right now, only mother and I and a few other servants are really able to communicate with her."

"That is amazing," Elly said, shaking her head.

"Indeed, it is," Troy agreed. "She is a very special girl."

They were now standing only a few feet from the stables which were located on the east side of the castle.

"Would you like to go for a ride?" Troy asked turning to face Elly. "We have a spectacular breed of horses and-" He stopped short when he noticed the stricken look on Elly's face. "Elly, what is wrong?"

Elly was standing as if she were frozen in place, her face filled with fear as she stared at the stables. Her dream from last night came crashing down on her like a tidal wave.

"Horses," Elly mumbled, shaking her head vigorously. "I do not want to see the horses." She could see the velvet black horse that the woman had been riding, spinning around inside her head. Elly tried to stop the image but it refused to release its hold on her mind. Elly felt herself becoming dizzy.

"Elly, what are you talking about?" Troy asked puzzled as he placed his hands on her shoulder to steady her.

"Her horse," Elly said in a barely audible whisper, "is in there. I can feel it."

Troy's eyes darkened momentarily. "Who's horse? Elly, what are you trying to tell me?"

Elly closed her eyes and took in a deep breath, trying to calm herself down. "She died on one of the horses in that stable." Elly said this softly hoping that Troy would not hear her but, he did.

"Who died?" Troy's face had also paled upon hearing Elly's words and his hands shook lightly as he held on to Elly's shoulders. "Who?" he repeated sounding a bit harsh this time.

"Your sister..." Elly dropped her head, not daring to look at Troy. There were tears in her eyes and she was fighting hard to keep them in check.

"How did you know that?" he asked softly, as he lifted her chin up with his hand, forcing her to meet his gaze.

"I-I slept in her nightgown last night- I had a dream." Elly began to cry softly as she recounted her dream to Troy.

"The horse was not responsible for her death," he told Elly once she was done. "It was not his fault."

Elly looked puzzled. "I do not understand. What do you mean?"

"He killed her," Troy answered simply not bothering to explain who 'he' was. Troy's eyes were fierce now, as the memories came back to him.

Elly still did not understand.

"Come," Troy took her hand. "Let us ride out to the lake on the other side of the hills. I will explain everything to you there." Slowly, they made their way down towards the stables. Elly felt a chill snake up her back as they entered the place.

"That there is Maine," Troy said pointing to a huge velvet black horse in a stall near the front of the stable. "That is the horse she was riding that day." His voice was sad with the memories of what had happened. Elly recognized the horse immediately. The way it stood with its head thrown back, its mane falling over on one side, its deep dark brown eyes...

Elly shook her head, desperately trying to clear her mind.

Without saying another word, Troy turned away from Elly and walked further back into the stable. He came back a few minutes later with two horses, one on either side of him. "You can ride Rancee," Troy told her as he handed the reins to the light brown horse with the white stripe down its nose to her. "And I will ride Shadow." Troy petted the gray horse that stood on his left.

Once the horses were saddled and ready to go, they headed out through the field, making their way towards the hills on the other side. They rode on until they reached a meadow that was deep within the hills. There, Troy halted his horse and dismounted.

"Why are we stopping?" Elly asked as she pulled up next to him. She could see no sign of a lake nearby.

"Because we will have to walk the rest of the way," Troy explained. "The lake is at the edge of the meadow and the only way we can get there is by walking. It will be harder if we have to maneuver the horses through the meadow. Here." He took Rancee's rein while Elly dismounted and then he led the two horses over to a large oak tree and secured them to it. Troy then took Elly's hand and led her down a narrow path that led into the meadow. Several minutes later, they were out of the meadow and, looking down from the slope where she stood, Elly could see a grassy bank a short distance away that was peppered with flowers and a beautiful lake that shimmered in the bright sunlight.

"It is beautiful," Elly commented as Troy led her down another path that took them out to the bank.

"Now," Troy said once they had settled themselves comfortably on the bank, "let me begin." He took a deep breath and closed his eyes for a moment, collecting his thoughts. Opening his eyes once more, he looked intently at Elly and began his story.

"Cierah, my sister, was a very beautiful girl and she was also very talented. She loved music and could play almost any instrument you can imagine beautifully. One day, she met this man, a very nice man, so he seemed. He claimed himself to be a rich merchant who had traveled over many planets to make his fortune. He said that he had heard many wondrous stories about the Golden City, which happen to be where you are now, and had come a long way just to visit and explore the place, and hopefully make some more money while he was at it. Cierah instantly fell in love with him and after a time, the two of them became inseparable. He would regularly come to the castle, and the two of them would sit out in the field all day long and just talk, happy by simply being in each other's company. Cierah would play her music for him and he became very much enthralled with both her and her music.

"But something happened one day between the two of them that angered my sister very badly. She never told me or mother what it was and still today no one really knows what went wrong or why. We suspect that perhaps she had found out who he really was and decided that she did not want to have anything to do with him. Anyway, after that, she refused to see him anymore. She ordered the guards to keep him away, and all day she would sit inside her room brooding and crying. By the way, I should mention that my mother was against her seeing him from the beginning, claiming that he was not who he said he was and nothing more. But, of course, Cierah would not listen. After a while I had even begun to grow wary of the man for some unknown reason. Cierah accused us of trying to spoil her happiness, so we left her alone, hoping that she would come to her senses on her own."

Troy shook his head, remembering how Cierah had adamantly defended the man against his and his mother's accusations. "After my sister ended their relationship, the man stopped coming by and shortly after that, my sister came out of her gloom and was once more her old cheerful self. My mother and I were relieved, sure that this whole mess was finally over and, as we later found out, it turned out that the man really was not who he had claimed to be. He was just a simple commoner who was lucky enough to be able to squirm his way into Cierah's life." There was bitterness in Troy's voice as he said those words.

"But, of course, we were wrong; the mess was nowhere near over. It was just the beginning. Several weeks later after my sister had finally gotten herself back together, he showed up again out of nowhere."

"What was his name?" Elly inquired.

"His name was Bali," Troy answered. "And believe me, he was no ordinary commoner. He begged my sister to take him back, but she refused and once more, she ordered the guards to keep him away from the castle. After that, things were all right again for a while. But then, my sister started seeing things, becoming delirious to the point where she would run through the castle, screaming as though she were being chased by demons. She could not sleep at night because she would have terrible nightmares haunting her constantly. She soon started getting sick with fevers, headaches, rashes. You name it, she had it." He stopped for a moment to catch his breath, overcome by the emotions that he was feeling. Elly reached over and took his hand in hers and squeezed it gently. He squeezed her hand back in response then continued.

"He came back again one day, got past the guards and broke into the castle. My mother tried to stop him but he only laughed at her and told her that Cierah's life was at stake and he was the only one who could save her. 'I hear that she has been having a little problem controlling her sanity,' he had said sarcastically to my mother."

"You were there?" Elly interrupted.

Troy nodded. "Yes, I was there out of sight, of course. I did not want him to see me. I watched him as he made his way up the stairs into my sister's room where she was lying sick with fever. When she saw him, she jumped out of bed and started yelling at him weakly. He pretended not to hear a thing she said. 'I came here to offer you a proposition,' he said to her with a sneer. 'If you marry me, I will spare your life and cast off the spells that I have placed upon you. If you do not, I will simply turn my back and watch you die. Believe me, you will only live long enough to regret having crossed me. Cierah had yelled at him, 'I will never marry you! You are a despicable man!' The words were barely out of her mouth before she was running out of her room, past Bali, out of the castle to the stables where she got on Maine and rode off. Till this day, I still do not know why she did that. The only solution I could come up with is that Bali made her do it. I do not know." Troy looked at Elly and shook his head, a troubled expression on his face.

"You do not have to continue," she told him as a tear ran down her cheek. She had a pretty good idea of what happened next.

"It is all right," he assured her, "I want to tell you the whole thing." He turned away and stared into the deep green water of the lake as he continued.

"He followed her, chasing after her through the fields and, of course, I followed close behind him, not quite sure about what he was planning to do. The hills back here were not always so lush and covered with grass," he explained. "It used to be all rocks and mountain areas a few years back. Anyway, once they got into the rocky terrain, Bali suddenly halted and yelled something at Cierah who was only a few feet ahead of him. I could not hear what he had said because a forceful wind had started blowing. But I know she heard what he said because suddenly she glanced back at him and the look on her face was nothing but horror." Troy's body became tense and he gripped Elly's hand tightly.

"It was at that moment that the horse started going wild. I tried to catch up with her so that I could help, but he knew, he had known all along that I had been following them and he kept me back...froze me there where I was until it was too late. Then he turned his horse around and rode away, leaving her there to die." Troy stopped, choking on his words. He turned and looked at Elly, tears streaming down his face. She, too, was crying silently by his side. Elly did not know what to do or say to him. So, she sat there holding on tightly to his hand as though to keep him from drowning in his sorrows as the tears spilled forth from him.

"I tried to save her," Troy explained once he had regained control of himself. "But she would not let me. She said if she lived through this, he would only return to torture her again and he would keep doing so until she killed herself by her own hands. She told me that she had rather die now and be at peace." He shook his head in disbelief. "I do not know why I did it, but I listened to her and did as she wished. She died in my arms not more than five minutes later. Sometimes, I still cannot believe that she is gone and I know the nightmares will never end."

Elly thought to tell him about how Cierah's painting had reminded her of Aimer's little sister, Christina, but something held her back.

Instead, she asked, "What happened to Bali?"

Troy shrugged. "No one knows. He disappeared after that and has never been seen since which is a good thing because had I laid eyes on him after that, I would have killed him for sure." He sighed and looked up at Elly, staring into her dark green eyes. "I guess Cierah is one of the reasons why mother and I are so concerned about you and your situation," he said after a long pause.

"What do you mean?" Elly inquired.

"Don't you see? You are almost exactly in the same position that Cierah was in with Bali. True, he never threatened to destroy the planet, but I am sure he would have done so had he been given the opportunity. But he did take Cierah's life, just as Navar had threatened to take yours. Believe me Elly, I do not want you to come to the same end my sister did. My mother and I will do our best to protect you through this, I swear."

Elly was deeply moved by his words. "Thank you," she said to him softly and slowly, she leaned forward kissing him lightly on the cheek. He smiled in response, his eyes glowing brightly.

"Speaking of which," he said, breaking the moment, although he really did not want to. "We better head back to the castle." He glanced to the east where the sun was slowly sinking below the mountains, leaving behind a beautiful trail of purple and pink light that radiated off the clear surface of the lake. "Mother and I will be heading to Sarcaun later tonight along with our own Battle men. From the news that was brought to us earlier before you were awake, Navar has already attacked another city, and they need some serious back up. The man is insane and has to be stopped as soon as possible or else-" He cut himself short when he realized what he was about to say.

"Or else my home will be completely demolished," Elly finished for him in a small voice.

Troy turned away, unsure of what he should say to her.

"I want to go with you," Elly impulsively told him.

"No!" Troy answered adamantly, swiftly turning towards her. "If you are even considering doing a thing like that, then you are just as crazy as Navar. You are safer here. You must stay." His eyes blazed in anger and it startled Elly to see him so upset.

But despite his reaction, Elly just shook her head sadly as she stared across the bank to where the sun was slowly continuing its descent and said, "I will never be safe anywhere until he is dead."

They were silent for a long while and Elly's words hung in the air. They both knew that much danger lay ahead and the outcome, if the situation was not handled quickly and appropriately, could be devastating. Finally, Troy jumped up from where he sat and offered Elly his hand.

"Let us go, Princess," Troy said, smiling lightly. "There is much work for me to take care of before mother and I head off." Elly nodded solemnly as Troy pulled her up to her feet.

Silently, they made their way back through the meadow to where the horses were waiting for them. When they were back at the castle, they discovered that dinner was ready and they went and joined Norla in the dining room. Unlike at breakfast, Elly did not enjoy her dinner very much. She was too absorbed in her thoughts, wondering how her family was dealing with this whole mess and concerned for her mother's welfare. Finding out that Navar was attacking her home again did not help improve her appetite. Afterwards, Elly excused herself and went up to her room to lie down for a while. She was exhausted. Climbing into bed, she closed her eyes and fell soundlessly asleep.

CHAPTER TWENTY-EIGHT

Before leaving, Norla and Troy came to check on Elly to see if she needed anything. Troy even suggested that maybe she should come with them instead of being left in the castle alone. He said this remembering what Elly had told him earlier about not being safe anywhere; he was afraid to leave her alone for fear of what may happen while he and his mother were away. He could not figure it out, but he sensed that there was something wrong, he could feel it in the air. His instincts were incredibly sharp and clear and he was rarely ever misguided so when his instinct sensed danger, he was certain that it was lurking around somewhere just waiting to rear its ugly head.

Yet he seemed to be the only one who noticed the sudden chance in the atmosphere. There was an electrical charge in the air that pricked the hairs on the back of his neck. Unfortunately, his mother was against the idea of taking Elly along completely, saying it was too dangerous and Elly sat sullenly on her bed, not seeming to care whether she stayed or went.

"Whatever is going to happen will happen anyway," Elly had said to them almost as though she were in a trance. "No matter what." And those words had sent a cold chill up Troy's back.

In the end, though, it was decided that Elly would stay and Norla would return as soon as possible to be with her. Troy was not completely satisfied with that, but what choice did he have? His mother would not relent to his suggestion that she should come with them. So, he departed with his mother, with trepidation, leaving Elly behind, alone.

Elly did not mind being alone. She was tired and worn out by the events that had been taking place in her life lately. In her wildest dreams, Elly would have never believed that her life could be turned upside down so completely. She felt depression closing in around her and as hard as she tried, she could not keep it away. There were no positive thoughts to hold on to. Everything appeared hopeless to her, she saw no possible way out-at least not alive.

Sighing deeply, Elly crawled out of bed, trying to push the dark thoughts that were crowding her mind away. She would take a nice hot bath, she decided, to relax and then she would turn in for the night. After bathing, Elly closed the curtains, turned out the light and crawled back into bed. She was asleep instantly.

Elly's dreams were filled with dark shadows that were chasing her around relentlessly, desperately trying to smother her to death. The shadows were not faceless beings, but ones that she recognized. Navar, of course, was the foremost in pursuit and Elly could virtually see the evil pouring out from him, primarily in his eyes; they burned angrily with hatred and a hunger to destroy that momentarily crippled Elly in her flight.

He forced her to run from him until her legs threatened to buckle under her. When she could not run from him any longer, she was forced to plead to him, begging him to spare her life and the life of the others that he so much wanted to destroy. But there was no mercy to be found from him, and once more he forced her to run, laughing as she did for, he knew she could not get very far before she would finally give up.

When she finally did give up out of fatigue, he was upon her instantly, tearing her slowly to pieces. Her screams pierced through the darkness, causing the other demons that had been after her to flee. And Navar laughed gleefully, his eyes gleaming red in the darkness, as he continued to torture her, tearing the life out of her piece by piece. Elly woke up with a start, gasping for air, the screams from her dreams echoing loudly in her ears. Despite the fact that she was perspiring profusely, she was shaking violently as though someone had drenched her with a bucket of ice water.

It had all seemed so real. Her body was aching, as though she really had been torn to pieces. Her heart pounded heavily in her chest, and her breathing was harsh and labored.

Troy, where are you?! her mind cried out. She did not want to be alone anymore. She wished she had taken the opportunity to convince Norla to let her come with them when Troy had opened the window for her with his suggestion.

But now it was too late. She was frightened and there was no one there to reassure her that everything would be all right.

Elly leaned back against the pillows and tried to calm herself down. She was still shaking violently but there was no one nearby that she could call to. She was afraid to leave the room, afraid to get out of bed, for that matter. So, she laid there for what seemed like forever, staring up at the white ceiling, wishing she was safely home in her own bedroom, wishing that the nightmare would come to an end.

Finally, after what seemed like hours, her heart settled and her breathing became normal again. And although she did not want to and tried desperately to fight against it, her eyes were growing heavy with sleep again. Soon, she slipped into oblivion once more, where, she knew, the shadows were waiting to chase her into madness once again.

But the shadows never came. Instead, she slept rather fitfully for a long time, slipping in and out of dreams, none of which she was able to get a grasp on; forgetting one just before she slipped into another.

Suddenly, her senses became aware that there was someone else in the room with her, watching. She forced herself out of her sleep and looked around the room. It was still dark outside and could see that the sun was just barely starting to make its ascent over the distant horizon. It would be dawn soon.

"Troy?" she called out softly, hesitantly as she untangled herself from the sheets and reached towards the night table to turn on the light. But no one responded.

She flipped on the light and turned her head to the left and immediately, her heart froze.

Right by the foot of her bed, leaning against the footboard stood Navar, watching her intently as though she were a puzzle he was trying to solve. He did not look like the Navar she had met on Aeshern. The man who stood at the foot of her bed was a man filled with rage and eager to destroy anything and everything around him. He was wearing Battle man clothing that were torn and dirty, covered with mud and blood from battle. His hair was filthy and disheveled and his face was covered with a thick beard that was also filthy and unkempt, as though he had not shaved in weeks.

He slowly walked around to the side of Elly's bed where the night table was, leaned down and peered down at her with a smug, cruel smile on his face. There was fire in his eyes and they bore into Elly with such intensity that Elly felt he could see right through her. She pulled the sheets up close around her in a feeble attempt to protect herself.

"Navar," Elly whispered his name in disbelief as her heart sank. She desperately hoped that this was still only part of one of her dreams, but her senses told her otherwise.

"Now come, Elly," Navar said mockingly, his deep voice vibrating through the room. "Do not look so disappointed. Did you honestly believe that you could hide from me?" He laughed loudly and the sound that came forth from him was cold and mirthless.

Elly felt her heart flutter in her chest and although she had begun to perspire, she felt cold shooting through every part of her being.

She was trapped, she knew. This time, there was no way out. "What do you want?" she asked icily, trying to stay in control of herself.

"What do I want?" Navar repeated, as he pretended to think her question through. "Why, you of course, my sweet." He chuckled and reached out to brush her hair away from her face. Elly jerked out of his reach, pulling the sheets up tightly about her.

Navar pretended not to notice her reaction to him as he continued to speak. "You are the only one I have wanted to get my hands on, Elly. Everything else was simply a distraction. Now it is time to get down to business."

In an instant, and without really thinking about it, Elly bolted out of the bed and headed straight for the door. Navar did not even flinch and Elly quickly found out why. She turned the doorknob and pulled but nothing happened. The door was locked apparently from the outside since there was no lock on the inside that Elly could see.

Elly turned and faced Navar, her back pressed against the locked door. There was fear in her eyes.

"What do you want from me?!" she screamed at him.

"You will find out soon enough, my sweet," he answered her, his voice cold as ice. He came around the bed and within seconds was standing in front of Elly, holding her tightly by her left wrist, pulling her close to him. Elly squirmed and tried to pull herself free, but it was useless. His grip was like an iron vise.

"Not this time, Elly," Navar informed her. "You are not going to get away again." With that, he grabbed her by the waist, lifted her up and swung her over his shoulder like a useless bag, holding her tightly in place with his right arm. With his free hand, he grabbed the handle of the door and twisted it to the left. The lock broke and the door swung open and he swiftly made his way down the hall to the left towards the stairs at the other end.

"Do not bother yelling," Navar warned her. "No one will hear you."

But Elly screamed anyway. She screamed at the top of her lungs until her throat became parched and raw. And still, she screamed.

"Enough!" Navar yelled at her as he tightened his grip around her waist. "Stop or I will finish you right now!" Elly complied and went still as she desperately tried to find a way to get herself out of this predicament. She worked on keeping her head up as much as possible to keep the blood from rushing to her head and making her pass out. That was the last thing she needed right now.

They were about halfway down the first floor hallway when Elly spotted a door that was opened just a crack. Instinctively, without even thinking, Elly began to yell and scream, kicking her legs in every direction. Caught off guard, Navar stopped in the middle of the hallway and loosened his grip around Elly's waist. That was all that Elly needed to make a move. With a burst of energy, she planted her hands on Navar's back and rolled herself off Navar's shoulders and landed with a loud thud on the cold granite floor on her side. She felt excruciating pain shoot through her left shoulder.

Clenching her teeth against the pain, she started pushing herself off the floor but Navar grabbed her ankle and pulled, causing her to sprawl back on the ground on her stomach. Desperately wanting to escape, she quickly rolled to the left onto her back and swung with her free right foot and caught Navar squarely in the jaw. Stunned he dropped Elly's foot and fell backwards.

In a split second, Elly was on her feet, heading for the open door just a few feet away to the left. She flew through the door and slammed the door shut behind her and was grateful to see that there was a deadbolt to keep the door locked. Navar was pounding furiously on the door just moments after the lock fell into place. Fortunately, the door was thick and made of steel- Navar would not be getting through anytime soon.

But Elly was not about to take any chances. She pressed her back against the door and surveyed the room. She was in some sort of storage room filled with various boxes and other items that apparently have not been used in a long time as everything was covered with dust and cob webs. She needed to find a way out. Carefully, she skirted her way around the boxes towards the back of the room hoping to find another door or a window she could escape from.

As she made her way between two stacks of boxes, her hand brushed against something hard in the crevice of one of the boxes she was holding onto to support herself. She stopped and yanked at the object and was surprised to discover that it was an average sized sheathed knife with a sharp, curved blade and two leather strips on the side. This could definitely come in handy, Elly decided as she quickly tied the knife around her thigh so that her hands could be free.

She did not stay distracted for long as she could still hear Navar pounding on the door behind her. She was dusty and covered with cobwebs by the time she got to the other side of the room. There was a narrow space about three feet wide between her and the wall but there was no window nor was there a door on either side, as far as Elly could see. The only way out seemed to be the same way she came in through the door she had entered. But Elly knew that was not an option.

What should I do now? Elly thought wildly looking around, tears stinging her eyes. She could not go back, Navar would get her for sure. There had to be another way out of here. Elly began to pace the floor and when she had gone halfway to the left of the room, she heard a loud squeak when she took another step. Pausing in mid stride, she knelt down and moved the rug that covered the floor.

At first, she did not see anything but then she saw the outline of what appeared to be a trapped door. After running her hand on the floor a few times her fingers finally fell into a small grove which turned out to be a latch. She struggled with the latch for a few minutes before it gave way and it was another minute before she was able to pull the trap door open. She peered down the entrance and was able to see that there was a steel ladder on the side but other than that everything else was dark.

Oh, well, Elly sighed, there is no other way out. Taking in a deep breath, Elly lowered herself through the trap door and hung on to the ladder with one hand to keep from falling while she pulled the door closed with the other. She was not going to take any chances. In the dark, she continued down the ladder slowly until her feet touched cold concrete. The room she found herself in appeared vast and empty and even though the immediate area was dark Elly could see a light in the distance to her left.

As she made her way towards the light her feet became frozen with cold and she was shivering intensely. She desperately wished she at least had a robe on and a pair of slippers to keep her warm. When she reached the source of the light, she was relieved to see that it was a window that was about two feet above the ground and reached almost to the ceiling.

She quickly pushed the window open and felt a rush of cool morning air against her skin. Maybe there was hope after all. She closed her eyes for a moment and gulped in the clean air which her lungs desperately needed after being cooped up in that dusty, cob web filled room. But she did not relax for long before she pushed out the screen in the window and hoisted herself up through the window and out onto the cool, wet grass. She looked around and noticed that she was on the east side of the castle towards where the thick woods were and she knew that on the other side was where the stables were located. She wondered if maybe she could reach the stable to get a horse to escape on.

But before she could decide what to do, she felt a sharp blow to the right side of her head that sent her sprawling on her stomach. Touching the side of her stinging head she looked up to see Navar reaching towards her, a look of pure rage and hatred on his countenance.

"No," she moaned as she tried to crawl away. She could not let him catch her now, not after the struggle she went through to escape. She suddenly remembered the knife she had found in the storage room and strapped to her thigh. She reached for it and her hand touched the handle just as she felt Navar grab her left leg. She quickly grabbed the knife from its sheath and in one quick motion she turned and swung to the right towards Navar, aiming for his right arm that was holding her leg.

The knife sliced through the material of Navar's shirt and went straight through to his right forearm causing a wide, ugly gash all the way to his elbow. He yelped in pain and surprise as blood started streaming down his arm and immediately let go of Elly's leg. Elly instantly scrambled to her feet, shoved Navar over and started running while Navar was still on his back, shocked by what had just happened. Elly ran as fast as her feet could carry her, down a slope and around towards the east side of the castle where she knew the stables were.

She reached the stables, yanked one of the doors open and looked around wildly. She was disoriented and could not seem to focus long enough to find Rancee, the horse she had ridden with Troy just the day before, so she let the first horse she saw out of its stall. To her terror, she discovered that the horse she had chosen was Maine, the horse Troy's sister had been riding when she had been trying to escape from Bali. Elly's heart skipped a beat but she realized that there was no time to hesitate; she needed to act fast. She threw a saddle on the horse and quickly put the reins on him.

Within minutes she was riding out of the stables going south in the direction of where the bridge was. She was hoping to get to a village to get help because she did not trust going back into the castle. Navar could trap her in there and she may never find a way out again. She was only several feet from the bridge when she saw a figure riding out towards her. Even though the rider was still a considerable distance away, she instinctively knew that it was Navar. She maneuvered the horse around and headed back in the direction that she had originally come from.

She urged the horse forward and was galloping at full speed. She reached the slope she had climbed down from just a short while earlier and had to slow down and gently guide the horse up the slope. She had no problem encouraging the horse until they were halfway to the top. For no reason that Elly could tell, the horse suddenly became agitated and refused to cooperate. Regardless of what Elly did, the horse would not budge and she realized that they were losing ground as the horse started stepping backwards.

"No!" Elly screamed, panicking. "Don't do this, please." Tears were streaming down her face.

The horse paid no attention to Elly. Instead, he continued to resist her efforts to get him to move forward. Suddenly, without warning, the horse reared, taking Elly completely by surprise. Her hand slipped from the reins and she felt herself falling backwards. In that instant, the image of Cierah flying off of her horse and landing on the rocks flashed through Elly's mind. She landed in a heap at the bottom of the slope. Her body ached from the fall but, thankfully, she was still alive and able to move.

Gritting her teeth against the pain, she forced herself to her feet. She looked around and noticed that the horse was gone. She looked to the left and could see him galloping away. I guess I am on my own, she thought sullenly and began climbing up the slope. The climb up was slow and very painful but after what seemed like hours to Elly, she finally reached the top. Elly took in a few deep breaths to get herself in control. She was shaking from the experience she had just had and did not know what she should do from here.

She had to fight, she decided. She could not just give up now. There had to be a way to get herself out of this mess.

Looking around, she realized that she was back in the same place where Navar had caught up to her before she had escaped, for the second time, and a few feet ahead of her were the woods. Without taking another moment to even hesitate, Elly headed straight into the woods.

The woods Elly found herself surrounded by were thick and tightly packed with huge towering trees all around. There were flower and strange looking shrubs, along with other plants, growing everywhere. As soon as Elly was several feet into the forest, she stopped running. She needed to get her bearing before going on any farther. Maybe there was a way she could circle around the forest and head back in the direction of the castle so she could reach the bridge. Maybe then she would be able to find someone who would be willing to help her.

Before it was too late.

Elly finally decided to head to the right, carefully mapping her way through the thick trees and brushes. She had no shoes on, making her travel even harder. Rocks poked at her bare feet and thorns from the flowers scraped against her legs. Soon, she heard thunder rolling in the distance and within seconds she was completely soaked, drenched by the onslaught of rain. But still she continued to pick her way through the forest.

She slipped several times, falling and rolling in the now muddy dirt from the rain. Her nightgown was torn in places and her feet and legs were sore from the rocks and the thorns. The nightgown had been long, covering her feet, so she had ripped it up to the knees to keep from tripping over. Now there was barely anything left of it. A strong wind picked up, blowing the rain directly at her, blurring her vision even more.

Elly did not know how long she had traveled before she finally collapsed at the base of a huge tree. She was exhausted, cold and wet from the rain. Her muscles screamed and her head ached. Elly began to cry softly, her tears mixing in with the falling rain. There was no way she was going to survive this. No matter how far she got, death would be waiting to take her at the other end she was certain.

Her exhaustion was overwhelming and Elly found herself slowly drifting off to sleep. She struggled and fought to keep herself awake, but to no avail. Finally, she gave in to her fatigue. Leaning her head back against the tree her eyes slipped closed and she fell asleep while the rain continued to beat coldly against her body, undeterred.

After what seemed like only a few minutes to Elly, her eyes immediately flew open as she felt the ground begin to shake underneath her, jolting her out from her slumber.

"What is happening?" Elly muttered in confusion. And then, it hit her and she became fully awake and alert.

An earthquake.

Elly panicked, not knowing what to do. She had never experienced an earthquake before, she had only heard about them. She never even believed that they existed, until now.

She had been sitting on a slight slope when she had fallen asleep and it was slowly beginning to slip away from under her as the ground continued to roll underneath her with a loud thunderous sound. The rain had stopped, but the ground was still slick and wet. Elly screamed in horror as she began to slip and slide uncontrollably down the slope. She grabbed at the shrubs that were near her, trying desperately to stop her descent, but they simply slipped between her fingers or uprooted from the earth like pieces of liquid paper.

Down Elly fell until her hands caught around a sapling tree that had managed to somehow stay rooted to the ground despite its vicious rumbling. Elly wrapped both hands about the thin trunk of the tree and hung on for dear life, all the while praying that it would hold until she was able to further secure herself.

Elly glanced down from where she hung and instantly wished she had not.

Below her, just inches from where she hung, the ground opened into a huge gaping hole that was almost ten feet across and as the earthquake rumbled on, Elly watched as it began to grow wider, as if preparing itself to swallow her up once she fell.

Elly fought to control herself. It was another five minutes before the earthquake finally subsided and the earth became still again.

Elly sighed in relief, even though she knew she was still in danger. The sapling oak was slowly bending under her weight. It would not be long before it uprooted, sending Elly down into the gaping hole that awaited her below.

She had to do something- and fast. But there was nothing else in sight that Elly could use to support herself or climb back up the slope with. Only dirt and loose shrubs surrounded her.

Navar is not going to kill me, after all! Elly thought. Because I am going to end up dying right here! Tears of frustration formed in her eyes and Elly had to fight to keep them in check.

"You are not going to die here," Elly heard a soft crystalline voice say from above her.

Glancing up, Elly saw a young girl's head with long corn silk yellow hair leaning over the edge of the slope. Her eyes were a deep green.

"Christina!" Elly cried out in a whisper filled with surprise, for that was who it reminded her of but Elly realized it could not be Christina because the girl looked older than the seven-year-old she remembered Christina to be from earth. If this was not Christina, then- "Cierah?" Elly whispered to herself. Was it possible? But how? She was dead.

"You ask too many questions," the girl said, an amused smile on her face. "I am here, that is what matters. Here," she threw a rope down to Elly. "Grab onto this, I will pull you up."

I must be hallucinating, Elly told herself. This is impossible! But even as those thoughts crossed her mind, she did not hesitate to grab onto the rope when it reached her, gripping it tightly with both hands. And, to her amazement, Elly felt herself beginning to rise up towards the slope's edge as the girl pulled on the rope from above. Before she knew it, she was at the edge of the cliff and the girl was pulling her up by her arm the rest of the way. Elly laid there on the ground for a few moments without speaking, trying to catch her breath and recover from what had just befallen her. She was lying on her back so she rolled over, catching a glimpse over the edge of the cliff, and pulled herself up into a sitting position.

"Who are you?" she asked the girl when she was finally able to speak.

"I am your friend," the girl answered simply. "Now, come. We must go before it is too late. I know a quicker way out of here." She took Elly's hand and hauled her up to her feet.

Elly felt as though she were in some sort of strange, fluid dream as she followed the girl through the forest. The girl was tall and slim and looked to be about Cierah's age from the painting in the room she had been using. Elly could not get over the resemblance to both Cierah and Christina the girl had.

Elly quickly discovered that the girl was very agile and apparently, she knew her way very well around the woods for she pulled Elly through the maze of trees expertly and without the slightest hesitation. And what was even more amazing to Elly was the fact that the girl was wearing a long white gown yet managed to move without difficulty and without getting even a smudge of dirt on the gown.

But soon, Elly grew tired and was not able to keep up with the girl's fast pace anymore; she needed to rest. She said as much to the girl as she leaned herself against a tree. She was also hungry. How long had they been traveling through the forest? Elly wondered. She had lost track of time. The girl found some wild berries and roots for Elly to eat. Elly consumed them within seconds without even bothering to ask what they were exactly. She had not realized how hungry she was until then. She could not even remember when she had last eaten.

But the girl would only let her rest for a few minutes, saying that they were running out of time.

Elly did not know how long they traveled before they finally broke out of the forest into an open field of grass. Elly was so thrilled that she would have laughed and jumped for joy had she not been so tired and scared.

Silently, they began to make their way across the field.

CHAPTER TWENTY-NINE

They were barely halfway across the field when he caught up with them. He was riding his black horse and charging towards them at full gallop.

Elly froze when she saw him.

"Come on!" the girl urged, pulling Elly along behind her. But Elly's legs could not carry her very far. Her legs buckled beneath her and she landed in a heap in the middle of the field.

Her dream from the previous night came crashing down on her like a lead weight.

The shadows. Her cries.

It had only been a dream but, Elly realized it was about to become a part of her reality.

Realizing Elly's plight, the girl stood protectively in front of Elly, her legs spread apart and her arms crossed before her.

"You!" Navar screamed as he came closer to them and jumped off his horse. He had a finger pointed towards the girl and an ugly look on his face.

"Stay away from her, Navar," the girl warned, her eyes icy with anger.

And in that moment, Elly realized that the girl who stood before her was only a young girl in appearance. Her voice was filled with wisdom and age. She was definitely something other than what she appeared to be.

And Navar knew this, too.

"You, my friend, are no match for me. Get out of my way!"

"As you wish," the girl said. But she did not get out of his way. Instead, she jumped- no, leaped towards him in a single motion and

Elly watched in fascination as the girl turned into a creature that Elly was not able to put a name to as she flew through the air towards Navar. She landed square on his chest, knocking him over backwards. Navar screamed. The beast momentarily turned in her direction.

"Go!" she heard it scream at her. Instantly, Elly was on her feet. And as the creature began to wrestle with Navar, scratching his face, and tearing his clothes, Elly began to run back in the direction of the forest as fast as her legs could carry her, without even glancing back. But she did look back just before she entered the forest. She turned just in time to see Navar hoist the creature up over his head and throw it at a nearby tree. The creature roared in pain as it slid to the ground.

It was no longer an animal; it had turned back into the young girl again.

And she was not moving from where she laid.

"Cierah!" Elly screamed at the top of her lungs, calling the girl by the only name she knew for her.

Do not worry about me, she heard the girl say in her mind. I will be fine. Now go. Save yourself.

Without further hesitation, Elly disappeared back into the woods. Once in the woods, Elly stumbled a few times and fought to maintain her footing. Breathing heavily, she leaned against a tree to catch her breath. She had no idea of how long she had been stumbling through the forest. She was lost, she knew. Without Cierah to guide her she had no idea where she was or what direction she was going in. To make matters worse, it was getting dark out and very little light was coming through the thick trees. Elly knew she needed to find a place to hide before it got too dark but had no idea where to go from here. She was ragged, tired and extremely hungry. She did not have any energy to keep going.

But she knew staying in place was not good; it would almost guarantee that Navar would find her. Taking in a deep breath, she started pushing her way through the forest once more. She had not gone far when she stumbled again, this time falling to her knees as tears streamed down her face. Covering her face with her hands she tried to control her sobbing and fought to overcome an incredible desire to just give up.

Still on her knees, she wiped the tears from her eyes and quickly surveyed the area she was in as best as she could. She could not see very far in front of her but she could have sworn she saw something that looked like a cave carved out of the side of the hill. Elly realized she must have reached the other side of the forest opposite from where the field Cierah had led her had been. Not wanting to get her hopes up, Elly slowly crawled through the forest towards the hill and her heart jumped when she was close enough to see that there was actually a cave in the hill.

Elly crawled inside and found that it was dark and narrow with barely enough room for her to stand in. She had no idea how deep the cave was but she kept going in deeper until the opening was dark and indistinguishable from the rest of the forest outside. Elly stopped going deeper only because she had no idea what was in the cave and was afraid of what she would encounter if she went any further. Also, she was exhausted and just wanted to rest for a while. Stopping where she was, Elly curled up against the side of the cave wall and fell asleep instantly.

While she slept, Elly felt as though she were flying, floating away somewhere. It took Elly a few minutes to realize that what she was feeling was not exactly a dream. Someone has taken her out of the cave and was caring her through the forest. It was dark and since she was not able to see anything, Elly panicked and instinctively began to struggle, trying to get whoever was carrying her to let go.

"Elly, relax! It is me, Troy."

"Troy?"

"Yes, Elly. Now go back to sleep."

"Navar-," Elly began but Troy cut her off.

"Do not worry about Navar. I will take care of everything. I promise. Now, close your eyes and rest."

Even though Elly did not want to, she felt her eyes giving in to her fatigue. Leaning her head on Troy's chest, Elly closed her eyes and fell soundly asleep.

When Elly woke up again, she found herself snuggly tucked into a warm bed in a room that she did not recognize. It was small with only the bed she was in and a desk covered with papers near the foot of the bed. Someone had washed her up and put a new light pink lace nightgown on her before putting her to bed. Suddenly, the events of the previous day came flooding back and Elly began shaking at the memory. It all seemed so surreal that if it were not for her aching muscles and bruises on her body, Elly would have been inclined to believe it had all just been a nightmare that she was just waking from.

Suddenly, there was a loud crash from somewhere outside and Elly immediately jumped out of bed and ran to a low window on the other side of the room. She was not able to see anything except for green rolling hills that expanded several miles. What she did see, though, was smoke coming up from between some of the hills.

"Oh, no," Elly whispered. She had a sinking feeling in her stomach and something told her that the smoke was not just burning wood. Turning away in despair, she noticed that there were some clothes stacked on a chair by the bed. Rummaging through them she found a comfortable pair of dark blue silk pants and a matching top that was long, wrapped around the front and tied in the back. Once she finished dressing, she was about to leave the room to go find out what was going on outside when Troy opened the door and stepped in.

"Elly? Where are you going? You should be in bed."

Elly hesitated then answered, "I just wanted to get some air."

"How are you?" he asked as he stepped further into the room. "You had us worried for a while. You have been sleeping for almost a whole day and no one could get you to wake up."

"I am fine," Elly assured him as she pushed the disturbing thoughts that had started to enter her mind away. "Where am I and how did you find me?" she wanted to know.

"You are in the lower level of the castle that leads to the tunnels. This is the only room that is above ground, which is why there is a window in here. We did not want to take you underground in case there was an emergency- we were not sure if you were all right. You gave us quite a scare." He paused for a moment, took Elly's hand and led her back to the bed, sat her down, and took a seat next to her and began telling her what happened from the time he left the castle.

"When Mother and I got to Sarcaun, we met with your father and the Battle men. Navar had pretty much obliterated the island along with a portion of the city before retreating. We figured the only reason he relented was because he realized you were no longer on the island. We were down in the tunnels planning on how we were going to go about finding Navar and stopping him when I got the strangest feeling in the pit of my stomach. I do not know exactly what it was but something kept telling me I needed to go back home. I tried ignoring the feeling but it just kept growing stronger. Finally, against my mother's wishes because she thought I was just being over protective, I left the meeting and came home. By the time I got here, you were gone and no one had any idea where you were nor had anyone seen anything that would help me figure out what had happened."

"So how did you find me?"

Troy took a deep breath, got up and started slowly pacing the room. Elly could tell that he was troubled but could not figure out why.

"Troy, what is the matter?" she asked as she settled back against the pillows and propped her feet up on the bed.

Troy shook his head. "I do not know if I should tell you this because you may end up thinking that I am crazy."

"Troy, no, I would not think such a thing. After all, you did find me and saved my life. Who knows what may have happened if I stayed out there any longer. Please, tell me what happened."

Troy stopped pacing and nervously ran his hand through his hair. He hesitated only for a moment then began telling Elly the rest of the story.

"Elly, this is going to sound very strange but Cierah is the one who led me to you." He said the words so fast that Elly wondered at first if she had heard him right.

"Did you say Cierah led you to me? How?" Yet even before the words were out of her mouth Elly already knew the answers to her questions but she said nothing as she waited for Troy to respond.

"I was sitting in Cierah's room on her bed trying to figure out what had happened when it seemed that I must have fallen asleep even though I felt like I was still wide awake. I saw Cierah standing in front of me, beautiful as ever wearing a long white gown. Her hair was flowing behind her as if the wind was blowing even though the window was closed and she seemed to radiate light. She held her hand out to me and said, 'Come with me, Troy. Elly needs your help.' I took her hand without even hesitating and instantly found myself in the woods floating through the trees. Moments later, I looked down and could see you stumbling through the trees. I could feel Navar somewhere in the area but I could not see him. I saw when you crawled into the cave and fell asleep."

"I do not know how it happened," he continued, "but I blinked and found myself back in Cierah's room sitting on the bed. Cierah was standing in front of me again. 'You must hurry and get to her,' Cierah was saying, 'she does not have much time and I have done all that I can to help her,' She took my hands and knelt in front of me before I could ask any questions. What she said to me next sent chills down my back. 'Troy, you must let go of the past and face your future. Please do this for me because if you do not both you and Elly will end up being destroyed and my soul will never rest if that should happen.' I started crying and said to her, 'Cierah, I love you and miss you so much.' She touched the side of my face and said, 'Troy, I will always love you and be in your heart. But now you need to go and do what you have to do before it is too late.' No sooner were those words out of her mouth, she disappeared and I was alone in her room again, completely shaken by what had just happened and her words kept ringing through my head."

Troy let out a deep breath and sat down at the edge of the bed. Elly was so overwhelmed by what she had just heard that she did not know what to say. She just sat there and quietly waited for Troy to continue.

"I did not have time to contemplate on everything that Cierah told me. I had to find you first. From what I saw in the woods I knew that you were somewhere on the other side of the woods but I was not exactly sure where. It took me a few hours but thankfully, I was able to find you. You had a slight fever when I found you and once you fell back asleep when I was carrying you back, I could not get you to wake up again. By that time Mother had come home and she felt so guilty about what had happened. She is the one who took care of you when I brought you back."

"Tell her I said thank you."

"She will be pleased to know that you are awake and all right. During the time that you were sleeping I have had some time to think about what Cierah had said to me and I realized that she was right; I needed to let go of the past. I still blame myself for what happened to her so many years ago and because of that I tend to shut everyone out of my life because I am afraid that they will get hurt because of me. I think somehow this was Cierah's way of saying she does not blame me for what happened and she did not want me blaming myself, either. Since I saw her, I have had such an incredible feeling of peace that never existed before within me. It is amazing."

"Troy, there is something I need to tell you," Elly took a deep breath and told Troy what had happened from the time he had left to return to Sarcaun until he found her in the cave. She told him how Cierah had appeared out of nowhere while she was hanging over the cliff during the earthquake and how she rescued her and led her through the forest up until she saw her fighting with Navar.

"I thought she was dead when I saw Navar throw her off like that," she confessed. "But now I realize that there is no way Navar could have destroyed her because she is alive forever right here." She touched Troy's chest indicating where his heart was. She could see tears welling up in Troy's eyes.

He shook his head and said, "This is amazing. I have never had such an experience in my life."

"You mean Cierah has never appeared to you before?"

"No, not like this. I have had dreams about her all the time but she had never appeared to me and talked to me the way she did the other day." He stood up and went to stand by the window and Elly felt a knot in her stomach as she stared out the window and wondered what was happening outside. As if reading her mind, Troy turned and regarded Elly closely. "Look, you need to get some rest. I will come back to see you later."

"Troy, wait I-" He interrupted her; it was as if he knew what she was going to ask him.

"We will talk some more later. Do not worry about anything." He turned and left the room before Elly could say anything else. Frustrated, Elly settled in her bed and finally fell into a fitful sleep that brought nightmares of Elly trying to escape Navar through the woods and being caught and tortured every time.

CHAPTER THIRTY

Elly woke up in a cold sweat, her heart pounding to the sound of chaos and gun fire outside. Elly thought she was still dreaming until another blast occurred and the room she was in shook on its foundation, jarring her fully awake. For an instant she thought that there was an earthquake happening until another blast shot out the bedroom window sending glass and stone everywhere. Elly screamed, fell to the floor and curled up in a ball to protect herself from the flying debris and glass.

"Elly! Elly, are you all right?" Troy ran into the room out of breath and covered in dirt.

"I am fine," Elly coughed as she climbed to her feet using the bed for support.

"We need to get out of here right now!" He grabbed Elly's hand and was about to lead her out of the room when he immediately stopped in his track as two Zirnam guards came crashing through the door with guns aimed and ready to fire. From what Elly could see the men looked exactly like what Lanaya had described to her. They were strange looking men: ghastly white but tall and muscular with eyes that were cold and calculating like a snake. Those eyes sent chills down Elly's spine as they bore into her. They were shouting in a language that Elly could not understand but one thing was clear: they were ready to kill them both without even hesitating.

"Elly, no matter what happens, stay behind me and do what I tell you," Troy whispered to her. Elly squeezed his hand in response as she was afraid to speak out loud. One of the troopers motioned for Elly to come forward but she pretended not to understand and stayed behind Troy. Slowly, Troy began taking a few steps back but stopped as warning shots were fired around them. The guards motioned for Troy to get down on the ground and he pretended not to understand. So, more shots were fired and once again they motioned Troy to the ground.

"All right, stop shooting," Troy said, holding his hands up in defeat. He bent his knees as if he were complying but in the next instant, he had pulled out his sword from his side, jumped in the air and kicked both men square in the chest causing them to drop their guns.

"Elly, get out of here!" Troy shouted as he kicked a gun out of reach of one of the guards who was now struggling to get up.

"I cannot leave you here," Elly yelled back tears streaming down her face. The other guard was also quickly recovering from the initial blow and was trying to get back on his feet.

"Elly, please," Troy pleaded, "you must go now before it is too late. Do not worry about me." He kicked the guard on the left in the stomach and sent him sprawling against the back wall. "You need to get to the east village located near the base of the third hill from here. There will be a ship behind the first house waiting to take you away. Mother and I will follow as soon as we can. Now go!"

Elly looked around desperately and realized that her only way out was through the shattered window. Without hesitating, she leaped out of the window to avoid the sharp edges and rolled onto the grass beneath the window. Glancing back, she saw Troy wrestling with one of the guards on the ground. She hoped that he was strong enough to fend them off because if anything happened to him, she would never be able to forgive herself. But knowing that he would not want her staying around to get caught, Elly took off running up the first hill.

When she was halfway up the hill, Elly heard a loud wail coming from behind her. The sound stopped her dead in her tracks and caused her heart to skip a beat. Against her will, she turned and looked behind her down to the base of the hill and saw a figure standing there looking up in her direction. She could not see the person's face but she knew without a doubt that it was Navar. Regaining control of herself, Elly began running up the hill faster.

Elly had no energy left by the time she started up the second hill but did not dare slow down her pace. At the top of the third hill, she stopped for a moment and looked down. She could see the house a short distance from the base of the hill and was sure that it was the one Troy had told her about. She took in a deep breath and gave a sigh of relief. She was almost there. But as she began her descent down the hill, she somehow lost her footing and found herself rolling haphazardly down the hill. She did all she could to protect her face. When she landed sprawled on her stomach at the base of the hill and raised her head, she caught sight of a pair of hooves right in front of her face. Her heart sank in despair as she looked up and saw Navar perched on the horse. She did not know how he had gotten ahead of her but at this point it did not matter; she had to find a way to escape. Gathering her strength, she got up in one swift movement ran under the horses' stomach to the other side.

Elly was thoroughly unprepared for when Navar attacked her. He jumped off his horse and landed right on top of her back just as she reached the other side of the horse, crushing her beneath him.

"Sorry, Princess," he said as he roughly turned her around so that she was facing him. There were red, sweltering claw marks on the left side of his face from where he had been scratched by the creature that Cierah had turned into and his clothes were in shambles. "This time, there is no escape for you!" he laughed gruffly as Elly struggled in vain beneath him, trying to loosen his grip on her arms.

"Please," Elly pleaded, tears filling her eyes, "let me go!" She had come too far to arrive at such an end. What made this even more difficult was the fact that she had been so close to escaping.

"That is right, Princess, beg! I want to hear you beg while I tear you to pieces!"

"But- why?" Elly asked meekly.

"Because you took away my life, my power, my freedom and sent me to my death, woman. I have waited a long time to pay you back for that. And believe me I am going to enjoy every moment of it!"

He raised his hand as if to strike her but stopped midway when he heard someone speak from behind him.

"Let her go, Navar. You need to deal with me first," the person said.

Navar quickly spun around and growled wildly when he saw who it was and almost literally flung Elly aside. She landed several feet away and felt a searing pain in her right shoulder as she made contact with the rocks and dirt in the pathway. She bit her lip to keep from screaming.

"Get away from here, Troy," he yelled, jumping to his feet, "before I am forced to kill you, too!"

"Troy! Be careful!" Elly cried out weakly as she rolled over onto her back to alleviate the pain in her shoulder. Despite their predicament, she was relieved to see him.

"Be still!" Navar whirled back towards her and bared his teeth at her like a wild animal. He was seething with rage as he turned back to face Troy.

"Do not threaten me," Troy said hotly, "because I am not leaving here without Elly!"

Navar laughed eerily. "So, you want to die, too? Very well, then!" He drew his sword out from behind him and pounced towards Troy. Before he reached him though, Troy disappeared, reappearing again behind him with a sword in his hand.

"Do not play with me!" Navar warned Troy. But he tensed a little when he saw that Troy also had a sword now.

Troy charged him first, and the sound of the swords clashing together was deafening in Elly's ears. She did not know for how long they fought as she kept sinking in and out of consciousness due to the searing pain in her shoulder, but the next time she regained consciousness she saw Navar throw something at Troy and he was instantly blinded by an incredibly bright light. Navar took this opportunity to disarm him and then shoved him to the ground on his back. Pouncing on top of Troy, he placed his sword beneath Troy's throat, pinning him to the ground.

"Now, to finish you so I can get on with my plans," Navar growled with a nasty grin on his face.

"No!" Elly screamed as she painfully crawled to her knees and made her way towards Navar who was only a short distance from her. She reached him and, disregarding the excruciating pain in her right arm, she grabbed his left arm which held the sword, pulling the sword away from Troy's throat, towards Navar's face.

"Get off of me, woman!" Navar cried throwing her off like an empty sack. Then he raised the sword above his head, poised to strike down at Troy.

Instantly, within a matter of seconds, the clouds darkened and thunder roared. The wind picked up and started blowing lightly at first but then, in the distance, Elly could see that the wind was getting stronger and the dark clouds were becoming thicker and seemed to be moving quickly in their direction. In utter amazement, Elly watched as a small funnel started heading towards them, growing bigger as it moved along picking up speed as the wind picked up speed. Soon the funnel was almost upon them and now reached all the way up to the dark sky so that there was no way to tell where it began.

Elly could see and hear electricity crackling from within the funnel and she watched in fascination as the dark funnel of cloud began sending blazing bolts of lightning in every direction at full speed, burning anything in its path. Elly huddled at the base of the hill and shielded herself as much as possible against the strong wind but could not take her eyes away from the scene occurring before her eyes.

Elly was so taken in by what was happening that she momentarily forgot about Navar until she heard him scream in such a horrific way it made her blood run cold. Turning in his direction, she saw that one of the lightning bolts had struck Navar's sword where it apparently had still been up in the air above his head, and was sending a surge of electricity through his body. Navar's eyes were opened wide in horror and his face contorted in excruciating pain as he realized what was happening. He continued to cry out in pain as the lightning bolt held him and repeatedly shocked his body with electricity.

It was an unbelievable sight. Finally, after what seemed like hours even though only a few minutes had passed, the wind died down and the lightning stopped but the funnel stayed where it was; dark and seething, looming above them all the way to the sky. It stayed in one place, twisting and turning as electricity continued to crackle both within and all around it.

Once the electricity stopped surging through him, Navar instantly dropped the sword and rolled onto the ground in Elly's direction. Despite what he had just been through, he reached out with his right hand from where he lay on the ground and managed to get a hold of Elly's left leg. Terrified and shocked, Elly tried to pry his hand, which was intensely hot and felt like it was melting her skin, from her ankle. Somehow, Navar still had enough strength in him to hold onto her leg despite her struggle and began pulling her towards him.

"Stop! No!" Elly screamed desperately clawing at the ground, trying to find something to hold on to.

"Elly!" She heard Troy cry out but could not see where he was.

As Navar continued pulling Elly towards him, several bolts of lightning flew out from the funnel and struck him again. He screeched in pain and finally let go of Elly's leg after the third bolt of lightning coursed through him. His body shook violently and he could not keep from screaming in agony. The moment he released her leg, Elly felt someone touch her shoulder and looked up to see Troy standing behind her. His armor was in tatters and he had several bruises on his face and arms. Elly saw him wince as he helped her up and moved her away from where Navar was thrashing on the ground.

"Navar!" a voice called from somewhere above them, "you have crossed the wrong person again."

Elly and Troy looked around but did not see anyone. It seemed as though the voice was coming from somewhere within the funnel. Elly found that almost impossible to believe but could not find another answer.

"You!" Navar screamed as his body wracked with pain from the electricity surging through him. The look on his face told Elly that he recognized the voice that had spoken and knew exactly who it was. "Someday-"

"No!" the voice, which was still unrecognizable to Elly, cut him off sharply. "There will be no 'someday'. With your passing, the gates to Infersity will be sealed forever as of now and no matter who shall pass through, it will never open to you or any of the other spirits again. I have seen to that. Now, go!" the voice ordered.

Troy and Elly watched in awe as Navar started changing before their eyes. He screamed in horror as his body began taking on shapes that were unidentifiable to either Troy or Elly until, suddenly, he exploded into what seemed to be a million pieces that were instantly pulled into the funnel. Once the pieces disappeared, the funnel itself instantly disappeared.

Immediately after that, the dark clouds vanished and everything was calm again. Within a few seconds, the sun was shining brightly in the sky as though nothing out of the ordinary had taken place. Elly realized that she had been holding her breath the entire time the transformation was happening and finally let it out slowly in relief. Troy wrapped an arm around her and held her tightly against him.

It was finally over.

They stood there silently for a long while until Troy gently moved Elly away from him and regarded her closely. "Are you all right?" he inquired, brushing her hair away from her face.

Elly nodded, unable to find her voice for a moment. "Yes," she answered after a few seconds. "I am fine." Her leg still stung from where Navar had grabbed her and her body ached from the whole ordeal but otherwise she felt that everything was as it should be. She was alive and that was all that mattered. As she looked around, she tried to comprehend what had just taken place. Standing here now in the beautifully bright sunlight it was hard to believe that what she had just experienced had been real. To her it seemed as though it had all been a terrible waking nightmare that somehow ended in a wonderful dream. But Troy was here with her and had witnessed everything.

"Is this nightmare really over?" Elly asked Troy.

Yes, it is," he assured her as he gently rubbed her shoulders.

Taking in a deep breath of fresh air, Elly could feel that this was the truth down to her soul.

The battle was over.

As she stared up at the clear blue sky, Elly could not help thinking of the voice that had come out from the dark clouds. In her heart she was certain that it was Lurcia who had found a way to destroy Navar. She had promised all of them that she would end this battle and, somehow, she had done so. Elly wondered if she would ever know what had led to the events that had just taken place before her very eyes. Yet in that moment, nothing mattered more to Elly except knowing that she and her family, including her mother whom she had not seen since Lurcia appeared, were safe.

As the sun warmed Elly's skin, she smiled, took Troy's hand in hers, and the two of them began walking through the field towards the house where a ship was waiting to take Elly home.

ABOUT THE AUTHOR

Simone Voltaire is a first time author who has always loved reading many different types of books particularly science fiction, fantasy, and mystery books. The creativity and captivating imagination that she enjoys in the books that she reads and have read over the years is what inspired her to start writing in order to put her own imagination into words to share with others. On her free time, she enjoys playing tennis, bike riding and spending time with family and close friends. She is currently working on book two of Sarcaun.

www.ingramcontent.com/pod-product-compliance
Lightning Source LLC
Chambersburg PA
CBHW020411110726
47899CB00006B/1942